DATING JUST GOT SERIOUS

BOOKS ONE - FOUR

〜〜〜〜〜〜〜〜〜〜〜〜〜〜〜〜〜〜〜〜〜〜〜〜〜〜〜〜〜〜〜〜〜

Four Romances About The Women of Philly
and the Men Who Love Them

DATING JUST GOT SERIOUS – BOOKS ONE - FOUR
Jacki Kelly
Copyright 2014 by Harris, Jacqueline
ISBN: 978-0-9899601-4-4
First Edition Electronic August 2014
Published by Yobachi Publishing, LLC

Table of Contents

Dedication

This book is dedicated to my husband who always nurtures my heart and soul.

BLIND DATE

Chapter One

I had made a promise and I intended to keep it. Even though the promise only existed in my head. This would be the last weekend I spent with my father sitting on the couch watching re-runs or going on blind dates with men he thought were eligible bachelors. They were more like regrets from the free dating website. Now I had to break the news to him.

I glanced up at my Philadelphia duplex and sighed. *I needed to get a life.*

A good one where I at least had sex on a regular basis. A summer evening deserved hot, steamy loving. How many twenty-seven-year old women relied on their father to provide their entertainment? I trudged up the stairs with my portfolio slung over my shoulder and unlocked the door to my brownstone.

My cell phone chirped as I entered. I fished it from my bag while kicking my heels across the room, into the corner. My best friend Yolanda's number flashed on the display.

"Hey, Yani." I dropped my bags on the kitchen table and opened the refrigerator. "Are we still on for shopping tomorrow morning? Please don't cancel on me. I need to hear the swipe of my credit card." I stared at the contents to find something to settle my nerves.

"Phoebe, of course we're still on. I want a dress for the Labor Day party." She laughed. "I can't throw a banging party with a drab dress from last year. Will you get your dad out of town in time to enjoy the weekend?"

"Don't remind me. I love him, but I plan to send him home first thing Sunday morning. I'll pay you to help me find him a girlfriend. Since Mom died, he thinks I'm his responsibility. He called this afternoon to tell me he's arranged another blind date. Some guy he works with is picking me up at eight o'clock tonight. I'm thinking about not answering the door. I could always tell my father I got held up with a client."

"He'll only reschedule it. Maybe this man will be better than the last few."

"Fat chance of that happening. Why can't he be like other fathers and just sit on the couch watching television? At least then I wouldn't have to pretend I'm happy with some nerd he's set me up with. I'm exhausted with the dating game. I'm ready for a serious relationship with someone who wants more than a quickie."

I close the refrigerator door and made my way to the living room. I flopped on the sofa, turned on the television, and flipped through the channels.

"As horny as I am I'd take a quickie right about now," Yani said.

"Stop it. You would not."

"When was the last time you two acted like a *normal* father and daughter? I think you're closer now than you were before your mother died." Her voice softened, it always did when she mentioned my mother. "Remember the time he entered you guys in the bike race with that club?"

"How can I forget? We rode two hundred miles in two days. My legs ached for a week. I think he learned his lesson, too. We haven't done anything that wacky in months."

I padded back into the kitchen, pulled a bottle of Merlot from the refrigerator and popped the cork. I poured a water glass full and took a long swallow.

"Girl, you have more dates than anyone I know. Where does your father find all these eligible bachelors?"

"He's a sneaker salesman. Don't you know that's an all-male profession?" I shot back at her.

"It is not," she laughed. "But tell him I could use a hook-up, too."

I took another gulp of wine, either to shore up my resolve for the evening or to numb my disappointment. Either way wine couldn't hurt.

"Yani, you know your parents wouldn't approve of you dating an average guy. I haven't approved any of the men my father has set me up with. But you can sub in for me tonight and we won't tell my father. He only does it because

2

he thinks I'm too fat to get my own man." I placed my elbow on the kitchen counter and stared at the glass. The sting of truth was bitter to swallow.

"Phoebe, you're a size twelve, you're not fat. Do you know how many women would love to be your size?" She paused. "You know, I haven't had a decent date in months. At least you're out of the house this weekend. I'm doing laundry. You'll have to tell me all about your date tomorrow."

Holding the phone between my shoulder and ear, I pulled a bowl of grapes from the fridge and ate a few off the stem.

"You might as well start preparing for your date. It will be eight before you know it and we both know it takes you more than a moment to turn into Cinderella."

I trudged up the stairs. My bare feet thumped on each step like the final notes of a funeral dirge. Wishing I'd brought the bottle of wine with me, I pulled off my favorite pair of jean and dropped them in the middle of the bedroom floor. While showering I tried to conjure up the best outcome for the evening. Every scenario playing in my head resembled a dream sequence from all my favorite romance movies, all of them so far from reality I snapped off the water and stepped out.

My closet was as chaotic as my life. While I was vowing to make improvements this was another area calling for my attention. I found the sexiest dress in the bunch and put it on. The matching strappy sandals completed the look.

I finished my make-up just as the doorbell rang. My heart sped up.

Cory arrived exactly at eight. Being prompt moved him forward five spaces on my board game of life. I descended the stairs and opened the door to glimpse his tall, lean frame. I refused to exhale until I saw his eyes. No use getting excited if his eyes were flat. And on cue, his thick lashes lifted, revealing the most striking peepers I'd seen in years.

"Hi. Cory, right?"

"Yes, and you must be Phoebe, I've heard so much about you. You're even prettier than your father described and I already had high expectations." His lips widened into a smile that I could have admired all night and the pretty comment advanced him ten more spaces. At this rate, he'd be down the aisle with me in no time.

His dark skin glistened like melted chocolate from the top of his gleaming bald head to the collar of his crisp white shirt. I ran my tongue over my glossed lips. Cory had the noble appearance of royalty, with an air of confidence positioned on his shoulders like a crown jewel. Maybe the wine was working magic because my insides heated up. I was able to give him a good once over. His long fingers and well-maintained nails said he took care of himself. His expensive shoes said he liked nice things. His firm cut chin and high cheek bone said I could look at him all night. The quick flash of white teeth drew me to him like a bolt of lightning had snapped my butt. I didn't have to worry that he could handle me and my curves. His biceps were huge.

I don't know why my father had kept him hidden. Maybe he was saving the best for last. Before getting emotionally carried away, I conjured visions of my last set-up date. Those images could help me ignore Cory's magnetism. But if this is what the men in sneaker sales looked like I needed to switch careers.

Cory held his hand out to me and I slipped my palm against his. Butter is smooth, silk is soft but my hand in his was even better than I could have imagined. He caressed my fingers like he'd made a career of holding hands.

"Would you like a glass of wine?" He was so fine I wanted to sit home and stare at him all night.

"I have a dinner reservation for us at eight-thirty. We don't want to be late. Maybe we'll get to the wine later."

Did he just invite himself back to my place after our date? He was zipping across my board at record speed as he advanced two more spaces.

Cory closed the door behind us and rested his hand on the middle of my back as he escorted me to the car. I guess he couldn't find the small indentation that was supposed to signify my waistline. At least he didn't move his hand away, for that I was grateful. I inhaled his crisp woodsy cologne. He smelled like a man who knew how to please a woman. My stomach started doing jumping jacks. I needed to slow it down a bit. I was already planning our next date and thinking up names for our firstborn son. I was always falling for someone well before they showed any real interest. But as long as I kept it to myself what was the harm?

We reached for the car handle at the same time. His large palm covered my hand. I skipped a breath as a tingle ran up my arm. He stood close enough to hear my heart pounding in my chest. I took a deep breath and released it slowly.

"Let me get the door for you." He slid his fingers under my hand and opened the door.

We drove down Broad Street to a quaint restaurant. From the corner of my eye I followed the sharp cut of Cory's jaw along his handsome face. He must have owed Dad a favor to agree to take me out. This man could have any woman he wanted. He was probably a serial dater.

"So tell me about you," I said after we were seated and had placed our drink orders.

"There isn't much to tell." He drummed his fingers on the table. "I've been in sales for several years and just transferred to this area. I don't know many people in Philly, so it feels good to get out with someone so attractive to see a bit of the town. I'm originally from D.C. My family is still there. When I have some spare time I like to bike and hike. I love being outside. Now it's your turn. What should I know about Phoebe other than she has beautiful brown eyes, flawless skin and a pretty smile?" He leaned across the table and gazed at me like I was a prize.

Before I could reply, the server arrived at our table to take our orders.

"If you like salmon, it's great here," he offered.

"Fine, that's what I'll have." I handed the menu back to the server and leaned against the cushion.

"Okay, now let's focus on you." He repeated as he folded his hand and placed them in the center of the small table. His dark eyes narrowed and focused on me. The intensity in his stare made me fidget with the water glass.

I swallowed the saliva collecting in my mouth and tried not to stare. "Let's see. You already know my father likes to set me up on dates. Since my mother passed away I tend to give in to him. It keeps him occupied and I haven't had the heart to make him stop."

He nodded. "That's commendable. Not many women would be so considerate. What do you do for a living?"

"I'm a freelance graphic artist."

"Wow that sounds like fun. No set nine-to-five for you, huh?"

"I tried it for a short while, but I like this much better. Sitting behind the same desk everyday stifled my creativity."

He nodded. Not until he'd asked did I realize how much I missed having a good conversation with the opposite sex. Usually a date bought me a cheap drink and then tried to wrangle an offer to come back to my place. I'd said no so often I started getting on my own nerves. But if my dad wasn't coming to my place for the weekend, I just might be the first to suggest Cory stop in for a nightcap.

"So, you don't have a girlfriend?" I pinched my leg. That wasn't the question I meant to ask. It sounded desperate.

He shook his head. "No. Not any more." He fingered his knife. "I've been mending from my last relationship."

"Been there, did that too," I laughed. "But why a blind date?"

"I tried the bar scene and got tired of all the games. My mother suggested I look for a recommendation. Benjamin is a good guy. He's been my mentor for a few years." He shrugged his shoulder. "So here we are."

"I see. Your mother sounds like a wise woman." Any man who said something positive about his mother couldn't be all bad. Even if his confession wasn't the endorsement I wanted to hear, at least my father hadn't twisted his arm.

Our food arrived. The savory salmon melted on my tongue. "You were right about this entrée. It's delicious." I ate another bite.

"My steak is unbelievable. Taste it." He leaned across the table with his fork and placed the meat in my open mouth. It tasted divine. I'm sure it was because he fed me. I couldn't remember the last time I'd share something so intimate with a man that didn't involve taking off my panties. I could only nod.

I pushed my food around the plate. Satisfied. Maybe Cory would think I was thick from breathing too much air and not eating too much food. I skipped dessert and drank another glass of water instead.

"Since this is Labor Day weekend what do you have special planned?" he asked.

Long-range planning. I moved his piece ahead another two spaces. "Let's see. By Sunday I'm going to shoo dad out of my house and back to Baltimore. On Monday a bunch of my friends are getting together for an end of summer party. We're gathering at Yani's house."

"Then it's back to your regular life?"

"Yeah, if you're around you should drop by. We're just going to have some good food and my friend Cat will be mixing the drinks." As the last of the invitation slipped out of my mouth, I stepped on my own toe. I knew him a whole hour and was already asking him out on a date. I could've waited until after dinner to see if he had money to pay the check.

"Sounds like fun."

With my index finger I massaged the knot growing in my neck. His response lacked the overwhelming enthusiasm I wanted to hear.

"Normally my day to day life is pretty uneventful. Most nights I'm home, drawing and watching the latest made for TV movie. How about you?"

"I like to leave my options open. So right now I have nothing planned. Phoebe, let's go dancing." Cory made my name sound like song lyrics. I wanted him to say it again and again.

"I haven't been dancing in months," I gushed.

"Are you saying yes?" He stood and reached for my hand.

"I am. Let's go."

We strolled down South Street toward a small club. My hand brushed his as we maneuvered the tight sidewalk, pretending this was a real date. A date we both opted for without the gentle persuasion from my meddling dad. He grabbed my fingers and slid his palm over mine. Just as I turned to gaze up at him, he brought his tender lips down on my mouth. His kiss was so gentle my body failed to cooperate, making walking almost impossible. He wrapped his arm around me to steady my pace and pulled me closer.

The posh club was packed with attractive people, gathered in corners, and engaging in whispered conversations. Several women turned to examine Cory as we walked through the crowd. The pulsating music and classy atmosphere mingled with my good mood. I rocked my head to the beat.

Cory pulled me into his arms when a slow Maxwell ballad filled the room. I pressed my soft curves into his rock hard body while he sang the song in my ear. Serenaded by a prince; my best date ever. He slid his hand along my back and down to my butt. Instead of pulling his hand away, I let it rest.

I'm not a lucky person, never won the lottery, and only once did I win the sorority raffle, the prize was a t-shirt two sizes too big. But as the other single women in the club shot Cory dreamy stares, I felt like the winner. A second slow song played and he continued to hold me.

"You are so soft." His breath caressed my neck.

"And you're so solid. Like you're made of steel." I squeezed his bicep, not even offended when he tightened his hold on my butt. Too many lonely nights had me ready to say yes, if he'd just ask.

I couldn't remain mad at dad after this. Of all his attempts, this was the best he'd ever done. Usually, after dinner my date rushed me home before the smell of my perfume evaporated. Cory's eyes never wandered to the pretty women in sexy, slinky dresses who sashayed around on the dance floor. I had his full attention. This felt like a real date, one I could write about in my journal. I had to suppress my growing elation. The night was still young enough for a lot of stuff to go wrong.

The song ended and he escorted me back to our seats. "How long have you known my father?" I asked when he cozied in beside me.

"We met at a business meeting in Florida a few years ago. He talks about you all the time and now I can see why. I had to meet you."

I averted my eyes. My cheeks warmed.

"Did I embarrass you?"

"No. No, my father does that. And sometimes I just have a reflexive action." I teased.

"He only wants to take care of his daughter. You shouldn't be embarrassed, he cares about you." Cory reached across the table and touched my hand as he spoke. Behind his dark eyes stirred a hint of tenderness.

"If your mother fixed you up on blind dates you probably wouldn't be as understanding." I chuckled.

"Maybe you're right. But it's always better to have parents who care than to have one who doesn't give a damn."

I stared into his eyes, his sincere tone made my stomach flutter. My whole body heated up. This felt like a real date. If I could erase my father's hand in the middle of it, I could see myself sleeping with him. I crossed my legs to ignore the stirring between my thighs as I tried to remember the last time I had really good sex. If I discounted my act in the shower the other morning then it was three months.

Cory was easy to talk to. My tongue didn't get tangled in my mouth nor did I muffle my words. Maybe I needed to ease up on Dad, learn to trust his judgment more.

"It's almost last call. I better get you home." Cory grabbed my hand and led me out of the club. If he'd asked me back to his place I would have said yes, even though I never slept with a guy on the first date. But this wasn't a normal first date. Nothing about the night was ordinary.

In the car, Cory turned up the stereo and focused on the road. Talking over the sound of the constant stream of music on the satellite radio was impossible. Somewhere between the club and the car silence had taken over. Maybe he was thinking of a way to get me back to his place.

"I had a nice evening, but it went so fast," I said with too much enthusiasm.

Cory nodded. "Yes, I had fun, too." The firm set to his jaw said his mood had changed. The talkative gentleman from earlier was now quiet. I clasped my fingers and pressed them into my lap. I shouldn't have been surprised. Just because he was tall, good-looking with manners, I had expected too much.

Again.

"Is everything alright?" I asked.

"Yes. I'm just exhausted. Long day at work—you know how it is, don't you?"

Cory pulled up in front of the house. My father's car was parked behind mine in the driveway. Any plans to continue the date inside were scrapped. As he walked me to the door he slipped his hand around my mine and brought his face closer. His luscious lips were inches from mine. My heart clutched against my ribs. His fresh breath swept over my skin.

"I probably should have told you this earlier tonight, but I'm not ready to get serious. I'm coming off the heels of a pretty bad break-up and for now I just want to hang out and have a good time. I'm just not ready for anything steady," he whispered. "But you were a lot of fun, I'll call you sometime." He kissed my mouth and sauntered back down the walk.

"But—but…" I stuttered as he strode down the walk and jumped into his car. How could he have hidden his

10

arrogance all night? Did I look so desperate that he thought I would be sitting here waiting on him to stop by and rub my ass? I moved him back to square zero with the other nothings I'd dated.

As his taillights faded into the night I shook my head. Maybe if I shook it hard enough I'd shake some sense into it for expecting anything more.

"What the hell just happened?" I mumbled. Up until the last few moments, the evening had been spectacular. Stunned in place, my arms hung limp at my side. Again. Sooner or later I was going to be smart and stop falling for everything man just because he had on a pair of pants and an Adam's apple.

I swallowed the threat of tears, daring myself to cry. I took a deep breath before entering the house. I didn't want my father to see my disappointment. He might be encouraged to keep up his useless dating matches. He wasn't used to the rejection like I was. I didn't get to be twenty-seven and single without my share of being spurned.

In the living room ESPN blared from the television while Dad snored on the couch with his mouth open and his head tilted backward. I started to leave my father where he was, but if he woke up stiff, I'd feel guilty.

"Dad, wake up and go to bed."

"Phoebe." He held out his arms. "How did it go, baby? Are you crying?"

"No." I dodged his out-stretched arms. "There was no chemistry between us. I know you think everybody is perfect for me, but it's just not true."

"You always say the same thing. I think you need to change your mental image, baby girl."

I groaned. "Dad I haven't been a baby in twenty six years. You've got to stop calling me that."

"No I don't." At the opposite end of the sofa, he removed his tie from the confines of his shirt.

"Dad, you don't need to come up here every Friday. You work hard. After a long week you should sit at home and put your feet up, or play poker with your friends."

"I can put my feet up here." He placed his feet, shoes and all, on the coffee table.

"I have more good news for you." He lowered the volume on the television.

I focused my attention on my new pedicure. I didn't need to see the blow coming to know I wouldn't like it.

"Guess what. I've arranged another date for you tomorrow." His eyes sparkled like a kid at Christmas.

I groaned and buried my face in the cushions on the sofa. "Dad, you didn't. Not again."

"I sure did." He grinned and nodded. "Isn't that great? One tonight and one tomorrow night.

"Where do you find these men? Sooner or later the barrel has to go empty."

"Not when it comes to my daughter. I'm not giving up."

"But I want you to. I'm begging you to stop this madness. What if I refuse to go?" In my head I saw Cory making his way back to his car and me standing at my front door looking silly. I'd endured enough humiliation.

He laughed and his eyes sparkled like a child with a new puppy. "You just can't stop trying, Phoebe. I didn't raise a quitter. You're a princess and some lucky fellow is going to realize it and treat you like one."

"I'm no princess." I kissed his cheek and stalked into the kitchen.

"You are to me!" he yelled. "Don't you want to hear all about your other date?"

"No, not really."

"Jonathan, that's the fellow for tomorrow night—he's not as good looking or as polished as Cory but he's a fun guy. There's a lot to be said about a man who can make a woman laugh and Jonathan is always telling jokes and kidding around."

My wine was back in the refrigerator, thanks to my dad, no doubt. I found a smaller glass this time and filled it half-way. He didn't need to dedicate his life to finding me true love. It didn't exist for everyone. Sooner or later I needed

12

to stand up to him and tell him to stop meddling. That talk might break his heart, but his weekend challenges were too much and the blind dates were torturous.

After a long pause he said, "Phoebe, your mother wanted you to marry and have children. You know that's why I do this, don't you?"

I stuck my head around the corner. "I know, Dad. But, maybe I'm not interested in getting married right now. Besides, I'm capable of finding my own men. I'm a grown woman. Stop worrying about me."

"And have your mother visit me in my dreams? No thank you." He strolled into the kitchen with his hands in his pockets. The sadness around his mouth had faded months ago. He was taking Mom's death better than me. "Do this for me and I'll try to stop being such a busybody." His eyes pleaded.

"You said the same thing after you planned the trip to Baltimore. I had to spend the whole day with a group of senior citizens."

"That wasn't my fault. The ad said day cruise for active adults. I had no idea—"

"Let's make a deal. I'll go tomorrow night only if you promise not to set me up on anymore dates unless I'm forty with no prospects in sight. Even then, I will have to beg you three times and hop on one foot for an hour."

He rubbed his chin while peering down at me. "I-I guess that's fair enough. "But suppose I come across the perfect guy?"

"Dad, there is no such thing as an ideal guy. You are a dying breed. Believe me, I've been on enough dates to know. Blind dates seldom work out." I poured him a glass of wine.

He took a sip then set his glass on the table.

"How about the movie we saw last weekend?"

I shook my head. "I'm talking about real life. Anything can happen in a movie."

"Movies imitate life, you know. I met your mother on a blind date and we were happy for forty years."

"This is it, Dad, the last one," I warned before finishing my wine and leveling a stern eye at him.

One down and one to go and then I could have my life back. Maybe he didn't think he was going to keep this promise, but I had every intention of helping him.

####

Even though I was in a residential area, I jammed the accelerator. Putting some space between me and Phoebe was what I needed right now. From the moment she'd opened the door I was mesmerized. I couldn't take my eyes off of her, my mouth watered like she was a tasty treat, my palms wanted to feel her golden skin to see if it was as soft as it looked. My brain was firing so fast I almost forgot how to speak.

I rubbed my sweating palm on the knee of my pants as I turned down Spruce Street and made my way home. The last thing I needed was another serious relationship so soon after my miserable breakup. Not every woman wanted to settle down, hadn't that been the reason for Wendy's unceremonious bail?

Phoebe's sweet scent lingered in the threads of my blazer. She wasn't just any girl, and since I wasn't ready to give her everything she deserved, I couldn't jerk her around. She had an innocence in her eyes that demanded more than I could give right now. I was still nursing my heart back to life so what did I have to offer her?

If for one minute I thought she was the kind of girl willing to play sex games, I would have taken her back to my bed for a night of fun. Just thinking about her now caused a reaction in my pants.

But the invitation to attend a party with her friends was enough to ring all the alarms I set to keep me from falling into the same trap. My mother had told me to stop being so serious and have some fun. I couldn't seem to have a good time without the entanglement of commitment.

Dating Just Got Serious

Did that mean I was supposed to just date and bed women like a commodity? From the moment I'd laid eyes on Phoebe I could tell she wasn't one of those women. For now I needed to stick with the women at the club. The ones who only wanted to dance all night have a little fun then move on to the next adventure.

The spacious interior of my condo was welcoming, with a view of the city that would have cost me a whole lot more if the previous owner hadn't been in such a hurry to move to California. But looking out over the city alone, night after night was about as enticing as waiting in line at the DMV.

I fell on the sofa and threw my legs over the arm. I had two choices and both of them had major drawbacks. I could sleepwalk through my life trying to stay uninvolved and never get shot down again. Or I could play like a champ trying to win the big game and find the women I needed. Spending another lonely night staring at the ceiling had to be the worst choice. Dad didn't raise a chump. The breakup with Wendy had been pretty bad, but it didn't deflate me.

I propped my hands behind my head. Since dropping her off, every other thought going through my head had Phoebe's stamp on it. I wasn't going to get any rest. She had me stirred up, like the beginning of a storm. But after my quick exit she might not be inclined to talk to me again.

I'd just have to use my charm to wear her down. She could very easily be the one. The perfect one for me. Before trotting off to bed, I knew what I had to do.

Chapter Two

I found a table in the center of the food court and waited for Yani. Getting out of the house this morning without giving Dad details on my date last night was like trying to sneak out of the house after curfew. He was so pleased with himself as if Cory were the prize behind door number three.

Yani wove her way through the tables and took the seat next to me. "Sorry I'm late. I overslept."

"I thought you were staying in last night."

"I did, but drinking wine and watching a Sex in the City marathon wasn't a good combination. Sure didn't make me feel better. But I want to hear all about your date. How did it go?"

I gave her a dreamy look, pretending to savory the juicy details.

"What? Tell me. What did he look like?" Yani almost bounced out of her seat.

"Let me see. Cory is tall and good-looking. I could stare into his brown-flecked eyes all night long. His skin is the color of milk chocolate, the kind of chocolate you want to linger over and savor. We had a nice dinner. He even asked me to go dancing."

"Wow. It sounds like a great evening."

"He held me in his arms as Maxwell crooned A Woman's Work. I was so high, my feet almost slipped out of my shoes. I actually believed we were in the beginning of a relationship, when the sparks are red hot and everything we do is new, blooming like spring. My heart was doing pirouettes."

"Phoebe, that's fabulous." She clapped her hands with glee.

"It was pretty special. Even when I think about it now, I can't help but smile. Then he dropped me off at my door,

16

lowered his face to mind and muttered he didn't want to get involved and ran off without even a good night kiss."

Yani felt back against the chair liked I'd shot her. "You're kidding me, right? Nobody does any such thing." She sucked her teeth with indignation.

"I wish I were lying." I hunched my shoulders. "And I get to press the reset button again tonight. But if this gets my dad to stop meddling in my love life then it's worth putting on my game face."

"Oh Phoebe, I'm so sorry."

"The worst part was I invited him to the party. I knew the moment the words came out of my mouth it was wrong."

"Based on the things you said, I don't think you have to worry about him showing up. Besides he doesn't know where I live."

"Why do I always do this? How can I always be so optimistic? I should know better by now. I've never thought of myself as a person who had to learn her lessons the hard way, but now I'm not so sure."

"You're just like the rest of us. Searching for that special person. Stop beating yourself up."

"You're right." I nodded. "I'm focused and determined. I'll find the love of my life. I just don't need help from my father."

"At least your father isn't always looking down his nose at your choices. My parents think if someone didn't attend an Ivy League School and doesn't wear custom-made suits, then they aren't worth a minute of my time. Do you know how many men they've turned their noses up over?" She shook her head. "I've decided if I ever get serious about another man, I won't let my parents meet him until after we've eloped."

I didn't feel so lucky. My mother was the only person who could harness my father's rambunctiousness. When he had to spend his weekends alone, what would he do? Guilt weighed on me, but breaking the tie would be best for the both of us.

17

"Let's go shopping. I need a dress." Yani stood. "We'll shop until we both feel better."

"Yeah, I think I hear a pair of shoes calling my name."

By that night, my father bubbled with his dating efforts. "Two dates in two nights. Your mother would be happy."

I expected him to say "hot diggity dog" and slap his knee like they did in old movies. Instead he smiled and crossed his arms over his chest. He apologized again about Cory. "I thought he was special. Hurting my baby girl like that…" He shook his head.

"The way he dashed to the car you would have thought I'd asked him for a bone marrow transplant."

"Don't fret. I'll talk—"

"Oh no you won't. We have a deal. I'll stick to my part and you have to stick to yours. After tonight, you're butting out of my love life."

He nodded then buried his head in the newspaper.

"Besides, he wasn't my type." I shrugged. My father thought every man should be interested in me. My mother would be proud of his efforts.

"If you want me to be happy, go drum up some freelance business for me." I wagged my finger at him.

"You're doing fine, there. If I thought you needed my help, you know I would. That's what parents do."

I rubbed his shoulder and held his eyes. "You promised, Dad. And you have to keep it."

"Okay, okay. This is the last one." He reached up and rubbed my hand. "But if I get to heaven and your mother is mad at me, I'll haunt you." He laughed.

"Deal." I wanted to shake his hand and seal the promise, instead I prayed he kept his end of the bargain or our relationship would be very different moving forward.

18

Dating Just Got Serious

We sat in the living room, waiting for my date to show up.

"Jonathan is forty-five minutes late. If he's not here in the next two minutes I'm changing into my sweat pants."

"He'll be here. He's a little unconventional, that's all."

The doorbell rang.

Jonathan was an inch taller than me, but he appeared shorter. His bald head gleamed under the foyer lights. Was every sneaker salesman required to have a bald head? My father was pretty thin on top, too. But Jonathan's head wasn't sexy bald like Cory's, it was ugly bald like my Uncle Byrd. A dark shadow outlined where his hairline used to be. His stomach hung several inches over his belt. I shot my father the stink eye, but he was too busy grinning to notice. He must be more desperate to get me paired up than I thought. Did he hear my biological clock ticking?

I stepped out the door, hopeful. Maybe Jonathan's overweight personality would understand and like my curvy personality. I smiled and sashayed to his car. I hoped his eyes were focused on my butt, it was one of my best assets and I knew how to work it to my advantage. The other day I'd gotten fifteen catcalls as I strolled by a construction site, three better than the week before.

He walked several feet in front of me, and didn't offer to open the car door.

He glided into the front seat and left me outside tugging on the handle. "It sticks a little," he yelled from his side of the car. "Just pull on the handle and lift at the same time."

I yanked the door open and looked down at the passenger seat.

"Push that stuff on the floor," he said. "I didn't get a chance to clean up before driving over. Let's just say I was a little tied up." He chuckled.

I squeezed in beside a pile of papers and oily take-out food bags.

Dating Just Got Serious

Since he was late we skipped the movie and went to dinner at Jerry's Rib Joint in Center City. The smell of fried food greeted us when we opened the door to the small shop. Grease hung in the air. We were escorted to a booth under a faded picture of some unknown musician behind a piano.

"I'm a little short on cash, so keep it light." He smirked.

I opened my mouth, but closed it without replying. I couldn't believe him. His eyes were beady and his ears were small and stingy. Maybe he thought I would gobble up everything on the menu.

The server arrived at our table. Without waiting for me to open the menu he blurted, "I'll have a full rack of baby-back ribs with extra sauce, french fries and cole-slaw. Oh yeah and two pieces of sweet corn bread." He ran his tongue over his lips, leaving a wet spit shine behind. "Oh yeah, and bring me a light beer, whatever you have on tap."

He looked across the table. "You probably only want a salad. I know you must be on a diet 'cause girl, you got some junk in your trunk. It don't look too bad though."

His cartoonist words floated across the sticky oak table and bit me like a thousand mosquitoes. He definitely wasn't my perfect match. Exhausted by his rudeness, I put the menu on the table. "I'll have a full rack of baby-back ribs with extra sauce, a baked potato with the works, a salad with extra dressing, two pieces of sweet corn bread, lemon poppy seed pound cake for dessert, and a large cola." Most of the time I drank diet sodas, but I felt a need to rub his face in his smugness and soothe the frustration rising in me.

His bottom lip dropped, exposing his pink swollen tongue. This date was already in the "do not repeat" column, so I didn't care. I nestled my chin in the palm of my hand and watched a fly buzz around his shiny head. I wanted it to land and secrete that stuff to make his head a tasty treat.

"I told you I was light in the pockets, girl. Are you trying to eat everything in the place?"

"I'm hungry," I said without parting my teeth. "If you couldn't afford a date you should have stayed at home."

20

"I'm doing your father a favor. Thought maybe he'd put in a good word for me at work. You know."

"Put in a good word? What are you talking about?" I sat up straighter, my stomach tightened into a knot.

He grinned at me like he was finally getting to the point of the evening. "The promotion to District Manager. The way I hear it, your father will make the final decision with the panel. So you know..." He hunched his shoulders. "I hope you tell your dad I'm a good guy. You know what I mean?" He reached for my hand and rolled his thumb across my knuckles.

The server set our drinks on the table. Jonathan slurped his beer and watched me over the glass rim.

My first instinct was to pull my hand away and slap him. But his comment slowed my reactions. This whole weekend was one grand farce. The dates, the pretend happiness to be with me, it was all about a job. Even Cory and the dancing were just a stunt to win the good graces of my father.

"I'll mention something to him, as soon as I get home." My voice was as cold as a February blizzard.

The idiot smiled. "I knew I could count on you, baby. Maybe after dinner you and I can go back to my place and have a little fun. I like big butts and I cannot lie," he sang.

I snatched my hand away and signaled the server to refill my cola. "I don't think that's going to happen."

He lifted one shoulder. "I know you might not believe this, but I'm dam good in bed. Don't let the looks deceive you."

"As tempting as you think your offer is, I'm not interested."

"Then why did you order so much food? If you didn't plan to party with me tonight, you should have stuck with the salad."

"Why don't you just shut up?"

He drummed his thick fingers on the table. His eyes rolled over my face and landed on my breasts.

21

"Ever thought about dropping a few pounds? You'd be cute if you lost a little weight. You should try running. I know women who run and pow!" He flared his fingers apart like exploding fireworks, "their figures are knockouts."

"I was going to ask you the same thing. If your stomach wasn't so big, you'd be a stud," I lied.

"I thought women liked beefy men. You know, they feel like I can protect them."

The only thing he could protect was his dinner plate. I folded my arms and placed them on the table between us, the barrier I wouldn't allow him to cross. He continued talking about diets and exercise, neither of which seemed familiar to him. "You don't get to the gym to very often either, do you?" I reached for my soda and twirled the straw.

"It's different for men than it is for women. I've got love handles. You know, something for a woman to grab on to." He smirked.

"I guess I wouldn't know. I'm not much of a grabber."

I needed to find a woman for my father, to occupy his time. Two bad dates in one weekend was too much. A record for him. I glanced at my watch. In a few hours, I would be back at home in my comfortable sweat pants in front of the television.

Dinner arrived and we ate without talking. He scooped food into his mouth like a pig at a trough. I had every intention of licking my plate clean, but I couldn't.

"If you don't plan to eat all the food I can take care of it for you. The ribs and cake, anyway. I don't want the salad." He grinned. "I've got a dog."

"I don't think so." My response was curt, just like I intended. His anguish and the tangy taste of barbecue sauce lingering on my tongue was the most pleasurable part of the whole evening.

When he pulled in front of my house I jumped out before he could insult me again. "Don't forget to put in a good word for me. I could really use a promotion."

I glared back through the window at him. "You can't be serious, can you?"

"Hey, I was a gentleman tonight."

"Yeah, you were a real gem."

"See you 'round," he yelled as I slammed the car door.

I stalked into the house like my thong was on fire.

"What happened?" My father ran across the room. "Did he hurt you?" His eyes were wide with fear.

"No, nothing like that." I patted his chest. "Just promise no more matchmaking … please."

My father gathered me in his arms like I was his little girl. "I thought Jonathan was a stand-up guy," he said.

"Dad, did you promise Cory and Jonathan anything to go out with me?" I asked without lifting my head off his chest.

"Of course not. Any one of them would be lucky to get a girl like you." He tightened his arms around me.

"Want to share my poppy seed lemon pound cake?" I flopped into the chair at the kitchen table and removed the plastic container from the bag.

"Sure, baby." He sat beside me. "He was that bad, huh?"

"Dad, are you blind? Didn't you see the word creep written across his face?"

He shook his head and popped cake into his mouth.

"I think Mom had a discerning eye. You on the other hand need to work on your skills just a wee bit more. Consider your matchmaking days over. You need to understand that I'm going to be okay. I love my work. I have good friends. I'm happy. Really, I am." I forced him to look at me. A glint of understanding registered in his dark eyes.

"Okay, Phoebe. I guess you're right. But promise, if you change your mind you'll call me. I work with a lot of single men. One of them could be right for you."

I pointed my fork at him. "Nope. Don't even consider arranging another date for me or filling my weekend with another crazy stunt."

"All right, all right."

"For the next several months, I'll come visit you in Baltimore. You don't even have to worry about driving up to Philly."

"Are you mad at me, baby girl?"

The lines in his face seemed exaggerated.

"I could never be mad at you, but you've got to let me go it alone. I'm going to be just fine."

"I know. I know."

We finished the cake, smashing the crumbs against the plate, and licking the sweet confection from our fingers.

"I'm going to turn in now." He patted my hand and stood up.

"Night," I cleared the table.

He stood in the kitchen doorway, with a wide grin on his face. His robe hung off his shoulder. "Cory called tonight. He said he'd call back tomorrow."

I spun around to face him and pointed my finger. "Dad?"

"I had nothing to do with it. All I did was answer the phone when it rang." His eyes sparkled. Then he winked and shuffled off to bed, his flip-flops slapping hard against the tiled floor.

Chapter Three

My phone rang as I stepped out of the shower the next morning. I ran into my bedroom and glanced at the caller ID. A quick check of the piece of paper my father had given me last night confirmed Cory's number. I had a strong urge to pick up the phone and drop it down, but the effect just isn't the same with a cordless phone.

I stuck my head out the bedroom door. "Don't pick up Dad, I'll get it," I lied, but I needed to handle this situation my own way. Cory had made a fool of me and there was no way I would let him do it again.

As I came down the stairs I could smell sausage frying. My father loved his big breakfasts, which explained my thick thighs.

"Who was on the phone?" he asked as he poured sausage gravy over a homemade biscuit.

"Dad, you really need to stop meddling." I placed my hands on my hips. "Now tell me, who do you expect to eat all this food?"

"Consider this my going away present for you. Since you're kicking me out today."

I sat next to him and helped myself to a giant biscuit. "You're always welcome here. Just give me a few weeks."

"Deal," he said round a mouth full of food.

"I really need to get a life." I laughed at him.

Finally, with breakfast eaten and dishes washed, Dad pulled his car away from the curve and my shoulders relaxed. For now we had a truce. If the balance lasted for the rest of the year, then I'd consider myself lucky for the short win.

I snatched my keys and ID off the table and bounded for the door. As I made my way down the porch stairs, I glimpsed Cory approaching my house. Just seeing him again made my body stiffen from rejection. I forced my shoulders back and refused to glance down at my feet. Dressed less formal today, his jeans rode his narrow hips and long legs like

25

they were custom made for him. His lean physique against the backdrop of the afternoon sun made my mouth moist. With my hair pulled back into a tight ponytail and my tightest pair of jeans on, I must have looked like a throwaway chick. But after his treatment, I didn't care. I stuck my chin up.

I took a deep breath before my heart got too excited and tried to leap in his arms. He stopped at my door and glared up at me. "If you came to see my father, you just missed him." I descended the steps and slipped passed him.

"I called you a few times this morning. I thought you had to be here."

"I was ignoring you, couldn't you tell?"

"I came to see you," he said to my back as I walked away.

"Well, you've seen me," I called over my shoulder and headed up the street.

He caught up to me. "I know I owe you an explanation for the other night."

I stopped and shoved my hands in the pockets of my pants. "You don't owe me anything. We went out, we had a little fun. It's done."

"Do you mind if I walk with you?"

I wanted to walk him right up to my bedroom and out of my panties. The way the sun gleamed off his head was so sexy all I could think about was rolling my hands over it and smothering him into my bosom. But neither of those things was going to happen and I couldn't afford to be foolish. The remnants of my last breakup still reminded me how I'd ignored all the signs that Barrett was a cheat. Cory wanted a promotion and I was his way to get it.

"Cory, what is it? Why are you here?" I tried to force him to be honest. He seemed decent enough to tell me the truth. Even Jonathan, the creep, articulated why he was willing to spend a bit of change on dinner.

Cory placed his hand on my arm to keep me from walking away. "I want to talk."

"Well, as you can see this isn't a good time for me. How about I give you a call when I have some free time? I'm really not into relationships right now." I tried to mimic him but he had to know I was faking.

I made an elaborate display of exhaling. "Cory, I know you want some time after your last relationship. So let's not torture each other."

I left him there. As much as I would have loved to take his hand, lead him into my house and listen to his sexy, heavy voice talk all night long, Instead, I willed my legs down the street to have lunch with my friends.

Cat and Yani walked up to the café just as I did. Yani's long hair was pulled up into an elegant French knot and Cat's hair was even shorter than when I saw her a week ago.

"You cut your hair again?" I said as I ran my hands through her short curls.

"Yeah. Who needs hair? Life is so much simpler without the hassle, so why bother?"

Once we were seated, I ordered a Cosmopolitan. As soon as the server took our orders I put my hand up. "Cat, I hope Yani filled you in on my weekend because I need to tell you guys the latest. Cory showed up at my house today."

"Oh boy," Yani said. "What did he want?"

Cat pulled her chair closer and propped her elbow on the table. "That's a good thing right?"

"Maybe under some other circumstances I'd be happy. But I think this weekend was more about a position my father controls than it was about me."

"You can't be sure unless you ask him, right?" Yani asked.

"I could and I could ask him to love, honor, and cherish me too. But doesn't that make me sound like I'm begging? Are you dating me to get the promotion from my dad?" I shook my head. "No way. I can find my own man. I don't need my father's help."

"But if he's as good looking as you told Yani, then maybe—"

"Enough. We didn't come here today to solve my dating problems. I'll work it all out somehow."

"Phoebe, give your dad some credit. He at least tries. My father has turned his nose up at every one of my boyfriends this year. Now, when he and my mom come to town, I don't even mention the men in my life." Yani could have any man she wanted. Tall, thin, and beautiful enough to grace the cover of beauty magazines, she was just as selective as her parents. Her list for Mr. Perfect had twenty-five must-have items on it. Including someone who could afford to take her on a date to an exotic location. I'd settle for a date that wasn't arranged by my father, or one without a string leading back to him.

Cat lifted her glass. "This is going to be our year. I just have a feeling that in the next twelve months we're all going to find love. If it happens on televisions and in movies then it can happen for us. You know I have a sense for these kinds of things." She pointed a finger at them.

We clicked our glasses. Even though I had a lot of doubt, I didn't let on. Cat subscribed to the same theories as my father. But the logic didn't work for me. I'd started dating when I was fifteen and I had a list of hard lessons proving love was as elusive as the pot of gold at the end of the rainbow.

By the time we finished lunch we were laughing and talking about something other than men, or the lack of them, and my mood was better.

Maybe I didn't need a man to be happy. I wanted to believe the idiom was true, because my life might not mimic my parent's with true love and years of devotion.

I rounded the corner of my block just as the late summer sun settled below the horizon. Cory was seated on my stoop and stood as I walked up.

"You're still here?" I was happy to see him, but I didn't want him to see my joy.

"I came here to talk to you and we haven't had that discussion yet."

I examined him from his clean head to the tips of his Italian loafers. "Are you a stalker? Because if you are, you ought to know I have mace in my bag." I slipped my hand under the flap even though the most dangerous thing I could pull out was a tube of lip gloss.

"I'm not a stalker. I just want to talk to you. Call me determined." He took a step toward me, towering over me like a giant.

I liked looking up at him. There was something comforting in his eyes. "Okay, what do you want to say? You've got three minutes."

He shoved his hands in his pockets. My eyes went immediately to his crotch.

"Why only three, why not five?"

"You're wasting time." I started toward the door.

"Can I come inside?"

"I'm really exhausted." I sighed and dropped my shoulders for emphasis.

"You invited me to a party tomorrow, what time should I pick you up?"

I stopped in mid-stride with my foot suspended in air. My reaction was slower than normal because I wasn't sure I even understood what he was saying.

I turned to face him. "You aren't still thinking about coming to our party?"

His face didn't change. The seriousness in his expression answered my question.

"You aren't rescinding your invitation, are you?"

I stomped back down the stairs with my hand attached to my hip. "After your confession on Friday night, I was thinking about doing just that. I don't want to be the one to cause you to change your course of direction."

"Let me worry about my course. What time should I pick you up?"

If I hadn't been looking up at his enticing lips I'm sure I would have said no. But I really wanted them to touch me again, at least one more time. I took my time replying, hoping I was making him sweat, but he looked so damn cool.

"Okay, Cory. Tomorrow. Pick me up at seven-thirty." I marched back up the stairs without giving him another look. I shut the door with a firmness that said what I couldn't.

Chapter Four

I felt strange having him pick me up and take me to a party I was helping to throw. In the past I didn't always date the classy men. I'm the first to admit my shortcomings and now I was going to make better choices. Even though Cory might not be a good one.

"I'm a little surprised you actually showed up." I could have given him a more welcoming greeting, but I had too many doubts about him.

"I said I'd be here." He glanced at his watch. "And I'm right on time."

"So I should be happy?" I was being difficult but I didn't want to fall for him. As handsome as he was, it would have been so easy.

"You shouldn't be anything but ready to go." He extended his hand and led me down the stairs. He might not be my one true love, but I wished he were.

I gave him the directions to Yani's place before buckling my seat belt.

"I know the area. She's not too far from me." He started the car. "You're sure she won't mind if I crash?"

"You're my guest. It's not a problem. As long as you don't try to ditch me after dinner, or at the door, I think everything will be just fine."

I had no intentions of helping him to get the promotion and as long as he wanted to pretend with me, I would do the same thing with him. Being open and honest was important to me, but I didn't consider my behavior as deceitful, I was just taking care of me for a change. Putting myself first, which is something I had to learn to do.

"I'm looking forward to meeting your friends." He made a right turn and merged into traffic.

"They're looking forward to meeting you, too. You just might get a thousand questions tonight."

"You've told them about me?"

"Only the bad stuff."

"I see. So tell me what I'm walking into. Will I have to defend myself?"

I made an elaborate gesture of rubbing my chin. "They're my girls. I told them about our first date. What do you think?"

He winced, but said nothing more. Torturing him a little was fun. Seldom did I have the ability to poke fun at a date gone badly, but since Cory had popped back up like a game of whack-a-mole, I decided to get all my emotional baggage out while I had the chance. I knew Yani and Cat were tired of helping me carry it around.

There was something lovable about Cory. As much as I wanted to dislike him for the way he'd treated me, I really couldn't. He had a gentleness that softened all the rough edges of my heart.

Cory wore a pair of dress slacks and a casual three-button polo shirt. No matter what he chose to wear, he would have looked good. The dress I'd purchased just for this occasion was worth every expensive cent. The jersey material hugged my hips and the deep cut neckline kept pulling Cory's eyes off the road.

"I'm not sure if I already said this, but you look exceptional tonight. But you looked fantastic both times I've seen you."

"Thank you." I smoothed my hands over my dress without looking at him. He was throwing off the charm, I had to be careful.

"I didn't expect to hear from you again. Your disappearing act was quite convincing."

"Can we put our first date behind us?"

"How about this, I won't mention it again for at least twenty-four hours. I can't promise you any more than that."

"Fair enough. I'll just have to work on something else to replace it with in your memory bank."

"You can try."

"Are you this tough on all your dates?"

"No, only on the disappointing ones." I turned toward the passenger window to hide the pleasure I was getting from giving him grief.

"I didn't mean to disappoint you. What I was trying to do was be open with you. I should have told you what was going on with me when I picked you up. I know that now."

"Her house is the one with the light in front." I pointed. He found a space not too far away, and jumped out to open my door before I could grab my clutch. The tension in the car eased. No matter what he did tonight, he was still going to be on square one. It would take a lot more than good manners to get him moving ahead again.

####

I deserved every smart remark she threw at me. After each one, she seemed to release a little more of her pent up anger with me. In a few months she might almost forget what I'd done. Actually it was funny to see how many ways she could think up to describe our first date. I only hoped years from now she'd still think our first encounter was worth talking about.

As I followed her up the walk to her friend's house my eyes wouldn't move past her shapely ass. That dress must have been custom made for her booty. And to think I'd almost passed on this beauty.

She looked over her shoulder and gave me the sultriest gaze with eyes that said way more than her body ever could. She might like ribbing me, but she also liked me, I could tell. When she thought I didn't notice, she was checking me out.

"Yani, we're here," she said as she opened the door.

"Hey, come on in, Phoebe. We're in the kitchen."

"Are you ready?" she asked me. "My friends can be as brutal as I am. In fact they taught me everything I know."

"Bring them on. If I can handle you, I'm sure I can handle your friends." I placed my hand around her waist and escorted her down the hall toward the laughter and chatter.

32

"Phoebe, that dress is spectacular on you. I'm so glad I talked you into buying it. And this must be Cory?" A tall woman with striking features stood in the entry of the kitchen with a martini glass in her hand.

"Yes. Cory, this is Yani, and the woman behind the martini shaker is Cat. Watch out for her or she'll try to get you drunk."

"It's nice to meet you both. I've heard a lot about you."

Both women gave me a thorough exam without even touching me. Neither threw anything, which meant Phoebe must have said some things to make it worth keeping me around.

"We've heard even more about you." Cat raised the metal shaker above her head and shook it along with her hips. "If you really want to give us a hand can you please get the grill lit? Both Yani and I tried, but all we got was a lot of smoke and no fire."

"All these men around here and none of them could get the grill started?" Phoebe asked.

"Cat's been pretty heavy-handed with the drinks, so the best they can do is strike a match." Yani finished her drink and set the empty glass on the counter.

"Just show me the way." Happy to get away from their scrutiny, Phoebe led me through the house and onto a back deck.

"I think they like you," Phoebe said as we stepped outside.

I lifted one eyebrow. "How could you tell?"

"Believe me, you'd know if they didn't."

My eyes landed on her cleavage for the tenth time before drifting back to her sparkling eyes. "Yeah, but the important question is, do *you* like me?"

Her curly lashes fluttered, but the smile tugging at her lips told me she was seconds away from giving me one of her beautiful smiles. "I'll let you know at the end of the evening. How about that?"

I pulled her into my arms, loving the way she had to look up at me. Her full, glossy lips dared me to smear them, but I'm always ready to test the boundaries. The sweet taste of her lipstick was nothing compared to her tongue. She followed my lead and the friendly dual between our tongues fired my desire. I tightened my hold on her waist, sinking deeper into the luxury of her warmth.

"Uh-huh. The grill may not be hot, but it looks like you two sure are." Yani set a tray of ribs and steaks on the table.

Phoebe stepped back and rolled her lips under her teeth. "You probably shouldn't kiss me."

"I never said I wouldn't kiss you. How can I keep my hands off of you when you're looking so tempting tonight?"

"I think you ought to give it a try. Remember, you're the one with the relationship issues. "I'll leave you to the grill, so we can eat sometime tonight."

"Yeah, let me get on that. But don't forget where we left off." I whispered the last part to Phoebe.

"I already did." She followed Yani back into the house and I watched every step she took before disappearing inside.

I spent the night watching Phoebe. Her graceful interaction with her friends displayed her softer side. She may have had a basketful of snide remarks for me, but for everyone else she overflowed with charm.

She crossed the room and headed straight for me. The luminous glow on her face seemed to draw everyone's attention, but her gazed was pinned on me, making me feel liked I'd won the golden ring.

"Are you okay? You've been pretty quiet." She ran her hand along my bicep. Her touch was gentle and left me wanting more.

"I'm fine." I placed my hand over hers, holding it in place. "Can I get you something? Refresh your drink?"

"No. I'm not drinking another one of Cat's infamous concoctions. I've got an appointment with a client tomorrow and I need a clear head."

I should have been listening to her. Instead I couldn't look away from her lips. All I wanted was to feel them again. With my finger under her chin, I pulled her toward me and took the kiss I needed.

"Get a room, you two," Cat remarked as she passed with a full blender of more drinks.

Chapter Five

Why did all the men who seemed so perfect have to have so much junk in their heads? Cory couldn't have been more engaging and attentive all night. But not once did he mention my father or the promotion. Couple his lack of openness with his need to stay unattached, and everything about him should have had me sprinting away from him.

I've done a lot of stupid things, most of them I'd like to forget, but standing on my door step gazing into Cory's bright flecked eyes and wishing we could have an exclusive relationship, was moving ahead on my list. I'm the level-headed friend who always has advice for someone. But I couldn't seem to follow the yelling in my own head.

"I better get inside. I hope you had a nice time tonight. My friends can be a lot to handle."

"I liked them. They obviously care about you."

I pecked him on the cheek, instead of curling up in his arms like I wanted.

"Aren't you going to invite me in? I still want to talk to you."

I pretended to think about his question. It's a good thing he couldn't see what was going on inside of my head.

I glanced at my door and back to him. I could make this easy on him, or hard. I wanted to make him sweat, but my stomach was full and it was too warm to haggle with him on the stoop.

"I guess I'll let you in. But you'll need to keep your hands and lips to yourself. I would make you talk out here, but I need to come out of these shoes. My feet were screaming for relief. The comfort of my five inch sandals had worn off long before the party ended."

"I think that's a good idea." He held my hand as I walked up the stairs.

I flopped on the couch without trying to look sweet or dainty. After he said his piece and was on his way, I'd fall into bed and dream about him. "I'm listening. What's on your mind?"

He settled on the sofa next to me. "Hand me your foot." He wiggled his fingers.

"What?"

"Let me."

I placed my foot in his lap. He unbuckled the gladiator sandal on my right foot. I held my breath as he ran his thumb down the sole of my foot, applying pressure at intervals along the way. His hands were warm and tender. As much as I wanted to pull away, my legs wouldn't move. Having him rubbing my feet was enough to make me happy.

"Cory, if your goal is to confuse, me you're doing a helluva job. What's your game? Don't you think you're leading me on?" I rested my head against the cushion. His touch was more than magical, it was sensual. Maybe he'd found the spot on the bottom of my foot that was connected to the spot between my thighs.

"I'm not playing any games. I like hanging out with you."

"Oh, I'm like one of the guys, huh? Maybe I should flip on the television and find a game we can enjoy."

"You know, instead of using your mouth for so much smart talk, you could use it to kiss me."

"I could, but this is much more fun."

He pressed his knuckles into the ball of my foot with enough pressure to make me melt into the sofa. He knew exactly what he was doing and I was too silly to resist.

"I'm listening, Cory." I used my head to nod at what he was doing to my feet.

"I wanted to talk with you. The other night we didn't get an opportunity to really have a discussion and after tonight, I think we need to give it another try. If you have to keep coming up with ways to take jabs at me, I'm afraid you might need medical intervention."

I shook my head. "No, the other night I was just fine."

"You are fine. That's why I had to come back. I think you are an amazing woman. You're beautiful, easy to talk to, and you have curves in all the right places. Look at you, I'm mesmerized by you." The way he looked at me without pulling his glance away made me uneasy. Usually when a guy is lying he has the decency to look away.

I tried to pull my foot away, but he loosened my left sandal and repeated the whole process. I nestled back against the cushion. I figured free massages didn't happen every day so I needed to enjoy this special treatment.

"Cory, you didn't need to come to the party tonight to tell me you think I'm attractive. I appreciate the foot massage and the compliments. But it's getting late and I've got an early meeting with a client in the morning. You want the job my father is posting, don't you? You know you should have just said so on Friday night." I didn't mean to blurt out the question, but I didn't like the tease.

His hands stopped kneading my feet. "Ah, I get it now. I should have known a woman as beautiful as you wouldn't continuously take jabs unless she had issues or she was misinformed." His eyes pierced mine, and with so much to say, I was speechless.

"Is that what you think? All this time you thought…"

"I don't know what to think." I pulled my feet away and placed them on the floor.

"I enjoyed our date and I had fun with you at the party tonight. Have a happy life." I jumped off the sofa like it was a battle ground.

He smirked. "You are a little spitfire, aren't you? Are you always this headstrong and stubborn?"

"Every chance I get. Are you always so imposing?"

"Always." His voice was like warm, sweet butter and just as smooth.

"I'm not interested in your father's job opening. But I am interested in his only daughter." He stuck his foot out and in a stance that was slightly intimidating, but just as appealing. "I want you to go out with me again. But you seem to have made up your mind about me already." He headed for the door and I started to let him. But his broad shoulders and tight ass taunted me as he reached for the doorknob.

"Wait a minute, Cory." I beckoned him back. "I had to ask. I'd always be wondering otherwise." I shrugged my shoulders.

"Let me try this, then." He seared my lips with a kiss that set my flesh to simmer. I surrendered my tongue to him knowing I was being led deeper in the woods just like Hansel and Gretel. And I didn't even have the sense to bring breadcrumbs.

He towered over me and wrapped his arms around me. His lips were less than an inch from mine and all I wanted him to do was to kiss me again. He placed his mouth over mine and my body relaxed. His tongue eased into my mouth so slow I drew it in deeper, wanting to taste him. His kiss was as demanding as my desire for him.

When his knee slipped between my thighs, I ground my pelvis against him. He pulled me tighter. Wrapped in his thick arms felt just right. But I was getting carried away. I pulled away from him. My lips felt warm.

"So now what?" I asked.

He looked down at his crotch where his erection was quite evident. "I guess I shouldn't ask if you want..."

"No you shouldn't." I gasped. "Don't you dare!"

"Then say you'll let me pick you up after your meeting tomorrow and take you out to dinner."

I hesitated. "You want to take me out?"

"I do. And I want to be real clear this time around. I'm asking you out because I want to be with you, not because your father suggested the idea or because he has an opening you think I want." He pressed his nose against mine. "As a matter of fact, I've already been offered the position of Director of Inside Sales. So you see, instead of working for your father, I'll be working along side him."

"Why didn't you say so when you came here on Sunday or when you first walked through my door?" I swatted his shoulder.

"I had no idea you were manipulating the facts in your cute little head and I certainly didn't feel the need to justify my behavior." He drew me close.

39

"Well, one thing you need to know if you decided to date me, you'll always need to defend yourself."

"There's something you should know about me too. In a relationship, I never defend my position. You have to trust me."

"So we're in a relationship now?" I held my breath waiting on him to reply. Asking such a bold question wasn't me, but I couldn't make another incorrect assumption. And the least he could do was tell me, like the boys used to do when we were in grade school. He should have slid me a piece of paper asking me to circle yes or no.

"Yes." A mischievous grin played across his mouth.

Chapter Six

The decision to pursue Phoebe had to be right. Visions of her full lips and tantalizing hips danced through my head, all night. Today, instead of concentrating on the transition to my new assignment, all I wanted to think about was holding her again.

I examined the slip of paper with the address scripted in her handwriting. The tall glass building wasn't what I'd expected. Her business contacts must be high-end not the mom and pop operations I'd imagined.

After only a few minutes, she strode out the door. The moment she came into view I couldn't take my eyes off her. She pulled her portfolio over her shoulder and glanced around. I blew the horn and waved to her.

"Did you have a good meeting?" I asked as soon as she was buckled in her seat.

"They liked my concepts and offered me the contract. It will keep me in high-end shoes for a while." The gleam in her eyes made her whole face sparkle. Her relaxed confidence changed the atmosphere in the car.

Resisting the urge to grab her and fill her up, I put the car in Drive and pulled away from the curb.

"Where are we going? You never said." She shifted her body to face me. Even though her blouse was buttoned to an acceptable level, I could still see the top mounds of her breasts.

"We're going to a picnic in the park." I used my head to point to the basket in the back seat. "See, I have the food, the blanket, and everything."

"It will be dark in an hour. What are you planning to eat by, flashlight?" Her voice was light.

"We're going to watch a movie under the stars."

"Sounds like fun. What are we going to see?"

"The movie isn't the important part of the night. Spending time with me is the bonus."

"Oh, I'm glad you told me, otherwise I would have been staring at the screen all night instead of at you. But really, what is the movie?"

"The best movie ever made, Casablanca."

She tilted her head to one side. "You really think that's the best movie, ever?"

"No, but that's what the flyer said."

"But won't we get cold when the temperature drops?"

"Don't worry, I'll keep you warm." I rubbed my hand along her bare arm.

Traffic into the park was congested, but I was able to find a space in the rear of the lot.

"I've got everything." I picked up the basket and blankets.

"So who prepared the food? I didn't know you were a cook." She pressed her body against me as we headed for an open patch of grass in the middle of the lawn. The night was only just beginning, but I was content already.

"Oh, girl, I can cook. I make a pasta dish that will make you fall in love." I snapped the blanket and straightened the edges.

She placed her hands on her hips. "You sound pretty sure of yourself, Mr. Casanova."

I sat next to her and propped myself on one elbow. "Just wait and see. I'll cook for you, real soon."

"Are you always so cocky?"

"Only when I have to be. You see, you pegged me all wrong, so now I have to show you who I really am."

There was a hint of skepticism in the twist of her mouth. "I think we better eat before it gets too dark to see the food."

I opened the lid and pulled chicken salad and fruit salad from the wicker basket.

As the sky darkened, the film began. She sat between my legs pressing her back against my chest. I wrapped my arms around her as the opening scene lit up the night sky. With my nose nuzzled into the softness of her neck, I inhaled

42

her clean scent and then I planted kisses along the column of her neck.

She gave me a playful swat. "You aren't watching the movie," she whispered.

"I'm seeing everything I want." With my fingertip I turned her chin up so I could kiss her. The slow dance of our tongues stirred my need for her. With my hand at the base of her neck, my tongue rolled over hers, tasting the sweetness of her mouth. My body responded and when she pulled away I didn't want to let her go.

"Why did you stop kissing me?" I tried to pull her back.

"I think we should take our little party inside. Let's go to my place." She got up on her knee, careful not to block the view of the folks behind us.

I pulled the ends of the blanket up. "I'm closer."

I don't normally go to a date's house until I've gone out on at least three dates with him, but I was really into Cory. At least he didn't take me to another restaurant or a movie theater. I liked sitting in his arms under the stars. Of all the conventional dates I've had, this was the most romantic one. At least he put some effort into the planning instead of just making a reservation.

As he drove the short distance to his house, I couldn't take my eyes off of the dimple in his chin. I kept wondering if he'd let me stick my tongue in it.

He pulled into the garage of a high-rise and then held my hand as we entered the elevator.

"What about the food? Are you going to leave it in the car?"

He ran back to get the basket. "You're right. We can always continue our picnic inside.

He unlocked the door to his apartment and allowed me to walk in before him. A single lamp illuminated the large living area. "I see you don't need much to get by," I said as I surveyed the room.

"I haven't lived here too long. About two months. I'm trying to see if this is a place where I want to put down roots."

The blood flow to my heart stumbled. I was planning a future with Cory and he wasn't even sure if he was staying in town. How many times was I going to let him trip me up? He was about as fickle as a butterfly, landing on one flower and immediately attracted to another. I picked up a magazine on the table and leafed through the pages, like I was really interested in Sports Illustrated. But at least I didn't have to respond to his reply.

"So come sit with me." He patted the sofa.

"This is an amazing view." I stared at the skyline with my back to him. Sitting beside him only meant one thing and I wasn't in the mood to torture myself. I had enough one-night stands detailed in my journal.

"Okay, we'll do this your way." He came up behind me and wrapped me in his arms. It felt so good to be held by someone other than my father. As much as I wanted to resist, my body couldn't. I leaned into him and vowed it would only be for a moment.

The way he swayed back and forth to a rhythm that was slow and steady shook loose the last of my resolve. As if it were scripted by Hollywood the night seemed so perfect for falling in love. My willpower faded like a setting sun. By the time he turned me around and parted my lips with his tongue I knew I was going to sleep with him. If not tonight, soon.

Chapter Seven

I had every intention of talking Phoebe out of her skinny jeans and into my bed, but once we were inside the condo, I wanted more than what resided between her legs. I wanted her to give me her heart. I wanted the smile she wore at her party to greet me every day when I walked through the door. I wanted to hear her say my name with the same lilting voice she used with her friends.

"I'm glad you gave me another chance. I hope tonight I showed you I wasn't just another jerk."

"Don't pat yourself on the back yet."

I threw my hands in the air in mock indignation. "Why? Tell me where I went wrong. I picked you up on time. I fed you a balanced dinner and provided good entertainment."

"You're very sweet, Cory." She reached up on her toes and placed a kiss on my chin, her tongue running along my dimple.

"I'm not trying to be sweet. I'm trying to charm you."

"Charm me or charm my pants off of me?" Her voice was lustful.

"I'd like to do both." I let my hand drop to her firm butt and gave it a squeeze.

I tilted her chin to reach my mouth, half expecting her to fight me. Instead she allowed my tongue through the golden gates. I drove deeper, trying to enjoy every inch of her. Her full breasts pressed against my chest and almost without trying I pulled her blouse from her jeans and slipped my hand under the shirt.

Her skin was even softer than I'd imagined. She didn't wear a bra, which made it easier to cup her firm breasts. She moaned as I rubbed my thumb over her nipples. Each one tightened under my touch.

"I just might let you, too."

"Tell me what I need to do." I slipped her blouse off her shoulder and kiss her. She kneaded my back through my

45

T-shirt. I wanted to feel her skin against mine, so I yanked off my top. She moved her hand down my abs. With each inch she wound me tighter. I wasn't sure I could contain my desire for her. Scooping her off her feet, I carried her to the bedroom.

The only light in the room came from the moon. The setting couldn't have been more ideal. I placed her on the bed and pulled her jeans down her long lean legs. She locked eyes with me as I undressed her. Without saying a word the lustful look in her eyes encouraged me to continue. Her thong came off with the jeans. Instead of unbuttoning her shirt she pulled it over her head. Her naked body should have been captured on a canvas. Every inch of her was exquisite.

"Aren't you going to undress, too?" Her voice was low and husky.

I stripped off my shoes and pants.

####

If I was as smart as I thought I was I would have got out of his apartment when he admitted he might be a short-timer. But when it comes to love, sometimes I listen to my heart and not my head. It's a fault that I need to work on. I vowed to find an Oprah recommended book on the subject just as soon as the sun came up.

Until then I listened to his heavy breathing and floated on the luxurious feel of having every inch of my body touched with so much tenderness.

"You're awake?" He spoke into my ear.

"I am." I pushed my body into the curve of his and just like I wanted he draped his arm over me and snuggled closer. I had to make a difficult decision. Cory was so near perfect it would be a shame to have to walk away from him. But I've had a one-way love life before and there isn't anything about it worth trying a second time around. The sooner I got out, the better.

"I better get home," I said.

"Don't tell me you have to get home to your cat. I know you don't have one."

"Um, yeah. It's not a cat. But I've got this thing I need to do." I reached for my thong on the floor. "If you have something to do, I can catch a cab." My fake bravery surprised even me.

"Are you sure you have to go?" Unless my ears were faking me out, he really sounded disappointed. I needed to get out while he still wanted me to stay.

I wiggled into my jeans, jiggling my breast in the process. Hoping my actions drove his desire up several more notches.

"I'll drive you, give me a minute." He climbed out of bed and bared his tight, firm butt as he sauntered out of the room. I covered my face with my hands, not sure I was happy or disgusted with my feelings for him. He had "stay away from me" tattooed all over that beautiful body and I wanted to ignore every single inscription.

As soon as he closed the door, I twirled around and buried a squeal in my throat. I found my shoes in his living room and was waiting on him when he came out.

He picked up his keys and tossed them from one hand to the other. "You sure you want to go home? I have an awesome hot tub I've been waiting to take for a test run."

"Maybe next time." I was more than willing to strip again and take him for another ride, but my sensibility warning flashers were blinking in my head.

He bobbed his head and reached for my hand. "Okay, let's get Cinderella home."

The drive back to my house was quiet. The buckle on my portfolio was the most interesting clasp I'd ever seen. Opening and closing it kept my hands busy, because I couldn't slow my thoughts. What if he decided to move away again? Was I just setting myself up for another disappointment to write about in my journal?

He parked the car and walked me to the door. I tried to gather the courage to ask him the question that haunted me all night. The insecure part of my heart was fearful of his answer.

"What time should I pick you up tomorrow?"

I tilted my head, hoping I'd heard him right. One minute he was talking about leaving Philly and now he was sticking to me like honey and being just as sweet.

"Tomorrow?"

"You know, the day after this one. I might not find anything as exciting as the outside movie, but I'll think of something."

I could have been a high school girl crushing over her first infatuation. I was a perfect example of good girls doing stupid things. My head was screaming no, but I nodded yes.

"What do you have in mind?" I was trying to measure the amount of stupidity I wanted to invest in this relationship. Already my mother was probably looking down on me and shaking her head.

He pinned me against the door. I could smell my cologne in the fibers of his shirt. "You've got to stop this, you know," he said.

I looked into his dark eyes and the smoldering desire flaming in them told me he was feeling something, too.

"Stop what?"

He placed his head into the curve of my neck. I could feel his warm breath on my flesh. "This pull you have on me. I can't seem to get you out of my head. When we're not together, I want to be. And when we are, I only want to think of ways for us to stay that way. You're not playing fair." His words stroked me the same way his hands had earlier.

"I think you're the one cheating."

He kissed my neck. "Tell me how?" His voice was barely audible.

I unlocked the door. "We better go inside, before my neighbors come out to see the show."

The moment I closed the door he pushed his hand under my shirt.

"There's just one thing I need to know before you go there again," I said.

He stopped. "Anything you want. I'll give you anything you want."

"Okay Cory, I promised myself I wasn't going to ask, but I seldom keep the promises I make to myself, so here goes. You made a statement earlier about not being certain you wanted to stay in Philly." I held my hands behind my back. "If you're a short- timer I need to know. I don't want a long distance relationship nor do I want a one night stand." I paused. "I guess I should have thought about that a few hours sooner."

He held me at arm's length. His eyes widened with a seriousness that wasn't there before. "I've known you the span of a holiday weekend so I know you might find this implausible maybe even impossible, but you're going to have to deal with it. I'm falling for you Phoebe, and if that means I have to put down roots in Philly or in Hicktown, U.S.A., then I'm there. Got it?"

My heart thumped so loud I barely heard the last of his sentence. I couldn't reply.

"Did you hear me, Phoebe?" He tightened the pressure on my arms.

I nodded.

"That's the second time you've misunderstood me. Instead of wondering what's going on in my head, you're going to have to come right out and ask me. I promise to always be honest with you."

I wrapped my arms around his neck and kissed him. "Okay. You've got yourself a deal."

ONE YEAR LATER

"Phoebe, what time is your father getting here?" Cory yelled from downstairs.

I ran down the stairs, buttoning the three remaining buttons on my shirt.

"He said he'd be here right after work. If you'd stop pestering me, I would've been dressed an hour ago." I nudged him.

"If you stopped walking around in those little things you call panties I wouldn't feel the need to pester you." He grabbed me by the waist. "After everyone leaves tonight, we'll move on to part two of what we started."

"I can't wait. Can we just sit the food on the front stoop and put out a sign saying we're busy?" I slipped my hand into his pants.

He pulled it out and kissed each finger. "No, now put your shoes on, I'll start the grill." He brandished a muscular bicep.

"Okay." I pretended to pout.

In the small bedroom, I rummaged for a pair of flip flops. The mixture of Cory's clothes and mine stuffed the closet. We'd talked about moving to a bigger place but we hadn't taken the time to look.

"Phoebe, your dad's here," Cory called up.

I found the two of them on the deck.

"Dad, I've missed you!" I kissed his cheek.

"No you didn't. Since Cory's come along you've exiled me to Baltimore." He laughed.

"Benjamin, you can visit anytime you want," Cory said.

The doorbell rang and I waggled my finger at Cory behind my father's back. Giving him an open invitation could mean he'd show up every weekend.

Yani and Cat came through the door followed by their dates. Even though Yani swore she didn't have a love match, at least she had someone to fill her empty nights for now.

"Okay, before we eat, I want to show the pictures from our trip to Bahia." Cory stood by the television waving his arms.

I scurried to his side. "Cory, you're kidding right? No one wants to see our pictures. You'll bore everyone to pieces," I whispered to him.

"Yeah we do." My father took a seat on the middle of the sofa and motioned everyone to sit with him.

I tried to give Cory the stink eye but he refused to look my way.

"You might as well sit down, Phoebe. I think he's going to do this whether you want him to or not," Cat said.

I plopped on the edge of the arm of the sofa and crossed my arms over my chest. I might have to sit, but I didn't have to do it willingly. Cory stood behind me with his hand on my shoulder.

"I don't believe you're doing this," I said to him without moving my teeth.

He massaged my shoulders as the video started. The grand entrance to our hotel with me waving at the camera came into view.

"Dad, stop clapping," I admonished from across the room.

When I turned back to the television, Cory was on the screen. But it wasn't a scene from our trip. From the screen he said, "Phoebe, the last year of my life has been blissful beyond my expectations. From the moment your father set us up a year ago you have made me happy by sharing my life with me. So tonight, in front of our family and friends…"

I turned to find Cory on one knee with an engagement ring in the palm of his hand. "Phoebe, will you marry me?"

"I-I…the whole picture thing was a set up?"

"Of course it was," Yani and Cat said in unison.

"You haven't answered my question, yet." Cory's voice was soft, pulling me in.

"Yes, Cory. Yes, of course I will."

He stood up, pushed the rock on my finger and kissed me. His game piece made the final move landing on the big,

Dating Just Got Serious

gold star, but I was the winner. I think I heard everyone clapping, but the sound of blood rushing in my ears was too loud to be sure.

A SINGLE DATE

Chapter One

Yolanda Maxwell glanced at the clock on the dashboard of her new sport coupe and winced. She had five minutes to maneuver through the thick Philadelphia traffic or risk being late again. Based on the conversation her assistant had with the contractor, this was his last trip to her condo. No matter what, he wasn't coming back. His condescending attitude set her teeth on edge. Every minute of her workday was busy, but he couldn't discuss her kitchen and bath renovation in the evening when she had more time.

She pulled into her designated parking space in front of her unit and shut off the engine. A battered truck plastered with vacation bumper stickers occupied her other slot. It had to belong to the ill-tempered contractor. Who else would have the audacity to use her spot?

With two minutes to spare she grabbed her new green Hermes bag and dashed up the walk. As she rounded the shrubs, he smacked a note on the front door.

"I'm not late. It's not five o'clock yet. I still have a full minute," she called to him as she approached.

"Yeah, but with your track record, I expected you to be a no-show, again. You are Yolanda Maxwell, right?" His voice had the same disapproving tone she'd heard before.

"Yes. Why? Who else would I be?" She thrust her chin higher, dismissing his reprimand.

"All of my interactions have been with your assistant and I assumed…never mind. Forget I said anything." He looked away but not before she saw the chagrined expression on his face.

He wasn't at all what she'd imagined, either. Instead of a fat dumpy guy with pants hanging below a big beer belly, he was tall and all lean muscles. His sleeveless T-shirt exposed biceps the size of her calves and his tanned skin only made his wheat colored hair and light brown eyes more

54

pronounced. The striking resemblance to Brad Pitt was amazing, only he was much taller and several years younger.

She stuck out her hand and tried to sound casual. "Please call me Yani. My parents call me Yolanda when I do something that doesn't meet their approval. And believe me, I hear Yolanda often enough. You must be Drew Sizemore."

He grabbed her hand in a firm grip.

"It's nice to finally put a name with a face. I was beginning to wonder if you really existed."

"I'm sorry about those missed appointments. I did show up a little late last time, but you had already left. I'm usually very prompt, but I just got stuck in the office." She stepped in front of him to unlock the door. "Sometimes getting away is not easy."

He gave her what could have been a smirk before crossing the threshold. "I know you're very busy, so instead of taking up too much of your time, why don't you show me what changes you want to make." His thick Timberland boots clomped across the hardwood floor. A tiny pink teddy bear dangled from the tool belt strapped to his waist. So, he was either married with children or single with children.

His hair was pulled back into a ponytail that hung to the neckline of his shirt. A man with a ponytail, she shook her head. Her father would have something negative to say about that if he saw it.

"Yes, certainly." She led the way toward the kitchen. "I bought the condo two years ago, but I'm only now getting around to making some changes. I want to open up the kitchen so it flows into the rest of the house, which means taking down this wall and this bank of cabinets. I want quartz countertops and a double oven in the wall." She stopped to see if he understood her chattering.

With his hip positioned against the kitchen sink and his clipboard on the counter, he looked uninterested.

"Aren't you going to write this down?"

"Don't need to." His deep voice was intimidating.

"Mr. Sizemore, I don't want to have to repeat myself over and over again."

"Call me Drew. And I have no intention of making you repeat yourself." He stepped closer to her, freezing her in place with his penetrating stare. "I heard everything you said. Please continue."

She swallowed past the tightening in her throat. This was her house. She should have feel in control. Instead, the way he towered over her made her nervous and clumsy. She backed away from him and made her way into the dining room.

"Now, should I show you the bathroom en-suite that I want to re-do, too?"

"Sure. Continue on, I'll follow you." His eyes took a long, slow tour of her hips and then down to her legs.

She tugged at her pencil skirt, uncomfortable with the unauthorized attention.

"So what's up with the teddy bear? Is it a hidden screwdriver?" She wanted to sound casual, and draw his attention away from her body.

He made a half laugh, half-snort sound.

"What's so funny?"

"You didn't think you were the first person to ask about my teddy bear, did you?"

"Then you know it's odd for a muscular man like you to have a pink bear hanging from his waist."

"My goddaughter gave it to me for my birthday two years ago. And just so you know, I don't care what people think of me. I only have to please myself."

His manifesto settled in her stomach like a load of bricks. She was still trying to muster the courage to stand up to her parents and he made it sound so easy.

She cocked her head and glanced back at him. "You're lucky, Drew."

"How so?"

"Never mind." With him behind her a strand of nervousness inched up her spine. She felt his eyes on her as she hurried down the wide hall to her master bedroom. Inside the room she stepped aside, allowing him to stand beside her. "The bathroom is right through there." She pointed, choosing to follow him now. Good thing nothing personal cluttered the counter, she already felt exposed.

"What would you like to see in here?" He stepped inside the small area, directing his attention to the ugly brown tile on the floor and the hideous beige Formica counter and old ceramic sink.

"I want something more modern, more feminine." She pressed her back against the wall to keep her distance from him. Even though they stood in her personal space, she tried to sound authoritative like she did in the conference rooms at work.

"You're not at all what I expected." He swung back around to face her.

She drew her eyes up to his face, realizing he'd changed the subject. "Yeah, you already said this. Since you feel the need to say it again, don't you think you should tell me what you were expecting?" She huffed.

"Maybe I shouldn't say." His voice dropped an octave, sounding even sexier.

"Now you have to tell me. I want to know." She folded her arms over her chest and stuck out a spike heel-shod foot. "Go ahead, say it." She almost dared him to insult her again.

"Well, I thought you were going to be an uptight corporate executive. While you're certainly uptight and you're obviously a corporate big shot, you're the best looking one I've seen in a long time." His deep voice floated over her like an invitation to something memorable.

"I...I—"

"I probably shouldn't have said that. But I tend to say what's on my mind. My filters are limited." He turned back and peered in the shower as if he'd just commented on the weather or a baseball game score. "Do you have any specific ideas for the bathroom or should I make suggestions?"

She cleared her throat. "Yes, I'd like to hear your ideas." She hurried out of the confined space and back into the kitchen where sun poured in through the window and a counter separated them.

Without asking, he grabbed his clipboard and took the nearest chair. While he scribbled she removed a bottle of pinot noir from the rack and poured herself a glass.

His pronouncement about her looks rattled around in her head like a loose marble. She was flattered by the comment, but his arrogance and brashness almost erased the charming side hidden under his low-slung jeans and slightly bowed legs.

"I'll have a glass, too." His voice drew her attention away from the window.

"What?" She faced him.

"I'll have a glass of wine, too." He lifted his foot across his knee and put the pencil down. "You meant to offer me a drink, didn't you?"

"Actually I didn't." As she reached for another wine glass she hoped her comment startled him for a change.

"I'm usually done at four on Friday's. But since you couldn't get here any sooner, you're actually encroaching on my weekend. It's the least you could do, don't you think?"

She filled the glass and placed it on the counter. Unable to decide if he was hostile or flirting was unnerving. She didn't know whether to smile or show him the door.

He strolled across the room and accepted the glass. She was almost five feet, nine inches tall, but standing next to him, she felt petite. Judging from where her shoulder hit on his arm, he had to be at least six foot, five. The hunky, handsome handyman had her imagining thoughts from lusty love scenes. This felt more like a date than someone she planned to hire.

"Are you always so forward?" she asked. "You know, the comment you made in the bathroom?"

"Most of the time. Are you always late?" Even though his comment changed nothing between them her heart pulsed with expectation.

"I'm sorry about our last appointments. I apologized already."

"Apology accepted." He tapped his glass against hers and took a sip. "This is pretty good. Now can we talk about timing and budget?"

She tried to focus on the reason he was standing in her kitchen, sipping wine from her special stash. Instead her brain acted like it was on an out-of-control merry-go-round. His shoulders were broad enough to hold up the world.

She blinked away the lustful thoughts. "The budget is fifty thousand and not a penny more and I'm hoping you can have everything finished in four weeks. I'm planning a Memorial Day party."

He put his glass down. For the first time since meeting him, his lips parted in a beautiful smile. His whole face brightened, which made him even more dashing.

"I should be able to get it done with that budget, but the timing is not realistic. We haven't got a design yet or any materials." He jotted something on his clipboard in bold strokes while squinting at her.

"What does that look mean?"

"It happens all the time. The owner delays the project then expects me to pull a rabbit out of my non-existent hat." He shoved the pen into the clipboard and turned toward the door.

"Wait a minute. Where are you going?" She grabbed his arm.

"Home. It's late and I'm exhausted." He stuck his thumb through the belt loop. "I'll be here tomorrow morning at eight. If you can get up early enough, we can finalize the design and start shopping. I can get your project done in about six weeks, but that depends on how committed you are and the materials you select. If those terms don't work for you, find someone else to rush your project through."

"Excuse you, Mr. Sizemore. The last thing I need is for you to come in here and give me ultimatums. I don't know what you think you know about me, but it's obvious most of your information is incorrect. You can let yourself out, I'll find someone else more agreeable to complete my project."

He swaggered towards the door. His T-shirt clung to the muscles across his back. His massive hands hung at his sides.

He yelled over his shoulder. "I'll be here at eight."

"Don't bother," she said without conviction.

Chapter Two

Drew downed a full cup of black coffee before stepping out of the truck. Yolanda Maxwell was no ordinary client. If she were he wouldn't have dreamt about her last night and woke up with a boner. Her dark eyes had held his attention but it was her flawless copper skin that he wanted to touch. The ice in her voice last night could have sunk the Titanic, but he was a professional. Difficult clients were just part of the business, but a difficult woman presented a challenge. And he loved a challenge. But saving Harrison Bryant Contracting was priority number one. His uncle had left the business to him, but failed to mention it was drowning in red ink. Without an infusion of cash, Drew would have to float the business a loan. A large one. His father thought he was crazy for trying to save the company, but his mother wanted him to try.

He made his way to Yani's front door, half expecting her to ignore the knock or bless him out when she recognized his face through her peephole. But he was willing to take that chance because something about her had crawled under his skin yesterday. And he intended to find out what it was.

She snatched the door open before he rang the doorbell. "What are you doing here?"

Instead of the straight, sophisticated hairstyle from yesterday, this morning her hair framed her face in springy spirals. Without make-up, her fresh, clean look was even more appealing. She wasn't wearing any shoes. Her toenail polish was a warm shade of blue that matched her denim shorts.

"Good morning, Yani. We had an appointment for eight." He glanced at his watch. "It's just five after, but I thought you could use the extra time. Aren't you going to invite me in?"

He stepped past her into the air-conditioned condo, without waiting for a reply. His arm brushed her breast, sending a pulse through his veins that his coffee couldn't match.

Her mouth dropped open just enough to show a row of even white teeth. "The last thing I said to you—"

"Yeah, I wasn't listening. Thank you for being up and ready." He strolled into her kitchen. The remnants of eggs and bacon cluttered a plate on the far side of the table. Steam curled out of a cup of coffee. "Did I interrupt your breakfast?"

She made a show of rolling her eyes like a child being nagged to do her chores. "You are a character, aren't you? After your comment yesterday what makes you think I want to do business with you?"

He studied her for a moment before taking a seat at the table. "Because I'm the best and you're a perfectionist. Besides, I need the money. Pretend I'm a friend and we're talking design." He patted the seat next to him. "Let me show you some of the concepts I came up with."

"What makes you think I'm a perfectionist?" Her eyes softened and sparkled like a precious stone.

"Because you try to control every situation. You haven't learned that's impossible yet."

"If you are going to be this arrogant, I'm not so certain I want to work with you."

He paused before answering. Teasing her was fun, her mouth twitched when she was flustered. "This is me, always."

"Good to know. Then I'll just have to ignore most of what you say or find someone else to do the job."

"Everything I say is worth hearing. You wouldn't want to miss out, now would you?"

"Show me the plans. I'll look, but it doesn't mean anything." She flounced into the chair. The smell of tuberose and white cedar wood teased his nostrils. The floral scent reminded him of a gathering of his sisters.

"Good. By the way I like what you've done with your hair. It looks playful and fun."

Her hand went to her mane. She ran her fingers through the loose curls settling at her shoulders. "I'll ignore that."

"What? I'm not allowed to compliment you?"

"I'm still deciding if I'm going to let you stay in my house."

"I see." He smiled and opened his computer, scanning through the drawings he'd developed last night. Based on their brief conversation he had two designs for the kitchen and bath. She gushed over each one like they were gifts and she wanted to pick the best one. Once he'd explained each one to her, he sat back in his chair.

"What do you think?" he asked.

"I like them all." She perched on the edge of her seat, even closer to him. The hint of cleavage budding from the low neckline curve of her T-shirt held him captivated. The skin on her chest was as dewy as the rest of her.

He cut his glance away and cleared his throat. "Can I get a glass of water?"

She jumped up. The angst from earlier had vanished. She was as perfect from behind as she was from the front. Her long slender legs were elegantly shaped like a dancer's and her butt was firm and round.

"Do you have someone you'd like to discuss these drawings with before you make a decision?"

"Umm, no. My parents live in Florida now and my brother is useless when it comes to design. He could live in a shoebox if his wife would approve."

"No girlfriend or boyfriend?"

"No boyfriend. I'll talk to my friend Phoebe when she comes back from her business trip. Anyway I'm used to making my own decisions. I don't like a lot of other voices in my head." From the refrigerator she filled the glass with ice then water before setting it in front of him.

With all the right answers, he drank the contents of glass in one gulp. "Well, which one will it be? Plan A is a little less expensive than Plan B, but with Plan B you get that huge walk-in closet that wasn't on your list of must-haves."

Dating Just Got Serious

"I can't believe I'm saying this but I want Plan B. That closet is fabulous. I should have thought of it. When will you get started?"

He stood up. "As soon as you put on some shoes."

Chapter Three

On her hands and knees of the floor of her closet, Yani paused to slow her breathing while looking for her shoes. Last night her dad would have been proud with the way she'd stood up to Drew. Today, he'd be disappointed if he could hear her heart thumping against her chest.

The man standing in her kitchen couldn't be the same person she met yesterday. Drew still sported his signature ponytail, but in his starched white shirt and jeans he didn't look like anybody's handyman. He could have been the Harvard graduate or professional man her parents would adore.

Drew's strong jaw and business ethic could even fool her highbrow father into thinking he was pure blue-blood through and through. But her father wasn't easily fooled, and once he found out about Drew, he'd start his traditional rant about her wasting time with men beneath her station in life. He found something lacking in every man she liked. Her mom and dad wouldn't be happy until she was marching down the aisle with one of those boring country club, shallow-minded elitist duds.

As long as her parents stayed in Florida, they'd never have to know she was interested in a man who made his living with his hands. She shook away the deceitful thought as she opened another shoebox.

The Silverman contract had her so busy she didn't have time to date anyone, much less cruise the clubs looking for the perfect man. If the handsome hunk in her kitchen giving her a hard time wasn't attached, he'd do just fine for a hot fling. He checked all her must-have boxes, even down to the big hands and muscular build. Just thinking about holding on to him made her feel carefree and careless. From now until Memorial Day, she'd figure something out.

She found the wedge sandals and slipped them on. Even if he wasn't the contractor for her, hanging out with him could be fun. Every stuff-shirt executive she'd dated in the last few months had as much personality as a dead fly. She could see her mother shaking her red lacquered acrylic nail at her for thinking about dating a man who swung a hammer. Yani's Ivy League education was supposed to put her in contact with doctors and lawyers. But if she had to spend another date listening to *the right man* talk about himself and his car and his stereo or investments all evening she'd expire. They might have the pedigree her parents thought was so important, but they had no passion.

"I'm ready," she said as she entered the kitchen.

Drew had a retractable tape measure stretched across the kitchen counter. With expert precision, he captured the dimensions of the counter and cabinets with a swiftness that was hard to ignore. He punched a number into his cell phone before snapping the tape shut and shoving it into the pocket of his jeans.

"Let's ride." He opened the front door and waited while she locked up. They made their way down the curved walk.

"I can drive." She dangled her keys on her index finger. She stopped at her car.

Without slowing his easy gait, his thick golden brow arched. "We'll take my truck." He pointed to the rusty blue bomb parked next to her car.

"You don't expect me to ride in that thing, do you?"

"I most certainly do. What's wrong with it? You know, if you were anymore uptight, you'd be wooden." He glanced at his truck, then back to her.

She saw laughter in his eyes as he opened the passenger side door, so there was no sting in his comment. The inside looked better than the outside, but not by much. At least the seats were clean, but a collection of empty water bottles and wrappers cluttered the floor.

"Put on your seatbelt." He started up the truck and backed into the street.

66

She held her feet close together in the only small clean space on the floor. Maybe her mother had a point. 'Right men' didn't drive pick-ups or work vehicles. "Does your truck always look like this?"

"Pretty much. I've had a busy schedule lately. The truck takes last place. You might as well breathe. You can't hold your breath until we get there."

"I don't mean to be…uppity…it's just—"

"I can tell you're not used to driving around in something like this, but it's efficient. If we need to pick up something today, it will fit in the back." He nodded at the truck bed.

"You have a habit of insulting me in the nicest way."

"I don't mean to. It's just obvious you only want the best. Look at you, even on a Saturday, while shopping for flooring and counters, you're dressed in four hundred dollar sandals and designer shorts."

"How do you know what my shoes cost?" She wiggled her toes, examining her new pedicure.

"I have sisters. All they do is talk about clothes and shoes."

"I work very hard for everything I have."

"Noted. Tell you what. Don't judge me by my truck and I won't judge you by your clothes. Does that sound like a deal?"

"Only if you promise note to judge me because I missed a few appointment, too. Then maybe we can work a deal. Now tell me how long you've worked for Bryant Construction."

He glanced at her with a smirk. "For about two years now."

"I actually thought I'd be working with Mr. Bryant on my reno."

"I hope I'll do. I'm more than qualified for this project." His clipped tone indicated she'd probably offended him. But when her father suggested she use Bryant Contracting he'd gone on and on about how wonderful the man had been when they added the addition to their house years ago. Mr. Bryant had to be near sixty now, so spending the day with Drew was the bonus for a day of looking at wood and kitchen stuff. At least he didn't keep looking at his watch or regaling her with tales of his 401-K.

She sat back. "Well, I imagine Mr. Bryant would have been easier to work with, but you might do," she said with satisfaction.

####

Drew suppressed the chuckle bubbling in his throat. Her comment was about as transparent and easy to read as a children's primer. But he'd allow her the little jab about his truck and what she imagined was his profession. History had taught him that flying below the radar had its advantages. A man on a mission had to keep his priorities straight even if a raven-haired beauty pushed him to distraction.

Part of her charm was the scrappy way she came at him. But he didn't feel up for a fight today.

Let her think Uncle Harrison still ran the business. As long as she let him re-do the kitchen and bath, he could prove his father wrong, and that was a good day. She probably thought he was some poor slug who worked for Bryant construction. The idea made him snicker.

"How long will it take you to do the work?" she asked without looking his way.

"So you decided I'm your man, huh? I knew you'd come around."

"I just don't have time to break someone else in. So I'll make do with you. How long have you been doing this kind of work?" She continued to stare straight ahead.

"Don't worry. He wouldn't have turned me loose on the public unless he thought I could do the job." He found a parking space in the lot of Kitchens and Cabinets and turned off the engine. She jumped out before he could open the door for her.

"Wow, look at all that granite," she squealed as soon as they stepped onto the showroom floor.

"Please don't get starry-eyed. Almost everything in here will look good. This is going to be a long day, so I need you to hang with me and try to visualize my recommendations."

The luminous smile she produced had him imagining her tangled between his Egyptian cotton sheets. He grabbed her hand and pulled her to the cabinet display. Her sex appeal was off the scale, luring him in subtle ways. She smelled good, she looked even better, and her walk could stop a high-speed train. Even though she was the complete package, she seemed unaware of the way she turned heads.

"How can I help you and your wife?" the salesman asked as he approached, wringing his hands.

"We're not married," Drew replied as he stepped in front of Yani.

"No." She gave the salesman a stern look. "We just want to see your kitchen displays."

The salesman pointed them in the proper direction and scurried away to help another customer.

"You didn't have to bite off his head," Drew said.

"Why would he make the assumption we were married?"

"He was just being very friendly, hoping to make a sale. Besides, I was holding your hand."

"Why are you taking his side?" she asked.

"What's really got you so riled up about his comment? You couldn't see yourself married to a man who makes a living working with his hands, or one who drives a truck, or is it both?"

The cheerful expression vanished from her face, replaced by uncertainty. She blinked. "You're a nice man, Drew. We're just different. But I'd marry anyone as long as they thought I was more important than how the Dow closed or the final football score. Do you think I'm asking for too much?" She cut her gaze away and focused on a contemporary kitchen setup, like she'd said too much.

He had to tilt his head down to see her. "No, that's not too much at all."

"Besides, he shouldn't make those kinds of inferences to people he doesn't know."

"Look at me and say that." He spun her around to see her if her eyes were in agreement with her words. He wanted to know the truth about her concern. Did she think he wasn't good enough for her?

"I think he was unprofessional. Nothing more. If it makes you feel any better, I'll prove it." She leaned over and planted her lips against his. The quick gesture surprised him. She pulled away before he could get a good taste. But his body perked up.

"Oh, you want to tease, do you?" He wrapped an arm around her waist and pushed his tongue into her mouth. He expected her to pull away. Instead, she welcomed him by sliding her tongue over his in a kiss so sweet, trouble had to be close behind. Together they performed an intimate performance in the middle of the store that only the two of them could enjoy.

She eased away from him. "Okay, I think we both made our points." Her eyes twinkled like ornament lights. "And you're a good kisser." Her voice was husky.

"That's because I had so much to work with." He held her gaze.

Several seconds ticked by. Her eyes zipped over his face and he wanted to say more, but the time wasn't right. "Look, we better start shopping or your reno won't be complete until Labor Day."

Chapter Four

Getting back in the messy truck at the end of the day was easy. Yani was too exhausted to care about the collection of refuse. She kicked aside as she placed her head against the headrest. After looking at an endless selection of stone, tile, granite, and cabinets, she should have been able to forget about her desire for him. But her attraction wouldn't tap out.

"That was more exhausting than I imagined. I don't think I've ever been this tired after shopping." She closed her eyes.

"We'll have to make a few more trips, but we've done enough to get started."

"I thought we'd have more than a hot dog for lunch. I'm starved," she said without opening her eyes.

He snorted. "I'm just trying to please the customer by not wasting time with fancy meals. You claimed time was of the essence. The sooner I can get started, the sooner I'll finish."

"You can tell Mr. Bryant that you were perfect. I didn't even mind having to go to three different quarries to find the right back-splash for the kitchen."

"I deserve hazard pay for trying to keep you on budget. I thought you were going to bite me when I tried to talk you out of that marble."

She smacked his arm, with a laugh. "Thank you. I do tend to get a little carried away. I have to work so hard because I live so well."

He pulled the truck to a stop in front of her condo and turned it off. She didn't want to leave him yet. Even though they hadn't been on a date, her stomach had turned into a nest of nerves. A single date with Drew would be better than all the dates she'd had in the past year combined.

"Why don't you come in? After the way I treated you the least I can do is fix you dinner. I can feed you better than you fed me. I might even have some beer."

He opened the truck door and walked around to help her out. "Dinner sounds good, the beer not so much. But if you have another bottle of wine, I'll accept."

"I'm sure I've got more wine, a bottle of sparkling red I've been dying to try, but I wanted to share it with someone." She waved him up the walk. The last man she'd invited to dinner was her father, and that was several months ago. The forward woman opening the door for Drew was unrecognizable to her. The only personal thing she knew about him was he had a goddaughter who liked teddy bears. But his swagger had secretly serenaded her all day and she didn't want to ignore it. Wherever her normally cautious alter ego was tonight she hoped she wouldn't return to spoil the fun. The pretend kiss in the middle of the showroom floor wouldn't release her thoughts all day. It was supposed to be a joke, but she wanted more.

"If you want to clean up first, the guest bath is right down that hall on the left."

The way he gazed at her face made her both uncomfortable and jubilant at the same time. There was nothing boring about him. He stood less than a foot away. The slight dimples in his cheeks puckered as he reached for her and drew her closer.

"This is what I want to do." He kissed her again, slower this time. The move was so smooth her body responded without hesitation. His big hands cupped the back of her neck, sending a spray of tingles cascading over her. She wrapped her arms around his waist and melted into him. The warm sweet taste of his tongue lingered on hers. He pressed her against the wall.

She released his tongue to breathe. Her heart raced so fast, she had to fist her hands to control the pace. Drew's intense gaze penetrated her thoughts. He leaned closer, his lips slightly parted. She pressed her palm to his chest, unable to bear anymore without losing the little self-control she had left.

"I've been thinking about doing that again, all day," he said.

"I thought only hard surfaces got you excited." She allowed her palm to linger on his chest.

"That depends on where they're located." He trailed a finger across her throat, a blaze of heat left in its wake.

"Wait a minute. This is happening so fast." She turned her head to get a breath of air that didn't have his scent in it. She wanted more, but fear paralyzed her.

"Not for me. But I understand." He held up his hands in surrender and stepped back.

"It's just that I don't know you very well. And...and you're going to be working on my house— I'm not sure this is the right time to get involved. Things could get very messy. I don't even know if you're married, engaged, or living with someone."

He nodded without breaking eye contact. "Well, let's see. I'm not married, or engaged, and I live alone. Do you require any more information before I can kiss you again?" He stretched his arms, pinning her between them as he pressed his palms against the wall.

"I think that's enough for now." She used her thumb to swipe her lipstick from his mouth.

"If you keep touching me like that, I can't promise I'll keep my tongue to myself."

"That's fair warning." She ducked under his arms and straightened her shirt.

"How about I meet you in the kitchen in five minutes?" Drew strolled down the hall.

The view of him from behind was just as awesome as the front view. She wiped her brow as he walked away.

Hanging with Drew felt comfortable. Worrying if her lip-gloss had stained her teeth, or if the mustard from the hot dog they ate for lunch was smudged on her cheek had never even crept into her head.

She hummed while pulling the dinner ingredients and the wine out of the refrigerator. The distraction helped her regain her composure. Since he paid for the hotdogs they ate for lunch, she was happy he'd accepted her dinner invitation. Expecting him to treat her to two meals in one day seemed

73

unfair. Besides, based on the condition of his truck, he couldn't afford to be frivolous. Drew looked like a man who enjoyed his steak and potatoes. The bone-in ribeye steaks were supposed to be for dinner next week when her dad came for a visit. "He'll understand," she murmured as she turned on the broiler.

"Who'll understand what?" Drew asked from the doorway of the kitchen. The red flush on his neck was gone now.

"I was talking to myself. I do that a lot." She seasoned the meat while looking at him.

"I see."

He came to stand beside her. "I live alone and I don't think I've ever talked to myself."

"Sure you have. You must hold conversations in your head. Everybody does. Just because you don't say it out loud, doesn't mean you don't."

He laughed. A hardy tone filled with happiness. "Shall I open the bottle?"

"Please." She shoved the steaks under the broiler, pretending not to watch as he removed the foil and the cork. His movements were swift and sure, like it was an everyday occurrence for him. In her kitchen, he was as natural as a knot on a log.

"You know, if you cleaned up your truck, you could get a date."

"You think so?" The dimple in his cheek deepened. "And what makes you think I need help dating?"

"You said you weren't married or shacking with someone." She shrugged and turned on the microwave for the potatoes. "Maybe that's the reason."

"Well, you're not married. It's obvious you live alone and your car is spotless. So what's your excuse?" He handed her a glass of wine.

The comment stung but she deserved it for venturing down this path. How many times had her parents tried to figure out why at twenty-six she didn't have a steady boyfriend and the promise of grandchildren somewhere in their future?

"You sound like my mother. To listen to her, you'd think I could pluck a man from a garden like a ripe tomato. My parents have set me up on dates with every eligible bachelor from their stable of affluent friends. If they aren't bland, then they're demanding."

"Ahh, I see. Then you know what I'm talking about and it has nothing to do with cleanliness of vehicles." He came around the counter to stand next to her. His elbow brushed hers.

"You're much nicer than I imagined." His voice was heavy. Standing so close, she could see the stubble on his chin. As hard as she tried she couldn't tamp down her rising interest in him. The kiss alerted her body and it seemed wide-awake now.

"I'm very nice. Ask my friends. I'm just very focused on a contract. You see, my father thinks I'm wasting my talents at the non-profit, so I'm trying to prove him wrong. Until I wrap up the deal, my time is consumed. I'm not usually late nor am I one to stand people up. Really, I'm not. You should never judge a book by its cover." She pulled the broiler pan from the oven and placed it on the trivet.

"I agree with you and I never judge by minor indiscretions."

"Let's eat." She pulled the potatoes from the microwave and placed them on a plate along with the steak. After handing him some napkins and flatware, they sat at the table and ate while swapping dating horror stories.

"When my parents moved to Florida, I thought I was going to get a reprieve from the constant meddling, picking, and inspections of all my dates and boyfriends. But with my mom so far away, she seems to have doubled her efforts to make sure her only daughter is firmly attached to something permanent before they leave this earth."

"I do the same thing with my sisters. If nothing else, at least their men know to treat them right because I'm watching."

Yani sipped her wine. Her mother's idea of ideal wouldn't be Drew Sizemore. Maybe it was time to take her own counsel on dating, because the playbook her parents used wasn't working.

He ate the last of his steak and put down his fork. "That was the best steak I've ever eaten." He wiped his mouth.

"You're just being nice, but thanks for the compliment."

"You're yawning, and it's getting late." He looked at his watch. "I better get out of here." Drew pushed away from the table and stood.

"Wow, I didn't realize what time it was." She stood too. "Thank you for a nice day. How soon will you start on the project?"

"So you've decided I'm the man, huh?" His smile was wicked.

She tried not to blush, but her cheeks got warm anyway. "Yes, you're the man."

"Then I better get my truck cleaned up." He gave her the most enchanting smile.

In the foyer, he loomed over her like a marble statute. "I'm very professional with my clients. I don't make a habit of kissing them, just in case you were wondering. But you're not like any client I've ever had." He leaned in so close she froze.

"I'll take your word for it." On her toes, she pressed her lips to his. Right now it was best not to analyze the commotion in her gut. Her parents' words were loud enough in her head. But as she slipped her arms around his neck nothing else mattered. Desire called her name and she had to answer. Drew was the mirage she dreamed about after every bad date. Maybe he wasn't the perfect man, but tonight he was close enough. The heat from his skin kindled a desire in her that no paper-pusher could match. But there was no such thing as a perfect man. She tugged his ponytail loose causing his hair fall to his shoulders.

The playfulness of their tongues grew more serious. He slowed the action down and increased the intensity. She relished each twist and turn. Instead of feeling like he wanted to be somewhere else, doing something else, he held her like she was the prize, the golden ticket to be won and treasured.

He unzipped her pants and slid them down along with her panties. She stepped out of her clothes and left them at his feet. He hoisted her against the wall, putting her at his level and granting easier access as he pushed his hand under her shirt. His flesh pressed into her, turning up the heat rushing through her veins. He ran his tongue over her earlobe. The touch was so pleasing, she sighed like a helpless jezebel. Everything she felt was wrong and right and good and bad, but she couldn't stop the mounting desires storming through her.

She ignored the disapproving words of her father floating in her head. Just this once she wanted to follow her heart and the desire stirring up the dusty corners of her soul. As his hand ravished one breast and then moved to the next, she discounted all the lessons preached to her by parents and opened her heart to the taste, smell and touch that Drew offered.

The moan that pierced the quietness surprised her, but she hadn't felt so helpless to her passion before. When his finger found her core, she released his tongue, threw back her head and gave in.

Suspended against the wall with only his arms for support, he fondled her like he was stoking a fire. Each gentle pull of his finger sent a spasm cascading over her body. With his free hand, he tilted her head and eased his tongue back in her mouth. She wanted to be the good girl her parents had raised, but she couldn't will her body to stop responding. Having sex on the first date would have been absurd. But here she was doing just that and they hadn't even been on a date, yet she was surrendering her soul to him.

All of the blood in her body seemed to pool between her legs. She squeezed her eyes shut as every muscle in her body went rigid. As each contraction jerked her she bit down on his tongue.

"Ouch," he said as she came to rest against him.

"It's your own fault. I couldn't help it." She was breathing hard.

"It's a good thing I was expecting your reaction or you would have hurt me."

The lust should have vanished when she landed back on earth, but the fire wasn't ready to be contained. She ran her index finger along his jaw. "Let me make it up to you."

He brought his lips to her ears. "What do you have in mind?" There was as much desire in his voice as she'd heard in her own.

She nodded to the back of the condo. He anchored his arms around her legs and carried her to the bedroom.

####

So the princess did have carnal desires, just like everyone else. He had begun to think his attraction to her was all one-sided. But Yolanda Maxwell continued to surprise him. Maybe she was toying with him, slumming while getting her renovation work done. And for now he was willing to be her boy toy.

She pulled him down on the bed on top of her. Moisture gleamed on her forehead. Standing back up he unbuttoned his shirt and pulled it off. As he stepped out of his jeans, he reached for his wallet in the back pocket and extracted the condom.

"Are you always prepared?"

"I try to be. You aren't complaining, are you?" He crawled between her legs and pushed his tongue against her swollen core. She knotted her fingers in his hair.

"No, this was supposed to be about you. Remember?"

"I don't. And this is about me." He rolled his tongue over her sweetness as slow as he could. She started a grinding rotation with her hips to let him know he'd found his mark. Right now, he should have been completing paperwork and submitting measurements for her renovation, but the nirvana between her thighs was so much better than he could have imagined.

When her movements increased with intensity, he pulled back then slipped on the condom. He eased into her warm depths, and for the first time, he released a groan that summoned all his willpower to contain his reaction to her.

She wrapped her legs around his waist which drew him in deeper. With her eyes closed she looked just as beautiful as she did in his dreams. Even though Yani tried to exhibit a tough edge, it hadn't taken him long to see she was tender on the inside. She was the kind of woman who could trip him up just when he had his future all laid out.

"Drew?" She said his name with urgency, demanding his attention.

"Yes." He plunged deeper into her, savoring every inch and every movement.

"I can't..."

"Yes, you can, baby." He buried his head in her neck and caught her soft flesh between his teeth. "Now," he demanded and right on cue she tightened her legs and her body contracted around him like a vice grip.

She pulled her arms around him and held him like a lover. He didn't want to start imagining things. Maybe she was holding on to him just until she gained her composure. But moments later when he rolled over, she continued to hold his arm.

Chapter Five

The ringing phone pulled Yani out of the magic of the night. She extracted her arm from his grasp and smacked around on the nightstand for the annoying interruption.

"Hello." Her voice sounded drunk with sleep. She was more irritated for having to move away from Drew than she was at the early morning wake-up call.

"Yolanda?" The terse sound of her father's voice erased the remnants of sleep.

Yani jumped out of bed and covered the phone as she hurried into the kitchen. "Dad, is something wrong? You're calling so early."

"I wanted to catch you before you left for church."

She flopped onto the kitchen chair and placed one foot on top of the other. "What's up?"

"I'm going to have to push my visit back a week. Your mother and I are going to see your brother. He and Olivia called last night. We're going to be grandparents. So we're going out to see him. Isn't that great?"

She wanted to be happy for her brother, but his wonderful life only made hers appear more tarnished. His life was purchased in a luxury department store. Hers was picked up at the thrift shop.

"Yeah Dad, that's great. I'll have to call him later today." She hoped she sounded better than she felt. How could one call from home wipe out such a beautiful night? She reached for the towel draped over the oven handle and covered her naked lap.

She ended the call and made her way back to the bedroom. The momentum she'd enjoyed during the night dissipated like rain on a hot summer day. Drew nearly bumped into her as he dashed out of the bathroom fully dressed.

"Is everything okay?" He pulled on his shoes.

"Yeah. That was just my dad."

"You look a little pale. You're sure you're okay?"

He pulled her into his arms while swaying back and forth. Just a few days ago her life was on track and content, even if there wasn't a significant other to cuddle up with. But now her brother had raised the expectations, and like always, she fell further behind.

"I've got a lot of work to do." Drew kissed her. The caress of his tongue was like a balm, but then he pulled away and headed for the door.

She rushed into the bathroom. Her hair must have looked frightening. By the time she came out, slipped on her bathrobe and ran into the kitchen, he was backing his truck out.

The day blurred in a pile of restless thoughts. As the sun slid below the horizon that night the sinkhole in her heart had grown, spreading like an ink stain on a fresh white shirt. She'd half-expected Drew to knock on her door, and recuse her from the loneliness, but the day waned, the moon glowed, and nothing.

Monday morning, Yani sat at her desk and tried to clear her mind. She shook all romantic notions from her head and turned on her computer. Expecting him to come back on Sunday was probably asking too much. Now he acted as if it was back to business as usual.

Instead of trying to dissect the events of the day before, she accepted them. She was horny, he was hot, and nature had taken over. It was simple and didn't require more scrutiny. Now with the hot fling behind her, she could get on with her life. No one had to know what she did, and no one could judge her as long as she kept the indiscretion to herself.

"So how was your weekend?" Cat slid into the chair in front of her desk.

Yani massaged the knot at the back of her neck. "Uneventful. I think the work on the house will get started today. So most of the weekend was spent selecting kitchen and bathroom stuff."

"Did you get stuck with the old man all day on Saturday?"

81

"Drew is a long way from old. He's actually quite good looking."

"Oh, I see. That's why I didn't get you when I called. I thought you said you were going to be home." Cat placed an elbow on the desk and leaned in like a detective questioning a suspect.

"Stop fishing, Cat. I have nothing I want to tell you." She gathered a stack of papers and tried to straighten them.

"Do I need to get Phoebe on the phone so the two of us can pump you for information?"

She sighed loud enough so Cat would know she was being a pest. "I know why your nickname is Cat. Because you're too curious."

"No." She laughed. "My mother was too lazy to say Catrina every time she wanted to reprimand me." She moved from the chair to the edge of the desk. "But something is going on with you and you know I'll find out what it is." Cat waggled a finger.

"There's nothing to find out, Cat. Go mind your own business."

After Cat closed the office door, Yani dropped her face into her hands. What would she say to Drew this evening? Thanks for helping me work out my sexual kinks, and please forgive my lack of judgment. There was only one small problem with her announcement. She couldn't get Drew out of her head. Flings weren't supposed to consume her thoughts but, all day little tidbits from the weekend kept popping up.

She shook her head. Even if she wanted to take Drew more serious, she couldn't, unless she wanted to give her parents matching coronaries. She massaged her temples. No matter how creative she tried to be, there was no way of avoiding him for the duration of the renovation. And after the way he fled on Sunday it was obvious neither of them knew what they wanted or what to expect.

Instead of shutting down her computer at the end of the day, she pulled more files from the drawer. Maybe by the time she got home Drew and his crew would be gone.

####

Drew helped his craftsmen pack up the tools. "Good work today, guys. We'll start back tomorrow morning, about eight." With his foot, he pushed the pack of marble flooring into the corner.

Finishing the project by Memorial Day was possible. A couple more long days and they could get ahead. Unfortunately Yani wouldn't have a useful kitchen or master bath for a few weeks.

From the window in the living room he saw her small red car pull up. Even after she dimmed the lights, she didn't get out.

He picked up his jacket, locked the door and marched down the path. "So how long are you going to sit in there?" he called to her as he approached the car.

"I was just getting out."

"Like hell you were, woman. I watched you for ten minutes." He bent low to see inside.

She unbuckled the seatbelt and grabbed her super expensive purse. He pushed his knee against the door so she couldn't open it. "What were you going to do, stay out here until I disappeared?"

"You're one to talk. Sunday morning you hightailed it out of my place so fast I thought something was chasing you. And what about the rest of the day Sunday? Not one word from you. But hey, it's okay. This doesn't have to get messy. Just do the work and we can erase everything else. Pretend it never happened."

Stunned by her tirade, he gripped the door handle. "Maybe I was getting started on the project to meet your timing. Did that ever cross your pretty little mind?"

"Are you going to let me out of the car?" She pulled the latch again. He stepped back to allow her to open the door. Leaning against his truck, he folded his arms over his chest and waited for her explanation.

83

"Okay," she said with a big breath as soon as she was out. "Look, Drew. About the other night, I think we both got a little carried away. We hardly know each other. Maybe we should try to act more civilized so you can finish the reno. Let's pretend the other night did not happen." Her chest heaved with each word. This wasn't easy for her.

"Suppose I don't want to?"

Her eyes widened for a moment before she looked down at the asphalt separating them.

"Sometimes, life doesn't give you choices." Her voice quivered.

She appeared to be trying to regain her composure. She was doing a better job than he was. He wanted to rewind the events of Saturday, and she was talking about pulling away. If dragging out this project provided time with her then he would.

She pushed her purse higher on her shoulder and headed for the house. He noticed she'd worn her hair long and straight today.

"The kitchen is a wreck. You can't eat in there."

Her purse slid back down her arm. Defeat registered around her mouth. "That's okay. I'm not real hungry, anyway."

He grabbed her arm. "Let me take you to dinner. I need to talk to you about some things I discovered today."

"No, I can't. Besides…"

"You don't have to argue with me over everything. Get in the truck." He opened the door.

After giving him a thorough look she acquiesced. "I can't eat fast-food, so let me treat."

He grunted but didn't reply.

"Did you hear me? I don't expect you to feed me while the kitchen is being done. I can make arrangements."

"Do me a favor, please, and just be quiet."

She sucked her teeth, but at least she stopped talking. The drive was quiet, even though she took several deep breaths.

"When I asked you to be quiet, I meant all the sighing too. You're making it hard for me to concentrate on my driving."

"Well, I wouldn't want to make you uncomfortable. Why don't I try to disappear?"

He pulled into the parking lot of his favorite Italian restaurant. "I hope this place is okay with you. As you can see, I'm not dressed to go anywhere fancier." He jumped out and opened her door before she could respond.

Red neon lights flashed around the large plate glass window of the restaurant, giving it a cheery welcome. Even though it was usually very busy most nights Drew knew he could get a table at his favorite place. He walked in behind her.

"Hey Drew. You haven't been here in a while. You want your regular table?" The hostess pointed toward the back.

"Yes and please bring us a pitcher of the white wine sangria."

"Do you want the usual?"

"I'm so hungry tonight I could eat two of them," he teased. "But can you bring a menu for my friend." He pulled out the chair for Yani. He opted for the seat with his back to the wall.

She ran her finger down the list of entrees.

"Want a recommendation?" he asked.

"Are you giving me permission to speak now?" She stared at him, thunderclouds gathered in her eyes.

"I just didn't want to hear you say no. You're good at shooting a man down."

"I'm good at sniffing a fake. Let's just say your behavior didn't pass my sniff test." She reached for her glass of water just as the server placed it on the table and took a swallow. "But I don't want to talk about the other night. Let's just talk about my house and nothing more."

The server showed up to take their order.

"I'll just have a Caesar salad," she said.

"Bring her the same thing you're bringing me." He picked up the menus and handed them back to the server. "Don't worry, Yani, I can cover this."

"No, I can't ask you to keep buying me meals."

He pulled in a deep breath to redirect his thoughts to a more positive place. If she were taller, she'd probably look down her nose at him. Did she think he was some pathetic shmuck who rushed his check to the check-cashing store to buy milk? He wanted to tell her he had enough money to buy her dinners and those expensive purses for the rest of her life. But watching her sweat it out was so much more enjoyable.

"Don't worry about the meal. My credit is good here."

She huffed either from exhaustion or from distress. "So what did you need to tell me about the house?"

Chapter Six

A few days later, Yani walked into Cat's office and dropped her briefcase on the floor before closing the door. "We need to talk."

Cat pushed away from the computer to face her. "Is it about the dreamboat working on your house that you keep talking about?"

"I'm glad my personal life brings you so much pleasure." She rubbed her forehead. "This is bad, Cat. I think I like him. I'm trying to ignore him and my feelings. He's the nicest man. Even though I keep giving him clipped answers or one word replies he remains unfazed by my attitude. I know it's the most ridiculous thing in the world but I can't help myself. Every evening when I go home, I hide in my office or bedroom until he leaves with his crew. Just so I don't look like a schoolgirl with a crush. But when he looks at me, I feel like he really sees me." She touched her lips.

"Wow, that sounds serious. What will you do?" Cat asked as she leaned on her desk. "You can't ignore how you really feel about him."

"Oh, yes I can. I hired him to do a job. Once it's completed, he can move on to another project. I can't romanticize the situation." She couldn't tell Cat what'd happened last night after dinner it would be like posting the information on Facebook.

"So you're going to let him walk away? Suppose this is your one true love. You only get one, you know." Cat pretended to swoon.

"He's not my one true love, Cat. He's…"

"What Yani, what is he?"

She masked her apprehension by laughing. "In the bright light of day, we don't have much in common. Can you just see us going out on a date? He'd probably want a burger and I'd want steak. The man drives a truck for God's sake."

87

She placed her elbows on the desk and cradled her chin in her palm. "He's my handyman. I can't date the handyman."

"Why not? Why can't you date him?" Cat sat back in the chair and gave Yani a stern look. "Is it because your orderly neat little life would be turned on its side?"

Yani pushed a stack of papers aside. "Save me the sermon. I'm supposed to marry a doctor or a lawyer or a CEO. My parents have preached that into my head since I was a little girl. I'm not ready to disrespect my family." Yani dismissed her friend with a wave of her hand. Cat was trying to be helpful, but her speech wouldn't change anything.

"But you are interested. You talk about Drew every day. I have a new car mechanic, but I don't mention him in every sentence, or sit around daydreaming about him all day, now do I?"

"I'm protecting myself," Yani shot back.

"From what—life?"

"It's easy for you to criticize me. You're in a relationship." Yani pushed a curl behind her ears.

"Yeah, and I didn't turn him away when he showed up at my door to deliver my pizza while trying to make a little extra money to pay off student loans for medical school."

"My parents would sign papers to have me committed if I show up for a visit with Drew on my arm." Yani shrugged, not wanting to admit Cat was right. "He's not a professional, and I only date professional men." Yani wanted to put an end to this awkward conversation.

"Are you sure that's the reason? Or are you just quoting the bull you grew up with?" Cat came around the desk and parked her butt on the corner.

"Okay, so I don't want to date handymen. What's wrong with that?" Yani leveled her gaze at her friend.

"Nothing, if you don't mind being alone or being a snob."

"I'm not a snob. It's just..." Yani couldn't finish the sentence. "Why bother dating a man when there isn't a chance it can work? I don't want to waste my time, and I'm sure Drew doesn't want me to waste his, either."

Cat threaded her fingers together. "I know you better than you know yourself. You need to put your fears aside and relax. Don't turn your nose up, because your condo can get pretty cold in the winter, especially if you're in it all alone."

Still smarting from Cat's comments, Yani smoothed her skirt over her narrow hips before picking up her briefcase and heading to the door. She waved at her friend before she walked out.

Cat could talk about staying warm this winter because every night she cuddled up with her soon-to-be fiancé.

Mr. Right was supposed to show up dressed in a Hugo Boss business suit and a crisp, white shirt, not a white t-shirt and ripped jeans. But, there was no denying Drew's sexiness; just thinking about him excited her.

Sitting at her desk she stared at the contracts. Instead of thinking about Drew she needed to get this deal signed. But Cat's words had rubbed her raw. Maybe her friend was right. The last time she had a serious relationship she was the only one vested in it. Drew seemed so different, but she knew so little about him, there was no way to be sure what kind of man he really was. He could be just looking to have some fun. The idea that he wore a teddy bear on his tool belt didn't prove he was a good guy.

The shrill ring of the phone shook her thoughts loose. The call was from Drew. She hesitated before picking up the receiver. He never called during the day.

"Drew, is something wrong?"

"I know you're real busy, but I need you to come home, now." His tone was sharp, like he was distracted.

"Did something happen?"

"Yes. See you in thirty minutes." He disconnected the call without waiting for her to confirm.

She shutdown her computer, grabbed her purse and briefcase. As soon as she got in the car, she dialed her friend.

"I have to get home, Cat. Some emergency came up. I'm waiting on the last changes on the Silverman Contract. Can you pick them up from my assistant when she's done and drop them off at my house on your way home?"

"Are you going home for business or pleasure?" Cat teased.

"Are you going to help me or not?"

"I'm having dinner with Phoebe tonight. We'll drop it off before we head downtown. We're going on a double date. Me and Robby and Phoebe and Cory. See, if you'd go ahead and let Drew into your life you could hang with us tonight, too."

"Do me a favor, give me a break, please."

"Okay, I'll stop pushing you. You know I love you. I just want you to be happy."

"Thanks, Cat."

Yani pulled in front of the house and jumped out as soon as she put the car in park. Drew stood in the doorway with his tool belt slung low on the side of his hips. The teddy bear caught her eye.

"You took your sweet time getting here."

"I came as soon as you called, but I didn't run any red lights. I figured if there was fire or blood you would have called 911 and not me." She pushed past him into the house, expecting to see the great disaster.

"What is it? What's wrong?"

"Well, there are a couple of things." He led her into the kitchen and pulled out a piece of insulation. "Do you see what I see?"

She inched closer with her fingers clenched tight. She saw five black spots. "You called me home because you found ants behind the wall? You couldn't kill them or spray them? You mean I had to come home for this?"

"They're carpenter ants, princess, and they've been eating the beams. So now we have to get an exterminator in here and we have to replace the studs. The contingency budget is already spent, so you'll need to come up with more money."

"Ants don't eat wood. You're talking about termites, right?"

"I wish. And I've found some other issues. In the bathroom, you have no insulation in the walls at all. It's a wonder you didn't freeze to death last winter."

She flopped in the nearest chair. "Okay. I get it now."

He sat next to her. "I know it's a lot to throw at you, but I needed an answer to keep this project on schedule."

"How much more money do you need?"

"I'll work up the numbers and get them to you later today. But we're talking a few thousand."

She glanced down at his work shoes. He was as solid as the Grand Canyon. His command of the situation reminded her of her father. Drew was a great guy. He could have been *the* guy. Without question, she trusted he knew what he was talking about.

"I believe I'm in good hands, so do what you need to do." Instead of looking at the wall in the kitchen, she focused on his crotch. She hopped up to put some distance between them. "I'm going to change clothes. I'll work from home for the balance of the day so if you need me, I'll be down the hall.

"Before you go, can I ask you a question?"

"If it's more bad news you might as well tell me now."

He stood and grabbed her hand. "No this is about us."

She swayed as the blood rushed to her heart and grabbed at the back of the chair for balance. She filled her lungs and waited for him to finish.

"Maybe we shouldn't have slept together on that first day," he said.

"It wasn't our first day. It actually happened on the second day." She had to correct him. It was bad enough she'd had sex with him, but at least it hadn't happened the first time she met him.

"Okay, my bad. Anyway, since then, you've been a little standoffish. I'll be honest with you, Yani. I think you're hot and I'd like to spend more time with you. Not time just working on your house, but real time." He rubbed his hand down her arm, leaving a warm trail behind. She refused to release a full breath until he lifted his fingers off her flesh and broke the spell.

"I-I…just thought we were having fun. I didn't want to take us too seriously. You understand, don't you?"

"No, I don't. I don't normally sleep with my clients. You are the first. It meant something to me." His rich brown eyes blazed, but there was no smile behind them.

"I get it, Drew. But I need to slow things down a bit. We started out so hot we were bound to fizzle. I don't even know anything about you."

"Let me take you to dinner tonight and I'll answer all your questions?"

"I need to make some phone calls. Can we talk later?" She inched away from him. There wasn't enough air in the room to sustain her.

She strolled down the hall. Her pencil skirt was so tight he was able to easily examine her smooth, round butt and wanted to grab a handful of it. He scratched his head, and gathered his falling hair into the elastic band used to hold it in place.

"Do you need any help getting out of your outfit?" he yelled to her before she disappeared into her bedroom.

She stuck her head out the door. "No. But thanks for the offer."

Would she be more willing to take him serious if she knew he owned the company instead of just working for it? No way would he open up to her, yet. If she wanted him, it had to be for him, tool belt and all. Not because of anything else.

Once she was out of sight, he dug through the clutter in the kitchen until he found his tablet and calculated the cost. Completing the project in the most economical way was a priority to her so it was important to him. He heard her close her office door. Did she think hiding from him would solve her problems?

The doorbell buzzed. "Yani, you've got company," he yelled down the hall.

"Can you get it, I'll be right there?"

His boots made a clumping sound as he headed for the entry. Now she wanted to treat him like a butler. He opened the door to find two women almost as beautiful as Yani stand there.

"You must be Drew." The shorter of the two stepped across the threshold with her hand outstretched. Her hair was in a pixie cut that framed her face.

"I am. And you are?"

"I'm Cat and this is Phoebe. We're Yani's best friends. Hasn't she mentioned us?"

"As a matter of fact, she has."

"Hey guys." Yani stood behind him, wearing a tiny pair of shorts. He got a good glimpse of her ass as he made his way back in the kitchen. Yani and her friends followed him.

"So Drew, where are you from?" Cat examined him like a lab specimen.

"I live in Philly, but I was born and raised in Maryland."

"Where did you go to school?" Phoebe asked. Did she invite her friends over to ask the questions for her?

"Okay, you two. Drew is a busy man, he doesn't have time for your question and answer session." Yani's voice was tight.

"I graduated from M.I.T. with a degree in engineering," he responded to Phoebe, but he watched Yani.

He expected her face to fill with delight, but there was no change. Her expression remained stiff as stone.

"Did Yani tell you she needs a date for my wedding next weekend?" Phoebe cut a smile at Yani.

"Cat, did you bring the contract? I know you guys are going to dinner so don't let me hold you up."

"No, she didn't. Are you inviting me?" He couldn't help but use the opportunity.

Yani put up both of her hands. "Enough, you two. I don't need a date for the wedding. As one of the maids-of-honor, I'll be too busy to entertain a guest."

"I'd love for you to come, Drew, if you're free. I'll get the information to you," said Phoebe.

Yani snatched the contract from Cat's hand and shooed them to the door. "Good-bye ladies enjoy your dinner tonight."

"He's cuter than you described," he heard one of them whisper before Yani slammed the door and marched back in the kitchen with the look of the Mad Hatter on her face.

"They were only kidding. Just ignore everything they said," she demanded.

"I just got a valid invitation to a wedding and I might attend." He chuckled. "I like your friends."

"You don't know them."

"I'm a good judge of character."

Her right eye narrowed to a squint and the left eye nearly closed. "I'm not hungry, so I'm passing on dinner tonight." She exhaled with exasperation and stalked out.

The sharp sound of the closing door rattled his composure. But if she thought he would let her brush him off so easy, then it was time to teach her a lesson.

By the time the house quieted from all the banging, it was seven o'clock. She hadn't come out since she'd stormed down the hall and slammed the door. No matter how many times he traipsed to that end of the house to check on the bathroom progress she didn't open the door. Princess was as stubborn as a cat near water. But she was dealing with a professional this time. Difficult clients were as plentiful as thorns on a rose. He could handle this.

He lifted his cell phone from his pocket and placed a dinner order from his favorite take-out joint. By the time the meal was delivered, he'd cleaned the layer of sawdust covering the table and set it with the paper plates and cups that'd come with dinner.

Before knocking on her closed office door he listened for activity. Nothing. Either she was asleep or stewing over their earlier conversation. He shook his head. Yani had crawled under his rough exterior, found his vulnerable heart, and now she was turning him to mush.

He knocked on the door with his ear pressed against it. "I know you're in there so don't ignore me."

"I'm very busy. Can we talk in the morning?"

"No, I want to talk now."

She snatched the door open and threw her hands on her hips. He had to choke back the laughter threatening to erupt in his throat.

"Okay. What's so important?" she responded, her eyes softened when she dropped them to the teddy bear.

He grabbed her hand and tugged her toward the kitchen.

"Drew, I really don't have time for whatever…" She pulled away from him.

"Make the time," he reached for her hand again and leading her down the hall.

Her reluctant steps were silent as she trailed behind him. In the kitchen, she studied the table and then him. She opened her mouth. Without speaking, her lips closed just enough to form a perfect circle.

"Let's eat." He pulled out the chair for her.

"I said I wasn't having dinner with you tonight." She huffed, but all the anger in her face had dissolved. Her eyes softened and instead of the fiery stare from earlier, now there was a sparkle.

"Why do you keep doing stuff like this?" She sounded like she was pleading with him.

"What? I'm hungry and there's no use in going home to eat alone. Plus, you haven't eaten since you arrived, so this is my solution."

"Where did all this food come from?" She circled the table and stopped next to him. Standing close to her was enough to warm him all over.

"I didn't know what you wanted and you were being too much of a bad-ass to disturb, so I got a little of everything. There's honey-glazed chicken, garlic and thyme

95

sautéed beef, steamed broccoli, string beans with blue cheese, and for dessert, cheesecake and brownies." He pointed to each dish. "I think I've covered all the bases."

She sniffed. "It smells wonderful. You shouldn't have done all this."

"Oh yes, I should. I figured if you ate something you wouldn't be so grouchy."

"I'm not grouchy."

He pulled out the chair for her. She took the seat, revealing her smooth thighs as he pushed her closer to the table.

He bent low to whisper in her ear. The view of her breasts caused his desire to wake up and demand attention. "Baby, you were in a mood and it wasn't a good one."

Her eyes grew large and her body was still. "Don't call me baby."

"Why not? Do you prefer I call you honey, or sweetie, or darling? I'll call you anything you want."

"My father calls me that just before he gives me another tidbit of advice that I'm supposed to follow."

"Got it." He turned to the counter and picked up the plastic martini glasses. "I made cocktails." He placed the martinis on the table.

She didn't hesitate before picking up her fork and placing food on her plate.

"You could have gotten something to eat on your way home," she said.

"Yes, but the company wouldn't have been as good." He held up his glass. She gave him a long stare before picking up and tapping hers to his.

"What are we toasting?"

He slid his chair closer to her. "I've been told that wise men say that if you're lucky you can find happiness in a single date."

She shoved a piece of chicken in her mouth while nodding. After chewing and swallowing, she asked. "Is this a date?"

"It could be."

She nodded again. "What about the night we screwed all over my house?"

"I don't screw, princess. I have sex with women I care about, and since I was feeling something for you I was making love to you."

She pointed her fork at him. "You care for me? You hardly know me."

"I know more than you can imagine." He speared some string beans and bit them in half. "What about those people who say they fell in love at first sight? Don't you believe them?"

She put her fork down and her face turned serious. "Yeah, I believe it can happen."

Her voice was barely audible. In the harsh glare of the kitchen work lights she still managed to look gorgeous. Her face was scrubbed clean and her hair hung loose just below her shoulders. He had to have her. There was no way he could shove his feelings for her back in the bottle now. The universe had placed the woman he wanted right in the middle of his project and in the center of his life.

He cleared his plate before pushing away from the table. She sipped the last of her drink and set the glass next to her empty plate. He reached for her hand. She hesitated for a moment as he pulled her into his lap. Before she could resist he planted his tongue deep in her mouth, tasting the mellow flavor of the olive juice from the martini. With his fingers intertwined around her waist he savored every inch of her that touched him. Her soft thighs against his legs, the thin indentation of her waist, the texture of her tongue as she played with his. If she could love him half as much as he loved her, they could live happy forever.

Just as he made his wish she circled her arms around his neck and held him tight. She wiggled on his lap for better position or to arouse him more. Either way it worked. He held her up and stripped off her little top, revealing the gentle slope of her shoulders and the dewy softness of her breasts. He eased his hand inside her shorts and stroked her core before pushing her shorts and panties down her long legs. He caressed her thighs as he drew his hands back up her legs, savoring each slow minute as he reveled in her beautiful body.

While he removed his clothes, she rubbed her hands over his back. Her movements were just as slow as his, unlocking his emotions. He couldn't tell her how he felt until she was ready to hear it. Tonight, she wasn't ready.

He sat back down and pulled her on top of him.

"Condom?"

"Yes, of course." He used his foot to bring his pants closer and then pulled the sheath from his wallet. She slipped it on him and climbed back into place.

He eased into her and into paradise.

Chapter Seven

Yani sat in the front of the restaurant, near the window so she could spot her friends the moment they walked in. She picked up the fork and pressed the tines against the table. The effort of tamping down her anger from last night left her with very little fight. Cat and Phoebe had been her friends since they stood up to the bullies together in fourth grade. But if the two of them thought they could change her mind about Drew, she needed to straighten them out now.

Their little intervention in front of Drew had led to wonderful, unforgettable sex, but she and Drew needed more than good sex to anchor a relationship. He'd grow tired of her soon enough if they tried to grab anything more than a few nights of fun.

It was easier to spot Phoebe because of her tall statuesque frame. Cat was so short Yani didn't see her follow behind Phoebe. Yani waved her friends over as they entered the restaurant.

"Okay, which one of you is the wise guy?" She glared at each of them.

"What are you talking about? Are you angry about something?" From the false tone in Phoebe's voice, she could tell the two of them had come up with their little scheme together.

Yani dropped the fork on the table and exhaled. The connection Phoebe and Cat had with their parents resembled nothing she'd grown up with. Phoebe's father was easy going and supportive. Cat's dad was quiet and left all the decisions up to his wife. But Brooklyn Maxwell was hands-on. His gripped reached so deep, he'd probably still be giving commands from the grave.

"Why are you doing this? If no one else understands my dilemma, I thought I could count on you two. Don't you remember what it was like for me when I started dating? My father almost chased one guy out of the house for kissing me in the front hall. I know I'm grown and should just ignore my parents, but it's not easy for me. They were very strict, and raised us to follow what they dictated."

"Oh, come on, Yani. What can they do to you now?" Phoebe nudged Cat. "Cat, help me out here. You thought inviting him to the wedding was a good idea, too."

"I know, but I didn't think she'd be this upset." Cat dropped her eyes to her lap.

"My parents just want the best for me. They always have. I've heard them say a million times how important marrying the right man is. If I pick the wrong guy, I could end up divorced, a single mother, or a battered wife. There are a whole host of bad things that can happen to me if I screw this up."

"Oh, you want a guarantee?" Phoebe folded her arms over her chest and sat back, as if she were scolding a child.

"Isn't the right man, the one you love?" Cat stepped in to take on the next round.

"Love doesn't last thirty and forty years, Cat. It takes more than passion to hold two people together for a lifetime."

Phoebe and Cat exchanged a glance like two detectives getting nowhere with their interrogation.

"Yes, it does. It's the only thing that holds couples together. Look I know Robby doesn't love me yet, but after the lonely nights and missed holidays while he's doing his residency rotation, we'll see where this relationship goes. It can't end as badly as my last one, now, can it? Either way, I'm seeing it through and giving it a chance. I trust him."

"Cat's right." Phoebe sounded indignant. "Love is the only thing that lasts. The way I feel about Cory I have no worries that he's the one. Even when I'm upset with him, I still want to be with him. And I wouldn't let some crazy belief keep him out of my life. Love can't be ignored."

"Are you falling in love with Drew?" Cat eyes registered the sympathy her voice didn't.

"No," Yani lied. "I don't know. I've only known him a few weeks."

"Love doesn't tell time. You can fall in love in a day, in an instant. But I have to respect your choices. Maybe we shouldn't have intervened, but we thought we were helping you out." Cat sat back with resignation, too.

After placing their lunch orders, Yani wrung her hands. Last night she'd try to envision her future and the image was blank. There was no white dress, no smiling groom at the end of the church aisle waiting for her. If she couldn't have the man she wanted, she wouldn't have anyone. Everyone else would be compared to Drew. But they were so different, having a fulfilling life together seemed impossible. Would she grow to resent the things he couldn't give her? Would he resent her wanting?

"So how do I uninvited him to the wedding, now? Drew has a stubborn cord running down the center of his spine. He'll probably want to show up just to spite me," Yani said as they finished their lunch."

"You'll think of something," Cat responded.

As they walked out of the restaurant, Yani turned to her friends. "Just so we're clear. You both know I'm going to get you back for this stunt of yours. You might not see it coming, but keep an eye over your shoulders." She pointed at them.

Back at her office, behind the closed door, was the safest place for Yani. Her greatest accomplishment this morning was getting out of the house before Drew showed up. She didn't need to see his fit body or penetrating eyes to know she was falling for him. She had driven to work wishing she could extricate herself from her brewing feelings without always thinking she'd missed her one opportunity for love. Maybe what they'd had would have to be a memory from now on.

That first Saturday they'd spent together, laughing and looking at samples had been the most fun she'd had in a long time. He wasn't pretentious and cautious. He was just fun.

Long after she left the restaurant with her friends, their words echoed in her head. Yani tried to shake the comments off. But the truth in their words stung. She liked

Drew, and ignoring her feelings for him didn't seem possible. What she thought she knew about herself and her future was less certain, now. She felt like she was pushing a gigantic rock uphill and at any minute she'd lose her grip and be crushed by the one thing she wanted, Drew.

The phone rang, pulling her away from the unhappy thoughts. Her father's number flashed in the display, making her palms clammy. After the third ring, she picked up with a deep breath. "Hi Dad."

"Yolanda, I know I shouldn't interrupt you at work, but your mom and I have decided to come up a little early for Phoebe's wedding. We'll be there on Monday."

Yani held the receiver above her mouth and sighed. He wasn't asking, he was telling. Always telling.

"Dad, I've got a lot going on. I'd rather you guys arrived on Friday like we planned." Her voice grew firmer. "If you guys insist on coming earlier, then I may not be available to see you until the end of the week." She held her breath.

For several moments silence occupied the line. Yani sensed the irritation her father was holding back, but she refused to give in. Instead of speaking first she remained quiet.

"Okay, Baby. Let me tell your mother."

She exhaled long and slow. "I'll see you then." She hung up the phone with a grin. "Boy, that felt good."

While tidying her office to go home, she recalled her last relationship, the one her parents had blessed. The first few dates with Glen had been promising. She was almost certain they could get serious. But the passion never erupted. They drifted apart. His only interest was his work. On the few days they managed to schedule time together, he talked on his cell phone or recapped the events of his day, in glorious, dull details. It bored her. He fit the profile of the perfect, professional man, but their relationship lacked sparks let alone a full-fledged fire.

She had become as boring as Glen. When she wasn't working, she was thinking about what she needed to do when she got there. Without Drew to hang out with or banter back and forth with the contracts, nothing could take her mind off all the emptiness in her day. Her life would go back to the monotonous loop that she was so familiar with. The routine she now hated.

She hurried down the stairs and out of the building to her car. Tonight she planned to get a good long look at Drew. Paste it in her memory so she'd never forget how he strummed her body like a precision instrument. With the bathroom now finished, he would be done with the whole project long before Memorial Day. Then he'd move on to his next job or next woman.

Yani pulled her car out of the parking lot. Maybe she could find another project for him.

Her.

Like her new kitchen, her life needed a makeover too.

Torn between what she really wanted and what she ought to want, her knees wouldn't stop shaking. Standing up to her father was like facing down Goliath. But she really hadn't slayed the big monster, yet, her fear. And until she learned how to do that, she'd be running from it forever.

The man in the car behind her blew his horn when she failed to move through the green light. The vision of Drew disappeared when she pressed the accelerator. She shook away the image of her fantasy handyman and focused her attention on getting home. It was silly to think she could be falling in love with someone so different from the men she'd dated in the past; men with lots of money, long lists of degrees and pedigrees. But those relationships were behind her for a good reason. None of them were memorable enough to make her heart yearn.

Yani slowed the car when she turned onto her block and examined the well-manicured lawn, pleased to see her landscaper had kept his promise to trim the shrubs and plant spring flowers in the beds. Now the house had character, it looked alive and happy...unlike her. Drew came into view in front of the French doors. His muscular shoulders strained against his white signature t-shirt. Her pulse quickened and so did her heart. She watched as he fished around in his large toolbox, and all she could think about was stepping into his thick arms and letting him capture her tongue again.

Before going into the house, she checked her make-up in the rear-view mirror to make sure she looked presentable. Her brown eyes stared back at her, revealing the loneliness she tried to ignore. Maybe they could have one more fling between the sheets before she watched him walk away. Nobody had to know about it. She took a deep breath to steady her nerves before climbing out of the car and heading inside.

"Yani, you're home." His husky voice greeted her.

She nodded. She wished she could run into his arms, instead she let the kitchen island separate them. The cold stone functioned as her chaperone. Again, she tried to slow her breathing.

The ripped wall from yesterday was now taped and spackled. The progress in one day was noticeable. Maybe he was in a hurry to get away from her crazy baggage.

"With the insulation and bug problems, I thought you would get behind, but you're making good progress."

"I called in a few more men. I know you're planning a party for the holiday. I don't want to be the cause of any delays, princess." He ran tape along a seam.

"Well, it wasn't just about the get-together. The place has been a little chaotic. I want my life and house to get back to normal. I work better when everything is steady."

He pressed the tape firmly into place and then dropped the roll in the box. He swiped his hand on his pants leaving white chalky marks.

It took a moment for him to answer. Yani felt uncomfortable with his penetrating gaze. "Is that the only thing important to you? Neatness. Following directions and work?"

She put her briefcase in the chair. "Isn't that why we work, to make a living?"

"Yeah, but it should be something you enjoy, something that excites you to get out of bed in the morning."

"Hammering all day does it for you?"

"Yes, hammering is fun. But it's a small part of what I do. It takes planning, organizing and imagination to complete a project." He gave her his infamous smile as he walked around the counter to stand closer to her. She wanted to touch him, feel his skin, to see if the sizzle still existed between them or was her empty life working her imagination overtime. It took extra fortitude not to move nearer to him.

"Before I begin hammering, as you put it, I have to develop a plan and fine-tune it until I come up with a design that works. Changing your kitchen was akin to working on a canvas. It's like art for me, creating something no one else has ever done. I took your old, non-functioning bathroom and made it into something you can enjoy using." He swung his arms wide to encompass the kitchen. "When I'm finished in here, I'm hoping I can say the same thing about it, too."

"Well Drew," she hesitated. "What you've done so far looks great." She ran her hand along the smooth quartz of her new kitchen island, admiring his work. The man knew how to use his hands. Too bad he wouldn't be using those hands to work a little magic for much longer. Everything else about Drew was perfect; he almost had her panting and he hadn't touched her. She could feel his eyes on her as she moved around the space.

"Are you staring at me?" she asked him when she caught him looking at her legs.

"As a matter of fact, I am."

"I think you are supposed to lie when someone catches you."

"Normally, but for you I wanted to tell the truth. I don't make a habit of lying."

"Uh-huh." Yani felt like a schoolgirl, fumbling for the right words. She turned her back on him and broke eye contact. If she didn't get out of the kitchen soon she just might rip his t-shirt off his tight abs and jump on him.

"Am I making you uncomfortable?"

"Only a little. But it's okay."

"What's okay, the fact that I'm staring at you, or your level of comfort?"

"Both." She laughed as she realized they were flirting. She wanted to stop flirting and listen to her heart. With her parents living in Florida it should have been easier to ignore their sobering advice. But Phoebe had listened to her father, and now she was getting married to a wonderful guy. Maybe following her parents' wishes would lead her to the right man, too. But no one could do to her heart what Drew had managed.

"You have a beautiful smile."

An uncomfortable silence hung between them. Could he sense her desire and her reluctance? She averted her eyes and tried to hush the demands of her body.

Finally, he said, "I think the new design will fit your lifestyle."

"Oh you do, do you?" She leveled her glaze at him wondering why she felt so uncomfortable. Her brain refused to function. Instead of his usual barbed responses, he was being gentler with her. Maybe he detected her angst tonight.

"I didn't mean to offend you. Judging from your full pantry and the new commercial range you wanted installed, you must like to cook. The new kitchen will make it easy for you to do that even more, because of the flow."

"I love to cook and I enjoy entertaining. Once you're all done, I can do both." She flashed a quick smile at him.

"You shut me down yesterday for dinner, so you still owe me a meal."

"What do you mean? We had a nice dinner. An even nicer night. And my memory does serve me correctly." She dropped her voice to sound sexy.

"Let me take you out tonight. A real date. Where I put on dress clothes and you put on a nice dress. We don't argue over the bill and I get to pick the place. You know, like real people do?"

Before she could reply he continued. "Why don't you change and I'll come back for you in an hour?" The alluring set of his mouth was like a serenade. Desire lurked behind his eyes. Every familiar emotion surfaced and held her body captive. She exhaled a little at a time, afraid to say yes, because doors would open that she could never close again and walking through to the other side was both scary and exciting.

With his stance wide and his muscular arms folded across his chest. He appeared comfortable and relaxed. Yet she was a bundle of nerves.

She pressed her weight against the counter for support. For a moment, she thought she misunderstood him, but he continued to stare at her. She nodded her head before she could get the words out. "Okay," she managed. Maybe tonight she could live out the fantasy that had chased her all day. The one where he gathered her up in his arms cleaned away all the old relationship cobwebs. The one where they were a real couple on a real date. Even if it was a single date.

"For a moment I thought you were going to turn me down and break my heart."

"Break your heart?"

"You heard me right." He pressed her body against his. She could see a tiny imperfection under this chin, a small half-moon scar that resembled his smile. "I'll be back in an hour."

Her eyes never left his masculine physique while he collected his tools and walked out. The invitation stunned her. As soon as his truck pulled away, she dialed Cat's number.

"He asked me out, again," she yelled as her friend answered the phone.

"What did you say?"

"I said okay. I can't believe I agreed. He gave me this look, this intense stare that almost dared me to say no."

"Maybe you're coming to your senses."

"This is crazy. But he seemed so confident and sure of himself. The way he looked at me was enough to get me excited. This feels so right. I'm so excited my stomach is doing somersaults. You would think this is my first date," Yani groaned.

"When are you going out?"

"Tonight. He'll be back in a few minutes. I'm supposed to change into a dress."

"Then you better get off the phone and put on something sexy. Forget the uptight suits you wear to work."

"Cat, all day long all I thought about was Drew. I have never had my thoughts so preoccupied by a man before. Now I know what you and Phoebe must feel for your men. I know you're going to think I'm crazy, but I think I'll pursue this. If Drew is halfway serious about me I'm going to do it. I can't believe how close I came to letting him slip out of my life. I don't care what my parents think. As a matter of fact, today I actually told my father he couldn't come early for the wedding. So somehow, I'll deal with my mom and dad. Once they get to know Drew, they can't help but know he's different. They can't stay mad at me forever. Besides, maybe my brother will do something really stupid and then they can turn their attention on him. What was I thinking?"

"I knew you would come to your senses. Now go and have fun. And do everything I'd do, if you know what I mean." Cat laughed as she ended the connection.

Yani raced upstairs to change clothes and tried to control her excitement. Not since her daring college days had she done something so far from her normal convention. Her heart raced as she pulled off her navy blue blazer and pencil skirt, and tossed them on the bed. Instead of putting on her favorite black mini dress, she rummaged through her closet until she found the silk butterfly halter sheath. The way it caressed her butt, he'd have a hard time turning her down. Maybe Cat was right, she thought as she dug in her closet for a pair of shoes to make her legs longer and sexier. She could keep her nose in the air and be alone or accept the crooked smile offered by Drew.

When the doorbell rang, she grabbed her purse and charged down the stairs. Before she opened the door, she took a deep breath to keep from hyperventilating. She had to calm down or she might just jump into his arms when he walked inside.

"Ready?" he asked when she opened the door.

She needed to breathe, but looking at him made it hard. If she thought Drew was handsome in his jeans and T-shirt that was only because she hadn't seen him in a suit. The black suit with fine grey pinstripes and the starched white shirt with black onyx cufflinks made him look like he was prepared for a boardroom.

She strolled around him while examining him from head to toe. "You look…you look like a different person. Where's the ponytail?" She brushed her fingers through his hair.

"Did you think I only had a closet full of jean and work shoes?"

She shook her head. "I sound like a snob, don't I?"

He cupped her chin to lift her face. "Only to people who don't know you like I do."

"Before we leave I need to say something to you." She paused long enough to manage the flutter in her heart. "I was attracted to you from the very first day I saw you. But I have been trying to resist the attraction. Some of the reasons aren't so important, but I will say I was afraid. I'm not afraid anymore, Drew."

"I think I know the reasons, princess. But you're right, they aren't important. I'm just glad you're finally ready to admit your feelings. I've been waiting on you to own them."

Could he understand what she was going through? He grabbed her by the waist, his fingers pressing into her. His lips hovered over hers. She couldn't wait another moment to taste him. She stretched up on her toes and kissed him. He yielded, accepting her tongue. Spending the rest of her life wrapped in his arms and attention would be wonderful.

"Anyway, one day I'll tell you all about it. But tonight's not the time to discuss my shortcomings. You'll know them all soon enough," she said.

His straw-colored hair hung damp and curled in ringlets around his face. Yani swallowed, almost overwhelmed by the heady emotions.

He stood several inches taller, so she had to tilt her head to see his eyes. They blazed with such intensity she took a quick breath.

Without saying a word, he lowered his mouth over hers. She accepted it and relaxed, savoring the moment. A warm commotion started at the base of her neck and flowed across her skin like a wave of heated oil. His hand electrified her skin through the thin fabric of her dress. If he was as hungry for her as she was for him, they'd have instant sparks.

"I like your style, Drew."

"If that's the case, you'll love me by the end of the night."

She reached for his hand as he led her to the car. She was a lot closer to loving him than he could have imagined. But that bit of information she needed to keep to herself for now. No use in scaring the man away when she just realized she was ready to change her life for him.

He opened the truck door for her.

"You cleaned up the truck?" she said

"Yes, yesterday, before you decided to stomp off to your bedroom. There's something I want to tell you, too. I'd planned to talk to you last night, but you weren't in a listening mood."

Before pulling her feet into the truck, she asked, "What is it, Drew?"

"I'll tell you at dinner. It's not earth-shattering."

"You're sure?"

He tapped her leg. She swung them around in the seat while still staring at him.

"I'm sure."

He closed her door and ran around to the driver's side. He climbed into the driver seat and strapped on his seat belt.

"Last night, your eyes were saying you were going to accept my invitation until your friends showed up and ruined your mood. They don't do their little double team thing too often, do they?"

"You knew what was going on?"

110

"Of course. But teasing you is so much fun. The more we piled on, the more your lips stuck out. You have the prettiest pout I've ever seen."

She faced him. "You've been working on my house for almost two weeks and we've been pretending or ignoring this thing between us. We really should talk."

"Maybe over dinner tonight, I'll tell you a few things about me. You said you had some questions, so I'll answer every one of them."

"There's a lot about you I want to know, I hope there aren't any convictions or zombie in your past. I really think that might be too much to handle in one night."

"I think I can manage your questions. I'll answer some tonight, the rest the next night."

"Maybe after dinner we'll both go running in opposite directions. You're that sure of yourself, huh?"

"Princess, I've been in your kitchen and bathroom, the two most personal rooms in your house. I've seen what you eat, I've seen those little things you call panties, and I've seen what they are supposed to cover. I have a pretty good sense of who you are, and I know you wouldn't have let me near your precious body if you didn't feel something for me. So yes, I'll be around tomorrow and the day after that and the day after that one." He nodded with certainty.

"You think you're so smart. Let me see what I know about you." She glanced over the seat and examined the car. "You love your big work boots. You must have ten pairs and none of them appear to get much wear. Even when you're wearing your ponytail, your hair is cut to precision, so you must have a streak of vanity. You clean up good, because even though I expect to see dirt under your nails, there's nothing there, ever, and you have a thing for pink teddy bears."

"Very observant. I have to hand it to you." He pulled into the valet lane in front of the restaurant on the pier.

"Yeah, but I don't know where you live. I know you have sisters, but I have no idea how many or if you have any brothers. I do know there is one goddaughter in your life that I'd love to meet."

"I would answer your questions now, but then you wouldn't be able to interrogate me during dinner."

Holding hands, they strolled toward the entrance. An attendant opened the door as they approached.

They walked inside hand-in-hand. All the apprehension about saying yes to him evaporated the moment she'd walked down the stairs in her house. Somewhere she'd find the courage to stand up to her parents. Drew was too good to keep hidden.

"This is quite an exclusive place. I hear it can takes weeks to get a reservation, so how…"

He pressed his index finger against her lips. "Again, hold on to the questions until after we've at least had a glass of wine."

"Mr. Sizemore, your table is ready," the hostess said as soon as they stepped up to the walnut podium.

"How does she know your name?" Yani asked.

"Shhh," he whispered.

Yani tried to squash the dubious angst stirring in her stomach. They were seated at an elegant circular booth. She slid in and Drew sat beside her. He didn't need to impress her. She was already committed to something with him, even if it was hot dogs a few times a week.

The server placed the wine menu on the table and disappeared. Drew looked as comfortable here as he did spackling drywall. After ordering a three hundred dollar bottle of champagne, he turned his attention to her.

"Are we celebrating something?"

"Yes. Us." He winked at her.

"Okay, Drew, I've almost bitten my tongue in half." She glanced around the elegant dining room. "This is very nice, but you don't need to go overboard to impress me. I'm hooked already."

"Princess." He placed his hand over hers. "I've got this."

112

She sighed and leaned back against the leather booth. "Don't you think it's time you tell me about yourself?" She folded her hands on the table and willed the butterflies in her stomach to settle down. It was going to be a long night.

"I would have answered your questions any time you wanted. All you needed to do was ask."

"You could have volunteered some information."

"Maybe you're right. I'm Drew Sizemore. I don't work for Brian Contracting, I own it. Brian is my uncle, and since he's retired, I'm trying to save his company." He shrugged a shoulder. "My father doesn't think it can be done and my mother is hoping I prove him wrong. I come from a very competitive family. I was only supposed to spec out your job then turn it over to my crew, but when I saw you strutting up your sidewalk, I knew I would find a way to stick around."

"So when you're not deceiving women, what do you really do?" In the dim light of the restaurant she had to shift to see his face.

"I own a consortium of companies, but I really like working with my hands. I didn't deceive you. I'm very hands on, and so I'm often at a site supervising the work. In your case, I decided to show up every day. It had extra benefits."

"So why are you riding around in the beat-up truck?"

"You don't expect me to do construction work in a luxury car, do you? Can you imagine what it would look like with toolboxes and mud-caked shoes in the back seat?"

"I thought you were a carpenter." She dropped her head, hoping he wouldn't see the stupid look in her eyes.

"I am, but I'm more than just a man with a hammer."

The server returned and popped the cork. After pouring the champagne, she disappeared.

"This whole time you let me believe all the wrong stuff about you."

He leaned away from her. With his hands resting in his lap, he studied her. "You weren't totally incorrect about me, princess. Around you, I was myself. I didn't have to worry about what I said or how I said it or you cancelling the

113

contract." He planted a tender kiss on her lips. "I didn't even have to dress up every day and you still let me get between those legs."

"Were you laughing at me behind my back the whole time?"

"Not once. Every day I hoped you'd invite me back into your bedroom. And I was thankful for every time that you did."

Chapter Eight

After their meal Drew paid the check without taking his eyes off her. If it was possible she grew prettier every time he looked at her. Somewhere between dinner and dessert she seemed to relax. After their meal, she knew everything about him except the name of his first grade teacher.

"I'd planned to take you to a private showing of some new movie release. But I can't remember the name of the film, and I'd much rather take you back to my place. There aren't any ripped out walls and I have a priceless view of the city. So how about it?" He placed his hand on her knee and inched upward.

She put her napkin on the table and folded it. With her palm on top of the neat squared linen, she said, "Are we a couple, now?"

Her boldness would never get old. "We've been a couple for some time. I haven't been seeing anyone and neither have you. So if you're ready to make it official, then we're a couple."

Her whole face brightened as her lips shifted into a big smile. "I kind of liked the idea of you being my handyman. Thinking of you as a corporate tycoon is going to take some getting use to."

"I'll be whatever you want me to be. If you need something fixed tonight, I've got just the tool you need." He kissed her again.

"Then we better get started on your new project. Me. Before all my plumbing goes haywire."

He escorted her out of the restaurant. In the car, her dress road up her legs, exposing her luscious thighs. At each stop light, he stole a quick glance. By the time he pulled into his garage he wasn't sure if he'd get her upstairs before his need to devour her took over.

"I should have known, she said the moment they stepped into the exclusive penthouse elevator. When the doors glided open, revealing his spectacular view of Center City, Philadelphia, she spun around to face him. "Why does a single man need a place this big?"

"To impress you."

"I was impressed the moment you told me about the teddy bear."

"You're easy. I could have made that up."

"But you didn't. Now it's my turn to impress you." She dropped her purse on the floor and slipped her left shoulder out of her dress, then her right one. She shimmed the dress over her breasts and past her hips until it landed in a heap around her heels. She discarded the dress and the shoes with a quick kick. The gesture was so smooth and quick he couldn't look away.

Standing in front of him in nothing but a thong and willingness, his brain went numb. Her creamy skin glowed from the city lights coming through the big window. He slipped off his jacket, unbuttoned his shirt, and slipped off his shoes and socks. He lifted her into his arms and carried her upstairs.

"Aren't you going to turn on any lights?" Her question was both a whisper and a giggle.

"No. I have a recurring dream about what I want to do to you. I can do them with my eyes closed. But believe me, they'll be open, because I want to see every glorifying second with you."

He placed her in the center of the king-sized bed like he was handling a delicate piece of priceless crystal. She watched as he stripped out of his clothes. From the nightstand he removed a box of condoms.

She reached for him and pulled him down on top of her. "You're taking too long."

He silenced her with a kiss. Her tongue was eager, circling his with so much intensity, his body hardened, threatening to explode. The palms of her hand caressed his back as he shifted to taste her earlobe and her neck. Just a hint of her of cologne lingered behind, but her sweetness was enough to fuel his desire. Never had his body responded with

116

such fervor. Controlling his eagerness was difficult, but he wanted the night branded on them like a song on continuous play in their heads.

She pressed her lips against his chest, searing like a torch as she glided lower. Her touch was so light and gentle he had to open his eyes to match the reality to what he was feeling. He cupped her full breasts, squeezing each one with just enough pressure to make her moan. She slipped out of his reach to plant lingering kisses along his torso as she moved down his body.

Her mouth surrounded his throbbing member. With a strong pull, she drew it deeper. Afraid he might bruise her delicate flesh, he released his hold on her breasts and grabbed the sheet instead. A blistering heat enveloped his body with every tug and twist of her tongue. She wrapped her tongue around him like she was sealing a delicate package.

Weeks ago when they first met, his impression of her had been so different from the passionate person he was falling in love with now. Just knowing she wanted to share a future with him was enough to make him happy, but he wanted more. A family. A life. Forever would be a beginning. Plans of introducing her to his parents were already on his agenda.

He pulled her away before she pushed him over the edge. The dark look glowing in her irises spoke to her passion, too. He traced his tongue over each nipple while she groaned and rotated her hips. Each seductive sway enticed him closer to the brink of bliss.

"Enough, Drew," she pleaded.

He reached for the condom on the bedside table and drew it on. He eased into her slick center, trying to stretch the moment into hours. The tempo of her hips picked up speed and nothing he did seemed to slow her down. They locked eyes just as his feelings flung him into the universe.

"Do you ever plan to let me go?" he asked moments later when her legs still held him in place.

"I don't think so." She ran her finger through his hair, tugging on the ends. "I hope you'll never let me go."

"It has taken me too long to get you to wade into this relationship." He held her tighter. "This is real for me, Yani. I love you." The words slipped out. Wearing his game face should have been so easy, but with her none of his negotiating techniques worked.

"I think you're supposed to say those words before we make love, not after."

He held her gaze. "At least I said it."

She placed her warm soft hands along his face, and kissed him. "I love you, too, Drew. But I think you already knew, didn't you?"

"A man can hope."

"I need you to do me a favor." She cradled his face.

He nodded. "Anything."

"When we go to Phoebe's and Cory's wedding, please let me introduce you to my parents as my carpenter."

Epilogue- Fifteen Months Later

From her seat on the dais with the wedding party Yani watched her father yakking with Drew. Her mother kept nodding as if it were the most interesting conversation she'd ever heard. Sitting with the bride's maids and ushers was so much easier than being at the table with her parents, but she'd promised Drew she'd recuse him as soon as possible.

Yani pushed away from the table and placed her napkin beside her plate. She gathered Phoebe's train and tucked it around the chair so no one would trip over the delicate lace

"I'll be at the table with Drew if you need me," she said to the beautiful bride.

"He must really love you if he hasn't run screaming from the interrogation your dad is giving him" Phoebe lifted her wine glass to her lips. Her constant smile hadn't wavered once all day.

"My dad probably won't let him leave," Yani said before hurrying through the cluster of linen draped tables. Drew's face softened the moments he spotted her. The tenderness in his eyes almost stopped her short of reaching him. Her mother followed his gaze. When she saw Yani the anxious lines around her eyes eased. Yani recognized the expression. She didn't see it often, but when she did it meant her mother was on her side.

She kissed Drew's cheek. "I got here as soon as I could." She whispered to him before sitting in the empty seat next to him.

"I'm fine." He mouthed and placed his hand on her thigh.

She relished the warmth of his touch.

"We've been having a nice chat with your friend." Her father's steepled fingers were a clear indication he wasn't happy with something. "So far I've been doing all the talking. Drew here seems to be a man of few words. "

"I've been enjoying your stories. You've lived a colorful life." Drew's tone was casual but Yani caught the taunt.

"I've had quite a bit of success. I'm not bragging, I'm just getting to know you." Her father tilted his head down and glared over his glasses. "How long have you and Yolanda been dating?"

"That's enough, dad. We're supposed to be helping Phoebe and Cory celebrate their big day not playing twenty questions." Yani reached for Drew's hand and threaded her finger's though his.

"We see you so infrequently. We're just trying to find out what's going on in your life." Her mother's voice was calm enough to charm the information out of me.

"Drew and I have been dating for a few months." Yani held up their united hands demonstrating they were a couple.

"What do you do, Drew? For a living?" Her father leaned in more, his shoulders hunched for business, indicating the frivolous talk was over.

"He's my contractor. We met when he did the renovation on my house." Yani spoke up, afraid Drew might not give the proper answer. Being with him gave her the courage she needed to confront her parents. She should have done it years ago.

Her father's eyes darkened, his lips tightened with disapproval. But for the first time since she could remember she didn't care.

"You're really quite charming, Drew." The lilt in her mother's voice said Drew had won her over, already.

"I'm glad you think so, Ms. Maxwell. Because I'm in love with your daughter and I hope you both will give us your blessing. I want to marry her." He spoke to her parents, but without taking his eyes off her, he got down on one knee and reached for her left hand.

"What did you just say...Did you..." Yani looked around the table. No one looked flustered. It was as if Drew had asked her parents to pass the salt.

"Yes, Yani, I'm asking you to marry me."

Her heart accelerated like she was being chased. She stared at his lips. He was talking to her.

He pulled a velvet turquoise ring box from his breast pocket and lifted the lid. The glow from the candle center piece captured the facets of the diamond. She covered her mouth.

He slipped the ring on her. His eyes held the promise of forever. She couldn't look away.

"Well, Yani. You have to say yes. It's so obvious this young man adores you," her mother said.

"Hold on a minute, Yolanda..."

"Oh shut up, Davis. Can't you see they are in love?" Her mother poked her father's arm with enough gusto to make him clamp his mouth shut.

Drew squeezed her hand. "Yani? Did you hear me?"

She nodded. "Of course I will marry you. I love you."

"Can you afford that ring? It's bigger than her mother's and it took me years before I could buy it. Starting out in debt isn't a good idea." Her father spoke fast, his words sounded more like a command than a comment.

She waited for him to point his index finger at Drew and snort.

"Actually." Drew released her hand and stood. The expression on his face was serious now. "I haven't been totally honest with you Mr. Maxwell. I own a construction company. A very successful one. Every now and then I like to get my hands on my tools, so I did the work on Yani's remodel."

She nudged Drew's shin. She was enjoying her father's discomfort. He'd certainly dished out plenty.

Her father smacked the table. "I knew it was something about this man I liked."

"Does this mean I get to plan a wedding?" Her mother held her hand together like she was praying.

"Soon, Mom. Soon," Yani said. "But for now let's enjoy this one." She pulled Drew onto the dance floor.

DATE ME

Chapter One

Cat Preston circled the huge kitchen island of Drew's Philadelphia penthouse. Each trip around the spotless quartz counter ended with an invisible period made with her index finger, before beginning the next useless loop. Not the most productive way to spend a Saturday morning, but her failed relationships wouldn't release their grip on her. No matter what, it was time to forget about the past. No matter what, it was time to stop wishing for a different outcome. No matter what, it was time to accept the way things turned out.

Two months was a long time to take up residence in someone else's home, but when her life disconnected from gravity and flung her against the cold, hard universe, this was the softest place to land. Surrounded by friends and sharing their laughter blurred the pain. But Yani and Drew were getting serious. No matter how delicate they tried to handle her, she was getting in their way. Just because her love life had ended up in a muddy ditch didn't mean she should ruin their chance at happiness. No one liked a third wheel and even if they were too polite to say so, Cat knew it.

The gentle pulling of the elevator cables sounded as she marked her fourth lap. Yani and Drew were home. Living in the elegance of their penthouse had been the balm she needed to patch her heart, but now she was fine and time to prove it. Today was the big step. The two of them were showing her a brownstone that they thought was perfect for her.

As the cables quieted she took a deep breath and squared her shoulders. Sooner or later she had to move out, but her stomach didn't agree with the idea, so all morning it had acted like a naughty child.

Instead of Drew and Yani stepping off the elevator Jeremy Gavin strolled into the foyer. Her Jeremy. The man she'd given her heart to. The man, who'd crushed his fingers around it, squeezed it tight, took her virginity, and then marched down the aisle with another woman. She'd spent months wishing she could take back her innocence, her love, and her life. He'd left her flattened on the pavement like road kill. She thought she'd found solace with Robby. Instead, he had been the buzzard flying overhead ready to pounce on the weak and naïve.

Cat drew her eyes up from his signature Italian shoes, creased wool slacks, and ultra-white starched shirt. Coal black curls framed his face, giving him a boyish handsomeness' that made her swallow. With his hands deep in his pockets and his narrow gaze, Jeremy could have been ten feet tall. His presence seemed to fill the large living area. She fisted her fingers, and sucked in air as if she were drowning. Staring at him was like having a room full of gorgeously wrapped gifts and not being able to open them. But she smelled trouble and this stench had Jeremy written on it.

The moment Jeremy looked at her, his lips widened to reveal brilliant white teeth, as if they were two old friends reuniting after a long absence. A little corner of her heart flared red-hot. The kiss they had shared the night he announced he was marrying someone else still felt like a torch on her lips. She'd been silly enough to think she could kiss him and make him love her.

Men must have a hidden switch that operated them. Unfortunately, she'd never found the one to unlock Jeremy and reveal his true feelings. But he sure knew how to lay her wide open and march over her soul.

Seeing him was like having her heart pulled out of her chest with a pair of rusty pliers. Her temperature spiked several degrees. If life gives everyone one great love, then Jeremy had been hers. He'd filled every empty spore of her heart, made her laugh at the silliest things. And then came the day he announced he was going back to his old girlfriend.

To marry her.

The news was so unexpected it punched a hole in her soul the size of a meteor.

Robby was the rebound guy. Robby's betrayal hadn't hurt as much as Jeremy's, but in her weakened state she'd ended up on the sideline of life.

Cat couldn't say what she wanted to her friends. How do you scream at the world that your life had been tossed off course and you can't find your way back?

The flutters in her stomach weren't supposed to happen. Three months of being alone hadn't been long enough to teach her a lesson. Perspiration broke out down her back, making her blouse feel hot and clingy. Her breath hitched in her throat, allowing only shallow gulps. Almost in an instant the memory of him kissing her goodbye vanished, replaced by a retrospective of what his touch did to her body. The warmth on her back spread to her arms. Cat tried again to draw a silent breath with only a little success.

She backed up to the cupboard and pulled out a coffee cup. Seeing Jeremy after more than a year required something stronger, but a cocktail at this hour would raise an eyebrow and start a new discussion about therapy. Jeremy didn't need to think she was still pining over the unceremonious way he'd broken up with her. Where had she picked up the propensity to date the wrong men? Finding the answer would require a visit with her mother to delve into her childish need to please.

Cat sucked in a deep breath. The fuzz in her head made it hard to think straight. "What are you doing here, Jeremy?"

He shifted his position. "Drew called me. They won't get back into town until late this evening. Something to do with Yani's parents. He asked me to show you the house."

She dropped her purse on the stool and folded her arms over her chest. "I'll wait. I can see the house another day."

"Someone else is interested in leasing it. Drew wants it off the market as soon as possible. So don't let your anger at me keep you from having a nice place to live."

"That's easy for you to say." She stormed to the opposite side of the counter.

"Aren't you even going to greet me?" A single curl of Jeremy's dark hair hung down the middle of his forehead. His olive skin still held its summer tan. By now he should have blurred into the fuzzy recesses of her mind along with everything else that'd happened since the Robby and Rea incident, but every detail about Jeremy was crisp and clear, front and center like the defining moment it was.

After taking a deeper breath and holding it until her lungs hurt she exhaled and straightened her back. "Hello, Jeremy." Her voice sounded casual as if she didn't dislike him anymore.

"You're looking as beautiful as ever, I see." His deep voice was a siren song calling her closer.

"Thanks. Being dumped must be good for my complexion. You're looking well, too." She kept some distance between them and reached for the coffee canister. Then realized the coffee was already made.

His smile vanished pulling his lips into a thin line. "Ah, there it is, the sharp tongue with the cutting quips, I've missed."

"Then you're in luck, because I've got a whole lot more of them and, if we had to spend time together, you'd get to hear them all. But since I'm not going anywhere with you, how about I record some and send them to you?" She poured coffee into the mug and doused it with creamer.

He tossed his keys from one hand to another before shoving them in his pants pocket. "It's up to you. Drew changed the place just for you. He painted the master bedroom the brightest yellow he could find, because Yani said it's your favorite color. There is a private patio off the kitchen. Like I said, if you don't want it, someone else does. There is a lot of interest." He shrugged one shoulder. "So what's it going to be?"

She picked up the sugar bowl and scooped some into the mug.

Hanging on to memories of another man was not something she ever intended to do again. Well, except for her dad, because he was different. He was perfect.

"Drew's right, the townhouse is ideal for you. I can see you living in the place."

"Don't pretend you know what's good for me, Jeremy. I'm not the same girl you used to know. You'd be quite surprised at how much I've changed."

He cleared his throat while his eyes bored through her. Years ago that look would have been enough to make her bend to his will. But the new Cat wasn't charmed so easily.

"Let's play nicely. The mission today is to look at the house," Jeremy cautioned in a firm voice.

"I'll be nice. I think I've worn out my welcome here and it's time to move on," replied Cat.

"We better get going." Jeremy pulled his sunglasses from atop his head and settled them on his nose. "Are you ready?"

"Yes." She pushed her purse on her shoulder. She followed Jeremy to the elevator.

They rode down to the ground floor in silence. Behind his dark shades it was difficult to see what he was looking at, but he faced straight ahead. She watched the numbers count down from twenty on the digital display. When the elevator came to a halt in the lobby, Jeremy allowed her to exit in front of him.

The doorman held the door for them as they walked outside. The sunny sky did little to warm the cool October air. Cat rubbed the goose bumps that peppered her arms. She should have brought a jacket. The thin blouse wasn't enough to ward off the dampness. It was chillier than she'd expected.

"So are you going to talk to me? If not, it will be a long ride." Jeremy pulled his keys from his pocket.

"Does me being quiet make you nervous? Are you wondering what's going on in my head, what I really think of you?" They stood at the traffic light waiting for it to change.

"I can imagine what you think of me. The few times I've seen you—"

She put up her hand. "Let's not stroll down memory lane. We both have some things to remember about what used to be and none of it matters, now. How do you like working

127

with Drew?" she asked without looking at him. If she kept them on neutral ground, the day would be fine.

"I like it. I especially like the benefits." He folded his hands in front of himself.

"Benefits?"

"Yes, like seeing you."

"Like seeing me? You've got to be kidding." She couldn't help but roll her eyes and dismiss his comment. Trying to read more meaning into his words would only make her brain whirl out of control. Thoughts of Jeremy and the wild nights they shared were now in the redacted portion of her memory. Her life was divided into parts. Before Jeremy, when she was the hot girl who everyone wanted. Back then she passed out her phone number like she was handing out water to survivors in the desert. That was a good part. Then there was the unhappy woman Jeremy turned her into and the one Robby took advantage of. That was a bad part. Now she was a recluse who everyone pitied and tiptoed around. The bouts of unhappiness ran on like a bad sentence. Another bad part, but not for much longer.

Who she'd be when she shed the last of the cocoon protecting her was still undetermined, but going backwards was never a good idea.

They crossed the street and walked into guest parking. He led her to a black SUV with dark tinted windows, and held the door for her. In the front seat she placed her hands in her lap and pretended to be interested in the dashboard.

"How long have you been staying with Yani and Drew?" he asked while backing out of the space and pulling into traffic.

She ran her fingers across her forehead. "It seems like forever, but it's only been two months."

"Are you running from something?"

"Didn't Drew tell you my whole sordid story?"

"No. And he wouldn't." His words comforted her.

"I'm pretty good at running. When trouble starts I seek shelter."

"You never let me explain what was going on."

"I didn't need a long explanation while you were tearing my heart out. It wouldn't ease my pain or the outcome." She looked at him wishing she could see his eyes through the dark glasses to determine what was going through his head.

"I told you then. It was best for both of us."

"So you said." They continued in silence for a few moments.

"How's your sister doing? Is she still up to her antics?" He glanced at her quickly before returning his attention to the road.

"Geeta's calmed down a bit. At least my parents haven't put her out of the house lately. She graduated from college last year and she has a steady boyfriend. But we don't like him."

"Who is we?"

"The family. And you know my family is pretty laid back about such things. Every so often they still ask about you. Imagine that."

"Oh, they do, huh." He grinned.

"You can wipe that silly grin off your face. They're just making conversation. Nothing more."

"Sure, Cat. Anything you say." Jeremy slowed the car. "The house is right here." He pulled into the driveway of a quaint brownstone with white shutters and a glass-paneled entry door. She glanced through the windshield. "At least there isn't a white picket fence."

"The off-street parking is a plus."

"You don't have to put on the hard sell." She unbuckled her seatbelt and climbed out. "How did you get stuck babysitting me today, anyway?"

He lifted his sunglasses and produced a quirky smile, revealing his teeth and narrowed his eyes. "I'm not stuck. I manage all the Sizemore properties, so just consider this part of my job description." He led the way up the paved walk, unlocked the door, and held it open for her.

The sooner she looked over the house and made a decision, the sooner she could put some distance between herself and Jeremy. Maybe she shouldn't be so hard on him. Even though he'd tried to soften their break-up, it still hurt.

"If you want to wait out here for me, I'll look it over and come right out. No matter what it looks like inside, I have to take it. I really need to get out of my current living quarters." She stalked up the three steps leading to the door.

The Cat that got away. That's what he always thought whenever she came to mind. Choosing the noble and gallant path hadn't served him well. But instead of being bitter, he'd decided to move on and enjoy life. The vivacious Cat hadn't changed much since the last time he saw her. Her hair was long and full the way he loved it. She looked a little thinner but her eyes still had a fiery quality he couldn't forget. But he needed to.

Leaving Cat was the hardest thing he'd ever done. He believed they could have had a wonderful relationship. Even though the idea of soul mates was foreign, the way he felt about Cat would last the rest of his life. He'd been so sure he was doing the right thing by marrying Natalie. Even though he hadn't loved her, he'd wanted to make it work for their child's sake. Instead she'd played him for a prized fool and he'd lost the best thing that had ever happened to him.

Cat wore her anger like a well-deserved medal, and maybe it was. He'd never meant to hurt her. Letting her get away had been his major folly in life so far.

She still had plenty of curves. However, the bubbly person he remembered must have been vacuum sealed inside her somewhere because there was no hint of her today. One lie had torn them apart, making them both very different people. No wonder they were relationship-shy. The woman he remembered from those lovely nights of exploration had been a lot more fun. What had happened to her? He blinked away the thought.

Jeremy looked at his watch before following her inside. Since she was bent on hurrying this tour along, his afternoon would be wide open. He'd make it to his pick-up basketball game with plenty of time to spare. He stomped up the stairs. This was going to be easy.

"I'm not staying outside, Cat. And as much as you might want to punch me, you can't, so let's do this." He unlocked the door. "I think I should point out a few features the house has to offer. Drew really pushed the upgrades. He's almost out-priced the neighborhood by adding so much. Let me show you all the extras in the kitchen." He opened the door and signaled for her to follow.

"No need. I don't cook. I don't care." She dropped her purse in the corner near the front door and wrinkled her nose.

"If you're going to live here you might as well know what you're getting into," he insisted. Without waiting to see if she would follow he walked toward the kitchen. At the entrance he stepped aside and let her walk in front of him. Her compact tush filled out her jeans and her low-cut leopard top showed she had just as much to brag about on top as she did on the bottom. So many nights he'd fallen asleep with his hand resting on her breast. The memory made him smile.

"What's so funny?" she asked as she pushed past him.

"Nothing you'd want to hear about." He shoved his hands in his pockets and erased the smirk.

While he showed her all the things she should have loved about the kitchen she clasped her hands behind her back, showing no interest.

"Okay, so I can see you really love this room, what can I show you next?"

"You'd make a terrible real estate agent. You're supposed to point out all the qualities."

"Good, because I'm not an agent. I'm doing Drew a favor. A big one, and he can bet I'll be collecting." He led her back to the living room.

"Should I be happy you swooped down from on high to spend the morning showing me this house?"

"Yes, you should. You seem to need a place to live."

She snapped her mouth shut. "Bite me, Jeremy."

"Where?" he shot back.

She stuck up her middle finger and he braced for another harsh retort. But the fire in her eyes vanished and she dropped it. "I guess I never imagined we'd be spending time together again. At least not like this." Her voice had the childish quality she used when she was uncertain.

"I feel like you would rather bake me in the new oven than look at this place. Don't let your anger at me keep you from seeing how ideal living here could be."

"I don't want to be angry with you anymore. But it's hard." She almost smiled. "By now I should have gotten over it. Rob provided a needed distraction. I guess I should feel guilty for using him. But, you loved someone else, how can I be mad at you for not loving me enough? I realized that would be like asking someone to like the color yellow just because it's my favorite." Her body seemed to go limp. "For now, I don't want to be interested in anything. I like being numb. As long as I don't feel, I can't get hurt."

"So you're going to live the rest of your life afraid of being afraid?"

She shrugged her shoulders. "It's a good place to start."

"What was it? Your last boyfriend ran off with all your money?"

Her eyes narrowed to a squint. "Well, there was you, and then there was Robby. He was a cheater. Robby pretended all the way up to the end. Exclusivity only suited him on a part-time basis."

"Don't lump me in the same category as your ex. I loved you and never cheated. Our timing was just wrong."

"It didn't make me feel any better knowing we only had a timing issue. It sounds good, but it hurts just the same."

It had been painful for him, too, but he'd had no choice. "If you don't move on, then your ex wins, doesn't he? Do you think he's living half a life, like you?"

"Look, I don't need a therapist. Can you just show me the house?" She stuck her hand on her hip and looked around.

He half expected her to say she'd seen enough already.

"Show me the master bedroom and the bath. If it's good, I'll have nothing to complain about."

"I just hate to see you so unhappy. You're acting like this is a trip to the dentist. It shouldn't be. This is a time for you to start fresh. Make a new life in a new place, and before you know it you'll have a new love."

She screwed up her face, scrunching her mouth up to her nose. The familiar expression almost made him laugh.

"I don't have time for love. Right now the only thing holding me together is the belief that every day will get easier and one day I'll walk out of this tunnel and see life differently."

He held her shoulders to get her to stand still long enough to hear what he had to say. "Cat, everyone makes mistakes. I can't speak for Robby, and believe me, I don't want to. What happened between us was just one of those things. It happened to the both of us, but we turned out okay."

He needed to get away from her, but seeing those sad eyes kept pulling him back. Getting to the game would give him something else to focus on, because standing around staring at Cat was like opening a cherished photo album and seeing the past that you never wanted to let go. After a stressful week he needed to blow off some steam, and now Cat had amped up the need times two. Having her cry on his shoulder would have been nice, but when the tears stopped he knew he'd want more. He wanted her. And nothing good would come from that desire. Maybe they could be friends, because she looked like she could use one.

"Follow me. I'll show you the bedroom." He led the way upstairs. The room was at the top of the landing behind paneled double doors. He opened them with flair to showcase the elegant flooring and color combination.

She walked to the middle of the room, paused for a moment and then continued into the large en-suite bathroom. Her strides were long and calculated for a woman with such short legs. The way her skinny jeans hugged her thighs and calves would make her the envy of every woman in America.

He sure wanted to take a peek under the denim to see if his imagination still remembered her precise measurements.

"Yeah, it's great. I'll take it. I guess I can move in next weekend," she said without focusing on any one thing. Physically she was in the room, but it was obvious she wanted to be somewhere else or with someone else.

He shrugged. After dealing with his ex-wife's drama, biting off another chunk of personal misery, even if the woman was as seductively good-looking as Cat, was not an option. Like her, he was staying in the single lane. Once burned was enough for him.

Jeremy exhaled and suppressed his delight. Soon he'd drop her off and get on with his life. The rough texture of the basketball in his hands as he went one-on-one with his buddies was all he needed right now.

She gave the large bathroom a cursory glance before strolling back into the bedroom in the same slow steady stride. Without saying anything more, she headed for the door and was halfway down the stairs before he reached the landing.

In the wake of her flower-scented cologne he caught a blur as she ran down the stairs. Her heeled boots hit the hardwood floor with a decided thud.

A woman as pretty as Cat, shouldn't look so unhappy. He couldn't rescue every sad woman, but helping her was the only thing he could think about.

"Listen, I'll bet you don't have anything planned this afternoon. How about you come with me to my basketball game? Usually there are a couple of people there cheering for us."

She turned up her nose and sighed. "Yani and Drew asked you to do this didn't they? They want me out of the house."

"Get over yourself, woman. You looked like you could use a change of scenery. Let's just say I feel sorry for you." He locked the door.

"I don't need your pity. I'd rather go to a laundromat and watch the clothes tumble in the dryer than go sit through one of your games. Save your sympathy for someone who really needs it." She walked out of the house and marched down the street swinging her hips and her purse. Just watching her butt aroused him.

Every intellectual neuron in his body told him to let her go. Troubled women were troubled for a reason. After getting burned by Natalie, he should have run in the opposite direction. Instead, every instinct told him to catch her. He locked the door before going after her. "Hey, Cat, wait a minute. You can't walk to the penthouse."

When he touched her arm she spun around like she was ready to strike him.

"Come on. Go with me, you don't want me to take you home, yet. Give the new lovebirds some time alone. Beside, you can see some of the old gang."

Her long lashes fluttered just enough to reveal her light brown eyes. She was going to give in. He could tell by the way she relaxed her shoulders. But knowing Cat, first she needed to give him a few more seconds of attitude.

"I just want to go home. I haven't seen your basketball team in over a year."

"Save the speech, sweetheart and just say yes." He led her back to the car and opened the door. She slipped into the front seat with her purse clutched to her chest like a shield. "How about we call a truce, put the past behind us? We were both wronged and now we're going to move forward. Our next relationships will be different. Better."

As much as he wanted to tell her the reason for breaking up with her, he wouldn't. That humiliation was behind him and that's where it needed to stay.

"You're right. I shouldn't spend another day being sad. Maybe seeing your friends is a good idea. It's got to be better than watching Yani and Drew paw each other."

"And if watching me play basketball doesn't work, the drinks afterwards should certainly do the trick."

Chapter Two

Cat stared straight ahead. She wanted to go with him and hated herself for feeling that way. Accepting the halfhearted invitation from Jeremy only validated her lack of judgment.

"Are you still playing with the same group of guys?"

"Same ones. It's fun. When was the last time you laughed?"

"You still ask a lot of personal questions, don't you?"

"I'm just making conversation. If you weren't so bent on trying to be unhappy you'd realize this is normal chatter. If you don't want to answer then don't. No skin off my nose."

She wrapped her arms around her stomach. "Just don't judge me. Unless you've been with me for the last couple of months you have no idea what I've been going through."

"You're not the only one who's had bad luck in a relationship. I'm divorced. If you've never seen a marriage falling apart I can tell you stories that will tear your heart out. But what good would it do?"

"I didn't know we were playing 'top that'. You win. Should we start our own broken hearts club?" Until today, everyone had left her alone to wallow in her misery. Leave it to Jeremy to think it was his responsibility to pull her away from her unhappiness. It was one of his most noble traits, the constant cheerleader of sad souls.

"I nominate you president of our newly formed club. Since you deserve an award for your portrayal of the wronged partner it's the least I can do," he said.

"As I should be. It all started when you dumped me."

"You sound like a broken record. I didn't dump you."

"Don't get self-righteous over the semantics. You wanted to break-up, I didn't. You can call it the moon. I felt dumped." She was getting worked up again, but she couldn't pull back. The role of drama queen belonged to her sister, but being with Jeremy churned up a whole lot of old emotions.

"You know, for a long time I thought something was wrong with me. Why wasn't I enough? What did she have that I didn't?"

"It was none of those things, Cat. You were perfect."

She tightened her arms against her middle.

He stopped the car in front of his condo and shut off the engine. "I just need to run inside to change real quick. Come on up."

He hopped out without waiting for her to reply and then opened her car door.

Deja vu simmered in her belly while standing in front of his building. Even the doorman was the same, with his brass buttoned uniform and anxious eyes, eager to please. Jeremy ushered her through the entrance without a flicker of nostalgia.

The minute he opened the condo door he threw his keys on the table and began to unbuckle his pants. "Make yourself comfortable." He disappeared upstairs.

Instead of sitting down, she strolled about the familiar surroundings. Sun streamed in through the large windows overlooking the city. If his wife had lived here there was no sign of her now. It was still very masculine with lots of leather and dark colors. The rug in front of the fireplace was new. The festive one had been replaced with a muted brown wool that looked unforgiving considering the way they used to make love on it in front of the fire. The crystal vase she'd given him no longer adorned the center of the coffee table. He'd probably gotten rid of it soon after he got rid of her.

Within minutes, he ran down the stairs in a pair of black basketball shorts that revealed his runner legs, long and lean with bulging calf muscles. He also wore a pair of high-top sneakers. Jeremy had the build of an athlete. He was the kind of man she wanted in her life, confident, determined and focused. He never seemed to doubt his judgment. But until she got her instinct sensors back on track, it was best to avoid all men.

"I'm not so sure I should attend your game. Seeing everyone would be nice but...maybe I need to head back home."

"Too late. You've already said you'd go and now I don't have enough time to take you back or I'll be late."

They stared at each other for several seconds. Neither caved in to the silence.

"Okay." She finally relented. Two more hours and she could be alone again. She could do anything for two hours.

He whisked her out of the condo, into the car, and across town. He brought the SUV to a stop at an outdoor recreational center. It was still as neglected as she remembered. Weeds grew in the cracks of the paved court and the hoops lacked netting. A small crowd filled the graying bleachers as they watched a few men charging each other on the court.

Spending the afternoon at a pick-up game was only marginally better than lying across the bed watching an endless montage of Lifetime movies. But at least this activity had the advantage of real people.

Jeremy jumped out and popped the hatch on the car. She opened the door and found him sitting on the bumper pulling on terry cloth wristbands. He lifted his shirt over his head, exposing layers of muscles. The tattoo on his upper arm caught her eye. How many times had she traced the outline of the bird while resting on his chest? To keep from staring she looked at the court, but couldn't resist returning her glance to him. He looked more like a body builder than someone who sat behind a desk every day.

"Why are you undressing?" she asked, pretending to watch the practice.

"I'm skins this week. Next week you can watch me play in my shirt." He flexed his chest and contracted his stomach. She couldn't look away from his six-pack abs. Jeremy had a fabulous body and he didn't mind showing it to the world. At least while she watched him run up and down the court she'd see a fine male specimen.

"So you're still playing with the brothers, huh?" She nodded to the court.

"That's the intention. Why?" He bent to tie his shoe.

"Haven't you heard? White men can't jump."

He removed his sunglasses and placed them in the car. "Then you're in for a treat. Watch my moves." He winked. Before closing the trunk he handed her a cotton hoodie and a towel.

"What's all this stuff for?" She held them in separate hands.

"The jacket is to keep you warm, the towel is for me. To wipe my sweat." He gave her a knowing smirk.

"And why do I have to hold it for you?" She positioned the towel between her index finger and thumb, and held them away from her body.

"Because it's your lucky day. Let's go, I'm late."

Cat settled into the bottom row of the bleachers. She used to love basketball until she and Jeremy split up. The constant sound of the ball hitting the court was too much of a reminder of what she no longer had.

She shook her head. All those thoughts were in the past. She focused her attention back to the game in time to see Jeremy charge down the court and lay the ball up. He looked over at her and winked. He was actually pretty good.

"Cat, is that you? What are you doing here?"

Cat glanced up to see Egypt approaching the bench. Egypt was the only woman she knew who came to a pick-up game in four-inch heels and enough make-up to open her own store. "Hey girl." Cat jumped up and embraced her friend.

"I haven't seen you since you and Jeremy—"

"Yeah, I know." Cat cut her off.

"Are you guys back together?" Egypt grinned like she'd made the match.

"No. He just showed me a house today. Nothing more. What are you doing here?" Cat asked.

"I came to watch my brother play. Sammy felt sorry for me and dragged me out."

"I know the feeling. But why is Sammy feeling sorry for you?"

"Because my roommate just announced her engagement and I'm still single and waiting. My family is beginning to think I'm going to be old and alone. Maybe they're right." She turned her head away, but Cat saw her swipe her eyes.

"I see." Cat pushed a lock of hair behind her ear. Would her family say the same thing about her? Was there more pity in her future?

Egypt rubbed her eyes again before turning back to Cat. Dark streaks smeared her face and, her mascara ran down her cheek. The weak smile said she was trying to be brave. "Are you and Jeremy a couple or something? He keeps looking at you. And from the looks Natalie's throwing your way, she doesn't like it."

"Natalie's here?" Cat spun around and spotted Jeremy's ex seated on the top row. The evil gaze forced Cat's attention back to the court. "Why is she here?"

"She comes to quite a few games. Maybe she's still interested in Jeremy, too. If he has women lining up, maybe I need to get in line to see what all the hubbub is about," Egypt stated.

"Jeremy and I aren't a couple. We're just hanging out today."

"I wonder if he'd like to have some fun with me. He might be the distraction I need." Egypt sniffed. "If you don't want him, I'll take him. He looks so fine." She licked her high-glossed lips.

Cat held her stomach as it churned. Egypt made Jeremy sound like a commodity to be had. If anyone deserved to pull him off the dating market, then she should be the first in line. Jeremy had a sensitive side most people never even saw. But gum-smacking, heel-wearing, loud-talking Egypt only wanted to trot him out for a party or two, then she'd move on to the next available hunk.

"Well?" Egypt persisted. "Can I go for him?"

Cat ground her teeth. "I'm not his keeper." She tried to concentrate on the game. Egypt used to be a good friend, but if she made a play for Jeremy she'd definitely cross the line.

A quick glance over her shoulder proved Natalie was glaring her way. Cat sat up straighter. Natalie had no right to be indignant. That honor belonged solely to Cat.

Channeling her pride onto the asphalt court by cheering for every shot Jeremy made left her throat scratchy by the end of the game. Jeremy shook hands with the other team before strolling over. He flopped down next to her, shaking the weakened bleacher with his weight.

"Hello, Jeremy." Egypt's voice was as smooth as Belgium chocolate.

"Egypt." He barely looked at her before turning back to Cat. "So what-cha think?" He grabbed the towel and swiped his face. His darkly tanned skin looked red and hot. Before their break-up, she would have helped him mop the sweat off his brow. But now she dared not touch him. She needed to keep her hands to herself. Today, too much of what'd happened between them was like foreplay, sending her body on wild emotional swings. What she had in mind wouldn't be very appropriate for friends, and with Natalie looking as if she was a hair away from going bat-crazy, she kept her hands at her sides. A quick glance at Natalie validated her impression. The cold glare in her eyes chilled Cat.

"Good game, Jeremy," Egypt cooed.

"Thanks." Jeremy grabbed Cat's hand and led her away.

"What is up with her? She's acting stranger than normal," Jeremy said with a backwards glance.

"She wants to know if you're available."

"For what?"

Cat smirked. "What do you think?"

He shook his head and reached in the pocket of the hoodie to extract his keys. Several feet from the car he pressed the lock, a chirp sounded as the door on the SUV lifted.

141

"Why didn't you tell her not to waste her time?" he asked.

"I thought I should leave those negotiations up to you."

He grunted before running the towel through his hair. She couldn't help but smile, happy to know he wasn't interested in Egypt.

"You played very well today. I guess you proven me wrong."

"Oh really, well, that's one thing I've proved to you. Maybe you'll listen to me on other stuff, too." He stood.

"What do you mean?"

At the car he pulled his shirt from the hatch and tugged it over his head. As his abs disappeared she decided to focus on his dark eyes. He had a pair of lashes she would have paid to own.

"You're the kind of woman who needs to see things to believe them. If you believe you can find happiness, even after a broken heart, then it's more likely to happen."

"That's a bunch of bull and you know it."

He burst into laughter and she couldn't help but join him. Today felt like old times.

He opened the car door and watched as she got situated.

"I enjoyed the game more than I thought I would," she said.

"The fun isn't over yet. We'll grab something to eat with the team, and then I'll take you back."

"I guess that's okay. I didn't know seeing a house would turn into an all day event."

"Consider this your lucky day." He shifted into reverse and backed out of the lot before turning on the radio.

"We'll listen to some comedy, which ought to make you laugh." He adjusted the tuner until he found the station. A series of short stand-up snippets had her giggling as they made their way across town. When he pulled into the lot of a small sports bar not far from the hospital, her stomach dropped. She knew the place well since she'd spent so many hours at the table in the corner just to catch a few minutes with Robby between his shifts.

Jeremy put the car in Park and turned off the engine before glancing at her. "Is everything okay? You look pale, like you've seen..." He peered out the windshield and then back to her. "What is it?"

She unbuckled her seatbelt with a quick jerk. "The cheater." She paused to push a lock of hair out of her face. "This was where we had quick meals when he made time for me. It feels odd being here."

"If you're uncomfortable, I can skip the beer. It's really not that important." He started the car.

"No." She put her hand over his, stopping him from putting the car in gear. "I'm not running away. I've lived in Philadelphia all my life and I'm not going to start dodging around. I didn't do anything wrong. He should be the one in hiding. From now on, he's just somebody I used to know. I'm going in with you. Besides the chances of him being inside this time of day are low. If he's not on call, then he's probably with... Never mind. Let's go." She climbed out as he made his way around the car. Before going through the double wooden doors, she took a deep breath. Every word she said was true, now all she had to do was live it. The familiar stirring in her stomach almost rendered her too weak to pull the door handle. She squared her shoulders, extended her arm, and blocked the uneasiness.

"You're sure you want to go in, or would you rather I take you home?"

"I'm not a sissy. I'll be fine."

Jeremy's concern was sweet. Falling in love with him again would be so easy. He always managed to make her feel special, like whatever was going on in her head was important. Had she been able to do the same thing for him? Is that why he'd decided to leave her, because she didn't understand his wants? He'd been so patient with her today even though she wasn't good company. The game was the most fun she'd had in months.

"Your call, pretty lady." He opened the door and let her walk in first. She stood close to him while their eyes adjusted to the dim lighting. He spotted his friends standing at several high tables near the bar, and guided her across the room.

His hand on her waist was casual, but it felt like so much more. Maybe it was because she hadn't had an intimate touch for months, or maybe it was because every touch she'd had from Robby in the last year had turned out to be a lie. Which meant she'd been alone, even while in a relationship.

Jeremy's friend Brooks waved them over to a couple of empty seats. Brooks had the same olive coloring as Jeremy but his hair was lighter and not nearly as curly.

"Hey everybody, this is Cat, a friend of mine. You all remember her, don't you?" Jeremy said to the gathering.

A group hello went up in unison. She responded with a girly wave. They were friendly and welcoming. At least this way she wasn't one-on-one with Jeremy, which made it easier to ignore the tingle in her stomach every time he looked at her.

"Come sit next to me, Cat. I want to know more about the woman who has held Jeremy's attention for so many years." Brooks pushed several empty glasses into the center of the table and slid his chair aside to make room for her.

"What do you mean, Brooks?" She searched his face for an explanation.

"Don't pay him any attention." Jeremy shoved Brook's shoulder. "That's the liquor talking."

"I don't know if I held his attention. He just got stuck with me. He's supposed to keep me out of the house for a while. I'm sure as soon as his shift is up he'll deposit me back at my doorstep."

"Oh, he's still stuck on you. Believe me. I hear your name all the time. Just give him a few beers and it's Cat this and Cat that." Brooks slurred is words.

Instead of glancing at Jeremy or gleefully squealing like a pig, she continued to stare at Brooks without grinning.

One simple sentence and now the day didn't seem so bad. At least she wasn't the only one with sweet memories.

Jeremy squeezed his chair next to her. "Shut up, Brooks. Ignore him, Cat," Jeremy commanded.

Brooks pretended to zipper his mouth.

"And she's twisting the truth. I'm enjoying spending my day with her. The lady has a vivid imagination. Maybe she needs something stronger than diet cola to drink." He placed his hand on top of hers while staring into her eyes. His gaze was penetrating, like he saw into her soul. She almost pulled her hand away, but she liked the pressure of his hand, it was like snuggling into a comfortable bathrobe.

"I think you're right," she yelled above the music and chatter. "I'll take a beer. The same brand you're having is fine."

"You're going to drink beer? You don't like beer. Don't you want something sweet and frilly with an umbrella?"

"I figure if I want my life to be different then I need to do some things different. Now it's time for me to switch to big girl drinks." She propped her elbow on the table and surveyed the restaurant.

"So you have been listening to me. And here I was thinking you were mostly ignoring everything I said." He nestled his hips against her. The connection was intimate. It felt more like a sexual contact than a casual one. She glanced at him and saw a glint in his eyes. Maybe he was feeling the same spark that was glowing in her belly.

"I haven't paid you much attention. I'm picking and choosing which advice to follow. But mostly I'm following my own counsel, and my inner voice is telling me to go with the beer."

"I think the lady has spoken and she's not afraid to use her words," Brooks said as he signaled the server.

Jeremy gave her an approving look.

While they waited for their drinks, Jeremy pulled his phone from his pocket, looked at the display, and returned it.

"Is everything okay?" she asked.

"Yeah. It's nothing." He didn't look at her.

145

By the time the drinks arrived, Jeremy and Brooks were rehashing the game. The conversation between them was teasing and playful. Cat took a small sip of beer and held it in her mouth. The sharp jolt was not what she expected.

"Do you like it?" Jeremy asked.

"It must be an acquired taste." She swallowed and placed her tongue on the roof of her mouth.

Jeremy gave her a warm smile before continuing his conversation with Brooks. She watched Jeremy's face as he pounded his hands on the table with each point he made. She focused on the cleft in his chin as he engrossed his buddies with details of the game. His lips held her attention. They were full and inviting. She forced herself to look away even though she wanted to taste them.

"Brooks are you still seeing Jourdan?" Cat asked.

"I'm not seeing anyone right now. But if you know the name of a chocolate princess like yourself, I'm interested."

"Back off, Brooks. She's not interested in you." Jeremy's deep voice sounded sharp. His eyes were narrow.

"Relax, man. I'm just inquiring if she knows someone." Brooks picked up his beer and drained the glass. "Cat, don't you think Jeremy could have done a better job at offense. How many points did he give up today, like twenty?" Brooks held his beer to his lips and waited on her reply.

"I think he played great. You guys won and he didn't miss one lay-up."

"Aw man! She's already defending you." Brooks pushed away from the table with a playful grin, turning around and asked the group behind them the same question.

"Just ignore him. He says the same thing after every game," Jeremy assured her when they were alone. "And if we hang around long enough, he'll say the same thing about everyone on the team. It's just part of his routine."

Jeremy's smile came so easy. Just watching him made her feel happier, as if all the moping around had been a waste of time and energy. All she'd needed was a change of scenery and personnel, and the stench attached to her past life seemed to evaporate. She finished her beer and placed the empty glass on the table with a solid thump.

"Want another?" Jeremy asked.

"I know I said I was going to make some changes, but I still need to take baby steps. Beer might not be my thing. Maybe instead of beer I need to switch to wine. Yani and Phoebe are always drinking their reds and whites like they can't live without them."

The bar door opened, throwing a brief band of light across the table and floor bar. As several people stepped inside she locked eyes with Robby.

Chapter Three

Jeremy looked for the server to order Cat a glass of wine. When he turned back, she looked stiff. Even with her tawny coloring she looked green.

"Are you okay, Cat? You look like you're going to be sick." He touched her arm, half expecting her to be ice cold.

"It's him. He just walked in." Her voice sounded panicked.

He glanced around.

She grabbed his hand. "Don't look. Please don't look." She dropped her head and leaned closer, almost hiding behind him.

"Do you want to leave?" he whispered in her ear.

"I-I don't know what to do." She talked to him without looking up, her gaze pinned to the floor.

"It's your call, Cat. I'll do whatever you want."

"Can you go over there and punch him in the nose for me?" She laughed but choked it off.

"No." He slipped his arm around her waist and pulled her chair closer. She was shaking like she'd stepped into a subzero freezer. "I think he's coming this way. Tell me what I can do for you. He's seen you so you can't sneak out the back door now."

She looked up into his eyes the same way she had in the kitchen earlier today. The doe-like innocence revealed a softness which only appeared when she was uncertain. He held her face between his palms and kissed her trembling lips. She slipped her tongue in his mouth and turned the fake kiss into something real. Her tongue began a twisting, swirling dance with his that no man could have resisted. She snaked her hands around his waist and squeezed him like she used to do on those late nights after they'd made love and lingered in the afterglow. He knew they were acting, but his body's reaction was authentic. If she couldn't hear his heart beat it was only because his breathing was drowning out the sound.

148

Her mouth was soft and wet and sweet. The more he tasted the more of her he wanted to relish. He held the back of her head at the perfect angle to get full access to her mouth. He wanted her back. He had to have her, now.

When her ex-boyfriend reached their table and cleared his throat, punching him seemed like a really good option as she pulled away.

"Cat, it's good to see you." Her ex sounded a little timid. He didn't look like Cat's type, his shoulders were too narrow and his hooded eyes looked secretive.

Jeremy dropped his hand to her waist before giving Robby his attention. She ran her tongue over her lips in a way that was as seductive as the kiss. "Oh, hi Robby." She said the words with so much confidence, he thought he'd imagined her case of nerves.

With his index finger, Jeremy lifted her chin just enough to give her another peck. If he was going to be used, he planned to make the whole scene worthwhile. "Baby, aren't you going to introduce me to your friend?" He ran his thumb across her cheek and along her jaw.

"Jeremy, this is Robby. An old, old friend of mine."

Jeremy stuck out his hand. "Nice to meet you, man. How do you know Cat?"

Robby wiped at his brow. "We uh—we used to date." He looked uncomfortable.

"Oh," Jeremy draped his arm over Cat's shoulder, allowing his finger to lie on her breast. "She's mentioned you, I think. But we don't talk about the past. Do we, baby?" He kissed her cheek. Her skin was so soft. He wanted to taste her again, run his tongue along her cheekbone, but not right now.

Cat swayed a fraction of an inch closer and placed her palm on his chest. The small gesture stirred him up. The warmth from her hand spread through him. Until today he'd thought he could get beyond Cat, now he wanted to get her in bed. To hold her, smell her, enjoy her.

"You're looking good, Cat." Robby stared at her like she was a lost jewel.

"You know, I told her the same thing this morning. She gets prettier every day." Jeremy pointed to the empty chair vacated by Brooks. "Why don't you join us for a drink? We're celebrating tonight." He signaled for another round of beers.

Robby took the seat. "Oh yeah. What's the occasion?"

Cat's fingers dug into his waist. He looked down at her. Her lips glistened under the dull bar light.

"Maybe we shouldn't say anything until..." Cat started.

"I want to tell the world. I asked Cat to marry me and she's agreed." Jeremy stared at her eyes and saw a sparkle.

She pinched him just as the server placed more drinks on the table.

Robby looked at her hand. "I don't see a ring."

"We're picking it up tomorrow. It had to be sized." Jeremy ran his hand along her ring finger. Half expecting her to pull away, instead she placed her hand on top of his.

"You guys are moving pretty fast, aren't you, Cat?" Robby glared at her. His eyes narrowed.

She batted her lashes at Jeremy, finally agreeing to play along. "Well, you can't fight love, can you, sweetie," she said without taking her eyes off Jeremy. This whole charade was working in his favor. Her hand slipped down to his upper thigh and rested there. If she was pretending, she was doing a hell of a job.

"Actually, Robby, Jeremy and I have quite a bit of history. We go back several years."

Robby's eyes widened. "Before me?"

"Yes, definitely before you." Jeremy said, while trying to keep the pride out of his voice. "You know how loyal Cat is. She'd never be unfaithful in a relationship."

Robby picked up his beer and nearly drained the glass.

"So how are you and what's-her-name doing?" Cat asked.

"Her name was Rea and we aren't together anymore." Robby finished his drink and stood. "I think I'll leave you two alone. Take care of yourself, Cat." He reached in his pocket.

"The drinks are on me, man. It's the least I can do since it looks like I stole your girl." Jeremy grinned.

Robby stepped back. "Yeah, thanks. Well, it was good to see you, Cat. I hope you'll be happy."

"Oh, I'm very happy. My life couldn't be better, thanks to this wonderful hunk." She flipped Robby a careless wave before sticking her tongue in Jeremy's mouth again. This time she was more demanding and he was willing to give the lady what she wanted.

She released his tongue in time for him to see Robby push his way through the crowd and back out the door, with his hands deep in his pockets.

Cat dropped her head, like the wind holding her up had suddenly disappeared. With her focus on the half-empty glass in front of her she spun it around, making slow wide circles.

"Are you feeling better?"

She nodded.

"Want to talk about it?" He rubbed his hand along her arm, trying to get the merriment from earlier to return.

"Let me finish my beer, and we can get out of here. Do you want me to get you something else to drink since you don't like the ale?"

She shook her head. "I thought our little act was quite convincing. It sure looked like your ex fell for it."

"I really wanted to get back at him. Now that I have, I still feel the same way. What he did was awful. But what really hurts was all the lying. It wasn't like we had this great love affair that would have torn me apart if it ended. It was the missed dates, the sneaking around, and the pretending. I used to think I was a nag, who didn't understand his long hours and hard work to become a doctor." She picked up her glass and put it to her mouth. The beer touched her lips, but she never took a swallow. "I was getting ready to move out when I found him having sex with another woman in our apartment. I'd come home early to pack a few things. I was going to spend some time at my parents' house. But once I

151

saw him and the woman he'd denied for so many months I couldn't stand to go back to the apartment."

She inhaled a deep breath and her shoulders relaxed as she exhaled. "Let's get outta here. Do you mind?"

"I'm ready whenever you are." He placed some bills on the table, nodded at his buddies, and guided her to the door.

Once they were outside he continued to hold her hand until she climbed into the front seat of the SUV. He closed her door and walked around to the driver side. The little scene inside the bar had unfolded all the emotions he'd packed away. It was almost like Cat had a key to his secret compartment. He rubbed his chin before getting into the car. The whole thing was make-believe. He had to remember she wasn't kissing him. He was just a stand-in for Robby.

"Do you want to talk about what just happened?" he asked, with his hand poised at the ignition.

"You kissed me." She folded her hands in her lap like she'd just finished preaching a sermon. A hint of laughter danced on her lips.

He nodded slowly. "My memory is a little different. I'm not complaining. But your tongue assaulted mine and I don't think it was all pretend."

"I freaked out. I knew I was going to see him sooner or later, but I didn't want him to think I was distraught over what happened between us."

"Are you?"

"No. I'm mad at me for being too trusting. Philly is a big city and I'm no country bumpkin. I should have known better."

"Oh, boy, does that mean now you're one of those women who has nothing good to say about men?" He started the car and backed out of the space.

"I'm not saying. I'm just saying."

"I don't know what you're talking about. I'm glad I could assist you. Anytime you want to borrow my lips for practice or to act out again, let me know."

"Was I wrong to use you to strike out at Robby?" Her voice softened.

He hesitated for moment. No way could he tell her he liked it as much as he did. Men were supposed to be tough but around Cat he never felt the need to act hard-bitten. "I'm glad I did something you could approve of today."

It wasn't a lie. She had the ability to bring out the best in him. In her presence, he always wanted to be the man she looked up to like she did her father. It was the only reason he'd walked away from their relationship. Fathers take care of their children and he had to at least try. How many times had she told him about the sacrifices her father had made for her and her sister? He'd forfeited so much for Natalie's imaginary child. His life would never be quite the same.

Her phone pinged from inside her huge yellow handbag. She pulled it free and glanced at the display before shoving it back.

"Aren't you going to take the call?"

"It's a text from Geeta demanding to know where I am. I'm not sure I'm up for her high strung antics. This day has had enough drama."

They headed across town. Without the car stereo, the only sound was the hum from the tires, a comfortable silence. Instead of the constant need to chatter, Cat had always been just as content as he was to enjoy the quiet. How couldn't you love a quiet woman? "Are you ready to go home now?"

"I wouldn't call their place, home. Yani and Drew have made sure I feel comfortable. But I've overstayed my welcome. I can see it in Drew's face.

"Think positive. Pretty soon you'll be in your own place and you'll have a whole new life."

She nodded as she reached across the armrest and placed her hand on his forearm.

"What is it, Cat?" He glanced at her while trying to maneuver past a car turning left at the intersection.

"I don't want to go back to Yani's place yet. I know this might sound crazy, but tonight I just can't take being there either. She and Drew are so...so happy. I feel like I'm in their way." She looked out the window as if she wanted him to deposit her on the next corner.

He removed his foot from the accelerator and tapped the brake. "Where do you want to go?" He swallowed, unsure what she had in mind. The nearest hotel was miles away. His king-sized bed flashed in his head like a motion picture. "You can stay with me tonight. I won't even try anything. You can sleep in the spare room. How about that?"

The idea was so ridiculous it was perfect.

She squeezed his arm. "You wouldn't mind? You don't have anything planned?"

"I don't mind at all, Cat. I've always hoped we would remain friends."

"Yeah, but Natalie made it clear she hated the idea. I think she has a mean streak."

Jeremy bit his tongue. Cat's perception didn't come close to describing the trouble trolling around in Natalie's head.

Chapter Four

Cat hesitated before getting out of the car. How do you go from being someone who had anchors and direction to someone shuffling from pillar to post with nothing to grab on to? Beginning tomorrow, she would turn the direction of her life around. She wasn't some weak, needy girl and the sooner she stopped acting like one, the sooner everyone would stop giving her the sad eyes, half smiles and syrupy voices. If she heard one more empty assurance she'd crumbled into a pillar of salt.

From the garage they rode the elevator up to his condo. At least this way she was able to bypass the doorman. The fewer people who viewed her regression the better.

Once inside the condo, Jeremy turned on the lights. "Are you hungry?" He was so handsome, just looking at him made her throat swell. He'd almost been the one.

"I'm starved and maybe a bit tipsy. I can call the Thai place you used to love." She pulled her cell from her purse to find the number.

"Great. I'll go shower. I should be back down by the time the food gets here. Make yourself comfortable. You know where everything is." He looked at her for several moments before climbing the stairs.

After placing the order, she sat in the huge window seat and gazed at the skyline. Robby's appearance at the bar had given the perfect opportunity to kiss Jeremy. Feeling his mouth again reminded her of all the dreams she'd had for them. They were supposed to travel together, learn to cook fancy French dishes, and share them with friends at their dinner parties. They were supposed to have at least two children, a boy who looked like her and a girl who resembled him, just to be different. She ran her tongue over her lips, hoping to taste him. But like everything else, there was nothing to hold on to.

Dating Just Got Serious

In the night sky she watched a jet began its descent into Philadelphia International Airport. The plane's blinking lights held her attention until it disappeared from sight. Agreeing to stay the night wasn't such a smart idea, but going back to Drew's would have been just as stressful.

Across the room in the same place she remembered, sat the massive dining table where they'd had their last dinner. The dark mahogany wood gleamed like always.

Jeremy came downstairs just as she sat in the same chair as that night.

"This is where I was sitting the evening I thought you were going to propose. I had on my expensive lingerie, all silk and lace just for our special occasion."

He shook his head and plowed his fingers through his hair.

"Instead you had something very different on your mind. Wasn't I silly?"

He stood ramrod straight, his eyes unblinking. The doorbell rang before he responded.

"I'll get it." Jeremy bounded off the last step and made his way to answer it.

Cat raced to the door with the money crushed in her palm. "This is my treat, Jeremy. I want to." She tried to step in front of him.

"I can't let you pay, Cat. You know I can't have a woman—"

"We're friends, now. This isn't a date. Besides, I think your phone is ringing, again."

He raised his palms and stepped back. "Okay. Today, you win."

She settled the bill and followed the sound of his voice. The rustling of the bag as she extracted the food made it hard to hear his hushed conversation. He had to be talking to a woman, but Cat had no right to ask. She was the intruder.

Jeremy ended the call and flipped through the channels on the TV. He settled on the sofa while aiming the remote at the set. "What would you like to watch, romantic comedy or thriller?"

She guffawed. "Romantic comedy, that's an oxymoron, don't you think? I've never found romance to be comedic. Have you?"

"Oh, I think romance can be funny. It certainly plays tricks on you. If you can't laugh then you better stay off the field." Jeremy unpacked the cashew chicken and pad Thai, and dished heaping spoonfuls onto the plates. The savory aroma made her stomach growl. Without waiting she ate several bites before he finished serving his plate.

He picked up his fork and shoved in a huge mouthful of chicken. Tightly curled black ringlets made his hair appear shorter. He must have shaved while he showered because the faint stubble from earlier was gone. She'd liked the rough feel of his face between her palms. Now she wanted to see if his face felt as smooth as it looked.

"I noticed Natalie was at the game today. Do you and her still hang out together?" She tried to sound casual.

"It's complicated," he replied before eating the bite he'd suspended in front of his mouth.

"Is that code for mind your business?"

"Would I say something like that to you? Now let me ask you a question." He took his time chewing. "Why did you kiss me like that? Did you just want to make your ex mad?"

She opened her mouth and closed it with a small pop. Lying used to be an option, but not anymore. One of her new credos was to live her life and to stop trying to make everyone else happy. "This afternoon started out being a prank, but you're a good kisser so I decided to go for more. I guess the joke's on me, huh? Always wanting something I can't have."

"We can always have another round." He put his plate down.

"Oh, I'm sure you think we can. I've never met a man who turned down a kiss, even from a stranger."

"I'm not like any man you've ever met, especially your ex. You'd be surprised at what I've turned away."

"No, I don't think I would be. I'm on your list, remember?"

157

"No, you're on a list, but it's a special one. Yours is the only name on it."

"And what is the filter for this list?"

"I haven't decided yet. I'm still working on which one to use."

You're just trying to taunt me, aren't you?"

His eyes twinkled with either teasing or lust. If she chose the wrong one her feelings could get pulverized.

She stood up. "I'm really tired. I'm going up to bed, okay."

Disappointment shadowed his face, but he said, "Fine. You know which room, right? Top of the stairs on the left. But you're more than welcome to sleep in my bed, just in case you're fearful of monsters or things going bump in the night."

"Aren't you sweet? But I think I can handle the boogeyman." She grabbed her purse and charged upstairs.

She closed the door and leaned against it. Her heart pounded so fast she couldn't move until she slowed her heart rate. Thank God Jeremy hadn't accompanied her to show her around. Having him this close to a bed would tempt her more than she was willing to test.

The chirping from her handbag indicated another message had come in. She reached for her cell phone and scrolled through her messages. *Where are you? Call me now.* Her sister's panicked text made her sit down.

"Geeta, it's me. What's wrong?" she asked when her sister picked up.

"I'm worried about Donny. He's acting funny." Geeta's high-pitched voice sounded urgent.

"You've called me three times to tell me your boyfriend is acting funny. Geeta, he's a jerk. Leave him." Cat stretched out on the bed.

"I can't. I love him," she whined.

Cat took a deep breath. She had to handle her sister gently or Geeta would end up in a fit of tears that would take all night to quash.

"Okay, okay. Look I'll call you first thing in the morning. We can have breakfast and talk about what's going on."

Geeta's loud hiccup indicated she was either drunk or crying.

"Did you hear me, Geeta?"

"Yes. Breakfast. Tomorrow. Call me." She hung up.

Cat shook her head. Her sister would never grow up as long as everyone kept babying her. She complained about Donny every week, but refused to dump him.

Before she could put the phone away, it buzzed in her hand. Phoebe's number this time. She sat crossed-legged on the high queen bed before pressing the call button. "Hi, Phoebe."

"Where are you? Yani said you left this morning with Jeremy and she hasn't heard from you all day. Is everything okay?" Phoebe sounded worried.

"Are you checking up on me or are you being nosy?" Cat sighed.

"Since you started staying with Yani, you have never stayed out all night. You hardly leave the bedroom except to go to work. Didn't you think we'd worry about you?"

"I thought Yani and Drew would be happy to have the place to themselves for a change. I guess I should have called, but so much has happened. Besides, I'm fine. Do you know I've counted the number of times Yani and Drew touch each other. And in a matter of minutes they touch no less than fifty times. Isn't that impossible? They aren't glued together."

Phoebe chuckled. "You actually counted?"

"I've got a lot of time on my hands." She paused wondering if she should confide in her friend. Almost whispering, she said, "I'm staying at Jeremy's house tonight."

She heard Phoebe sigh. "Do you think that's wise? You can't keep rebounding between the same men. When you and Jeremy broke up you were so devastated, why would you even consider staying with him?"

159

"Calm down, Phoebe. I'm not sleeping with him. I'm in his spare room with the door closed. I just didn't want to be around Yani and Drew and their constant petting."

"How long will you stay in the bedroom?"

"Cut me a break. I'm fine and I know what I'm doing."

Phoebe sucked her tongue. "Yeah, sure you do. I'll bet you ten dollars he creeps down the hall and into your bed sometime during the night. Isn't that what always happens?"

"He won't. Even though he did offer me room in his bed." She fell back on the pillow. "But I want him to. I never stopped loving him. I thought I would. I thought I could. I thought I did when I was with Robby, but today I realized I still love him." She pushed back the tears.

"Are you okay, Cat?"

"No. I woke up this morning, thinking this was going to be the day I freed myself from all the old stuff, but now I feel as knee-deep in it as ever." She moaned.

"I'll come get you. You can stay with me and Cory and I promise we won't touch each other while you're here," Phoebe said.

Cat choked as she tried not to laugh. "Thanks, but I'll be fine. I'm moving out next weekend. And I'll start looking for a new man. One I haven't had before."

"Are you sure?"

"I am. Goodnight, Phoebe." Cat disconnected the call.

With the phone nestled beside the pillow, Cat stripped off her clothes and fell on the bed.

Several hours later she was still staring at the ceiling. Sleep should have descended on her like a cloud, but knowing Jeremy was just a few feet away made it harder. She flipped on her side and squeezed her eyes tight, willing Phoebe's words to come true. Listening for Jeremy's footsteps in the hallway. Hoping. If he came to her room tonight she wanted to be tough enough to turn him away, the way he'd done her, but she wouldn't. She pushed her face in the pillow. Who was this indecisive person?

Kissing him, even if it was for a good cause, had been a mistake. The idea of not moving beyond her love for

Jeremy was haunting, always wanting a man who didn't want you had to be a lonely existence. Next, she'd start adopting cats until she had hundreds and no way to take care of them. People would shake their heads and remember when she was vibrant and full of love.

She flopped on her back like a fish flung from a fishbowl, tired of ignoring the desire blooming between her legs. All day she'd pretended it wasn't there. Every time Jeremy looked at her, touched her, talked to her, it was like a love song to her heart. But now in the quiet the only thing she heard was her body calling. Wanting someone to touch her. Maybe, not a hundred times, but ten good times would be a good start.

She eased her hand between her thighs. The throbbing between her moist folds was unbearable. Just a few feet away from her was the best lover she'd ever had and she was forced to find her own pleasure. Life was cruel. She grunted and pulled her hand away.

Moonlight lit the room through the vanes of the blinds. She slipped out of the bed and followed the ray. The full moon comforted her. Always promising something fresh and different.

A draft blew through the poorly insulated window, cooling her fevered skin. After a deep breath she tiptoed to the door, cracked it open, and peeked into the darkened hall. While balancing on her toes, she found the bathroom.

She edged the door closed before turning on the light. She stood still until her eyes adjusted. After splashing cold water on her face she examined it in the wall-to-wall mirror over the sink. A nose. Two eyes. A mouth. She looked exactly like she expected, but she didn't feel normal.

She turned off the light. Her shoulders rose as she took a deep breath. The pebbled skin on her arms tingled with fear, but she continued, without over analyzing her actions.

At his bedroom door, she tapped with one knuckle and waited.

Chapter Five

She held her breath, waiting for Jeremy to respond.
After a few seconds, she tapped again, harder.

"Cat, is something wrong?" His sleepy voice was
barely audible.

"No. I'm fine. Can I come in?" Her knees turned to
powder. It was too late to run back to the security of her
room. And even if she did, she'd always want to know what
if. If this was her one chance to win Jeremy back and she let
it slip away.

He opened the door. His eyes rolled down her body,
stopped at her Brazilian wax, and returned to her face. "Wow,
Cat. Nice."

"Did I wake you?" She pushed hair behind her ears.
She expected him to be naked too. When they were together
he'd always slept in the nude, but tonight he wore a pair of
lounge pants.

"I won't lie. I was asleep, but I'm wide awake now."

She saw his penis jerk. The anxiety melted away.
Even if nothing else happened tonight, she'd always be
thankful he didn't escort her back to her room.

"I can't sleep. I kept hoping you'd tiptoe into my room
and hold me. But..."

He reached for her with both arms and folded her
against his chest. His warm, hard body pressed into hers. She
snaked her arms around his waist and laid her head on his
chest. He'd held her this same way the night they broke up.
They'd had the most civilized breakup in the history of
romance. He'd been stoic and determined. She'd been weepy
and childish. But he'd held her until she stopped crying, and
then he'd driven her home.

"Cat, if I had tried to cross the threshold of your room,
you would have cut me off at the knees. I know you well
enough to know you do things in your own time. What took
you so long, tonight? I fell asleep, waiting."

Jeremy lifted her chin. The way he stared into her eyes, he must have been reading her thoughts. His penis, fully hard now, pressed against her pelvis. He lowered his mouth to hers. Their lips connected, wet and moist, for several moments, before he slipped his tongue in her mouth. Unlike in the bar, this time every movement was slow and measured. His hands roamed across her back, warming her flesh as he made his way to her neck. His fingers thread the stands of her hair. Just like someone hitting the Rewind button, she was melting for him again. Her body luxuriated in his touch, almost knowing where his hand would land next, and which direction his tongue would take. It was like returning home.

Without releasing, they staggered to the bed, all arms, legs, and lips. They landed on the mussed sheets. She could smell his woodsy scented cologne in the fibers. All the memories they'd shared drifted back to her, light and full of emotion. They could have been watching a trailer from an action film the way her heart began to pump. She held him tighter as their first time together paraded through her mind in vivid detail. His kiss tonight was as tender and reassuring as it had been the first time he touched her.

His warm, rock-solid body pressed her into the mattress. She fumbled for the drawstring on his bottoms, but with their bodies locked, she couldn't release the string.

"You've got to remove these." She flicked his ear lobe with her tongue.

He pushed away from the bed without taking his eyes off her. With one hand he looped his thumb through the string and released the knot. The pants dropped exposing his massive erection.

She sat up to reach for him. He grabbed her hand and held her gaze. "Cat, are you sure you want to do this? It's been an emotional day for you. I don't want this to be something you regret in the morning." The desire in his eyes betrayed his words. He was just as needy for sexual release as she was.

"The only thing I regret is not being woman enough for you before. If I had, maybe you wouldn't have left me. I

163

believed we had something special." She closed her mouth with a snap. Those words were supposed to stay in her heart until the day she died.

Jeremy kneeled beside the bed, coming level with her. His soulful eyes brimmed with emotion. "I never wanted to leave you, Cat. She said she was pregnant. What could I do?" He took her right hand and held it while rubbing his thumb over her flesh. There wasn't a sound in the house and nothing filtered in from outside.

She wanted to pull her hand away. Was he confessing to cheating on her, too? "We had been together three months, Jeremy. How could she have gotten pregnant unless—"

"You know me better than that. Don't pretend you don't. If you're looking for a way out there's an easier way." He sounded exasperated. "She told me it happened before we broke up, before I even met you. I thought I was doing the right thing by trying to make a home for my nonexistent offspring. I wanted to be a good father, like my dad."

"Let me guess. You found out she wasn't having a baby after you walked down the aisle."

"About a month after we went to city hall." He let go of her hand and sat beside her. "I wasn't going to tell you the details. Natalie played me for a fool, and because I wanted to be a standup guy, I fell for it. Something about the whole ordeal changed me."

They sat in silence. He'd finally given her the explanation she thought she needed. But his confession didn't open the door for the two of them again. Too much debris cluttered their path.

"Why didn't you tell me?"

"Would you have felt better if I'd told you? I thought if you knew I was marrying Natalie and starting a family that would have hurt you even more. And once I found out my life was a farce, I hardly wanted to shout the mistake to the world."

"Why does she still hang around?"

"She's always creeping around the edges. She likes playing head games. Her life revolves around crisis."

"Karma is a bitch, isn't it? You broke my heart and your wife broke yours. If the whole incident wasn't so sad, I could almost laugh."

"No matter how I look at the whole charade, I never laugh. And just so you know, she didn't break my heart. I wasn't in love with her, but I didn't trust her to raise my child by herself."

"Why didn't you come back to me?"

He caressed her chin. "No, baby, it doesn't work like that. I made a mistake. I let you go, I lost you. There are no take backs. I had to live with that decision, no matter how painful."

She brushed his forearm with her fingertips, words stuck in her throat.

"Cat, I know I hurt you. That was never my intention. Jeremy's breath on her face fueled her desire.

She couldn't resist another moment. Either this was going to be the stupidest thing she'd ever done, or the smartest. She wrapped her arms around his neck and bent him to her as she eased back into the bed. The moment their lips connected, all the old magic guided her movements. Her tongue found his like it was welcoming an old friend back to her life. How many nights had she imagined tasting him again?

She placed her palms on his cheeks, pulling his strong jaw closer. His face was as smooth as she'd imagined. She held him in place while her hips ground against his erection. He pulled his face away and placed kisses along her neck and shoulders until he reached her breasts. His tongue blazed a trail around each nipple, drawing a deep throaty moan from her. His large hands cupped each breast, kneading them until they felt feverish and sensitive.

Every part of his body was familiar. She explored his back and shoulders as she made her way to his pounding member, cradling his shaft as it pulsed against her palm. She squeezed him tight, receiving the reaction she wanted. Jeremy's moans filled the room as he ran his tongue around one nipple and moved slowly to the next. His mouth was like a match, leaving hot spots everywhere he touched. She ran her index finger along the ridge of his shaft, coaxing his silky essence into her hand. He pulled on her nipple, grazing his tongue over the sensitive blossom until she arched off the bed.

Making love to Jeremy was so wrong, she couldn't think about what she was doing. Right now she should be back in her room getting a good night's sleep. But with this much man just a few feet away no way would her body let her rest.

He slid his finger inside of her and she melted. A frozen treat lying in the sun on a hot summer day couldn't have thawed faster. Every touch was magnified. The earth could have skidded off its axis. Nothing else mattered as his finger worked her tender flesh. Each tiny movement sent a wave of pleasure rolling through her veins. Just when she thought she would expire under his touch, he pulled away.

"Hold on." He kissed her cheek. From his nightstand he pulled out three condoms and tore one loose. She reached for the packet and ripped it open with her teeth. Instead of rolling the latex into place, she teased the tip of his erection with the latex. When he finally slipped inside her they hummed in unison. For a few seconds neither of them moved. She couldn't. So many times she'd wished for this, she needed to linger in the moment. It was like someone had given her a spoonful of the most delicious chocolate ice cream and she needed to savor the taste before the cool, sweet flavor dissipated into nothing. She relished in the pure indulgence of having him again. With her ankles locked around his back she pulled him deeper. Together they reached a natural flow, the to and fro of a seductive dance. Her body welcomed each thrust. She squeezed her eyes tight to draw out the moment. Willing the feeling to last through the night, through the weekend, through the rest of her life.

Just when she thought she could control her lust, her body switched gears. The wave of animalistic desire flooding through her veins consumed her. Instead of fighting, she surrendered to the ecstasy encapsulating her. The sensation

Dating Just Got Serious

was so phenomenal she wondered if the sensation was really an orgasm or something more ethereal.

Chapter Six

Cat's muscles contracted forcing him to release everything he had. This is exactly what he wanted and exactly what he didn't need. Having her back would have been perfect, but so much had happened in two years. Jeremy couldn't forget those hurtful days after they broke up. Cat was the kind of person who held on to the bad stuff, nursing it like a starving baby.

Tonight he knew she wouldn't stay on the opposite end of the condo. The only surprise was how long she took to knock on his bedroom door. He'd fallen asleep willing her to walk down the hall. What was next?

After several minutes, his breathing slowed and he rolled beside her. She cuddled closer, fitting against the length of his body. This was how they used to fall asleep. Tonight was like finding the lost puzzle pieces and finally putting the picture back together again. He slipped off the used condom, dropping it on the bedside table.

"Wow, that was nice." There was genuine pleasure in her voice.

He pushed up on one elbow to get a good look at her. The only light in the room was from the dim bedside lamp, but there was enough to see the satisfied glow in her cheeks. "We were made for each other. I know that might sound like a cliché, but it's true."

"I can give you a good explanation for my behavior tonight. But I won't."

"I wasn't looking for any details. I'm just glad you did. Before you went to bed I almost dared you to come to my room. Then I could be certain you would."

She poked his arm with her index finger. "You remember that about me, huh?"

"How could I forget? You've never met a dare you didn't take, have you?"

The phone next to the bed rang. With his back to the table he contemplated not answering. No one needed to talk to him at one in the morning. It had to be Natalie. She was off her meds, which meant a butt load of trouble was coming his way. The second ring sounded even louder.

"Aren't you going to answer the phone? Suppose there's an emergency." Cat pulled the sheet over her breasts.

"I wasn't." Jeremy sat up and shifted away from her, as he picked lifted the receiver. "Yeah," he barked.

The only response was heavy breathing.

"Hello," he said. Cat's eyes widened at his harsh tone. She made a move to climb out of bed, but he pulled her back before her feet could touch the floor.

"Where are you going?" he mouthed.

"It sounds like you need some privacy," she said over her shoulder.

He put the receiver back on the base. "No, I don't. What I need is this." He pulled her down on top of him and locked his mouth over hers. He knew exactly who was on the other end of the line and he'd find a way to handle her.

Chapter Seven

Thinking Jeremy was unattached was foolish. Of course there were probably lots of women standing on the sideline just waiting for an opportunity to get with him. The ringing phone in the early morning hours brought the sobering fact back to her so fast Cat almost forgot to breathe. Jeremy brushed off the incident, like it wasn't important, but only someone who thought they had a claim would call so late.

The loose curls along his forehead held her gaze. Focusing on his hairline was easier than pretending they could have something again or to accept the truth devouring her consciousness.

She was making a real mess of her life, which had seemed impossible just a few days ago. All she wanted was a place to live. Now she was on a road that led to nowhere, without the good sense to take a detour. Jeremy lay on his side. His breathing was soft and regular. She eased to the edge of the bed. The goal was simple, get dressed, get out, and get control of the emotion tugging her apart.

She tiptoed across the hardwood floor and out of the room without waking him. Back in the spare bedroom, she dressed and pulled her unruly hair into a ponytail. Her phone was still on the bed next to the pillow. After grabbing all her belongings she placed her ear to the door before opening it.

From the living room she called a car service to take her home. Standing on the corner trying to catch a cab at this time of morning would only validate her poor choices.

She closed the entry door and caught the elevator to the lobby. The car was waiting at the curb in front of the building. The driver hopped out and opened the door for her. A sudden movement across the street caught her eye. She looked back for the doorman, but he was tapping into his cell phone. Before ducking into the backseat she tried to get a better look at the person dressed in black, but they were already heading in the opposite direction. A cold finger slid down her spine, as the figure disappeared in the shadows.

As soon as she the driver closed the door, her phone pinged with a message from her sister.

Can't make breakfast. Catch u later.

Under other circumstances the short notice cancellation would have upset her. This morning not having her sister drone on about Donny's shortcomings was a blessing. All she wanted was to process her thoughts and behavior.

In the predawn light Cat told herself everything about the night before was no big deal. No more significant than an event like shopping for shoes or watching a movie. She leaned her head against the seat rest and closed her eyes while repeating the mantra to herself. If she said it often enough it would stick. It had to.

The car pulled up to the curb in front of Drew's condo. Cat tipped the driver and made her way to the elevator. Yesterday seemed like a dream. The details leading up to screwing Jeremy seemed fuzzy now. Calling what they did making love would have felt better, but he didn't love her. At least her mind could accept that truth. And there wasn't a man in the world who would turn down a naked woman knocking on his bedroom door at two in the morning. They were only screwing and she vowed not to pretend it was more.

In the seclusion of her bedroom she stripped off her clothes and placed everything in the laundry bag. Nothing about yesterday was worth reminiscing about unless she wanted heartbreak to become a constant companion. Cat turned on the showerheads at both ends of the stall and stepped between the hot sprays. For several moments the water pelted her skin, massaging the doubts gaining momentum in her head. Finally, she reached for the soap.

An hour later she was stretched across the bed with the remote in her hand. The faint smell of Drew's big Sunday breakfast for Yani seeped under the closed door, but she refused to be lured downstairs.

A sharp knock on the door startled her. "Yani, I'm not hungry for breakfast. You and Drew enjoy your meal. I'll be down later," she called out.

"Cat, it's Jeremy."

She jumped up. Her heart and breathing fought for control of her body. "Shit,'" she whispered as she looked around the room. The need to hide was overwhelming.

Before she could invite him in, he pushed the door open. He stood in the doorway, his eyes dark and his arms hanging at his side like two stiff poles. He had on the same clothes he'd worn last night, only now they looked a little rumpled. He took a deep breath, his chest expanded with the effort.

"Jeremy, what are you doing here?"

"What are *you* doing here?" He remained in the doorway. Each breath he took was punctuated with a rise of his chest. All he needed to do now was turn green and his Hulk impression would be perfect.

"I live here."

"And you couldn't wake me up and tell me you were leaving. What the hell is that about, Cat? Why the hell did you sneak out?"

"Don't get it twisted. Last night was just a booty call. You're not supposed to chase me down the next morning."

"I don't follow the rules. Sue me."

She wrung her hands and dropped on the bed. "This is why I left. I didn't want to have this conversation. I can't explain what happened last night."

His shoulders seemed to relax a little. At least his breathing didn't seem as labored. With one hand in his pocket, he stalked across the room and sat beside her. His eyes were so dark she couldn't make out the gold flecks that usually made them sparkle.

Earlier today the most important thing had seemed to be getting out of his house and away from him. As if she could ignore all the turmoil slugging through her brain just by putting some distance between them. But it wasn't going to be so simple. Hours after he'd touched her she could still feel his hands on her body, him buried inside of her, and his scent in her nostrils.

"I asked you if you were sure last night, remember?"

"I was so horny I wasn't thinking straight." She sighed.

"So now what, Cat?"

"I don't know. I wish I did." She wanted to touch him, but refused to lift her hand. No good would come of lingering over what used to be.

His cell phone rang from his back pocket. He made no move to retrieve it.

"Aren't you going to answer that thing? It rings all the time." Her bones told her Natalie was on the other end. Maybe she was reclaiming him. How long did Jeremy think his little charade would last?

"No, I'm not." He reached for her hand. "We're taking a walk."

She looked at her baggy sweat pants and oversized t-shirt before allowing him to pull her from the room and down the stairs. What he hoped to accomplish was unknown. His macho act wouldn't change her mind. She'd been on this road before with him and had no intention of putting her foot in the same trap twice.

"Cat and Jeremy, don't you want to join us for breakfast?" Yani called to them from the kitchen.

"We can't." Jeremy yelled over his shoulder as they walked out the front door. Cat caught a glimpse of Yani's big smile as the doors closed.

On the elevator she said, "This isn't necessary, Jeremy."

"I think this is exactly what we need," he said without looking at her. The elevator stopped in the lobby and they stepped out.

"Why don't you answer your phone?"

He moved his head so slow to face her she almost thought he hadn't heard the question.

"Why?"

"It's Natalie, isn't it? The two of you aren't through. She still has a hold on you. I'm not going to get in the middle of another relationship. Not again. The last time this whole ordeal put me through a meat grinder."

He gripped her shoulders. "You're right, it's Natalie. But I'm not talking to her. There is nothing between us."

Cat nodded. "Talk to me after you've convinced her."

"What are you saying about me? You think I can't handle my business?"

"Can I go back upstairs, now?"

He glared at her. "Not yet. Let's get some breakfast. You owe me that much."

Chapter Eight

A week later Cat was standing in her new townhouse directing the movers to place the last of the boxes in the upstairs bedroom. She looked around and blew a wisp of hair out of her eye. Jeremy was right, this was the perfect place to jumpstart her new life, even if he wouldn't be in it. Not a word from him this past week drove home that fact.

"Cat." Yani ran down the stairs. "Where do you want me to put these books?"

Cat positioned her hands on her hips, trying to fight off the exhaustion pulling at her. "Put them on the table and get out of here. You and Drew are trying to be helpful, but I want you guys to celebrate having your privacy back. Let me get used to my new place." She shooed her friends toward the door.

"Are you sure? I can help you unpack more stuff." Yani surveyed the room.

"Yeah, Cat. We're here to help. So point us in the right direction." Drew pulled up the lid of a box to peer inside.

"No. I insist. I want to do this. I have a whole weekend to put things away, and I have no idea yet where I want stuff to go. I'll take my time and enjoy my new life as I unpack it. So go, please."

After a reluctant look around, Yani strolled out behind Drew. Cat locked the door behind them and leaned against it as she examined the clutter. Never had such a mess felt so liberating. For the first time in months she was in charge, again. Even the constant bombardment of scenes from her hot night with Jeremy didn't derail her. The last time she got between Jeremy and his baggage, the surprise wasn't a bargain. A girl's entitled to a little fun, but she needed to be careful. She picked up a box labeled kitchen and trudged toward the island.

175

Thinking about him was stupid, a waste of time. She needed so many things right now, like a new coffeemaker, but not a man unless he knew how to make a great mocha latte.

The doorbell rang. She loved the whimsical sound it made through the whole house. Living here was going to be fun. She'd even pay the neighborhood children to ring it and run. But if Drew and Yani were back she wouldn't let them in.

Cat checked the peephole to see Jeremy peering back at her. Her heart raced. It explained why every night she fell asleep with him in the little bubble above her head.

"I saw your eyeball so you have to open the door."

She glanced down at her faded jeans and oversized t-shirt with dirty smudges across the front. The next time she saw Jeremy she had planned to be smoking hot, but today she resembled a bag lady. Being back in the dating rotation required a step up in her game. Instead of washed up *girlfriend* she needed hot-on-the block clothing. She tried to brush the splotches away before opening the door.

"What are you doing here? You have a way of showing up in the strangest places at the strangest time." Cat motioned him inside. He wore an expensive pair of jeans that weren't made for hard work, and another pair of pricey shoes. Her sneakers were flecked with drops of green paint. Remnants left over from her last attempt at homemaking.

"I know today is moving day and I've come to help." He pulled a bottle of wine from behind his back. "Look what I brought. You said you wanted to give wine a try since beer wasn't your thing, so let's give my selection a taste."

"I don't have a corkscrew and I don't know where to begin to look for one." She glanced at the stack of boxes lining the kitchen wall.

"Good thing I thought to bring one." He pulled a corkscrew from his jacket pocket as he placed it on the chair. "I didn't think about glasses though. We can take the bottle to the head or open the boxes and find some." He gave her a wicked grin.

She pretended to contemplate the idea, but the moment she saw him through the peephole, she knew she'd buy whatever he was selling. "Okay, let's find some glasses."

"I was hoping you'd say that. You had me worried for a moment." He walked ahead of her into the kitchen. "Why don't you have a seat and I'll find them." He pulled out a chair for her and ripped the lid on the nearest box. He pulled out the wrapping paper, dropped it on the floor, and pulled out a red square plate.

"Try again," she laughed.

He went through the same maneuver and managed to find the toaster and the broken coffeemaker.

"You're sure we can't just drink from the bottle?" she asked.

"Part of the joy of drinking wine is using the nice glasses. Rolling the stem between your fingers. You do own wine glasses, don't you?" he asked as he opened another box.

"If it holds liquor, I have it. Let me help you look." She stood.

He raised his hand. "Nope, I've got this." He dropped more packaging paper on the floor. "Voila. See what persistence gets you? And I can be very persistent." He held the glasses up to the light before rinsing them, popping the cork with flair, and pouring the wine. His comedic actions helped erase the stress of moving. Unpacking and getting settled didn't seem as important as he raised his glass to hers.

She took a sip, and allowed the liquid to linger on her tongue. "This is good. I could learn to like this one. What is it?"

"Since you like sweet drinks with umbrellas, I decided to start you on a Riesling. This is sweeter and milder than some of the other wines."

She took another swallow. "I like the taste. Switching my signature drink might be easier than I thought. Good job, Jeremy." She motioned for him to take the seat next to her as she refilled her glass.

"To starting over," he said.

"Is that toast for you or for me or for us?" She held her glass in midair.

"Let me make this simple for you. To us." He tapped her glass and took a swallow. She followed his lead.

"To us, huh? When did you and I become us?"

"Last Saturday. We sealed the deal when you marched into my bedroom and seduced me." He took another sip of wine.

"You can't judge our relationship by my behavior. I was horny. I would have done almost anything for a night of...a night of—"

"Yeah, sure. Well you took my stuff and now you owe me," he said.

"Just try to collect," she whispered, then climbed off the stool and backed away from him. She set the glass down to pull off the headband. After running her fingers through her hair, she put it back in place.

"Since I haven't seen you since our breakfast last week, I thought you'd run off," she said.

"I had some things to take care of." He turned his back to pick up the wine bottle. After refilling his glass, he met her eyes, but didn't elaborate on his whereabouts.

She drank half the contents of her glass. Tonight she didn't need to think clearly, not even a rational thought. There was lust in his eyes and if he made a move, she was willing.

He came around the counter, towering over her. He lifted her chin and kissed her. His mouth was sweet and cool. Her mind yelled stop, but she ignored the warning and accepted his tongue. The slow tender roll of this tongue over hers eased all the apprehension out of her shoulders. This was happening way too fast, but she couldn't stop thinking she deserved the moment.

After several minutes she pulled away to breathe. She was a mess and so was the house. Nothing had been put away and the now half open-boxes resembled the mess her family created on Christmas morning under the tree. She stepped away from him and pushed a strand of hair back in the band.

"As you can see I haven't done very much. I've only been in the house a few hours." She emptied her glass. A warm feeling enveloped her body.

"There's only one thing you should do right away. And that's to get your bedroom straight, so when you're ready to pass out, you can. Believe me, I learned the hard way."

"I can always just curl up on the sofa." She pointed across the room. Unfortunately it was covered in clothes that hadn't fit in a box.

He grabbed her hand and tugged her toward the stairs.

"Where are we going?"

"Upstairs to make your bed. You'll thank me round about midnight."

"You're planning to still be here at that time?"

"Only if you play your cards right, sweet-cheeks." He pinched her butt.

By the third step Jeremy released her hand and continued ahead of her.

He stood in the middle of the master bedroom. "Okay, is your bed where you want it?"

"Yes, this is fine." She rushed to the box where the bedding should have been and tore open the lid. Priority number one was getting Jeremy out of her bedroom. Seeing him so close to where all her naughty dreams of him occurred was like living out the erotic dream in real time. Thanks to the wine, nothing seemed as sharp as before, not even the peril.

"I think the bedding is in this box. I remember putting a blue mark on the outside." She pulled out her rose-colored satin sheets and tossed them to him. The sooner she got this done the sooner they could get back downstairs.

"I didn't say I was going to help you. I only planned to watch." He was pretending. Cat saw the smile. He relaxed his arms and draped the sheet over her shoulders like a cape.

"Oh buddy, this was your idea, you're helping." She threw the linen at him.

He held it above her head out of her reach while dancing it around her shoulders. He dropped his arms encircling her. His fingers caught her hair at her shoulders. Together they seemed to be fighting to grab hold of something that would quickly disappear.

Jeremy ran his hands along her back. His touch woke up every part of her and every fiber welcomed him. She thought she was going to be okay with just a single kiss, but even with the wine her body told her otherwise. She would never be okay until she had Jeremy back.

He placed his lips to hers, pushing his tongue slowly into her mouth.

She matched his movement in precise steps. They were made for each other, this much was true. But that didn't mean being with him was going to be easy.

He extracted his tongue from her mouth and the void was immediate.

She didn't want to let him go, she'd made that mistake before and stumbled into another relationship that was doomed from the beginning.

"Cat, I want to hear you say you forgive me. Tell me you understand why I did what I did."

"I don't want to talk about what happened. Not tonight. Tonight can't we just pretend we never knew each other? No history."

He pressed his nose against hers. Something he used to do before when he wanted to get her attention.

She stared up into his penetrating eyes. They blazed with such sincerity; she had to clamp her tongue to the roof of her mouth to keep quiet.

"Tonight we can do whatever you want. But we're going to have this conversation. I want to put everything in the open so there aren't any questions or secrets. If I'm lucky enough to get you back, nothing, and I mean absolutely nothing, is going to come between us again."

Her tongue wouldn't work, and even if it did, she didn't know how to respond to him. So many nights she'd dreamt Jeremy would come back. She had the whole conversation mapped out in her head, ready to tell him exactly how she felt. But with him so close, her senses filling up with him, none of those words seemed appropriate. Her heart wanted to do the speaking for her head and it was open, willing, and ready. The wine unlocked the door to her hesitation.

"Tomorrow, we can go through the details. Tonight, let's just do this." She grabbed the ends of his shirt, tugged it over his head, and threw it over one of the boxes. The abs she remembered and missed so much, pulsed under her touch. She ran her hands over his chest, her fingers greeting each muscular bulge like a long lost friend. "I forgot how awesome your body was. When did you get this tattoo?" She rubbed her thumb over the finger-length blue mark.

He pulled her big t-shirt off and dropped it at her feet. "I remembered your birthmark right there." He poked his finger at the imperfection just above her right breast. "I always thought it looked like a bolt of lightning. So I got the same thing tattooed on my chest. I wanted to do something to mark the special bond we had." His eyes glazed over, making it hard to interpret what he was thinking.

If he was looking for a way back into her life, he was doing a good job. Every woman dreamed of a man who remembered the small things. She shook the thought away. Why couldn't she forgive and forget as easily as her sister? By now Geeta would be buying bride magazines and picking a band.

"I didn't see it the other night."

"We were in the dark."

"When did you get inked? Before or after?" She continued to press her finger to the design.

"I thought you didn't want to talk about this stuff right now."

"I want to know."

He paused for a moment, breaking eye contact as he watched her finger trail along the marking. "The day after I broke up with you. I felt like a heel and I needed to do something." He shrugged his shoulders.

"You could have come back to me."

He nodded.

Tomorrow everything could be different. The resentment might return, making it impossible to move forward. The shame of him leaving her still resided in a corner of her heart. She'd be stupid to let him walk back into her life after the way he dumped her.

He gathered the fitted sheet in a ball and shook it over the mattress. Instead of helping him, she clasped her hands while he made the bed.

Jeremy admired his handiwork before turning to her and covering her mouth with his in a move so hot and swift she felt sexier than she'd felt since the last time.

Jeremy picked her up, walked backwards without releasing her tongue until he placed her on the center of the bed. He climbed between her legs, pushing them apart with his knees and capturing her mouth again. This time was even more sensual than before. More tender than she remembered, and she remembered every sexual moment they'd spent together. The new ones and the old ones. Cat relived those memories in the middle of her lonely nights. Everything Robby did had been measured against the supremely high standard she grown accustomed to with Jeremy.

She placed her hand on his chest. His heart thumped against her palm, promising her something she had given up on over a year ago. He seemed as excited about tonight as she was. She sucked in a short breath as his penis came to life against her legs, beckoning her with pleasure.

Tonight needed to last forever, because tomorrow held no promises. One thing she'd learned was not to count on tomorrow. The only thing worth holding on to was today. She ran her hand across his back and chest, exploring his body. Reacquainting her senses to every inch of him. The sound coming from him vibrated in her ears waking up her body like nothing else could.

He cupped her breast and held it firm, like he was checking a melon, drawing her closer. His touch was hot against her flesh. Almost in slow motion he switched to the other breast and her reaction was the same. He ran the tip of his finger between her breasts, just the tip, skimming along her skin like a wisp of summer wind. The intensity was almost too much to bear. As much as she wanted to believe she had moved beyond Jeremy, she hadn't. The story of her life would always be scripted around him. Cat couldn't erase the things he did to her body or the place he occupied in her mind.

She arched her back, easing closer to his warmth. She kissed his fingers before running her tongue along each one like she was licking a lollipop.

He struggled to release her belt. She helped by guiding his hand through the motion. Together they eased her jeans over her thighs and down her legs. Then he teased the elastic on her panties before drawing them down with the same agonizing slowness. Tonight she couldn't be level-headed or sensible. She wanted to feel the magic that only Jeremy provided. Even if it meant being vulnerable, tonight she was willing. She slipped her hand inside his pants, holding his length firmly in her palm. Slowing the quick passage of time for a moment.

She wanted to hurry his movements to satisfy her mounting desire. With his hand resting between her thighs, he slipped one finger between her moist folds. The simple act was enough to charge every cell in her body, waking them up like flowers on a spring morning. She'd almost forgotten what real ecstasy felt like. He clutched the back of her head, pulling his mouth to hers. She attacked his tongue like a woman grabbing hold of a lifeline.

He pulled away. Unprepared for the separation she reached for him. Willing him to return to the bed. Before removing his pants he extracted three condoms from the pocket and then dropped the trousers on the floor without taking his eyes off her. His raw, open stare rolled over her body. The desire flickering in his gaze made him as vulnerable as her. He opened the package and rolled it on before easing back on the bed.

"Just a minute, Cat. I need to do this for both of us."

"Hurry, please," she begged.

"I am, baby."

183

The moment his body pressed against her, she couldn't contain her passion. She opened her arms, accepting him back into her bed, her life, and her body, even if it was for only one night.

He eased into her, stripping every thought and doubt away. With her legs wrapped around his back she pulled him in deeper. Together their bodies pulsated in unison, using a language only the two of them could understand. Being a part of something more than the singleness that'd dogged her since their break-up was so alluring she banished the thought. A melody played in her head, soft, sweet, and promising. Even without trying, their bodies melded together like warm butter. The easy dance was sinful.

Unable to control her hips they took on a rhythm of their own. At first very slow and checked, but the more she had, the more she wanted. Longing for completion, she raked her fingers across his back.   With his head buried in the curve of her neck, planting wet, warm kisses in the tender spot above her collarbone his scent added to the fervor. His breath brushed her skin intensifying the heat gathering in her groin. To extinguish the flame, she'd have to end the connection, but letting go wasn't an option, yet.

The pressure mounting in her core threatened to consume her. She tightened her hold, driving her hips against him. Reaching the top of the mountain and looking over was nothing compared to the leap she was getting ready to take.

He mashed his lips to her ear. "Now, Cat," he demanded just as she sailed off the edge of the cliff and touched heaven.

Chapter Nine

The shorter days of fall were perfect for sleeping later, but he was wide-awake. The room was dark, the sheets hanging from the window barely kept the dawning sun from flooding the room with a morning glow.

Cat slept curled in the bend of his elbow. At least this time she hadn't slipped away before he woke up. Last night she refused to talk about their past, but it was right there, in every move, in every thought. The relationship they used to have had been special and getting it back used to seem impossible. But there was hope.

"How long have you been awake?" Cat rubbed her eyes.

"A while. I didn't want to disturb you."

"I guess you were right about finishing the bedroom first." She surveyed the room. Several boxes were toppled, the contents thrown across the floor.

"I've been to this rodeo before. I know what needs to be done." He tightened his arms around her.

"You're sure you weren't looking out for your own interest?" She nudged her arm against his rib.

"Oh, you enjoyed yourself as much as I did. I wanted to have a conversation, remember?"

"Yeah, but last night wasn't the time to be serious." She looked toward the window, where the sun was beginning to brighten the sky. "I'm afraid to have that talk." She climbed out of bed. Shuffling through a box, she pulled out some fresh clothes.

"Where are you going?" He sat up.

"To shower. I smell like wine and sex." She placed a towel on top of the things in her arms and ducked into the bathroom.

"I like wine and I like sex, so I think you've got the perfect scent." He reached the bathroom just as she stepped

185

into the glass-enclosed shower. He draped his hands on top of the stall door as she soaped her body.

"Why are you ignoring me, Cat?"

She turned away from him. Water rolled off her shoulder, down the curve of her back then over her buttocks. The sweet fragrance of the lather as it caressed her luscious body was enough to make him forget the need to have a discussion.

He pulled the door open and stepped inside. Water spilled on the marble floor as he spun her around and kissed her forehead. "I'm not going away," he said as he tangled his fingers in her hair and kissed her neck.

She lathered his chest with the pink bar of soap in her palm making small circular strokes without looking at him. Her touch was superb. The need to talk slid down his legs and through the drain. She couldn't evade the conversation forever, but he wouldn't press her right now. He'd find the time and the right words to win her back.

He removed the soap from her hand and rubbed it over her shoulder and each breast. She moaned as his hand caressed every inch of her body. "You're purring like a cat," he whispered in her ear.

"How many times have you said that to me?" She stroked his shaft with slippery hands.

"Every chance I get." He dropped the bar and kissed her. Her moist mouth opened enough to accept his tongue in a playful tug of war. Life with Cat stretched him to a higher level.

Her moans grew louder when he slipped his finger into her. She arched her back, her head fell backwards. Water poured through her hair, slicking it to her scalp. He placed small kisses along the column of her neck and throat. Every time she allowed him to touch her was a treat. Her moans heightened his desire. With deliberate slowness he continued kissing each breast until her nipples hardened, and then he turned his attention to the space between them. Trailing his tongue along the divide in the middle of the voluptuous mounds was like enjoying the final run down a ski slope. She grabbed his hair by the roots as he neared her navel. He ran his tongue around the small indentation before slipping it inside. Warm water splattered her breasts and his face. When he reached the small thin strip of hair leading to her treasure, she loosened her grip enough for him to dart his tongue into her sweet nectar. The slow sway of her hips increased, building to a feverish pitch. Her knees buckled and she began to slide down the glass.

"Hold on, baby." He placed one arm around her waist to support her while he continued to stroke her nub.

"Jeremy," she cried above the noise of the water.

"Do it baby, let go."

She hummed while the last pancake bubbled around the edges. Jeremy used to love it when she cooked a big breakfast. She eyed the sausage, eggs, pancakes, and juice laid out on paper plates. The plastic knives and forks completed the table setting. Maybe this was too much. Why was she trying so hard? Was this the part in the story where they hold hands and walked off into the sunset?

Jeremy bounded down the stairs. His hair was still damp and his shirt unbuttoned. At least this morning she looked better than when he showed up. The skintight yoga pants and sports bra were a strategic move. He liked her belly and this morning he could enjoy it as much as he wanted.

"What smells so good?" He looked at the spread and his smile widened.

"For you, the bed was the important thing to get ready. For me, the kitchen needed to be in order. Besides, I think we need nourishment. The last few hours have been pretty wild."

"Now I know why we are perfect for each other. Between the two of us, we've covered all the bases." There was a sparkle in his eye, but only for a second. He removed a box from the chair before taking a seat.

187

After sliding the last pancake from the pan, she took the seat beside him. He picked up a sausage link and bit it in half. This time he tried to hide the desire in his eyes, but the erection in his pants gave him away.

"This is just like old times," he said.

"Are you talking about what's lurking in your boxers or the breakfast?"

"Both." He continued to chew. "There's just one thing missing."

"Yeah, what?" She pierced a chunk of egg and shoved it in her mouth.

"Direction. I have no idea where we stand." From his tone, she knew she couldn't delay this conversation a moment longer. She lifted the juice to her lips and took a swallow. He removed the glass from her hand and placed it on the table.

"Seriously, Cat. You know me. I'm straight up. I've always been honest with you even when what I had to say wasn't easy. So you can pretend you're thirsty as hell and drink juice all day long, but I'll still be waiting for a reply."

"I can't answer your question because I just don't know where we stand. I've been through a couple of rough patches and I made a promise to take better care of myself. So that means I need to stop following my heart and listen to my head, too. And my head is telling me to slow down. There is no need to hurry."

He nodded and pushed his empty plate away. "Okay, Ms. Preston. We'll play this your way. I think I'm man enough to let you handle my strings for a while. Remember, with great power comes great responsibility. I'm making a commitment, here. If you're not up to it you need to tell me now."

"Why do we have to decide now? Can't you just date me for a while and see how we do?"

His lip twitched just enough for her to notice. He wanted his way, but she'd won this round.

"Okay, we'll try things your way for a while. A real short while."

She pushed a lock of hair behind her ears. Walking back into a relationship with Jeremy was the stuff that used to keep her up at night. All she had to do was nod her head, open her arms and be happy. But for how long? She'd trusted him with her heart before, put everything on the pass line and she'd crapped out.

"Phoebe and Cory are celebrating their first wedding anniversary in a few days. I could use a date." Her voice was so sweet he couldn't say no.

"If that's your way of saying yes, I'm there."

His phone rang before she could respond. His brow tensed, revealing the furrow that meant he was unhappy, but he didn't reach for the dang thing. Before they could step forward she had to find her own answers. She snatched his cell and backed away. Before Jeremy could wrestle the cell away from her she, answered it.

"Hello, may I help you?" She stood on the opposite side of the table, dodging Jeremy as he tried to grab her.

"Give me the phone, Cat," Jeremy demanded.

She shook her head and yelled into the phone. "I can hear you breathing so you might as well answer me. Who is this?" She had to run to the opposite side of the table as Jeremy lunged across the top.

"You want to know who this is? It's Natalie." Her voice was raw with anger. "You think you can take my man. You should know by now that Jeremy will always come back to me. Didn't I teach you that the last time? Do you need another lesson?" She released a ragged breath. "You are just a booty call. He will be coming back. He always does. Ask him where he was last week. He was between my thighs."

The phone went dead just as Jeremy pried it from her hands. "You had no right to..."

"I had every right. You're asking me about our future and you're still dragging around your past." She ground her teeth. "Get your things and get the hell out of my house. And while you're at it, get the hell out of my life. You've crapped in my life once and you won't get another chance to do it." She plucked his plate off the table and threw it in the trash.

Dating Just Got Serious

"Cat, I just placed my heart in the center of your hands. You know you trust me."

"I don't trust anyone anymore." She stepped closer to him. Her chest heaved, trying to pry the weight off of it. "Where were you last week?"

Chapter Ten

"Cat, are you even listening to anything we're saying?" Phoebe asked.

Cat looked up from her seat in the dressing room to see her friends staring at her. "I'm sorry, what did you say?"

"You've hardly said anything all through our shopping excursion. And you haven't made one purchase, so something must be bothering you. You've never met a shoe you didn't like." Phoebe eased into the chair next to her. The tight satin sheath she was trying on didn't look easy to move around in, but it was perfect for the party.

"The dress is fabulous, Phoebe. All eyes will be on you this weekend." Cat sat straighter and focused her attention on her friends.

"What color did we agree to wear to the party, Cat?" Yani stood in front of her.

"I'm not very good company today," Cat admitted. "Maybe I should head home and call you guys later tonight. Whatever color you decide is fine with me."

Yani placed her hand on Cat's shoulder refusing to let her up. "What's going on? Friday, you were excited about the house. You pushed Drew and me out the door like we were unwelcome ants at a picnic. Don't you still like it?"

Cat shook her head. "The house is great. I love it."

Yani flopped in the seat on the other side of her. Flanked by friends should have made her feel better. Instead, they both looked ready to pounce.

"Then what is it?" Phoebe insisted.

Cat dropped her head. The knot in her stomach tightened. Telling them wouldn't help, but hiding would only make things worse. "Against my better judgment, I started seeing Jeremy again." Cat rubbed her forehead. "I can't blame him for anything that's happened. I knew better. I just wanted to have someone in my life. Jeremy and I can be so good

191

together. But he has so much baggage, it's like poison. I ignored my common sense. So I deserve what I got."

"What happened?" Phoebe's eyes widened.

"I don't want to talk about it." Cat tried to smile.

"Well, you have to. Whenever Phoebe and I are going through some stuff you bulldoze your way right on in, so now it's our chance to be here for you." Yani leaned so close Cat could see the glue from her false lashes.

The store clerk stuck her head into the large dressing room. "Is everything okay in here?"

Phoebe waved her hand. "Yeah, we're fine. We're just discussing color. We'll be out shortly.

Cat huffed. "Okay, let's get this over with. Jeremy and Natalie are a long way from over. I thought since they were divorced, I had nothing to worry about. She told me to keep my hands off."

"How? Did she come to your house?" Phoebe asked.

"No, the phone."

"She called you?" Yani sounded appalled.

Two pair of eyes narrowed on her. A fireball rolled up her neck and settled in the center of her scalp. She tugged at the turtleneck, trying to conduct air to her flesh. "She calls Jeremy's phone every hour and he just ignores it. So I picked it up. I won't be blindsided again."

Phoebe glared at her like she was a creature from a lost planet. "Are you ready for me to put you in a home? You shouldn't have answered his phone without permission. You were looking for trouble. Don't be surprised now that you found it."

"And if I hadn't, I could have ended up in the same predicament as before. I'm not doing wounded again. I've tasted that apple and I don't want another bite."

"Whew." Phoebe looked relieved. She rubbed Cat's back like she was trying to burp a baby. "I don't blame you. Maybe, I would have done the same thing."

"But Natalie is off her rocker. Cat can't take her seriously." Yani demanded.

"She sounded pretty sane to me. If Natalie isn't an issue then its Jeremy's responsibility to handle her. And I'm not going anywhere near him again until he does," Cat replied.

"You know we invited him to the party. He indicated he was coming." Phoebe continued to rub her back.

"Let's hope he doesn't bring Natalie," said Yani.

"It's okay. We can be in the same room, and I can keep my hands to myself." Cat stood up, wanting to believe her declaration. "Now let's finish shopping. We've got an anniversary to celebrate. And watch me this weekend. My performance will be so good, you both will nominate me for a gold statue."

Jeremy had to walk faster to keep up with Drew. The final examination of the income property wasn't going well.

"What do you have on your list, Jeremy?" Drew called over his shoulder as they approached the kitchen again.

"I've got cracked molding, water damage in the ceiling, and the pantry door is broken. We had our folks in here last week. These items should have been repaired." Jeremy flipped the page on the clipboard. "I've been a little distracted or I would have been on top of this."

Drew slowed his pace. "Something you want to talk about?"

"Does it ever do any good to discuss women? I can't figure them out." Jeremy snapped the metal clip on the board and shoved it under his arm. If he could erase the last few days he would, but discussing them with Drew wasn't the solution.

The way Cat had narrowed her eyes and ordered him out of her house and her life was like a blade through his heart. Being with her again had been fantastic. As if the love gods had come to their senses and brought them back together. The only thing they forgot to do was to make sure Natalie stayed on her meds and out of his life.

193

"I hear you, man. At least Yani and I have found our groove and things are really good. You'll be okay."

"About the house, I'll get my head back in the game and have all this stuff corrected before the end of the week."

Drew slapped him on the shoulder before leaving. Jeremy circled back through the house and turned off the lights. In the foyer his cell phone chirped with the ring assigned for Natalie.

He pulled it from his pocket and accepted the call. "Natalie, you need to keep your doctor's appointment today." He tried to keep the emotion out of his voice.

"What I need is for my husband to come home tonight," she cooed into the phone.

"I'm not your husband. We've been divorced for over a year. Remember?"

"No, no, no, Jeremy. Don't say that." She slurred her words. "We can still save our marriage if you just stop seeing that bitch. I know you're fucking her. I know everything."

Her voice tightened, she was getting agitated.

"Make sure you stay away from Cat! Do you hear me?"

His fingers contracted around the phone.

"And what if I don't?" she screamed. "I got rid of her before, I can do it again. Permanently."

"Stay the hell away from her, Natalie. If you don't go back on your meds you know what's going to happen." Maybe Natalie's family was right. But hospitalization seemed like a drastic move.

"I'm trying to be good, Jeremy, but you won't play right. You know if you just come home, everything will be fine. Like it used to be. We can try again to have a baby, a real one this time." Her voice softened.

"Is your sister taking you to your appointment?"

"Jeremy, you aren't listening to me. You know how I get when you don't listen. Just come by tonight, baby. I know how to please you. I can do everything you like and it will be better than that bitch."

He disconnected the call and dialed her mother.

194

Chapter Eleven

Cat pulled into the small driveway and turned off the engine. Her sister, Geeta was seated on the front step, bundled in a black down coat with a leopard print scarf wrapped several times around her neck. With the two shopping bags piled at her feet, she could pass for homeless.

Beads of sweats rose on Cat's back. "Oh shit," she muttered before opening the door and stepping out of the car.

Geeta looked up. Her red, puffy eyes were enough to grant a clue. The absence of her elaborate make-up palette provided another. Not a good sign. Her stomach twisted like someone was trying to get the last few drops of water from a towel.

"What the hell happened this time, Geeta? I've had a bad few days and I don't need any of your drama." She unlocked the door and helped her sister carry her stuff inside.

Geeta collapsed on the sofa next to the last box waiting to be unpacked. The pure wail Geeta released dropped Cat to her knees beside her sister. She gathered Geeta in her arms and rocked her until she quieted a bit.

"Did you have another fight with Mom and Dad?"

Geeta cocked her head.

"Well, what was it? Did something happen to Donny?"

"He was arrested this morning." She started sobbing again. Every time she tried to talk, a new wave overtook her.

"Please try to calm down. You're going to make yourself sick." Cat continued to hold and rock her sister.

After several minutes Geeta stopped shaking. Cat relaxed her arms and sat crossed-legged on the floor.

"Do you want to talk about what happened?" Cat whispered, hoping a tender voice would help calm Geeta.

"We were asleep. At least I was, when this loud banging started at the door. Donny rolled out of bed and onto the floor just as the police kicked the door in."

196

"Oh my God, Geeta. Were you hurt?"

Tears ran unchecked down her face. She nodded. "By the time they got to the bedroom, I was standing naked in the middle of the room. A policeman shouted for me to put on some clothes. There had to be at least seven or eight of them. They all had guns. I still don't believe it," she said as a new wave of sobs wracked her body.

"The whole time Donny was under the bed. They were yelling at me, wanting to know where he was. I couldn't talk. I couldn't." She wiped her nose on her coat sleeve. "They snatched open the closet and the bathroom door, and I finally pointed to the bed."

"Did they hurt you?"

"No. But I think I peed myself. I can't remember." She sniffed the air as if detecting the smell of urine.

"They let him put on some pants before they handcuffed him and dragged him out. The whole time he's shouting at me. 'Why'd you tell em where I was?' Like they weren't smart enough to look under the damn bed. They even carted me to Police Plaza. Can you believe that? Did you know the back seat of a police car is made of hard plastic?"

"No, honey, I didn't." She patted her sister's knee. "What did they arrest him for?"

She shrugged a shoulder and looked away. "Drugs. He was selling drugs. Evidently, lots and lots of drugs. "

"Oh my God! Did you know?" Cat hoped her question didn't sound like an accusation, but Geeta liked to walk on the wild side. A man in a suit and tie was like kryptonite to her.

She drew back. "Of course not, Cat. How could you even ask? You're as bad as the police."

Cat unfolded her legs and sat on the sofa beside her sister. "I'm sorry. You're right. The whole thing is just so...unbelievable."

"Can I stay here? I can't go back to that apartment. The police tore it up, the lock is busted and I..." Geeta dropped her head and took several short breaths.

"Of course you can stay. Man, do we have some crappy luck when it comes to men. I think Mom and Dad must have taken all the Preston love luck." Cat trailed off as her comment induced a fresh flood of tears from her sister. But between Donny and Rob and Jeremy and a host of others, they had their share of bad luck. She spotted Jeremy's jacket still lying on the chair near the door where he'd left it. Even the best of relationships sometimes had to come to an end.

"Let's get you upstairs and settled." Cat stood and picked up the heaviest suitcase. "When did you have time to pack?"

"I peed myself, Cat," she wailed again. "At the police station I did it again. I was so scared. Do you think I'm incontinent now?" Her eyes widened with fear.

"No. I'm sure you're not. It could have happened to anyone."

"I hope it happened to Donny."

It had taken over an hour to get Geeta settled enough to even close her eyes. She couldn't stop trembling. She had no idea how long her sister planned to stay with her. The two of them couldn't live together for very long before they'd start bickering like they did at seven and five. Having a younger sister as rambunctious as Geeta was hard enough. Growing up, she didn't get much better as they grew older. But now, her antics weren't of the grade school variety and policing her should fall on the shoulders of their parents.

Before heading back downstairs, Cat cracked the bedroom door to find her sister curled in the fetal position sound asleep. Cat left the door open in case Geeta needed something.

Cat carried the packing boxes into the basement and trudged back into the kitchen. At least now everything had been put away, and the mess in the basement would get put away in the spring. At the kitchen sink, she glanced out at the patio. It was supposed to be a major reason for leasing the house, but she hadn't managed to enjoy it once. With the sudden drop in temperature, it wouldn't happen now. Leaves fell from the tree in a continuous sprinkle, blanketing the ground in yellows, reds and oranges.

The doorbell pulled her thoughts away from the leaf-covered patio. Without looking through the peephole she opened the door. Jeremy stood on the landing, his hands shoved in his pockets, a frown buried on his forehead.

"What are you doing here?"

"Aren't you going to let me in?" The sound of his voice made her heart soften.

"Whatever you need to say you can say it from there."

He folded his arms over his chest. The way his eyes bored into hers made her uncomfortable. "Fine, Jeremy." She stepped aside and allowed him in.

He unbuttoned his jacket and began pulling it off.

"Don't take off your coat. And this is something you left the last time you were here." She lifted his wrap from the chair and pushed it into his hand.

"You're being silly, you know that, don't you?"

"No, I'm being smart. And it's about time." She left him standing in the living room and made her way back to the kitchen. Even though his shoes made no sound she could feel his presence right behind her.

"I'd offer you something to drink, but you're not staying long," she said over her shoulder.

"I'm staying here tonight." He pulled off his jacket and positioned it on the back of the kitchen chair.

She spun around to find him seated with his foot over his knee, just the way her father always sat. "Like hell you are."

"Cat, sit down a minute." He reached for her arms and pulled her into the chair next to him. She tried to wrench away, but he held her forearm. "Natalie isn't well. She hasn't been for a very long time and now she's refusing to take her medication. Her family is in the process of having her hospitalized. They've found a good place near them in New Hampshire."

"But what does this have to do with me or you staying here tonight?" She tried again to pull away, but he continued to hold her in place.

"She's fixated on you. She might even come to your house. I figure if I'm here I can diffuse her and—"

"Is she dangerous? Does she want to hurt me?"

"I don't know and I don't want to take any chances. We've been looking for her for two days. She knows what's about to happen, so she's hiding."

Jeremy loosened his grip on her arms and she flopped back in the seat.

"But why me? I hardly know the woman."

"Like I said, she's not thinking clearly. I just don't want to take any chances." He wrung his hands. His eyes were bloodshot and he looked exhausted.

"You care about her, don't you?" Cat steeled her stomach for his reply. Maybe one day the love she had for him would fade into something bearable.

"I'm here because I care about you. I tried to be honorable and do the right thing before, and I was miserable." He removed his tie and draped it over his shoulder. "I'm staying here until Natalie is found and until I can convince you to give me another chance."

Cat exhaled slowly from her mouth while staring at the floor. "Wow, I wasn't expecting that."

He leaned forward and cupped her face. "Then you better start." He pressed his lips to hers and she responded without hesitating.

When he released her she continued to stare at him. "What about you going to her place? I asked you about it that morning and you never responded. I thought...I thought—"

He rubbed his forehead. "I was wrong to leave you the first time. I'll regret doing that for the rest of my life, but I won't keep apologizing for it or have you questioned everything I do and everywhere I go. So tonight, I'm putting it all on the table and we have to agree to leave it there."

Cat nodded.

"I went to her place because she was cutting. She called me and told me she had slit her wrist and was about to do the next one. When I got there she had a superficial cut on her right wrist. I bandaged her up and called her sister. It was never anything more, but it was enough for her family to get serious about her care." He sat forward and dropped his elbows on his knees. "Now can you feed me something and take me to bed?"

"I'm sorry Jeremy. I should have trusted you. It's just...when you picked her instead of me, I—"

"You were always the one, Cat. I never stopped loving you. I can't help feeling a little guilty about marrying Natalie. I knew I couldn't be what she needed, but I thought she was pregnant. I saw her pee on the stick."

Her heart opened up like a slow sweet melody. Even the Christmas when she got the Barbie house she didn't feel this good.

"You've never said you loved me before."

"I should have."

Cat moved to his lap and draped her arms around his neck. "I love you, too. I always have."

"Does this mean you're willing to let me hang around, act like a couple, go on dates? Not one where our friends have manipulated us like hand puppets."

"Yes, it means exactly that."

Chapter Twelve

Jeremy couldn't control his euphoria as Cat rode him to the door of pleasure.

"Shh, or you'll wake up Geeta. She doesn't know you're here, and as upset as she was yesterday, I don't want her to." Cat pushed a pillow over his head and fell on his chest.

"I can't help it. How can I control myself if you won't keep your hands off of me? Can't you tell I haven't had much sleep in the last twenty-four hours?"

"You could have slept on the sofa in the living room." She ran her hand over his chest.

"Then you would have had to come all the way downstairs. You know you can't resist this package." He laughed.

"You got that right." She kissed him. Her lips were soft like sweet butter. He could spend the rest of his life in her arms.

She held his face between her palms. "The last time you were here, you asked me to commit to you. I was afraid to say yes. I'm not afraid anymore." She paused. "Well, maybe I am a little, but I'm more afraid of what will happen if I don't. If we stand a chance, I want to do everything I can.

He swallowed even though his mouth was dry. Relief flowed through him. A transformation descended on him. His life had found its course. "Are you giving yourself permission to love me?"

"I am. I do." She kissed him, again.

"You know, I was going to hang around until you came to your senses. I'll never jeopardize our relationship again."

"And I'll never doubt you again. You're my prince charming."

"I'll be everything you want me to be." He cradled her in his arms.

"Are you going to work today?" she asked.

"Not until I know what's going on. Hopefully, this whole Natalie thing has been resolved." He climbed out of the bed. "Let me shower, then I'll make some calls. Go back to sleep."

She pulled a pillow to her chest and waved him away. "Okay, but if you go downstairs, try to be quiet. I don't want to spend my morning calming Geeta again."

"Got it." He closed the door to the bathroom. At least the salty feeling in his eyes was gone, but now, his shaft was so tender. All night he'd tried to make up for time he missed with Cat. His back had the scratches to prove it.

After showering and finding a spare toothbrush in her drawer, he felt rejuvenated. As soon as he had some answers about Natalie, he'd take Cat away someplace nice, where they could really enjoy each other without the world interrupting. Having her back was like winning the championship game. He wanted to celebrate where they wouldn't have to tiptoe around her sister or threats.

He opened the bathroom door and dropped his cell phone on the tile floor. Natalie stood over Cat with a kitchen cleaver gripped in her hands. Cat's twisted mouth and tear-filled eyes made his heart thunder against his ribs. Her bottom lip trembled as she lifted her lashes to look up at him.

"Natalie, what are you doing? Put the knife down." He extended his arms, palms down. His voice was steady and calm.

"I told you to stay away from her. She can't have you. You belong to me." Natalie's face was streaked with tears. Her eyes weren't focused. She stepped closer to Cat, pointing the knife at her stomach. He shook his head, hoping Cat would keep quiet.

"Natalie, look at me. How did you get in here?" He inched closer to the bed.

"Shut up, Jeremy. You're just trying to distract me. If I get this bitch out of the way, we can be happy again." She looked from Cat then back to him.

"When was the last time you took your medicine?"

"I'm not taking them anymore. Ever. You don't know what it's like to have your head filled with fog all the time. I'm not living like that." She continued to cry. "You said you understood, Jeremy."

"Natalie, let Cat get out of here. We can sit and talk." He was beside the bed now. One swift move and he could snatch the blade from her hand. But Cat looked so scared he needed to get her out of the room.

Natalie's eyes softened, losing some of the manic glow. "You'll talk to me?"

"Yes, just you and me. We'll talk if you let Cat go downstairs."

"No. Talk to me now." She lowered the blade closer to Cat. "Tell me you love me so she can hear it and leave us alone."

His mind raced. This wasn't happening. But it was. 'Firm, determined voice', that's what the counselor said. "Natalie, let her go, now. Then I'll talk to you."

For several seconds no one made a sound. With his eyes locked on Natalie, he motioned Cat toward him.

She narrowed her gazed on Cat. "Did you screw her, Jeremy?"

Tears glistened in Cat's eyes.

"Just tell me if you fucked her." Natalie yelled.

Cat jumped, drawing her legs up a little. The knife wavered closer to her chest now as the sheet dropped below her breasts.

Natalie's eyes fell on the birthmark, and then jerked back up to him. He watched her process the matching marks as her eyes shifted between him and Cat. Her face crumbled. "Because of this bitch you got that ugly tattoo the day before we got married, didn't you?" She pressed the knife into Cat's firm stomach until a drop of blood appeared.

"Natalie, look at me," he demanded.

She raised her head to meet his eyes. The blade hung at her side.

"Cat isn't the issue." His voice boomed against the wall. Natalie's shoulders drooped. She was running out of fuel.

"Cat, why don't you climb out on this side of the bed and leave us alone?" He pulled back the bedding, exposing Cat's nudity. Without breaking eye contact with Natalie, he draped the sheet around Cat while hurrying her to the door. Everything seemed to be happening in a slowed pace. When Cat left the room he closed and locked the door.

####

Cat charged down the stairs so fast she came to rest in a heap of arms and legs at the base of the stairs. Her thoughts in a jumble, like the rest of her body. The sheet discarded as she tumbled down.

She knew Jeremy was trying to protect her. She knew he loved her. She knew Natalie wasn't ready to let him go. The coldness in Natalie's eyes clouded everything.

Afraid to move, she remained still, refusing to even try to straighten her legs. This was the final act of cruelty, butt naked and lying in a heap like a bunch of used clothes, her blood frozen solid in her veins. Her body ached from the inside out. How could this be happening? Maybe she'd wake up and realize it was all a bad dream. After holding back the dam of tears pushing at her faÃ§ade, she surrendered.

"Cat, what the hell are you doing? Why are you naked? Are you okay?" Geeta charged in from the kitchen with a cup in her hand.

She wanted to pull out of her sister's way, but couldn't move.

Being stoic while crumpled at the foot of the stairs would have been noble under the circumstances, but the tears wouldn't hear it. Along with the crying came the tortured sobbing she'd never learned to control. She couldn't think, every thought seemed to be the same and vanished before she could put them to words as if they hit a massive wall and crumbled.

"Where are you hurt? Can you get up? Did you break something?"

"Look Geeta, call the police. Just do it now. Now!" she snapped.

"Okay. But why—is something wrong with your friend?" Geeta picked up the cordless and dialed.

"Tell them to hurry. She might hurt..." she choked.

Geeta gave her name and address, she returned to Cat's side.

"Did you let her in here, Geeta?" Cat pulled up slow, straightening her legs.

"She said she was your friend. She wanted to surprise you. She even had a gift, wrapped in pink tissue paper. Did you two get in a fight?"

"Get me the throw off the sofa. I need to cover up."

"What the hell is going on, Cat? First it's me naked with the police and now you. What happened?"

Cat wanted to reassure her sister, but her heart was thumping so fast it was hard to talk, and with no idea what was going on upstairs, she wanted to get Geeta out of the house.

"Look, help me up and let's get outside."

She winced as Geeta put her arm around her waist and pulled her up.

Within seconds a squad car pulled up in front of the house. Followed by a dark blue sedan. Just as it came to a stop, several people climbed out and raced toward her.

"Is Natalie okay?" A middle-aged woman with worry lines asked between gasps.

"Ma'am, I'm going to ask you and your family to stay out here while we go in," the first officer instructed.

"But, she's my daughter. She's troubled. I can calm her down." The woman insisted.

"Stay here." His voice was sterner than before. With his hand positioned on his gun he turned to Cat and Geeta. "Who else is in the house?"

"Jeremy and Natalie." Cat tried to clear her throat. "Just the two of them," she repeated louder.

Before the police reached the door Jeremy led Natalie out of the house. With his arm around her shoulder, she appeared normal, but a deranged look in her eye said otherwise.

"Natalie, are you okay?" Her mother and father rushed forward, gathering Natalie in their arms, greeting her like a runaway child.

Cat tightened the throw around her, as she tried to steal a little body heat from her sister. Sandwiched between Jeremy and Geeta, her teeth began to chatter. She couldn't stop.

"Are you okay? Did she hurt you?" Cat examined his face and hands for cuts.

"I'm fine," Jeremy scooped her up like she was a rag doll and carried her back inside. She clung to his neck, crying with earnest now. She sniffed to keep her nose from running.

Inside, Jeremy eased her down until her feet touched the floor. Her left ankle collapsed under her weight, but he caught her before she fell again.

"We better have someone take a look at that to make sure it's not broken." He picked her up again.

"It's probably broken. With the luck I'm having..."

"Our luck is fine," Jeremy said before easing her on the sofa. "Geeta, can you get Cat some clothes so I can take her to the clinic? After we get your ankle examined, I'll take you both to breakfast."

"Is someone going to tell me what is going on around here? Are you two back together?"

Jeremy looked at Cat. His dark eyes gleamed. "Haven't you heard, Geeta? We're engaged."

Epilogue

"Sit still, Cat." Geeta tried to unpin the veil.

"I can't, I'm nervous."

"Has he told you yet where you're going on your honeymoon?" Yani inquired.

"No. All he said was that I needed to bring lots of swimwear," Cat responded while Phoebe tackled the long trail of tiny buttons on the dress.

"It sounds fabulous, Cat. You'll have to send us a text letting us know where you landed," Yani said.

Cat stepped out of the beautiful princess gown, and reached for her sundress just as Yani took it off the hanger. The last few hours seemed surreal. One moment her life was in the toilet, and now she was so full of love and joy she could float away.

"When I think about everything Jeremy and I went through this year. Whew, it was a wild rollercoaster ride in a scary house."

"Well, you don't have to worry about Natalie anymore. After that last incident, she won't be bothering you again."

"The police said the same thing after she held me at knifepoint. But she managed to run my car off the road two weeks later."

"Okay, stop it," Geeta admonished. "We're not discussing that chick today. The only thing that matters right now is you and Jeremy."

"She's right," Phoebe added. "So let's get you changed and back downstairs. There is a very handsome hunk waiting to take you on a honeymoon."

Cat applied lipstick while Yani zipped her dress. "Okay, I think this is it. Phoebe and Yani, I need you to promise me something."

Everyone turned to her, all conversation on pause. "You guys keep an eye on my sister. Geeta's been speed-dating and we all know how that can turn out."

"Oh no." Yani lowered her head and massaged her forehead. "Say it ain't so, Geeta."

"What? What's wrong with speed-dating? I'm not looking to get married like you guys. I just want to have some fun."

Cat raised an eyebrow. "You two can handle her. I'll be gone for two weeks. But right now, I've got to get back to the reception. We have a flight to catch."

In the large hall Cat surveyed the gold and white centerpieces and decorations. She couldn't have wished for a better reception. She spotted Jeremy talking with her parents. The moment he noticed her, his smile widened.

He made his way across the room to her. "Every time I look at you, I think you get more beautiful."

"You don't have to say stuff like that anymore. You've got me, now." She reached up to kiss him.

"I just want to make sure." He wrapped his arms around her. A round of applause filled the ballroom.

"Your charter flight leaves in two hours. You better get out of here." Jeremy's friend Brooks patted him on the back. "You'll have plenty of time for that when you get where you're going."

"Do you know where we're going, Brooks?" Cat asked.

"I do. But if I told you, Jeremy would kill me." He winked.

"He's got that right." Jeremy reached for her hand. The crowd followed them to the entrance.

"Cat, about your sister, is she seeing anyone?" Brooks asked.

Cat gripped his arm. "Brooks, I like you, so I'm going to tell you straight. Geeta is going through a rough patch. Give her a little time."

He nodded and fell back in the crowd. "Pairing them as best man and maid of honor was probably not a good idea," she said to Jeremy.

"He's a big boy. He'll be all right."

Cat gave the crowd a final wave before getting into the limo. Jeremy climbed in behind her.

He waved from the window as the car pulled away. He'd removed his tux, but he was just as handsome in his jeans. "I'm glad you took off that big dress, I couldn't find your legs under all that tulle and lace or whatever that stuff was."

She leaned into him. Her heart beat with excitement. "When we get to the honeymoon suite, I promise to let you touch anything you want for as long as you want. Now, are you going to tell me where we're going?"

"You'll see when we get there."

"Well, just so you'll know, I have a secret, too." She batted her lashes at him.

"Tell me your secret and I'll tell you mine."

She placed her hands in her lap. She'd planned to tell him tonight no matter what. If she had to keep it to herself a moment longer she would expire. She gathered his hands in hers and faced him.

"What is it, Cat?" A hint of concern gathered around his mouth.

"I'm pregnant."

His eyes widened. "You're...are you sure?"

"I'm sure. I took three tests."

"Are you teasing me?" The smile that he'd worn all day was gone, his eyes blinked rapidly.

She squeezed his hand. "I know what this means to you so I wouldn't play a cruel trick on you. Are you ready to be a daddy?"

"You've given me the two best gifts I could have ever wanted. You and a baby, all in one day. If you never buy me another present, I will still be the luckiest man in the world."

ONE DATE AT A TIME

Chapter One

The warm Philadelphia afternoon sun warmed Geeta Preston's back. Two days ago she meant to retrieve the mail from the box, but another jail house letter from Donny while he tried to come up with bail money kept her away. She shuffled through the thick multicolored pile of correspondences. Bill. Bill. Bill. Junk. Letter.

She stared at her name in Donny's messy script. Her stomach twisted in a hostile knot. What would it take for him to understand they were through? After ignoring him since he was arrested he should have gotten the message, but Donny was never one to see what was right before him.

She scanned through the words, skipping to the last sentence. Each week his letter ended with the same sentiment – *'I'll be coming home to you, soon.'*

He couldn't think she was waiting on him or that she was even interested in what he planned to do while out on bail. The pressure in her belly expanded. She curled her fingers around the loose-leaf notebook paper. The satisfying scrunch of his letter undid the weight threatening to make her sick.

Now he had plenty of time to tell her how much their love meant. If only he had cherished her when she was begging for his attention. Selling drugs had clouded his views, ruined their relationship, and pushed her into reevaluating her life. For that she was thankful. It appeared sharing an eight by eight prison cell with a total stranger had changed his perspective on life, too.

She glanced at her watch and rushed out the door. Showing up late for Cat's party would send her sister into a homegrown tirade. Since this was her first visit in months the least she could do was arrive on time. There wasn't anything pretty about an angry pregnant woman. Their sisterly bond had settled into a cozy rhythm and today wasn't the time to test the boundaries.

Before opening the car door her cell phone rang. She fished it from her purse and stared at the screen. Unknown Caller. After hesitating for two seconds she answered.

"Geeta, it's me." The moment Donny's voice filled her ear her heartbeat accelerated. All her anger from the moment the police had dragged him from under the bed and threw him in jail pulsed through every vein in her body.

"Donny, it's over. I'm not interested in anything you have to say." She kept her voice firm and level.

"Let me stop by, so we can talk in person."

"You're out of jail?" She opened the driver side door and heaved her purse into the passenger seat. "When...your letter didn't say..." she stuttered.

He chuckled, his cool throaty laughter mocking her. "Yeah, baby. Sometimes mail gets hung up. Where are you living now? I'll drop by."

"No. I don't want to see you. Didn't you read the letter I sent you?" She pushed a stray lock of hair behind her ear.

"You were just mad. Now that I'm out, I can make it up to you." He poured on the charm. She could tell by the way he spaced his words.

"You're out for good?" She flopped behind the driver seat. The conversation zapped her energy.

"I'm out on bail. It took me a few weeks to get the money together. But I ain't going back. I'm sure I can beat this charge, especially with my baby by my side. Now tell me where your crib is so I can come see you."

With her index finger Geeta smashed the Off button. Her pulse quickened. After several deep breaths she shook her arms, trying to dislodge Donny from her life. The next call from him would go unanswered. Maybe the gesture was overkill, but watching the police drag him from under the bed, handcuff and shove him into the back of the squad car required a grand gesture on her part. If Donny refused to listen then she wouldn't waste another moment on him.

Dating Just Got Serious

Philadelphia's cross-town traffic put her in her sister's crowded parking lot with minutes to spare. She rode the elevator to the penthouse condo.

Ever since the authorities cleared her name and gave her life back, she was hardly recognizable. She had a new place to live, she couldn't stay in the place where Donny had committed his crimes. A promotion that paid enough so she didn't have to sponge off her family. And no hassles from men, since love was no longer on the table. The moment she packed up her heart for safekeeping life became much less complicated to navigate.

The one time she almost went too far was at her sister's wedding, but thankfully Brooks DiNardo vanished after the nuptials. She couldn't take him seriously anyway. He wasn't her type. He'd been a delightful distraction, but never anything more.

Her roommate, Egypt, thought speed dating was a good way to have some fun without the inconvenience of commitment. The whole hermit persona was a front for her sister. Cat worried too much about everything. Her hormones were on high alert since she became pregnant.

She was more than ready to slough off the old maid boredom, and ease back into a real life, like a gangly child outgrowing her summer wardrobe. Staking claim to a life that let her walk on the wild side without the threat of brushing the wrong side of the law didn't seem like to much to ask.

Life was remarkably better now. Too bad she had to almost get arrested to unveil this new normal. The elevator doors parted and she bounced down the hall towards her sister's condo.

Cat enjoyed entertaining. Any reason was good enough to cook mounds of food and call everyone over.

Without knocking, she opened the door. In true Cat and Jeremy fashion, the large living room was stuffed with their friends. Mellow music wrapped around the large area easing the guests together in whispered conversations. There were so many things about Cat's life to covet. She had good friends, a man who adored her, and now they were expecting a child. Maybe some of Cat's treasures would spill over and land in her life.

Spending time with her sister and brother-in-law hardly seemed like a major sacrifice. Cat had picked her up out of a sinkhole more than once. Coming to her party tonight was another way of saying thank you. Her sister made a point of calling daily and visiting often. How else could Cat give their parents the latest update on her baby sister's mental health?

Ensconced in the corner of the bar she spotted a familiar figure. Brooks DiNardo, a ghost from her past. This one with sweeter memories, though. The best man to her maid of honor at the wedding. A warm sensation enveloped her, much like his touch had back then. Tall and lean, her arms had fit around his waist like a custom tailored suit.

He'd swept Geeta off her feet like he had been sent by her fairy godmother to erase any lingering vestiges of Donny. But after the wedding he disappeared. Vanished like fog on a warm summer morning. He was a smooth talker, filling her up on the balcony before Cat and Jeremy cut the cake.

With a cell phone pressed to his ear, he poured a beer into a tall glass. Without looking up, he handed it to a waiting hand. After ending the call he scanned the room. His green eyes were as sharp as she remembered. His search stopped when he noticed her. He made his way around the makeshift bar towards her, a big, bright smile stretched across his face.

The first kiss tells everything about a relationship. At least that's what she thought after a few hours with Brooks. His heated kisses and the passionate way he'd embraced her sent her body into sensory overload. She couldn't have been more wrong. He was only interested in a few hours of fun. Now no matter how hard she tried, those moments kept visiting her dreams.

Sometimes, even now, echoes of the way he made her laugh still filled her ears, making her smile.

"Well, hello. I was hoping I'd see you here today." His deep throaty voice was like a sexual melody, pulling up memories of the two of them behaving like sex starved teenagers at the reception. Today he was casual, as if the last they'd seen each other was at some church picnic.

She shifted away from his touch. They weren't picking up where they left off.

"Brooks you're looking well." She faked sweetness. Today, she'd already expended all her extra energy on one ex-boyfriend. She couldn't swap words of wit with Brooks.

He was as strikingly handsome as she remembered. He still wore his blond hair short on the side and buzzed on top, which gave him a no-nonsense appearance, like a strict teacher or principal. Fresh out of a dysfunctional relationship with Donny was no time to get serious with the ultra-conservative Brooks. Another insurmountable obstacle she wasn't ready to tackle. Today he wore a button-down shirt and a pair of khakis, amplifying his stiff persona. If he could lose the good boy charm surrounding him, he might be worth a try.

She shook the thought away. What she needed right now was a real bad boy to loosen the cobwebs in her life. Even with the bulging muscles and sharp chin, Brooks didn't have the edge she was looking for. Since he was a friend of Cat and Jeremy she needed to keep him at arm's length. Her sister didn't need to know how she planned to treat any man in her foreseeable future. Use them and lose them was her new plan.

"You're the bartending tonight?" She was afraid to look at him or all the emotion she'd held back would rush through her well-placed shield.

"After all the things we did on the balcony at your sister's reception, you're going to kiss me like I'm your brother?"

"You ought to be foot stomping happy I kissed you at all, since I haven't seen you in such a long time," she retaliated.

"I've been away. But that doesn't mean I wasn't thinking about you. I've got some really fond memories." The wicked smile he gave her warmed the ice around her heart, but not enough to defrost it. His sincerity kept her from pushing him away when he embraced her waist with one hand.

The snug hug was both intimate and sensual. Too many lonely nights had left her horny. Her wayward senses telling her every man in the room wanted to take her to bed. Maybe he only wanted to greet her. The idea of being with someone…at least for a night, stroked the desire she'd been trying to ignore. A one-night stand would fix her immediate problem.

"Vodka and cranberry juice, right?" He led her back to the bar and reached for the bottle of Gray Goose before she could reply. With the flair of an expert he splashed liquor and juice into the glass at the same time, and then added the ice cubes.

Charming. Brooks produced an easy smile. His classical good looks reminded her of a much younger Sean Connery. The one in the James Bond movies her mother adored. If she hadn't been on maid-of-honor duty during her sister's wedding she probably have gone to bed with Brooks that night.

He dropped his elbow on the bar and peered at her. "You're more beautiful than I remembered. How come I haven't seen you in at a basketball game or at one of Cat's parties in months?" With flair he plopped a lime rind into the glass and handed it to her.

"I've been avoiding you. I didn't expect to see you here today." She tried to sound nonchalant. After the wedding he'd dropped out of sight, another sign that their moment together was just a way to kill some time. "I figured I couldn't let you keep me from coming to Cat and Jeremy's party."

"I've been away for a while. You're looking good, as usual." He stared at her as if this were their first introduction. "What have you been up to?" He ogled her breasts like they were on display at a buffet.

She pulled her hair behind her ears, drawing his attention back to her face. "I've started a new job that keeps me very busy. The publisher gave me my own by-line, which means I have to step up the stories."

"Philly E-News, right?" His expression turned humorous.

"Yes, and I know you think the whole idea of an e-paper is crazy, but we've landed some major advertising accounts. The paper is doing well."

"You call the e-pub a paper even though it's not printed on paper?"

She stepped closer to him. With her lips almost pressed to his ear she whispered. "What do you suggest we call it?" People always made fun of her new career choice, but the money was good. If Brooks thought he could materialize back in her life and offer his opinion then now was the time to correct him.

He swayed towards her so that her mouth touched his cheek. Her glossy lips left an imprint on his face. "Sweetheart, you can call it the moon. As long as you're happy, then I'm happy with you. Your career is working out, what could be better? Maybe the basketball team will place an ad in your paper about our upcoming charity event. We need to make sure we fill up the ballroom."

With her thumb she wiped the lipstick off his face. His smooth skin felt warm. "That would be great. Are you serious?"

"I am. I wouldn't joke about something this important to you."

"The owner is always encouraging us to bring in ads, if you're serious, then please let me know."

"You'll hear from me real soon."

His cell phone chirped. He put up his index finger, and reached in his pants pocket. "Give me a minute."

With his back to her he moved away, speaking too low for her to hear. With her drink in hand she inched away from him. Even at the wedding he'd snuck away several times to whisper into his phone. If he was in a relationship he ought to stop making goo-goo eyes at her.

218

Men always wanted what they couldn't have. Why couldn't they be happy with the plate they had? She glanced back over her shoulder at Brooks. He had his finger stuck in one ear and his phone pressed to the other. She hoped whoever was on the other end of the call was giving him a hard time.

"Ah, you're here," Cat yelled when Geeta wandered into the kitchen. "I have some people I want you to meet."

Geeta kissed her sister's cheek. "Cat, I already know your friends. And I'm not interested in any of your male friends. They're much too square for my taste. If I'm still single when I turn fifty, I'll let you do some matchmaking. For now, I'm happy with the small circle of acquaintances I currently have. We've had this conversation, before. Why don't you listen to me?"

"Just because none of my friends have been arrested for a DUI, or drug dealing or haven't check into a rehab center for an addiction to prescription drugs, like your last few dates doesn't mean they are boring or old fogies," Cat countered. "I wanted to introduce you to a higher class of men."

"You've got to stop worrying about me, Cat. I'm fine, now. Those guys didn't want much and I didn't have to give them much. They were perfect while they lasted."

"Not according to Egypt. She said most nights you're watching reruns of old sitcoms on your computer."

Geeta wanted to say something to erase the concern in Cat's eyes. The only thing she should have been thinking about was the baby she was carrying. The last thing Geeta needed on her conscience was Cat's health.

Geeta drew back. "You were the one who told me I needed to take a break from dating." She paused. "What did you call it? Cleanse my relationship palette. Egypt and I have a pledge. We're not sleeping with anyone for at least six months. Remember?"

"Yeah, but I didn't think you would draw it out so long. Do you have to take everything overboard? I said take some time, not forever." Cat lifted one eyebrow, something she'd picked up from their mother to accentuate her disapproval.

"It's only been two months. I wouldn't call that forever. If it makes you feel any better, Egypt invited me to Club Swiss. They have a speed dating night for singles. I'm checking it out this weekend."

"Picking up men you don't know is dangerous, Geeta. I won't say any more… for now. But let's talk tomorrow. And you know how wild Egypt can be, please be careful."

"Didn't you meet Jeremy at a club?"

Cat drew her eyebrows together. She hated being corrected. "Do as I say, not as I do. Besides, I was older than you and times were different back then."

"It was only three years ago, Cat. But I'm a big girl. Now can I just have a good time, without the match making?"

Cat positioned her hand on her spreading hips. Pregnancy made her look even prettier. Geeta wondered if she would look as luminescent if she ever decided to find someone to settle down with and have a baby.

"No matter what you choose, baby sister, I'll always have your back."

"Well look who it is, my favorite sister-in-law." Jeremy crushed her in his big thick arms.

"That joke was old the last time you told it, Jeremy, and it's not getting any younger. I'll always be your favorite since you have no sisters or brothers and Cat doesn't have any other siblings."

"You see how special you are." He gave her a final squeeze. "You know everyone here. Make yourself at home. The bar is fully stocked. Brooks is over there and he's been asking about you."

"I've already seen Brooks. Why is he asking about me?"

"Geeta, why does a man ask about a woman he already knows?" He bumped her shoulder with his before strolling away.

"The way he hugs his phone, he must already have a woman in his life. And just in case she likes to brawl, I'm keeping away."

"Brooks doesn't have a girlfriend. No one special, anyway."

"If a man spends as much time on the phone as he does, then he's either in love or doing something illegal. Either way, I'm smart enough to stay away from both, now."

"I think you're wrong," Jeremy said before one of his friends pulled him away.

She surveyed the room. Cat's friends were nice. They liked to have fun, but excitement for them was sitting around telling stories about what happened the last time they were sitting around. Boring. She stifled a yawn. Being outside, with the sun on her back or listening to loud music would be a lot more fun. Anything had to be better than being cooped up inside on a beautiful day like today.

The vodka and juice might be strong enough to get her through an evening with this bunch. She took a swallow from the glass. Processing Brooks' words was easier with a little alcohol. Why was he being so nice? If dating Donny taught her nothing else, at least she learned to steer clear of men presenting themselves as falling down nice. The pleasantness only preceded some major flaw lurking behind the kind words. Never again would she be caught off guard by a handsome smile and a little sweet talk.

Brooks advanced on her from across the room. With his height and broad shoulders he looked like a missile plowing through the crowd.

"Where were we?" he asked.

"I was enjoying my drink and the party." She turned away from him. There had to be a friendlier person to talk to.

"No, we were talking about your paper and the possibility of me taking out an ad." He stepped in front of her, blocking her path.

"You told me at the wedding you didn't like the idea of e-publication. Why would you be willing advertise in the

221

paper for something this important? Why not put your ad in the city paper?"

"I trust you. Besides, I've checked out your publication and it's not bad. In fact, Philly E-News is pretty good. I'm a subscriber."

"Since when?"

"I saw your column last week on that building collapse. Your writing was thorough and sensitive."

She fought back the smile that would have said all was forgiven. Compliments on her work were like a shot of adrenaline to her ego. Cat hadn't mentioned the piece until Geeta called her and requested she turn on her computer and read the article. Of course she was full of praise afterwards, but she had to be. That's what older sisters had to do. Brooks, on the other hand, was probably more interested in what was between her thighs than what was on the page.

The only thing she and Brooks had in common were Cat and Jeremy, hardly the solid foundation for a relationship.

"Brooks, let me be honest with you. I'm more than willing to work with you on an ad for your event. I'll give you some recommendations. If you like them then we can move forward. But if you're looking for anything more, I'm not interested."

"How do you know you're not interested? You don't know me. And why do you think I'm trying to hit on you? I only offered you some business. I'm not asking you to marry me."

His words drew her defenses in play. "Wouldn't you like to take me to bed and curl around these voluptuous D-cups you keep staring at?" She glanced down at her breasts and back at him.

"Is that an offer?"

She studied his face. Was this his way of flirting with her, some new dating technique where he pretended to be half interested until she opened up her arms and let him in and then he crapped in her life and walked out?

"The only thing I've got that would be of interest to you is an ad in our next issue," Geeta said. "I'd recommend you make a decision soon, because our space fills up fast."

His unexpected laughter knocked on her defense shield. Her heart warmed to his direct stare as if he had nothing to hide. But everyone had a secret.

"Do you want the space or not?"

"Wow, are you going to shoot me down like that?"

"Believe me, you want me to."

"Why would I want you to bust my bubble?"

"I'm not in a good place right now. I'm being selfish and living to please nobody but me."

"Maybe I can please you, too."

She shook her head. "Not interested. There's a pretty little blonde over there in the corner who looks like she needs pleasing."

"I don't want help finding a woman and I don't want just any woman." He popped open the lid on a can of beer. His pronounced adam's apple bobbed up and down as he swallowed. Brooks might not be the one, right now, in the future if she ever decided to do serious again, she'd look for someone exactly like him, minus the buttoned down attitude.

"Thanks for the offer, but no thanks. When you're ready to do business, let Cat know. She can tell you how to get in touch with me." She set the glass down. "If your goal is something else, than you're wasting your time and mine."

Chapter Two

Geeta repositioned the dining room chair in front of the window with the most sunlight. Instead of writing the article, She stared at the gray computer screen, with her fingers poised on the keyboard. Why the conversation with Brooks kept looping through her head was a mystery. After Cat's wedding it took her some time to get him out of her head, but she couldn't. Now a few choice words from him last night and he occupied space in her head, again.

Without knowing how much longer she could dodge the pressure from her sister, maybe the best thing to do was to avoid Cat for a while. For certain, Cat would not approve of her new lifestyle.

There was only one thing wrong with it. The pledge with Egypt seemed like a good idea. There was no sexual activity. The big question now, was how much longer she could remain celibate.

The hideous doorbell sounded through the house. Leasing Cat's townhouse probably hadn't been a good idea. Geeta lifted her fingers off the keyboard. Anyone ringing her doorbell between the hours of nine and five was trying to get her to buy something or giving advice on how to get through the pearly gates. Either way, she wasn't interested.

She positioned her fingers back on the keys to finish her article. The insistent ringing continued. What Cat loved about that damn doorbell she could never figure out. The sound seemed to roam through the whole townhouse like a thick fog.

"What is it?" She snatched opened the front door.

"Is that the way you greet your guests?" Brooks thick arms hung at his sides. He seemed unmoved by her rudeness.

"What are you doing here, Brooks?" She looked over his shoulder as if a clue stood behind him, somewhere.

"I followed your instructions. I got your information from Cat and I'm here to discuss the ad. If this is how you

224

handle your clients, your paper won't be in business very long." His smile broadened, amplifying the fact he was used to getting his way.

"I work from home. If I don't discriminate on whom I let into my day it becomes all scrambled. Usually people make appointments by picking up the phone. Don't you have a phone?"

He pulled his cell from his shirt pocket and waved it in front of her nose. Without replying he made a few taps and placed the device to his ear. From the office she constructed on the dining room table her cell rang.

"Very funny, Brooks. Can we do this later in the evening? I'm in the middle of something right now."

"You can turn business away?"

"I'm not turning down business. I'm only trying to schedule a time that's more convenient for the both of us. Do you let people barge into your office without appointments?"

He stepped across the doorsill without waiting to be invited. "This time works best for me." He reached in the breast pocket of his jacket, removed his leather bound checkbook, and grinned. "And I'm a paying customer."

####

Every time Brooks laid eyes on Geeta, his mind conjured up one of two images. Either her standing naked in the middle of the bedroom watching her boyfriend get arrested, or the softness of her kisses and body at the wedding. Both visions competed for attention, either one made him happy.

With all the chaos the day of the bust, she didn't seem to remember him and he didn't recognize her until Cat's engagement party. Hardly the time to tell her he'd been thinking about her perky breasts and nice round butt since their first encounter.

Her body was so exquisite he'd almost forgotten he was on a mission the day of the arrest. But he made a promise. Once the case was closed he'd get to know Geeta

225

Preston on more common ground. Unfortunately, waiting for the slow grind of the legal system didn't meet his needs.

Brooks strolled to the white sectional sofa and took a seat. She might have tried to look like she wasn't happy to see him, but the moment she opened the door her smile lines appeared. To an untrained eye it would have gone unnoticed, but he noticed everything.

Bantering with her was fun. The more she told him no, the more attractive he found her. This cat and mouse game intrigued him. If the chocolate princess had any idea that playing hard to get only made him want her more, she might dial down the venom.

Two things needed to be accomplished with this visit. The ad in the paper was the easy one. Telling her about the part he played in arresting her ex required a lot more finesse. He couldn't avoid the subject much longer.

He patted the spot on the sofa next to him. "I want a full page. Something colorful and eye catching."

"I'm not in advertising, Brooks. I don't have those kind of creative ideas. If you had called me I would have put you in touch with the marketing team then you would have saved yourself some time."

"That would have worked well, if I was interested in saving time." He tried to keep a casual look on his face without letting her see his examination of her curves under the Capri pants and spaghetti strapped top. Without the constraining refines of a bra her breasts bobbed when she strolled toward him. Keeping his hands to himself was going to require restraint. Thankfully, he was a patient man. One thing he'd learned a long time ago was women didn't like to be rushed. If she were hell bent on keeping him at a distance, then he'd let her think he wasn't within reach. He could wait as long as it took.

She plopped on the opposite end of the sofa and tucked her legs under her butt. She had to be teasing him, but taking the bait would disrupt his plans.

"Let me get the marketing team on the phone for you. They can help you and I'll get the credit." She reached for her cell.

"Give me the number, and I'll call them, myself."

She recited each number slowly, allowing him time to tap it into his cell phone.

"Well, okay then. I'll catch you later. Good luck with your charity event." Not the smoothest brush off, but a little less intense for Geeta.

"Why don't you come with me? It will be a lot of fun."

She swept the hair off her face. Her flawless skin gleamed. Those dark eyes held the promise of forever. She was taller than most of the women he dated, and she had more curves than the Schuylkill Expressway. His arms could encompass her waist with space left over.

He returned his gaze to her face. Hopefully, he hadn't missed anything she said.

"Because if I go, that would be considered a date, and I told you yesterday I don't want to date you." She shifted her position.

"I'm just trying to fill seats. The more money we raise, the more kids we can help. So think of it as doing something good for others in need."

She pursed her full lips into a seductive pout. He forced his gaze lower to the soft hollow of her neck, then lower. The waistband of her pants slipped below her perfectly round belly button, revealing skin as smooth as milk chocolate.

"I'll think about going." She unfolded her long slender legs, pushed off the sofa and glided towards the door. The doorbell rang before she could open it.

She glanced back at him, a questioning look centered in her eyes. He shrugged. More company meant he couldn't continue to charm her.

"Don't look at me. I came alone," he said.

She yanked the door open with the same bad attitude she'd used with him.

She released a sudden gasp. "Donny, what are you doing here?"

Brooks sprang off the sofa, his feet shoulder length apart. The flesh under his collar warmed. Donny might not remember him, there were so many officers in the small apartment when the arrest took place, but he couldn't take any chances.

"You should have known I'd find you. I wouldn't stop until I did." Without being invited, he stepped into the living room.

"And with all that, you didn't get the message?"

"Come on, baby, you can't still be mad at me." Donny tried to gather her in his arms, his lips puckered, but she sidestepped him. His slight build was hardly any match for the furor burning behind Geeta's eyes. The atmosphere surrounding them changed. An uncomfortable tension charged the room.

With his knees flexed, his arms at his side, Brooks stiffened his back. "Is everything okay, Geeta?" He moved next to her, touching her shoulder.

Donny looked him over, starting with his face then his eyes traveled to his shoes. "You look familiar, man. Do I know you?" he grunted.

"No, you don't know me," Brooks responded. The idea of telling her he was with the DEA and the lead on Donny's case faded. He suspected Donny would reach out to Geeta as soon as he was released.

"This is your new man? How long was I gone before you hooked up with him?" Donny pushed his crooked nose in the air. His hands pushed deep in his baggy pants pockets.

"I don't have to answer any of your questions. After what you did to me, you ought to be happy I even opened the door for you. And if I had looked first I wouldn't have bothered. Now I think it's time for you to leave."

"I thought I could count on you for a character witness at my trial. I've changed baby, and I want you to see the new Donny. I even joined the church."

"I think you better ask someone else. You don't want anyone to hear what I have to say about your character."

Brooks crossed his arms over his chest and widened his stance. Would Donny recognize him from the bust?

From the door he spotted Donny's thugs seated in the front seat of a swanky new luxury car. Donny had a line of cash and it probably wasn't from a payroll check. Since being released he hadn't wasted any time in picking up where he left off. The only thing new about him was probably his underwear.

"I'll wait outside, it sounds like you two talk want to talk."

She placed her hand on Brooks' forearm, halting him. "Can you please wait a moment?" she dug her fingers into his flesh.

"Of course." He stood behind her, giving her the support she seemed to need. He'd get another chance to capture the license plate, idiots always screwed up again.

"What, Geeta. Do you think I'm dangerous? Like I'm going to hurt you or something?" Donny's shoulders hunched and stayed that way.

The tension thickened. If she wanted Donny out of the house he'd grant her wish.

Brooks moved to stand in front of her. "I think she's done talking, man. You better leave now."

"Wait a minute." She pointed her index finger at Donny. "You already hurt me enough. There's nothing else you can do. Good-bye, Donny." She opened the door.

For a moment nobody moved. Donny glared over his shoulder and locked eyes with Geeta. Brooks' body tensed, the blood pumping through his veins accelerated. Damsels in distress were always landing at his feet. This one he couldn't step over, she was already getting to him.

"You gonna treat me like that? After all I did for you. All the stuff I bought you?"

"I never asked you for that stuff. As a matter of fact, I didn't keep any of it," she lashed back.

"Well, you can't treat me like a punk just 'cause you got a new man," he yelled.

"I think you better leave, now." Brooks moved forward.

Donny's shoulders relaxed, but the menacing glared hinted at his anger.

"Don't pull that sad-ass line on me. I'm not falling for it again. Step." She waved her hand at the door.

"Baby, we aren't done, yet. You know it and so do I." Donny walked out without looking back.

After she closed the door she sighed so heavy Brooks expected her to collapse under the weight. He extended his arms to catch her in case. Instead she marched to the dining room table plopped in the armchair and began to type.

"Geeta?"

"I've got to get back to work. I hope I've given you what you need." Her fingers flew across the keyboard.

"Are you okay?"

"I'll be fine. If you pull the door closed behind you, it will lock," she said without looking up.

"How well do you know Donny?"

She stopped typing. "I didn't know him well enough. Why?"

"Are you still in love with him?" he asked.

"Donny was a jerk and will always be a jerk. I'm just mad he showed up here like what he did was no big deal. He must think I'm some all-day-sucker. Why?"

"Maybe he's not ready to let you go."

She spun around, resting her elbow on the back of the chair. "He didn't let me go. I let him go."

"Then why are you upset?" He had to have some answers. Until today, chasing her had been an enjoyable game. But if someone else consumed her heart, he needed to know, now. Finding out months down the road wouldn't be helpful for either of them.

She didn't respond. Neither did she look at him. Her eyes were fixed on a nonexistent spot on the floor.

"Did you hear me, Geeta?"

230

"I really need to get back to this article before I lose the whole thread. Don't you have somewhere you need to be?"

Her tough façade was as flimsy as her tank top. He wanted to shed some light on everything, but if she was still in love with Donny then she might share the information with him. The time wasn't right. Not yet.

"What I need is an answer to my question."

She spun around so fast papers fell from the table. Without touching the computer, she said, "I'm upset because I was stupid, and Donny played me." She paused. "Now you know, are you happy?" Her eyes blazed, daring him to challenge her.

"About the charity event—"

She directed her attention to the keyboard. "Not interested."

Chapter Three

Geeta pulled the casserole from the oven. The cheese bubbling around the edges of the lasagna was a great start to an otherwise not so wonderful evening. Having Cat over for dinner was Cat's idea. Their parents had to be behind these frequent get-togethers. Another way for them to check up on her without having to put in an actual appearance, themselves.

"Brooks told me he stopped by last week." Cat pulled her chair up to the table.

"Did he also tell you I put him out?"

"Geeta, tell me you didn't do such a thing." Cat sipped her milk.

Egypt sauntered into the dining room on four-inch boots, and leggings so tight she sported a severe camel toe. One day Geeta vowed to gather the nerve to ask if Egypt would consider a makeover.

"Oh she did, alright. She told me all about it when I got home." Egypt popped the cork on a bottle of merlot and filled two wine glasses.

Geeta reached for the glass and took a long swallow. Thinking she could avoid Cat was silly. After all, this had been her townhouse and she still had a key. Mental note, change the locks. She took another gulp of wine. Cat seemed certain Brooks was a wonderful catch. If he was that fantastic, why hadn't someone snatched him up by now? She needed to break the news to her sister that nobody wanted to date the old fashioned blow-hard.

"He also told me Donny stopped by."

Geeta sliced the casserole into large pieces and dished some onto the plates. "Brooks talks too much. What did he do, call you as soon as he walked out?"

Egypt propped her elbows on the table. "He's not her type, anyway. He's much too conservative. I swear the man is older than you claim."

"Maybe what Geeta needs is a man with traditional values. After Donny, she should be more discriminating.

What's wrong with that?" Cat sat up straighter, like she was delivering a lecture to a bunch of students.

"I know this is between you two." Egypt pointed to Cat and Geeta. "But Cat... you don't approve of any of her guys. And a girl's got to take care of things, if you know what I mean." Egypt blew on her food before taking a bite.

"Hello. The girl is right here and can speak for herself." Geeta waved her hands. "Cat, I know you mean well, but I'm okay. You've got to stop checking up on me. "

They ate in silence for several minutes.

"What kind of work does Brooks do? I've never heard anyone say." Geeta focused on her plate, hoping to hide her interest.

"I have no idea. Jeremy never said. Whatever he does, no one talks about it much." With her brow wrinkled Cat said, "I'll have to ask, Jeremy. Now I'm curious."

"Let's change the subject. Enough talk about Donny and Brooks. They're both history." Geeta focused on her sister.

"Tell me, am I going to be the aunt of one or two bundles of joy?"

Cat's eyes sparkled. She moved both her palms to her stomach. "Twins. We're having twins!" She bounced in the chair.

Geeta dropped her fork. She circled the table and kneeled beside her sister, hugging her growing waist. "Oh, Cat, I can't believe it. That's fantastic news." She resisted the urge to squeeze her sister tighter.

They managed to finish their meal without any more talk about Brooks or dating. Cat was content to discuss babies and nurseries.

After dinner, Cat tugged on her coat. "Jeremy should be here any minute now. I better get ready to go. "Promise me you'll think about some of the things we said. You're much too young to give up on men. You don't want to end up like Aunt Charlene, do you?"

"Oh, God, Cat. Did you have to bring her up?"

"The woman had a nightstand full of vibrators. Why would one woman need ten toys? I'll never get over Mom's shock when she packed up the house. Now we know why Auntie was always in a hurry to get home."

"Just because you're pregnant doesn't give you the right to be disgusting," Geeta laughed.

"Do you own a vibrator, Geeta?"

For several seconds, she stared at her sister, not liking the direction of this conversation. "I have one, Cat. Only one. Not twenty. Okay?" She adjusted her sister's coat collar. "And I only use it once a week. How else do you think I've made it this long without sex?"

"Maybe it's hereditary. Watch yourself." Cat lifted an eyebrow.

The doorbell sounded.

"Oh good. That must be Jeremy. Saved by the bell." Geeta opened the door and waved goodbye to her sister.

Chapter Four

Geeta promised Egypt she would go to the club. She just hadn't expected Friday night to come so fast. There was no backing out now. She'd tried.

From the edge of the bed, she eyed her brand new stilettoes lying at her feet. Relationships were supposed to be a two way street. So why did it feel like a one-way highway? But everything Cat said was right. She was hiding, and it was time to stop.

Going out with Egypt was a good way to ease into being more social. How serious could anyone be at a speed-dating club? She'd flirt a little, have a few drinks, and come back home and report in to Cat. Then her sister would leave her alone for a few more weeks.

A perfect plan.

"You have to put those shoes on if you're coming with me." Egypt stood inside her bedroom door. Her short sequined dress shimmered. Egypt only had one look. Even when she was slumming she seemed to glitter.

Geeta looked down at the dress Egypt had insisted she needed to put on. Black, tight, and short. The plunging V-neck exposed a little too much cleavage, but that was part of the plan. According to Egypt's expert advice, she had to wear something that would make her stand out next to the other women competing for dates. The shoes completed the ensemble.

She pushed her feet into the black platforms. "I'm ready. Let's go have some fun."

"We're catching a cab. I expect lots of drinks will be purchased for us tonight. We look hot," Egypt laughed.

"Before we go, let me say this. If you find your true love tonight, don't worry about me. Have a good time. I'm not a rookie, I know how to handle myself and I know my way home."

"That's what I'm talking about. Welcome back to the real world, girl. Now, let's go break some hearts. I'll try to honor our pledge, but…"

"I know how you feel. I didn't think it would be so hard. I don't think I've ever been this horny," said Geeta.

The minute they stepped into the bustling club, Egypt hurried off to a table with a man sporting a mouth full of gold teeth gleaming like a treasure chest.

Geeta shook her head. Maybe class wasn't something you learned. For sure, Egypt seemed to enjoy life. She never let sadness stop her from having a good time.

She tugged down her tiny black dress and adjusted the deep cut V-neck before slipping onto the empty barstool. The South Street club was busy tonight, everyone jostling for attention. See me. Notice me. Look at me. She could have been on an isolated island. The loneliness the atmosphere was supposed to drive away clung to her like dead skin cells, instead.

Twenty-five women waited to get into the speed-dating pod. Every man making his way into the tightly knitted tables glimpsed her cleavage as if she were a sight along the way. She wasn't providing a peepshow. Tonight was supposed to be about finding someone to have fun with, not voyeurism.

If only she knew what she wanted. A string of unfortunate decisions, one that almost landed her in jail proved she needed to reexamine her choices. The idea was scary and exciting. Could she really become a serial dater?

According to Egypt, the whole idea of speed dating was supposed to help her move from heartache to euphoria. There was only one thing wrong with the analogy, her heart wasn't broken and euphoria didn't exist. What she needed was some good old-fashioned loving. The kind that worked out all the kinks and cobwebs.

Tonight was supposed to be fun. But if one more person bumped into her she was going to march out the door and scratch this club off her list. Right now the only thing she felt was out of place. Next Saturday she'd don a pair of sweatpants and head to the hardware store. According to her Facebook dating group hardware stores were full of willing testosterone.

"Hello, Geeta."

The moment she heard Donny's voice she shuddered, and sucked in a short breath.

"Donny, what are you doing here? Did you follow me?"

"Egypt told me. Getting information out of her is pretty easy. The girl's an air-head." He slipped his hand around her waist.

Everything about his touch was familiar. Her body reacted without any assistance from her head, leaning against him like they were still a couple.

"Let me buy you a drink." His baritone voice sounded like a melody luring her out of Eden.

"No." She pulled away, wanting to be tough, but her resistance was slipping. "I don't want anything from you. Why haven't you answered my question? Why are you here, tonight?"

"Come on, Geeta. Just a drink. We can at least share a moment, can't we? All of our time together wasn't bad, was it?"

Donny could be charming when he wanted something from her. He wanted a character witness and the only thing she wanted from him was a good night of sex. No way was she ever going back into a relationship with him, but he knew how to satisfy her—most of the time. Tonight a couple of well-placed kisses and a hard shaft with a real pulse would make her happy for weeks to come.

"One drink, Donny," she said.

With his hands on the rail of the bar, he ordered the cocktails. "I'm real sorry about how things turned out. I was planning to leave the business behind. I really was. But I wasn't fast enough."

"How did we live together for so many months and I didn't know? You must have thought I was an airhead, too."

The bartender set two glasses in front of them. Donny handed him two twenties and waved him away. She picked up the drink and gulped a mouthful.

237

"I didn't want you to know. I kept it from you. You know…handled my business away from home. You were the best thing to happen to me, Geeta. I should have never put you in harm's way like that. I hope you can forgive me one day."

His hand dropped to her knee. Either the vodka was working faster than normal or she was more desperate than she realized, because she didn't push his hand away. The idea of taking him to her place for a round in the sheets was enticing.

The crowd around the bar thickened, pressing them closer together. Donny reached for the bowl of nuts and pressed against her breasts. His touch was too deliberate to be accidental, but she didn't care. Another bad choice stared at her and she couldn't find the strength to say no. At least she wasn't as bad as Egypt—picking up complete strangers for mindless one-night stands. Instead she could have mindless sex without worrying if he thought her butt was too big or too small or if she was pleasing him. Having sex with Donny could be perfectly idiotic and, perfectly satisfying.

She nodded at him. "I'm not mad at you anymore. I'm not even going to question your choices. I hope everything works out well for you."

He leaned in close, brushing her nipple this time with his forearm. "How about we go back to my place? I have something special for you." He stuck his tongue in her ear. The hot tip sent a sensation right to her core.

Donny gave her a seductive wink. His lovely dark eyes twinkled with amusement. Tonight he could be the distraction she needed. After so many lonely months the intimate warmth he could provide would be a lot better than the blanket on her bed. His massive arms caressing her set her body in a panic. She wasn't supposed to feel this way. This was really happening.

She gave him her prettiest smile, the one she'd perfected in the bathroom mirror when she was fifteen. Donny whispered to the man standing beside him and his knee brushed against hers slow and steady. The man nodded and walked towards the exit.

"You look like you need my undivided attention tonight," he said.

Donny sat so close his cologne stung her nose. The scar on his forehead appeared larger than before. The liquor dulled her need for scrutiny.

"Obviously you've missed me. You're not dating anyone. Not that dude I saw at your place. Tell me you were waiting on me to get out." His voice was deep and lusty.

"I'm alone because of you. After what happened why would I trust anyone, ever again?"

"I'm home, baby and I'm ready to take care of you the way I should have. Now that I'm out, you won't have to worry about anything."

She leaned away from him. The bullshit still flowed like jewels from his lying mouth. "Who was the guy that just walked out?"

"Nobody, baby." His hand was back on her knee.

"You're lying. Who was he?" She searched Donny's face. He was such a lair.

He sighed. "Geeta, you know I've only been out for a few days. I needed someone to help me out, give me a place to stay…you know. Clay is my go-to guy." He peered into his glass.

Whenever Donny told a lie, he couldn't look at her. Tonight his lies didn't even matter. They had no future and all she wanted was about twenty minutes of his body.

"Don't worry about Egypt. She's a big girl. She can find her way home," he said when she looked around.

Geeta continued to gaze into the pod where desperate people recited rehearsed speeches, hoping to find the perfect person. Tonight she couldn't muster the faux persona required to be successful in the pod. It was easier to sit at the bar and nurse the vodka and pretend with Donny.

"Tonight I'll keep myself company along with this glass. Vodka doesn't ask any questions and after a while the sting will erase all the answers." She sipped her drink allowing the liquor to warm her insides and drowned out the warning sounding in her head. She didn't need to know how stupid she being now.

"All I could think about in jail was you. My body longed for you like a starving man." He looked her over, his eyes stopping at her hips.

Donny could be fun. His bad-boy appeal was everything she wanted. The spiky hair, five o'clock shadow and pierced ears were like a magnet. Even the dragon tattoo sprouting up through his V-neck sweater was enticing. She wanted to swear off the roughneck type, but maybe she'd been too hasty.

"I could use another drink." She tapped her glass.

"Let's get the lady what she wants." Donny signaled the bartender and then leaned even closer. Since when did a drink give him the right to ogle her?

The bartender placed another round of drinks on the bar. Donny pulled more bills from his pocket and peeled off a fifty.

Cat's voice echoed in the back of Geeta's mind, watching over her like the constant guardian. Contemplating spending the night with Donny would cause her sister to screech like a cat caught by the tail. But Cat had someone to love. She never did anything wrong, never miss-stepped, finished school on time, married the right man, never spent time in a holding cell. If Geeta could buy that kind of confidence, she'd run home, leaving a trail of scattered disasters and bust her piggy bank and buy a better future.

From the way Donny peered at her cleavage he'd be drooling in a few minutes. If spending one night with him would erase some of the unhappiness clinging to her bones than she was willing.

She sipped her drink. Vodka—her new drink of choice—worked faster than the sweeter varieties. The music notched up louder making conversation even harder to hear. She could pretend the uneasy silence had nothing to do with their incompatibility. This wasn't the place to examine things too closely.

Donny's hand inched up her leg. Not high enough to offend her, but certainly not in the friendly zone. The wild response from her body reminded her she hadn't made love to anyone. For a twenty-five year old woman that was a crime.

"I think Egypt has abandoned me." She wiggled off the barstool.

"Let me take you home, Geeta." His words were simple enough, but his intentions were screaming in her ear. The drink, the touching, all meant he wanted to weasel his way back into her life. She wasn't so far removed not to understand the nuances. The idea was intriguing. One good night could make her forget some of the history dogging her. Getting together could satisfy both of their itches and then she could move on.

This past year was the worst she'd ever had. Even at the gangly age of thirteen, life wasn't this lonely. A man as handsome as Donny could help her forget. Drowning her troubles in his dark brown eyes and a layer of lust, were the perfect prescription for something. After a good night of loving she'd sweep him away like the dust bunnies under her bed.

"Yeah, okay. Let me go to the ladies room first." She stood and tugged the edges of her dress. Wearing skin-tight dresses and five-inch heels weren't her normal attire. She longed for her jeans and running shoes.

In the ladies room she nudged her way to the sink to reapply her lip-gloss. Even before the shocking red hue touched her lips the dull glow in her eyes caught her attention. In the bar with music thumping against her ear taking Donny home seemed like a good idea. Between here and there the whole image turned seedy. Trying to erase her drought with an ex would be about as successful as trying to dream without falling asleep.

She couldn't do it. Sleeping with Donny wouldn't solve a thing. The gaping hole in her heart would still ache and the loneliness lining her soul would continue to chase her. Somewhere in the last year she'd forgotten how to live, how to be happy. Nothing he did tonight would change her.

He wasn't the one. Thinking he could pull her out of the sinkhole was as much a fallacy as Santa Claus.

I'm not that horny or that desperate, she mouthed to her image in the mirror. Without smearing the color on her lips she shoved the tube back in her purse and walked out, right into the massive chest of the man exiting the men's room.

"I'm so sorry," she looked up.

"Geeta, is that you?" Brooks braced her by her biceps.

His thick blond buzz military cut and meaty shoulders looked as good tonight as they had in her apartment a week ago. He'd been chivalrous that day, standing up to Donny with her. But he was an apple and she was passion fruit. He was so conservative and a little boring. All those good looks in a button down shirt seemed like such a waste of time.

"Brooks, what…what are you doing here?" She looked around. "I'm surprised to see you in a club." Donny and Brooks on the same night couldn't be a coincidence. "Did Egypt tell you I would be here? Or was it Cat, sending you to chaperone me?"

He grinned a little too quickly before looking down. "I like music, I love to dance and I like getting out. I'm here and it doesn't have anything to do with you. Imagine that."

"Um-hm, exactly." Her instinct might now be great, but she knew deception when she smelled it. "Does this mean you'll tell Cat all about this little meeting, too?"

"Wow, Geeta, you really do have a war raging in your head. If you don't want me to say anything, don't do anything worth talking about. That should be easy for you, right?"

"Oh, shut up." She looked up into his bright eyes and laughed.

They studied each other for a moment.

"You're looking good. I take it you're doing better now?" Instead of examining her body he looked in her eyes.

"Better? What do you mean?"

"The last time we talked you were determined to hold onto your solitude and write your articles. Something must have changed.

"Any luck in the pod?" He nodded to the tiny tables across the room.

"I didn't sit down tonight. I changed my mind after I got here. But Egypt must have found a love match. I think she left me. Are you speed dating?"

"Nope, one date a night is enough for me. I didn't even know this place had turned into one of those dating clubs."

There was a tone to his words, a judgment. Of course he wouldn't speed date and he most surely had an opinion of those that did. A negative one. She shifted her feet.

"Do you need a ride home?"

She bit her lip before glancing over her shoulder. "What I need...Can you do me a favor?"

The corner of his mouth lifted, transporting her back to the dance they had at the wedding.

"For you, anything," he said.

She wrung her hands, trying to form the right words. "Here's the situation. Donny is in the bar, he offered me a lift home, but I'm sure it's got strings attached and I can't." She shook her head. "I'm not interested. But I don't want to go through all the hassle of why and why not." She paused. "Can you tell him for me?"

His head snapped back. "You want me to cancel a date for you?"

"I'm not on a date. Not with him. It's a lot to ask, I know. But I just need to get out of here." She looked beyond him to the exit a few feet away. Freedom was only a few feet away.

He folded his arms over his thick chest in a slow methodical gesture. "Wait here for me. I'll take you home."

"No, I don't want to impose on you. I can get home."

"Well, it's too late for that. Stay here. I'll be right back." He pointed to the spot on the tiled floor before spinning around and heading into the center of the club.

####

Brooks squared his shoulders. Keeping surveillance on Donny was easy. Running into Geeta was the surprise. What were the odds of her being here, too? No matter how much she protested it seemed like the two of them had more unfinished business. During the investigation, her name had been cleared. She had nothing to do with Donny's illegal activity, but if Donny continued to hang on the fringe of her life, trouble had a way of spreading.

Tonight he'd tell her, everything. This was the perfect opportunity to discuss everything with her. If he'd learned anything, he knew delaying the conversation only made matters worse.

Maybe it was time to hand off this assignment to someone a little less involved. His objectivity could be compromised.

He strolled behind Donny, sizing him up. Tonight he was alone. His crew wasn't in sight.

"She's not coming back, man. You might as well get going," he said, standing over Donny.

"What the hell." Donny spun around on the stool and jumped up. "What are you, her keeper now?"

"The lady asked me to deliver a message. That's all."

Donny tried to look around him. When he wasn't successful he took a step to the right of Brooks and peered to the back of the club.

Brooks blocked his path. "She wants you to get lost. Take the hint."

"Who the hell are you, anyway? Why are you always hanging around my girl?" Donny demanded.

"She doesn't think she's your girl. Maybe you need to get an update on your status."

"I swear I know you. I've seen you somewhere, before."

Brooks narrowed his eyes. "Maybe, you ought to get out of here." He used his chin to indicate the door.

"Who's going to make me?" Donny yelled. The crowd in the bar quieted, and gave them a little more space.

Brooks stepped close enough to whisper. "Your crew's not here and punks like you are nothing without your boyz. Take some good advice and head home."

Donny's face tightened like a prune. He picked up his glass and drained it. After slamming the glass on the bar he glared at Brooks. "I'm out," he paused. "For now."

Brooks held his breath until Donny stepped outside. Activity in the Pod had never stopped, but the bar took a moment before returning to normal.

He strolled to the back of the club to fulfill his promise to Geeta. Maybe chasing her would have to wait until the case against Donny was tried. He wasn't some two-bit drug dealer. He had been moving large quantities of cocaine, to Philly, Jersey and Delaware. Getting him behind bars was the first priority.

The woman crowding the restroom was thick. Geeta wasn't in the horde. He searched the small area, again.

Nothing.

With his hand in position on his belt he looked around one last time.

"Excuse me, can you please go into the restroom and see if a woman by the name of Geeta is inside?" he asked a petite woman who smiled at him.

She nodded. Her seductive stroll into the ladies room could have been a lot faster if she'd stopped looking over her shoulder at him.

To find out Geeta was gone wasn't a surprise. The way her eyes had danced like an out-of-control marionette, he would have bet she was going to make a break for freedom the moment he turned his back.

Less than a minute later, the petite siren returned and shook her head.

"Since she's not here, I'll go home with you," she cooed before rolling her tongue over her red lacquered lips.

Chapter Five

Geeta slumped on the sofa and placed her feet on the coffee table. Her life wasn't miserable, it was just unrecognizable. In the last few months she'd molted the life she knew and the new one was foreign. Sidestepping trouble last night pulled her out of one bad situation and dropped her into another. By now she should have known better, but learning from her mistakes was a shortcoming she hadn't mastered yet.

She slipped lower on the sofa, burying her head against the throw pillow. But Brooks didn't deserve being dragged into her drama. He probably thought she was a flake.

Brooks was like a white knight, saving her when she didn't even know she needed rescuing. But that was as much a problem as it was a blessing. Why she kept tripping over the wrong men was a big mystery. Brooks had her tied into a massive emotional knot. She liked his calm exterior, but didn't want to. The collared shirts he was so fond of were better than the loose jeans Donny wore that hung so low on his butt, his boxers showed.

Thinking about dating Brooks made her uncomfortable, like living in a country where she didn't know the language. Somewhere out there the right man for her was waiting. She needed to be patient until their paths crossed.

She heaved a big sigh. Guilt churned in her stomach, growing thicker with each revolution. Getting out of the club before stupidity and loneliness landed her in the wrong bed seemed like the smartest move at the time. But like most of her decisions, now she had another problem. The loud music, the tight dress and the vodka had clouded her judgment. It would have been easier to stand in front of a Septa bus.

The evening was supposed to be fun. A few unexpected incidents and it was anything but. The leering bunch of salivating men, Donny's appearance and running into Brooks made last night a colossal disaster.

She exhaled through her mouth. Not since her prom date came down with chicken pox had a fun evening flipped upside down so dramatically.

Whatever Brooks expected as payment for his good deed would have been more than she was willing to pay. He might not know it yet, he'd thank her one-day for leaving him in the club. She had enough life issues to work out without involving Brooks. At her door she probably would have jumped on him like a horny hog. A year without sex made dry humping sound appealing.

She reached for her cell phone and dialed her sister.

"What time do I need to be there and what am I supposed to bring?" she asked when Cat picked up.

"You were supposed to be here at noon, it's already one and the game starts at two. I thought you were going to help me set up?"

"I was out late last night. My ass is dragging this morning. Can I skip the get-together this weekend?"

"Not an option." Cat's voice was screechy, which meant she'd slipped into big-sister role. "Tell me about your night. Where did you go?"

"Egypt and I went to the club. Friday night is speed dating."

"Ugh, Geeta?" she moaned. "I begged you not to do that. Anybody worth going out with wouldn't be caught dead speed dating. Have you ever heard of anyone who said they met the perfect person on a date that lasted five minutes?"

"Yeah, well, if it makes you feel any better I didn't go into the pod. I sat at the bar and let Egypt do her thing."

"Egypt is more than a free spirit. Her issues will require time on the sofa of a good psychologist."

"She's not the only one. I might have to ask her to slide over." Geeta placed her arm over her forehead and closed her eyes to block out the events of last night.

"Why? What happened?"

"Donny was there, and so was Brooks," she said.

Cat's laughter crackled through the phone line. "You're kidding me, right? Are you dating Brooks, now?"

"No. I'm not dating either one of them, which makes it that much weirder. But that's not the worst part of the evening. If I didn't have to come to your party I could avoid an unpleasant discussion a little longer."

"Since I'm pregnant I need help getting stuff done. My stomach is always in the way. Please come. You know I like having my sister here. You can tell me all about your adventure."

Cat knew how to use her pregnancy to get everyone to follow her rules. For the next few months it was easier to let her have her way than to argue with her.

Geeta sighed. "Okay. I have some icky business I need to take care of anyway." She disconnected the call and stood. Before she could make it upstairs, Egypt walked in.

Well, look what the cat dragged in," she said.

Egypt wore the same dress she had on last night, but her once-beautiful coiffed hair was a tangled mess and she carried her heels on two fingers.

Egypt put her hand up. "Don't go there. I just need to go to bed. I've got a hangover."

"I hope that's all you've got."

Egypt flipped the finger and trudged up stairs. "You're one to talk. I saw you cozying up to your ex."

"You shouldn't have told him we'd be there. Donny is the last person I need to spend time with."

"The way you've been acting I thought you could use a friend. What could be the harm? You're alone because you are too picky. Donny is good looking, he likes you and he's got money."

Geeta massaged her forehead. "He also has a criminal record and a shady background. You don't get it. In the future, please don't tell Donny anything about me."

Egypt shrugged her shoulders before continuing up the stairs. "Sure. No problem. Wake me for dinner and not a minute sooner."

"I'm on my way to Cat's. You're on your own, today." Geeta looked down at her jeans and blouse. Before grabbing her keys. "I hope the guy you spent the night with was worth it."

"I haven't decided yet." Egypt yelled down to her.

Geeta closed and locked the door, before turning around. The moment she laid eyes on the luxury car with dark windows parked in front of her townhouse her arms started to itch. Donny eased out of the car. His face was as tight as a mask.

"So you gonna dis me like that?" He threw his arms up, which meant he wasn't going to be reasonable. Instead of the gentleman she'd seen last night, today he wore faded jeans, a big army green sweatshirt that was torn at the neck. His thick work boots were untied. "You sent your fake-ass boyfriend to step to me?"

She squared her shoulders, trying to ignore his bullying tactic. "I told you as soon as you got out we were over. I don't know why you're stalking me. Go find some hoochi-momma that will put up with your antics. I am not the one."

He crossed the small lawn and stopped in front of her, standing much too close, blocking her path. "You can't dismiss me. I'll tell you when we're done." His nostrils flared, but he fingered the collar of her blouse with a tenderness she hadn't expected. The smell of liquor on his breath overpowered her.

She didn't know this Donny. This man was a thug. The Donny she wanted to remember was the sweet guy who acted a bit goofy on dates and fought over who'd hold the popcorn during the movie. She inched away from him. His sweatshirt lifted, exposing his flat stomach and the shiny black handle of a gun. The panic in her stomach rose up, almost strangling her. She couldn't avert her eyes from the cold steel.

"It's over, Donny." Her voice was a whisper. She inched backwards.

"You're my woman for my trial." He pushed his face closer, his whisker, looked stiff and dull.

249

"Find someone else." She pointed her key fob at the car and released the lock.

"It doesn't work that way, baby. I picked you. So it's going to be you." Donny spoke with that cocky assurance people used to throw others off track. He grabbed her arm.

"Let me go. I'm not a piece of property." She tried to wrench away, but his grip was too tight.

"You are if I say you are." He jerked her closer.

Her heart pounded so hard it was difficult to breathe. Now she understood how Cat felt when Natalie started stalking her. She pressed the alarm button on the key fob. The flashing lights and blaring horn were enough for him to release her with a shove.

The window in his car slid down. "Come on, Donny. We gotta ride. Something's up."

Geeta didn't recognize the face in the passenger seat. Nor did she want to. Getting away from Donny was the only thought she could hold.

She tried to pull away again. "I've got to go."

This time he released her with a slight shove. He backed towards his car without hiding the exposed weapon.

She settled behind the wheel of her car and started the engine. Her breathing came in short spurts. Without lingering she backed out of the driveway, making sure to head in the opposite direction of Donny's black sedan.

Her heartbeat didn't return to normal until she was near Cat's condo. Donny's menacing demeanor used to be thrilling, watching him get his way. But now that she was on the receiving end she wasn't enthralled. This Donny scared her. And when did he start carrying a gun? She took several short shallow breaths to slow her heart rate.

This morning when she woke up, the static in the air indicated the day was charged with negative energy. Which meant the odds of running into Brooks were pretty good, and the outcome with him wouldn't go well. At least he didn't carry a gun. He probably didn't even run with scissors. She needed to apologize. There was no way the two of them could coexist in such a small circle of friends, until she asked for forgiveness and then she could return to the safety of her bedroom and lick her disappointment like a cat.

One day she'd stop digging holes that required stepladders to get out of. What was it about Brooks, anyway? He was always showing up, always in her thoughts. She could have used his do-good attitude in the yard a few moments ago. But he wasn't her type. She couldn't count on him saving her every time Donny showed up. It wasn't fair to him. Donny was her problem and she had to find a way to deal with him.

At the stoplight, she dropped her head to the steering wheel. The idea of staying in her room until she got beyond the dark cloud hovering over her head was beginning to seem like a good idea. During half time, she'd find a reason to excuse herself. How bad could it be?

She pulled into the condo garage. After turning off the car she tapped her fingers against the dash. A glimpse of her image in the rear-view mirror showed her ponytail had come loose. She gathered her hair and stuck out her tongue. Pain is not a good thing for anyone. If she didn't get her life together, no one would do the job for her.

She hopped out of the car and made her way upstairs. By the time she reached the door, she wasn't shaking and she was able to breathe like a normal person. At least Brooks was easy to talk to. As soon as she explained her behavior to him, he'd understand.

"Cat, I'm here." She let herself into the spacious condo.

Her sister waddled toward her from the kitchen with her hands positioned at her waist.

"Every time I see you, your stomach gets bigger and bigger. I don't know how you are going to make it to the ninth month." Geeta kissed her sister's cheek.

"Shut up. The doctor's going to test me tomorrow."

"For what? To see if you're having triplets?" She squeezed her sister's shoulders.

Cat put her hands up, halting the conversation. "Let's get the food set up. We can talk about babies later. Yani and Phoebe are already here." She led Geeta into the kitchen.

Phoebe and Yani were Cat's best friends since grade school. She couldn't remember a time when the three of them weren't together. She needed girlfriends like them. She had no history with Egypt. They'd only known each other a few years. They'd hardly interacted at all, until she needed help paying the rent on Cat's townhouse.

Geeta took the seat at the counter next to Yani. Phoebe stirred something over the stove.

"Make the dip, please." Cat pushed a bowl and a jar of mayonnaise at her.

"So who's attending this shindig?" Geeta stirred the vegetable soup package into the bowl.

"Jeremy invited all the guys on the team. They had to pick up some award for the ball team then they're heading straight over here," Yani replied.

"Drew will be here late. He's coming straight from the airport." Phoebe dropped the utensil on the spoon-rest. "Geeta, how you been?"

Geeta knew Cat told her friends everything, so the probably knew about the whole embarrassing incident when Donny was arrested. Hopefully, she left out the part when she peed herself. Telling Cat about Donny's latest visit would only upset her. Maybe later.

She stirred faster. "I'm sure Cat keeps you all abreast of my activity. The only meaningful thing I've done lately is landed a new national account."

"That's wonderful, Geeta." Cat put her hands on her large belly and rubbed her stomach like a genie bottle. "I hear Jeremy's basketball team is thinking about taking out an ad in your paper, too."

"I guess I ought to thank you for sending Brooks my way." Geeta pushed the bowl away. "Is he coming, today?"

"Of course. Why?"

Geeta looked around the room without meeting their eyes. "I want to see him, but I was hoping to put it off for as long as I could."

Cat pulled the dip bowl closer to finish stirring. "What did you do this time, Geeta?"

Her sister never came to her defense. "Maybe Jeremy's creepy friend did something to me."

By now she should have been used to defending herself to Cat. But for once she wished her sister would take her side, like she used to do when they were younger. Before Cat thought she was a major screw-up.

Yani and Phoebe snickered.

"Did *he* do something to you? He's so nice. I can't imagine he ever did anything inappropriate."

Geeta paused as her sister's words registered. "You're right. He was actually a gentleman." Explaining now, allowed her to prep for the conversation with Brooks. Cat and her friends stared at her. "Don't judge me ladies. You're all married so you can't understand a single girl's desperation."

"Drew and I aren't married, yet." Yani commented, her voice a little sad. "Anyway, we've all been there but we didn't commit any crimes against humanity."

"Well, I did," Cat admitted. "Why don't you just tell us what happened, Geeta?" Cat had no patience now that she was pregnant.

Geeta recanted the club incident for them. The whole time Cat's mouth hung open.

"And you're going to face him today? Here?" Yani asked. "This should be fun to watch."

Geeta swung her foot. "I'm still going through some stuff. I thought I wanted to have sex with Donny, but I changed my mind. I'm entitled to do that, aren't I? Haven't you ever changed your minds?"

"Ugh, Geeta, it's disgusting you even considered having sex with that sleaze bag."

"Yeah, I get it, Cat. The whole idea is appalling to me, now. But last night..." Phoebe shook her head and turned back to the stove.

253

"This is going to be fun," Yani said. "I think the guys just got here."

"Great." Cat pushed her tank size belly out of the chair. "Remember this is my gathering, don't put on a show."

Geeta stayed behind as they all exited. She exhaled long and slow from her mouth. "Put on your big girl panties and get out there," she muttered before climbing off the stool.

Geeta hung to the edge of the room, allowing all the greetings and kissing to take pace. Brooks stood near the door, his cell phone glued to his ear. He didn't look angry. Whoever was on the other end of the call held his attention. He paced in a tight circle.

He wasn't as tall as his friends, but he was several inches taller than her. Even from her distance the twinkle in his eyes was prevalent. He seemed to be smiling even though his lips hadn't moved.

When he caught sight of her he lifted his chin and ended the call. Without breaking stride he crossed the room to stand over her. She'd never seen him angry before, but the goose bumps on her arms warned her that was about to change. She braced for his outrage. After asking for a favor and sneaking out she deserved whatever verbal assault he delivered. Why she acted so flaky was a question her sister often posed to her, too.

"I thought you'd be here." His deep voice held no humor.

"About last night, I should try to explain," she began. "I owe you an apology, but if I didn't get out of there I was going to have a full-fledged meltdown. I was getting ready to do a stupid thing and I have enough of them under my belt already."

"So I saved you from humiliation?"

Was he making fun of her? There was a hint of laughter in his question, any other man would have been yelling.

"Yes. That's it exactly. Leaving the club with Donny would have been an awful mistake. I'm trying to get my life together, which means no more stupid incidents." The urge to touch him overwhelmed her, but she kept her hands at her sides.

"Don't you think leaving me to handle your little mess was not a wise decision?"

She twisted her hands. "Yes. I shouldn't have gotten you involved at all, but I needed to bolt. Was he terribly upset?"

"No. By the time I realized you were gone and went back inside he was leaving with someone else. The schmuck deserved to hear the news from you. He was so angry I thought I was going to have to deck him."

She balanced her shoulders and mustered a bad girl attitude. If another person told her how to behave or what to say she swore to give it right back two times heavier.

"Brooks, I'm trying to apologize."

"You're not very good at it." He shifted his weight, modifying the way the sunlight streaming through the window hit his face. His strong chin jutted out. He was teasing her.

"I admit I've got some ugly stuff with me. But you could have said no."

He gave her a slow nod. Not in agreement, he was evaluating her. Comparing her to someone better. Maybe the person on the phone who made him smile without moving his lips.

"Look buddy, you must have some stuff of your own. Why else are you always wearing those stiff dress shirts? Who wears them to watch a football game?" She grabbed the tip of his starched collar.

"What does that mean?" He looked down. "I'd never insult you even though every time I see you, you're in a pair of jeans so tight your crotch must gasp for air…or dresses so snug you can't walk."

She huffed, "I'm stylish."

"You're trying too hard, honey. Maybe if your britches weren't so tight you wouldn't get into situations you couldn't get out of."

She pointed a finger at him and stepped close enough for him to feel her anger. "I said I was sorry. What? Did you expect me to wait around so you could take me home and screw me?"

Cat glared at them, putting her finger to her mouth to quiet the ruckus. Since she'd become pregnant she gave up cussing. She swore the baby could hear everything.

Geeta looked around the room. These were her sister's friends. Everyone was stiff and way too uptight. Her skin prickled to get out of the confined space.

"Maybe, this is a conversation we should have in private." He placed his hand on her elbow and steered her into the kitchen.

If one more person manhandled her today she would lose it.

The whole conversation wasn't going the way she'd planned it in her head. Why was Brooks always pushing his way under her skin? She wanted to pull her arm away from his grasp, but instead of making a scene she hurried out of the room.

Once they were alone in the kitchen she placed her hands on her hips. "I've said all I need to. I think you get my point."

He positioned his elbows on the granite counter putting him at eye level with her. His eyes were the perfect shade of green, sparkling like sea glass.

"Now I get to have my say. I don't know what kind of guys you usually go out with, but judging from Donny, don't put me in the same category. The only thing I intended to do last night was get you home. Don't be so full of yourself to think every man with a dick wants to get in your pants."

She swallowed her anger, unsure of how to respond. She glared at him for several moments. "Well, I hope you feel better now that you got that off your chest."

He straightened up as if his point had been made. "One other thing." His smile returned. "I'm not saying I don't want to get in your pants, I just had no intention of trying last night."

He left her standing at the counter. Her brain tried to absorb his words. She wanted something witty to snap back at him, but nothing came to mind.

At her sister's wedding he'd been so nice, maybe too nice. But today he seemed like a different person. Her heart fluttered against her chest. His comment should have rolled off of her like water, but she liked the idea of him in her pants, and not only because she was horny. She rested her hip against the counter and closed her eyes. The best thing to do was to steer clear of Brooks. He wasn't her type, forcing a square peg into a round hole was a prescription for heartache.

"Are you okay?" Cat stuck her head in the kitchen. "Is he upset about last night?"

"Not as much as I thought he would be. But he got a few digs in anyway."

Cat rubbed Geeta's arm. She was always rubbing something, now. Maybe rubbing had become a craving for her.

"The game is getting ready to start, aren't you coming out?"

"Cat, what do you know about Brooks?"

"Why? Are you interested in him?" Cat came closer, her face scrunched with worry. "He's a nice guy. I think you two would be a cute couple."

"I'm just curious. Besides, aren't you supposed to be looking out for your younger sister?" Geeta tried to remain nonchalant.

"You have a heart of gold and after what Donny did to you, I can understand why you chew through men. But you're going to be okay. Don't screw over Jeremy's friend. It will make for some uncomfortable family gatherings. "I think he's the same age as Jeremy. Thirty-two, thirty-three, maybe?"

"Did you ever find out what he does for a living?"

"No. Why?"

"I just wanted to know. Don't you think it's odd that we don't have any idea? We know Cory is a sneaker salesman. We know Drew owns his own contracting and real estate business, but Brooks…we don't have a clue. Do you think he could be doing something illegal?"

"Go ask him, if it means that much to you. But sweetheart, don't judge everyone by Donny's yardstick. You've had a row of bad luck, but you're a good person. You'll find your happiness." The gentleness in Cat's voice was enough to make Geeta feel better.

Geeta shook her head. "No. I'm not asking him. Whatever he does for a living doesn't matter to me."

"All I know is that he's seems like a good guy. Come back in the great room and watch the game." Without waiting for a reply Cat spun around and headed back into the huge game room.

Cat threw around advice like it was manna from heaven. If giving Brooks an opportunity were as easy as she made it sound, Geeta would have done it by now. He had the qualities any woman with a sound mind would want, but his meticulous manner was intimidating. She couldn't live up to his expectations. She never bothered ironing her jeans, and Brooks looked like he didn't step outside the door until his creases were razor sharp.

Geeta trailed behind her sister. Everyone gathered around the sixty-two inch television looked up when they entered the room. The only open seat was beside Jeremy and Cat plopped in it.

Geeta pivoted around to grab one of the straight back chairs from the dining table.

"Here, Geeta, you can sit next to me." Brooks slid over making enough room for her on the love seat.

If she didn't already feel like an idiot for swearing in front of everyone, she sure did now. Instead of objecting she parked her butt on the corner of the sofa, as far away from him as possible. Pretending the game was the most interesting thing going on she dropped her chin in her palm and stared at the play-by-play action. All she needed to do was sit still for one quarter, then she could remember she needed to go home and feed her non-existent cat.

"You can get comfortable. I won't bite you," Brooks said.

"If it would get that bug out of your ass, I wish you would," she said without turning to look at him.

"I'm fine, doll. I said what I had to say and let it go. Are you feeling guilty?"

"No. So I guess we are all square now."

Why she let Brooks rile her was a puzzle. The rare feel of dating anxiety churning in her stomach only added to her discomfort. Next to him her emotions blurred into fuzzy lines and colors. Watching the game should have been easy, but every player could have been the same. For once she didn't care what happened on the field. She shifted in her seat. The Eagles took position on the line of scrimmage. If she focused on cheering for a win Brooks might fade into the background. If she focused on her work, she wouldn't have time to think about how loneliness visited her each night. If she focused, really focused, maybe she'd find something worth holding onto. Something like what Cat and Jeremy shared.

####

Brooks watched Geeta nibble her thumbnail. She contained her movement, ensuring she didn't touch him. The smooth milk chocolate skin along her jaw line looked lickable sweet. She'd managed to resist his charm, which only made him more determined.

He'd gotten under her skin. It was obvious from the way she held her back straight and stared at the television. If he wanted to be a gentleman he could move a little to the left and let her have more room on the seat, but watching her fake interest in the game was much more fun.

Right now he had her exactly where he wanted. She felt guilty about leaving him in the club. If that gave him an inroad, then he'd use it. Even her little crack about his attire didn't matter. The secret he was keeping was as bad as what she'd done last night. He detested lying to her, but there

259

didn't seem to be any other way. At least not right now. In a few weeks he could tell her everything. When Donny was off the streets for a nice long time.

"Can I get you something to drink, Geeta?" He stepped over her to make his way to the bar.

She looked up, met his eyes, but didn't reply.

"I'm not going to poison you or anything. I only asked if you want something to drink. This is me being nice."

The expression on her face changed. Relaxed. The tightness around her mouth disappeared. It was enough for now.

"Okay, please. I'll take a vodka and juice."

"You'll be here when I come back, won't you? I mean if you plan to make a mad dash for the door, save me the trouble." He looked over his shoulder.

"Very funny." She faked a laugh.

From across the room Brooks stared at Geeta while plopping ice into the glass. She glanced up, locking eyes with him. Even though she tried to portray a tough exterior, she looked like a wounded bird, one that needed to be held tight and nurtured. He could be that for her.

He returned and handed her the glass. "Oh, look, you're still here."

"Your joke wasn't funny when you first said it, and it's still not." She took a quick sip without looking up at him.

"Is everything okay over there?" Jeremy yelled from the comfort of his place on the sofa.

Brooks leaned back on the love seat. "I'm fine, man."

Geeta was a beautiful woman. Her hair was gathered in a loose ponytail at the nape of her neck. The dark brown wavy tresses shone like varnish. She could be his chocolate princess. If only she'd relax enough to trust him.

The time to tell her about their first encounter had passed. Backing up now to explain the situation would sound clumsy. There was a chance she'd never even believe him. He skipped over the painful thought, for now.

She finished her drink, and stood up. "I've got to be going," she announced to everyone in the room. "There are some things I need to take care of before Monday. I promised to get my article submitted before the end of the weekend."

"Are you sure? You haven't been here long." Cat tried to push off the sofa.

"Don't get up. I'll call you tonight," Geeta leaned down to kiss her, giving him the perfect view of her round butt.

There was no way he'd let her get away today without at least trying again. He followed her into the kitchen and watched as she gathered her things.

"I think we need to start over again." He positioned his shoulder in the doorway to keep her from walking out.

She exhaled so loud he could hear the air leaving her body.

"Brooks, it's like you said, you don't hold grudges. But I do. And right now I have a whole stockpile of them I'm trying to get over. I shouldn't have gotten you caught up in my mess. I told you to stay clear of me. Now you see what I'm capable of." She pushed the purse onto her shoulder and tried to maneuver past him.

"Let me take you out tomorrow night?" He blocked her exit.

She looked him over, from head to toe. When her gaze came back to his face she studied his eyes.

"I'm not joking," he said.

"Brooks, what do you want from me? Can't you see I'm coming from a broken place right now? I've done some real dumb stuff with my life and I'm trying to get it together."

"I'm not asking you for anything, Geeta. And I don't want anything from you, other than some of your time."

"Is this about last night?"

"I don't want a pity date. If you're only going to say yes to ease your conscience about what happened in the club, then say no." He stepped aside, opening the entrance for her. "But if you want to go out and have some fun, then that's what we'll do."

"This is only a date, right?"

"Just a date. Nothing more."

Several moments ticked by without her blinking.

"I'm only asking you out, not for your hand in marriage. How hard can it be to make a decision? You ragged on me about being out of style, but now you're acting like an indecisive old lady."

"Okay." She nodded. "How about tomorrow evening. We can do something simple, like dinner or a movie."

"Since I'm asking, I'm planning. I'll pick you up at seven."

Chapter Six

Geeta glanced at the bed covered in discarded outfits. Almost everything she owned was tight or snug or short or all three. Tonight required something simple, understated, and bland. The only problem was she didn't own those types of clothes. Which exemplified the fact that she was going out with the wrong guy.

She should have asked some questions about what he had planned. She rubbed her chin and examined the pencil skirt and lace top. Judging from Brooks' conservative nature, they probably were going to the opera or even more boring a symphony. She yawned.

At least Donny hadn't called or surprised her with another visit. She expected him to blow up her phone after their discussion yesterday, but all was quiet. Maybe he'd gotten the message. Even before his incarceration, she knew their relationship was doomed. But somehow it seemed easier to go out with the man in front of her instead of taking the time to unearth Mr. Right. Which explained why she said yes to Brooks. He was the polar opposite of Donny. What she needed was a man with Donny's edge but without his propensity for criminal activity. Even if she wanted to tone her life down a bit, she wasn't ready to put away her tight jeans and put on the ugly sweater.

She unzipped the pencil skirt, letting it drop to her ankles, and pulled the lace top over her head. She found a red peplum dress that was halfway between hoochie-momma and librarian. A red pair of platform heels made the outfit pop to her taste.

"So what are you up to tonight?" Egypt flopped on the bed next to the pile of clothes. "I'm going to the club tonight, wanna come?"

"I have a date." Geeta examined her reflection in the door mirror.

"Who is the lucky guy?"

"Brooks."

263

"He wore you down, didn't he? You've got to love a man with tenacity."

"I'm not even sure why I agreed. There's something about him that I like." She placed her hands on her hips. "But I don't know what it is."

"Maybe he won't show up dressed like a preacher tonight." Egypt laughed. "He looks like he's got money. If you play your cards right, you can order the most expensive meal and if you're real lucky you could get those designer shoes you've been wanting."

"I'm not like you. I don't want anything from him. He might be happier dating a church lady or a kindergarten teacher."

"Sounds like it's going to be a long night. Should I break open a bottle of wine to help you take the edge off before you go?" Egypt bounced on the bed.

"No, if Brooks thinks I've been drinking before the date he might freak out." She sat on the bed next to Egypt. "So, you never told me what happened to you in the club. Where did you disappear to?"

Egypt lay on the bed and hugged her knees to her chest. "His name is Jay. We really hit it off."

"How did you get beyond the gold teeth?"

Egypt grinned. "The way I figure, any man who can afford to put gold in his mouth can put gold on my finger." She held her left hand up and flexed her empty ring finger.

"Does that mean you ended up at his place?"

"Noooo. I didn't go to his house. Nor did I have sex with him. I'm sticking to our pact. We went to a little diner and had apple pie."

"Sure you did. You must think I get up in the morning and screw my head on like Frankenstein. If you left that club, you had sex."

"I did not. But we're going out again tonight. I'm not sure how much longer I can hold out. Why I let you talk me into such a silly pledge is beyond me. What is abstinence supposed to prove, anyway?"

Geeta fell back next to her. "According to Cat, as soon as you mix sex into a relationship everything gets all muddled. You stop thinking with your head and start listening to your loins. The pledge is not supposed to be easy, but it's supposed to be worth it."

"Your sister is wonderful, but she has too many rules to live by. Who cares about all that stuff and who can remember all those rules?"

"Cat doesn't let me forget." She sighed.

"You better not sleep with Brooks tonight, either."

Geeta shoved her. "Are you kidding me? Sleep with Brooks? You're joking, right?"

"No, it's been a long time since we took that pledge. God knows you must be horny. You might slip up."

"Not with him I won't. One date and I'm out."

Egypt jumped off the bed and stood in the doorway. "Good luck tonight. Are you sure you don't want to ditch Brooks and come out with me? If we decide to ignore Cat's golden rule, we can take our secret to our grave."

"I stiffed him once. I can't stand him up again. Even I can't be that flaky." Geeta sat up. All she needed to do was get through the night. How hard could a simple date be? If he didn't take her to a symphony she could fake her way through the evening, pay her debt and move on. If he chose a symphony, she'd be asleep in five minutes. This was going to be a breeze. She'd done worse.

"I think your date is here," Egypt called to her from the bedroom down the hall. "You'll have to get it. I've got to get dressed to meet Jay."

"Yeah, it's probably Brooks. Leave it to him to arrive early," she yelled before traipsing down the stairs. After tugging her dress down over her hips she opened the door. Brooks stood on the small porch. She couldn't help but notice how handsome he looked. Her body tingled in that familiar way when sex was on the horizon. "Brooks...what...?"

He stepped inside. "You were expecting someone else?"

He had on a pair of well-worn jeans, a black leather jacket, and a pair of scuffed brown boots. Instead of the conservative beau he resembled a regular guy with an extra douse of good looking. The lust hugging her libido, squeezed tighter.

"I was expecting the starched shirt and khaki pants. I hardly recognize you in these clothes. Where are we going tonight, and what…?"

He snapped off his black leather fingerless gloves. "Wow, you look fantastic tonight. A big change from the outfit you had on Friday night. But unfortunately you'd better change. Put on a pair of pants and flat shoes. Boots if you have them, but not the fancy kind. I hope you have a pair that you wear when you want to get something done." Brooks said with a hint of laughter.

"Oh, you're granting me permission to put on my skintight jeans? Where are we going?" she asked.

"You can put on any kind of jeans you want. They can be baggy jeans or a second skin, but that pretty little dress isn't going to work. I'll tell you where we're going after you change. Go. Hurry up." He waved her away.

She charged half way up the stairs before stopping to look at him again. "Is this about my statement regarding what you had on yesterday?"

He smirked. "You better hurry up." His green eyes danced, making her excited about the date. The idea of a surprise made her flustered like a child.

Back in her bedroom she shucked the dress and heels, throwing them onto the pile on the bed. She pulled a pair of jeans and a cotton hoodie off the closet shelf. She wiggled into the pants and shoved her feet into a pair of riding boots. Before charging back downstairs she snatched a short leather jacket from the closet.

With his back to her, facing the entry door he whispered in his cell phone. She stopped, waiting for him to finish the call. He had a life she knew nothing about and part of it was handled at the other end of the phone.

She cleared her throat, loud enough to announce her presence.

"Gotta go, bye." He ended the call and faced her. "Sorry. That was work."

"Yeah, I heard those excuses before. Let me say this prior to us crossing the threshold on what is supposed to be our date. If you're involved in illegal activity, tell me now. I don't want anything to do with it. I'm not flying close to the sun, again. And I will snitch you out." She pointed her index finger at him.

"Why would you think I'm doing something illegal?" he asked with amusement.

"Donny was always whispering into his phone and until the police dragged his ass from under our bed I had no idea. After an incident like that a girl learns to pay attention. So you can walk out now, no harm, no foul. But if you pretend to be something you're not and I find out then I'll call the authorities on you."

"Good to know you're such an upstanding American citizen. I have nothing to reveal. I'm on the right side of the law. You can relax."

She descended the remaining stairs. "Don't say you weren't warned."

He zipped her leather jacket, and then zipped his. "Are we ready to go now?"

"Are you going to tell me what you have planned for tonight?" she asked.

"We're taking a ride." He opened the front door for her.

In the driveway behind her car, gleaming in the night like a dragon, sat a massive black motorcycle. The streetlight beamed off the chrome finishes, making them sparkle. The square image she had of him vanished in a poof. Her stomach went into a free-fall. She gazed at him and then back at the bike. Making the link between him and the huge bike wouldn't materialize.

She pulled up short behind him. "Is this you?" She pointed at the machine.

"It is."

"Did you buy it today for our date?"

He turned to face her, mischief danced at the corner of his mouth. "You're kidding me right? You think I went out this morning and dropped eighteen thousand to impress you?"

"No, I don't think you did. But I never...you don't seem like the kind of guy who drives a motorcycle. I was expecting a black four-door sedan. The type police officers drive," she said without moving. The halo above his head started to disappear. Maybe he wasn't Mr. Goody-Two-Shoes.

He walked back to stand in front of her. "I'm keeping count and, this is the second time you've tried to put me in a box where I don't fit."

"And whose fault is that?" she demanded.

"Yours. You put all men in the same basket, and you shouldn't."

He was right but she couldn't tell him that. After years of dating, there hadn't been much difference in the men she'd come across. A few were better than others, but in the end the relationships always fell apart. Sometimes she led the charge, most times she was run over by it.

She tightened her fingers into a fist, preparing for a monologue on why she was wrong for judging him. If he didn't want people to think he was in line for the priesthood he needed to stop acting so churchy.

"You don't expect me to get on that thing, do you?" She inched away from him.

"It's the only way we'll get to where we're going. You said yes to the date, so you have to ride." He walked to the bike, lifted a helmet off the back and handed it to her. Then he unsnapped a second helmet and positioned it on his head.

"Are you serious?" Her voice was barely a whisper. "I've never ridden on the back of one. Are you trying to get even with me or something? Besides my hair will get all messy and I styled it special for tonight."

"I'm glad you went through all that trouble. You look beautiful." He kissed her cheek before reaching for her hand and pulling her closer, as if taking small steps would ease her anxiety.

He rubbed the seat like he was taming a lion. Seeing him next to the beastly machine shaded him a different color.

"How long have you been driving this thing? How do I know you won't crash?"

"I've never laid a bike down. I'll be extra careful tonight. Now come on. Or we'll be late."

"Don't you have a car like regular people?"

"I do, but this is more fun. Loosen up a bit. You can trust me." He swung his leg over the machine and patted the seat behind him. "Hop on and hold me around the waist."

She hesitated and looked back at the house. There was still time to cancel the date. Anything was better than ending up in an emergency room or in the morgue.

"Come on. You aren't chicken, are you?"

She narrowed her gaze on him. He was taunting her and seemed to be enjoying making her uncomfortable. Instead of releasing the blur of obscenities waiting on her tongue, she mounted the back. The seat was wider than she anticipated. She had to spread her legs to fit behind him.

"Keep your feet right here." He pointed to a metal peg. "And keep your arms tight around my waist."

"Suppose I need you to stop or I have an emergency?" she asked.

"You mean like a bathroom emergency?"

"Yeah, maybe, or any kind." She adjusted her butt on the seat.

"Then squeeze me tighter. Or lean in real close and run your tongue against my neck."

She couldn't see his mouth but he sounded like he was laughing.

"You wish," she retorted.

A quick jerk on the crank and the machine thundered to life. The deafening sound was startling. Her heart tried to outpace the roar. She intertwined her fingers just to make sure

269

she stayed in place. The vibration between her legs only added to the angst.

He started out slow, keeping a lot of distance between the bike and the cars. The moment they merged onto the Vine Street Expressway, he picked up speed. The crisp air cut through the leather jacket. She eased closer to him, hoping to keep warm. Every time a car raced by her stomach flopped to the opposite side. Her inner body played ping-pong, anxiety bounced from one organ to another. She tried to relax when they crossed the Walt Whitman Bridge. The idea that they'd only spend a couple of hours together before she'd be back home in front of her computer slipped away when he paid the first toll on the Jersey Turnpike.

The expert way he maneuvered around a slow moving car in the right lane eased her heartbeat. Just to be sure she tried to increase her pressure around his mid-section. She held him so tight he should have demanded she loosen her grip, but he never said a word.

She buried her head in Brooks' back, afraid to see where they were going and afraid not to look in case he ran into something. Through a tiny squint she saw everything in one long colorful blur.

His muscles flexed with every turn. He leaned back into her chest, giving passerby the impression they were long-time lovers. The intimate position on the bike was like snuggling. Being this close to him had never entered her imagination when she considered the date. It was kind of nice having her arms wrapped around him. Holding on at what seemed like warp speed.

Maybe he was testing her. The super conservative, clean shaven man sitting between her legs couldn't be the same man maneuvering this dangerous machine with the grace of a ballerina performing Swan Lake. Brooks had his own kind of charm. His rock solid steadiness was calming. No matter how much she threw at him he simply smiled and stepped around her mess.

By the time he slowed to a stop, her arms and eyes ached from being clenched for so long. She didn't take a full breath until he pulled into a parking slot between two other bikes that were as big as his. The small bar didn't look like it would fit her style. The hip-hop music drifting through the wooden doors was out of place in this desolate area. He hopped off like the hour-long ride was no big deal. After helping her down she couldn't straighten up.

"Where are we?" she pressed her thumbs into her spine.

"Jersey. How did you not know that?" He helped her remove the helmet.

"I had my eyes closed most of the time. I know we're in Jersey, but where and why? I must have bugs in my teeth and my body is one big knot. Look at my fingers." She held out her hands to him. Her fingers were gnarled and cold.

He removed his gloves and massaged her fingers, one at a time. Slowly at first before picking up the tempo, with so much vigor she laughed. His hands were warm and firm.

The gentle pressure he applied released the kinks in her fingers. Gazing in her eyes, he worked his way to her elbows, heating her entire body each inch of the way.

"Let's go inside. You're cold."

She stopped him. "Brooks, I'm used to going to clubs where you have to dress up. I've never been to one where jeans were the requirement. Maybe this isn't my scene. I know you've gone through a lot to get us here, but a honky-tonk bar...is..."

"You can't back out now, Princess. Give it a try."

"Are you trying to prove something? I was expecting the symphony or the opera, but not this."

"Oh, I've lots of things to prove to you." He opened the door for her.

"Have it your way," she acquiesced.

The rustic interior was crammed with dark wooden tables and clusters of people. The bar could have easily fit into a western movie. Brooks looked quite at home in the crowd of casually dressed men. Her jeans and jacket helped her to fit in, too.

271

He found a small-scarred table in the center of the room. There was nothing plush about the bar. The hardwood floor was worn smooth in several places. A server arrived at Brooks' side almost instantly. "You want the usual?" She began scribbling before he responded.

"Yeah, and bring the same thing for my date."

When the waitress walked away, Geeta asked. "Usual? You come here often?"

"Only when I want to relax or need a change in scenery."

"What are we drinking?"

"Beer. They make some special blends here. There's one dark brew I think you might like."

She settled back into the hard chair, wishing for the soft leather seat of the motorcycle. The way Brooks took charge at just the right times reminded her of her father. "What makes you think I'd like it?"

He leaned across the table. "Because you have good taste. You agreed to come out with me, didn't you?"

####

The ride to the shore was harder than he'd expected. Every time Geeta squirmed on the bike seat his body responded, their bodies already in sync like lovers. Paying attention to the road was difficult with a boner. If she had any idea of the impact she was making on him, she'd demand to go back home. Who could blame her, she was afraid of something.

At Jeremy's wedding he'd misjudged her. Back then she seemed like a runaway looking to experience an exotic new flavor. Getting under her frilly dress had occupied his thoughts that day. Now that he knew her better, he wanted so much more. To protect her, love her, build a life with her.

Someone had hurt her, and turned her world around. His bet was Donny. The two-bit-punk was a borderline psychopath. His behavior was about as unpredictable as a grenade. She needed a hero. He was ready for the job.

The server returned with two tall ice-cold glasses, placed them on the table and hurried away. Geeta pushed her fingers through the handle on the mug and took a big swallow.

"Was that to calm your nerves?" he asked.

"Yes. And I was thirsty, too," she said before taking another smaller sip.

A woman who likes beer had great potential. He picked up his glass and allowed the cool liquid to saturate his mouth before swallowing.

"This is a date. Dance with me." Without waiting for her to answer he pulled her to the floor. The moment she settled into his arms, the whole evening made sense. No matter how much she objected, they made a perfect match. All he had to do was be more convincing.

Her body felt stiff in his arms, she was trying not to get too close. He pulled her into his chest. One hand rested just above her hips, the other caressed her neck. She was softer than he'd imagined.

"Are you playing with my hair?" she asked.

"Yes. It smells good. You got a problem with that?"

Instead of responding she turned her head and rested it on his shoulder. Until she was ready to accept what was happening between them, he'd always have that beautiful image of her delicate, naked body the morning they busted Donny. Her wide eyes couldn't hide her vulnerability then, and they couldn't now.

"So tell me why you're so resistant. What is it about me you don't like?"

She didn't respond. The chorus on the song finished and the band started another ballad before she pulled away enough for him to see her face.

"I don't understand why you're interested in me. Are you the savior of lost souls?"

"Who hasn't made some bad choices in their lifetime? If I sat down to add all mine up, you might go running in the opposite direction, too. Besides, there is something about you that I find so irresistible I couldn't stay away even if you flew on a broom."

She studied his face. A twinkle in his eyes bounced with the beat of the music. "Not only are you an enigma, you're a sweet talking enigma. I've been sweet talked by the best and usually I'm out of my panties during the first chorus. But not anymore, so if that's your strategy you're not going to be happy by the end of the night. I glued my panties in place just to be on the safe side."

He spun her around and gathered her in his arms, again. "I'm in no hurry and when I get too horny, I've got the perfect solvent for glue."

"You're wasting your time," she sang in his ear. Her words should have turned him off. Instead she could have been stroking his libido with her tongue.

"I never waste, my time. You'll see. I want more than to get you in bed. I think we can have something special once you let your guard down." He planted a kiss on her cheek and led her back to the table.

Somewhere between their dance and several songs, Geeta stopped looking around the room like she wanted to make a break from the yard. The crazy glint in her eyes disappeared, too.

He rapped his fingers on the table in tune with the beat. "Would you like another drink?"

"Only if you'll have one with me."

"I never have more than one when I'm riding the bike. And since I've got a nervous passenger tonight, I need to be extra careful. Besides, this is only a pit stop. We've got one more place to go."

She gave him an appreciative smile. "Okay, I'm game. Where are we going? I might get back on the bike."

"I have a little place not far from here. We're having dinner there."

She nodded and turned her attention back to the dance floor. How often do you come to the shore?"

"Not as much as I'd like. But, I figured your backside might need a break, and this is the perfect place to stop."

She patted her butt. The solid sound could be heard over the thumping of the music.

"Are you ready to ride?"

She sat up straighter. "Let's do it."

Outside, she sighed before climbing back on the bike. "You know we could have gone to a movie, like normal people."

"Oh, but haven't you realized, there's not a lot of normal in me?" He cupped her chin before settling her helmet on her head and fastening her strap.

"I'm starting to notice a lot of things about you I didn't know." This time she wrapped her arms around him without hesitating.

Chapter Seven

The off-season drive along Atlantic Boulevard was easier than the first leg of the trip. This time Geeta opened her eyes, making the adventure seem more like an extended roller coaster ride. The only thing she missed was being able to talk to him or look at him. But he felt good in her arms, like he could belong to her. If he felt this solid in his leather coat then having him totally naked could only be better.

She blinked the thought away. Thinking about him undressed would lead to trouble. She hardly knew this complex man. Everything about them said they were complete opposites. Was this another bad choice?

Even though she couldn't hear the crash of the waves on the shore, she could smell the fresh, crisp scent in the salty breeze. The moon hung low over the horizon.

What seemed like hours was really only a few minutes before he pulled off the street. The smell of saltwater stung her nose. Her legs tingled. She needed to stretch them. Riding on the back of a bike must be an acquired taste, one she'd never cultivate.

Finally, he came to a stop in front of a seafront townhouse, shut down the bike, and help her climb off. The ocean air was much cooler than in the city. She shivered.

"Now what?" she asked.

"We're going to have a real dinner. Come on, let's go in."

"Whose place is this and do they have food? I'm starved."

He grabbed her hand and led her up the walk to a simple structure that looked blue in the full moonlight.

"I know the house may not look like much, but it's mine. This is the place I come to when I need to escape reality. I've asked my people to prepare a simple meal, just for us. On the weekend I like to shed my corporate persona and relax."

"Your people? Do you have servants?"

Inside he flipped on the light.

"Yes, the pizza should be delivered as soon as I call my favorite joint. What toppings do you like?"

They settled in the kitchen. He rummaged through a drawer several seconds before pulling out a pink flyer and handed it to her.

"You mean you're feeding me pizza? I thought we'd have something a little fancier than that." She glanced at the advertisement.

"You see, I'm full of surprises. And instead of beer we're going to drink plain-old soda."

"I understand why you're single now. You're not doing a good job of wooing me."

"You've made it very clear, you're not interested. The only reason you agreed to come out with me tonight was because you stood me up in the club. So you see, you're not fooling me at all." He paused. "So what do you want, pepperoni or sausage?"

"Let's get both."

"Nice choice." He picked up the house phone and pressed one button to place the order. There was a tuft of hair in the center of his head that stuck up like menacing little boy. The urge to smooth it in place rushed her.

"Do you want cola or ginger ale?" He produced two cans and held them out.

She reached for the cola. Her hand brushed his, lingering against him, absorbing his warmth. What started out involuntary turned into something very deliberate. His hand was cold, either from the long ride or from holding the soda.

He popped the lid before handing it to her. After opening his can, he took a long sip without breaking eye contact. His eyes smiled in the most compassionate way.

Brooks reminded her of a childhood super hero. Like Superman, he slipped in and out of character as required. Her heart started bucking like a wild stallion. Whatever was happening between them was so raw she couldn't compartmentalize the emotion. Like. Love. Lust. Or just plain horniness. It could have been any one of those things...or all four. For sure he had to be better than her weekly visit with her bedside toy.

They could have been old friends enjoying the evening. She didn't have to pretend to be someone different—an intellectual, a good time girl, or miss congeniality.

"Come on. We'll wait in the great room."

She followed him out of the kitchen like a newly trained puppy, begging for treats. He stacked logs in the fireplace. The solid sound of the wood thumping against the metal grate helped relax the apprehension in her shoulders. The relationship fear haunting her disappeared, but the fear of breaking the pledge still hung over her head. Maybe there was some truth in waiting.

####

At the sliding doors she stared out into the darkness. It was impossible to see the ocean in the starless sky. From behind, her butt looked like two perfect mounds of fun. At the bar she had loosened up a little, but now in the privacy of his house, her defense shields were back in place. Nothing out that window was interesting enough to hold anyone's attention for more than a few minutes. It was the ocean, for God's sake, she'd seen it before.

"Is that where you plan to spend the whole evening?"

She spun around rubbing her arms, like she was trying to warm them.

"I wanted to enjoy the view. It's not often I get to the ocean, so I have a rule of taking it all in when I can." She strolled across the room. Her tight jeans outlined the shape of her legs.

"You can come here any time you want."

"It's not a place thing, it's a time thing." She pushed her hair behind her ears. The brilliant blaze from the flames captured her attention. "The ocean has strange powers over me. Whenever I'm near the waves all I want to do is relax be a bum. The last few months my life has been in turmoil, there was no time for anything as decadent as a trip to the beach."

"Your ex—he's the one that hurt you, right?"

Without looking away from the crackling fire, she said, "Yes. But not for the reasons you think."

"Then what?"

She faced him and nodded. "We were together about two years. Neither of which was great. It wasn't a romance, but I was trying. Donny is a drug dealer. He made his living from his stash in the closet. I should have known. I was trying so hard to make our relationship worth something I missed his one, big, glaring fault. How crazy is that?"

"Why do you blame yourself for his activity? You didn't do anything wrong."

"Oh yes I did. I ignored the obvious. My ignorance almost got me arrested." She wrung her hands. "After that, I decided to take a little time out and get my head back in the game. Cat is always telling me I need to think things through, now I know what she means."

The pizza arrived. Without any fanfare he positioned the box on the table in front of them. After pulling a slice away he handed it to her. She was quiet until the pie was half gone.

"So aren't you going to say something about what I just told you?" she asked. "My little stunt in the club is evidence that Cat might me right, don't you think."

"If you're asking if I'm going to judge you, the answer is no. When you get to know me better, I'll tell you some of the crazy things I've done for love. Some things I'll never mention again."

She took a bite of the pizza, leaving a long string of mozzarella dangling from her chin.

"You've got cheese on your face." He pointed.

She swiped at her cheek.

"Let me get it for you." He slid across the sofa and used his thumb to clean her chin. Before she could pull away, he pressed his lips to hers. The first kiss was quick. The second was slower. His tongue lingered on hers, tasting the

279

salty remains of the sausage. Her lips were plush and inviting. He couldn't help going back for a third and fourth kiss.

She caressed his neck, drawing him closer. The tenderness of her touch was everything he'd imagined. Without releasing her, he repositioned his arm, getting it out of the way to allow him to touch every part of her.

She slipped her hand under his shirt, caressing his chest, kneading his muscles like she wanted to consume him.

He wanted to do the same to her, but he resisted the urge. Geeta needed to take things slow and he would.

Every inch of his body pressed for attention, willing those delicate fingers skim over his flesh. She climbed on his lap, facing him, straddling his legs. Tonight was going better than he'd hoped.

He held her by the waist, their hips moved in unison against the sofa. The only thing that mattered was making her happy. Erasing whatever haunted her ability to accept a new relationship or the thoughts that pulled her away just when she seemed ready to open up to him.

The silky top barely provided a barrier between her skin and his hand. She felt hot against him.

Before he could draw her closer she placed her palm against his chest, pushing him away. She wiped her mouth with the back of her hand, like she was trying to erase his essence.

"I can't do this." She shook her head and stood. "You see, I know this isn't a good idea. You and I have nothing in common. You're conservative and I have a wild side that you'll eventually come to resent. I don't want to change. I want someone to love me for who I am. Besides, if I meant something to you, you wouldn't have disappeared without a word."

"Because you meant something to me is the reason I stayed away. I was giving you the time your sister said you needed. If you keep running, how will you know when somebody comes along who's worth a try?"

She hunched her shoulders. "I'll know. I'll just know. I will."

Dating Just Got Serious

Was she convincing him or herself?
"Can you take me home now?"

Chapter Eight

A rainbow of color hung from the trees. The changing leaves clung to the branches like patchwork quilts. The crisp morning air promised another glorious day in Philly. Not too hot, not yet cold. Traffic had even cooperated this morning.

Two days later and she was still grinning every time she thought about her date with Brooks. The giddiness ground away at the blotch left behind by Donny.

The black lettering over the receptionist desk welcomed her to Philly E-News. A small group of staffers gathered around a box of donuts in the break room acknowledged her with a nod. The steady buzz of low whispers and ringing phones was the reason she was happy to work from home. But this weekly meeting dragged her out of the house for a change.

The glass-enclosed conference room was full. Every seat at the long mahogany table was taken. Hal, the business owner, waved her in to a chair against the wall.

"Geeta, you're just in time. We were getting ready to start." Without waiting for her to sit, he began the meeting by discussing the latest editions. No matter how many new subscribers they acquired, Hal was never satisfied. He wanted the paper to be successful yesterday.

Doodling along the edges of her pad allowed her to meander through snatches of her date with Brooks. Everything about it had been fun. Riding the motorcycle had been a thrill, but the way he touched her was far better. The only problem was she wanted more. Horny people did strange things, the toy in her bedside drawer was testament to that fact and the vibrator had fallen woefully short of satisfaction this morning.

"Did you hear me, Geeta?" Hal's words startled her.

She looked up to see everyone in the room staring at her. She cleared her throat, hoping he'd repeat his comment without her asking.

"The Jumpers' Charity Ball is next Saturday. The mayor likes the event and will be attending, so covering it will give us some publicity." He shuffled papers. "And Anna, next week I want you to meet with one of the Mummer's String Band."

"Wait a minute. You want me to go the ball?" Geeta knew she was whining but a ball required more than a pair of jeans and a sweatshirt. "How about I switch with Anna?"

"Oh, no. You're the new girl. The newbie always gets the ball. Hope you've got something formal to wear." Anna's smile said she was happy the problem was someone else's.

Geeta huffed. "What kind of ball is it?"

Hal looked over his glasses at her. "It's a fundraiser for the inner-city basketball team. They're raising money for kid programs."

Even before he finished the sentence, she knew. A whirlwind started in her stomach and moved up to her chest. Hal continued to talk, but the only thing she heard was Brooks asking her to go to the affair with him. Somewhere, little minions had stepped in to manipulate the script. She settled back into the arms of the chair. This was Brooks' and Jeremy's event. The very one she'd said no to. Now she had a perfect excuse for calling Brooks and asking him to escort her. The idea made it hard for her to remain seated for the balance of the meeting.

"I think we're done. Everyone has his or her assignment. Please get them in on time, people." Hal pushed away from the conference table and walked out. Her chance to plead a case for a different assignment vanished out the door before she could stand.

After the meeting, Geeta stood on the sidewalk in front of the building. The air was still warm even though a breeze blew. Any other time she would have been thrilled to hang out at a gala with handsome men. But this was different. Brooks was already in her head more than she wanted. She needed to stay away from him.

She dialed her sister. "Cat, can you meet me for lunch?"

"Sure, just pick a place near me. I want to stick close to home today. How about the Red Line? I can be there in ten minutes."

Geeta rounded the corner to the parking lot and pulled up short. Donny sat on the hood of her car, tapping the display on his cell phone. The cold finger of dread inched down her spine, making her gasp. She widened her stance. The swish of cars and the hum of foot traffic should have eased the pounding in her heart. With so much activity, what could Donny do?

He pushed his hands and phone into his pocket, leaving them there. Without moving he glared at her.

"Get the hell off my car." She hoped her voice sounded more courageous than she felt. Fear chewed at her kneecaps threatening to bring her down.

"Listen to you, trying to sound tough." He slid off the car. "We got some unfinished business, girl."

She took a step back. It was hard to believe the two of them used to have fun together. Being this close to him now, made her flesh pebble.

"I have nothing to say to you." Her voice wavered.

"I'm meeting with my lawyer in a few weeks and I want you to come with me. Understand our strategy, you know."

"Did you lose your hearing while you were locked up?"

"People don't walk away from me. You should know that about me. I don't want to get ugly with you, but I will if I have to. You're going to walk in that courtroom, do what I tell you, and then I'll think about letting you have your life back." He was almost yelling.

"I'm not a piece of land or a car." She slapped her hands against her thighs. The sting did nothing to quash the rage simmering in her belly. The man standing before her was a stranger. What had she seen in him?

"Go to hell, Donny." She turned back to the building, marching away from him.

"I tried it the nice way. The next time you see me, I won't be this pleasant." His crazy laughter pierced the air.

She pushed her shaking legs to keep moving, to get back inside the building.

In the lobby she gripped her cell phone, just in case she needed to dial for help. In the beginning she thought Donny would give up and go away. Now she knew better. Her knees continued to jump until the black sedan with darkened windows pulled out of the lot. From the crack in the car window, Donny sneered at the building entrance, his arm draped on the steering wheel. He drove by unhurried. She waited another five minutes before heading back outside again.

Geeta arrived at the restaurant before her sister and was seated in a booth along the far wall. The only thought crawling through her head since leaving the meeting was fear. Until lately her life had been a fairy tale. She'd never worried about much but now the only thing she did was worry. It was as if she'd stepped into someone else's life and couldn't find the door to get out.

She didn't notice her sister until she slid into the seat in front of her.

"What were you thinking about? You didn't even see me come in."

Cat looked glorious. Being married and pregnant must have been a balm. Never had Geeta been jealous of her sister, but now she wanted everything Cat had.

"Are you okay? Your hands are shaking."

"Donny keeps showing up. He wants me to testify at his trial." She shredded the paper napkin into a small pile.

Cat reached across the table and held her hands. "Let's call the police. He might be violating some bail rule, or you could get a restraining order."

Cat sounded so confident. Nothing scared her.

Geeta nodded. Her sister's concern was obvious.

"Do you think we should? I don't want to make him even madder. He carries a gun now." The words plopped out before she had a chance to scrutinize them. This bit of information would only make Cat worry.

Cat's eyes grew unusually large. "A gun? Did he always carry a gun? Has he threatened you with it?" She caught a breath, enough to fuel her interrogation. "Do you think he's selling drugs again? Why would he need a weapon? Surely you can get a restraining order if you tell the police he's carrying a gun. That has to be against his bail orders."

"Cat, stop it. You're getting worked up. That can't be good for the babies. I'll file a report after we eat." She tried to sound calm.

Cat pounded the tip of her index finger on the table. "Don't ignore this, Geeta."

"I won't. I promise. But he's not stalking me like Natalie stalked you."

"He sounds more dangerous, if you ask me." Cat fell back against the booth as if she was exhausted from the conversation.

The server arrived and took their order.

"I wanted to have lunch with you today to tell you I got a new assignments today, and guess what I have to do?" Happy to channel the conversation to something upbeat, Geeta fumbled in her purse for the notes she'd taken without waiting for her sister to reply. She placed the paper on the table and smoothed out the creases with her finger. "I have to attend the Jumpers Charity Ball."

Cat sat up. "That's great. Right?"

Cat's expectant eyes proved the two of them lived in different worlds. Everything surrounding Cat was shaded golden. She would even be happy if the sky opened up and dropped twelve feet of snow on the day of the marvelous event.

"Yeah, sure. It's just that I've never been and I don't know what to expect. I was hoping you could fill me in."

"Oh, Geeta, that's great! Even though I'm bigger than a house I'm going. Everyone will be there, Yani and Phoebe. The Ball is a fundraiser. You're going to have a good time."

The server returned with glasses of water. Cat's reassurance made the ordeal seem less onerous. The worry lines around Cat's eyes disappeared, her pregnancy glow returned.

"Brooks invited me to the event a few weeks ago. I told him no, but now since I have to go, I'm thinking of asking him to escort me. "

Cat slapped the table with her palm. "What a wonderful idea. Do you like him? The last time I saw you two together I thought you might bite his head off."

"We went out on a date last week…I had a good time." Thinking about the ride to the shore, the pizza and the kiss made her smile. "I hope he hasn't asked someone else."

"I'm almost certain he hasn't."

"Why, what do you know? Has he said something?"

"No. But I know he likes you. He's always talking about you." Her voice sounded extra sweet.

Geeta tried to ignore the warm feeling her sister's words stirred in her stomach, but she couldn't suppress the smile. "Well, we'll see how it goes. So far I've taken your advice and I'm proceeding slow. Dating isn't as much fun as it used to be. Nowadays you have to do criminal checks and credit checks on everybody, and even then you still can't be sure."

"Oh stop. Nothing is as bad as you make it sound."

"Says the woman curled around the love of her life every night."

"Relax, Geeta. All you need to do is take one date at a time. Stop thinking everyone needs to be the finish line. Have some fun. Lots and lots of fun."

Chapter Nine

Winter was over a month away, but the fall wind couldn't hold back the frigid temperature.

Brooks adjusted the thermostat in the car, giving him another opportunity to take his eyes off the road and look at Geeta. At every stop he stole a glance. Her hands were fisted in her lap, something had her uptight. Tonight with her hair swept up, exposing her long elegant neck, and the cinnamon-colored gown showing off her glowing skin.

He'd gotten word she'd filed a report on Donny. Not once had she mentioned it to him, and he waited. Even the hints he dropped went unnoticed and he'd given her plenty of opportunities to tell him about her fears. The twenty-four hour tail he'd arranged for her was another secret. They were piling up like skeletons.

When she called, his first thought was she wanted to talk about Donny's threats. But she had no idea he was working the case or circling the rim of Donny's existence. Waiting. The moment Donny made one unlawful move, instead of being free on bail he'd be behind bars.

Escorting her to the charity ball was an even better reason for her to call. When he realized the invitation wasn't a joke, he'd been happier than when the basketball team won the city championship.

Since their night at his beach house she'd been skillful at keeping just beyond anything more intimate than telephone calls and a quick dinner at a less than romantic place. But tonight an air of confidence sat on his shoulders.

The gown hugging her exquisite body rekindled his favorite memory. He had to be closer to seeing her naked again soon. When she called to accept his invitation, there was an undertone to her voice, a much more seductive quality than before.

"Geeta, before you get too busy taking notes tonight, I want to say you look gorgeous. Those things I said about your tight jeans before were out of line."

"It's okay. I didn't take you seriously. You only said that to get back at me for the stuck-up comment I made about your clothes."

In the darkness of the interior of the car he saw her eyes soften. Maybe she was deactivating the force field surrounding her heart.

"I was surprised when you called about the ball. You were adamant about not going. What changed your mind?" His gaze lingered on the elegant sway of her neck before returning his attention back to the road.

"I have an assignment. You'd asked. The idea seemed perfect."

"Well, I'm almost flattered...I think."

They rode in silence for several minutes. He couldn't help wondering if she was warming up to him. The hello kiss she'd given was more tongue than lips.

"What can you tell me about your organization?" she asked.

"Umm..."

"Tell me the stuff people don't know about the ball team. The inner secrets."

"I can't reveal any confidential information. If there's stuff you want to know, you have to hang out with me."

"I might do that. Your persistence is wearing me down." She ran her palms over her dress.

"Such encouraging words. You really know how to excite a man, don't you?"

"I used to let my body do all the work, but I've gotten so much better with my words."

"Too bad I didn't know you when your body had so much to say. It sounds like you were a lot of fun back then. "

He slowed down and pulled into the valet lane behind a line of cars at the hotel. A small huddle of people stood to the left of the entrance puffing cigarettes in the crisp fall air.

The moment they climbed out of the car, the wind whipped her wrap off one shoulder, exposing velvety skin. He repositioned the shawl and then escorted her inside. Her steps were short, restricted by the tight sheath hugging her hips. He allowed his hand to drop to the small of her back.

With a tender glance she smiled as they entered the ballroom.

"Are we seated at the table with Jeremy and Cat?" she asked.

"Of course. The captain and co-captain always sit at the head table. Consider this your lucky night. You get to spend time with me plus you I'll give you the inside scoop."

She stopped and held his hand. She could have been the royal princess from some opulent country.

"I want to thank you for escorting me tonight. I haven't been very nice to you, but you've always..." She cleared her throat. "You always make me feel special. No man has ever made—well you know." She pressed her hand to her throat, as if she wanted to pull the words back.

The pleasure swelling in his chest pushed aside everything. She'd moved beyond the invisible line between them. Now wasn't a time to show excitement, but the chord of excitement racing through him made it difficult.

"I like the sound of that. Tell me more." He stared into her eyes, hoping to coax more from her vault of emotions.

"Maybe later.

She leaned forward and brushed her lips across his.

Startled by her boldness, he captured her face in the palms of his hands and slipped his tongue in her mouth. Half expecting her to wrench away, she didn't.

She accepted the kiss with a seriousness bordering on improper for the middle of a ballroom floor.

But he couldn't resist, couldn't stop tasting her, couldn't stop his growing feelings for her.

For a moment Brooks remembered the vision of her mounted on his lap. He thought she was ready to accept him, but the look in her eyes tonight revealed a depth of emotion he hadn't seen before.

Somewhere in the middle of few words confusion his heart opened up for her. The foreign weightless feeling left him speechless.

The voice was hers. The tone was hers. The words didn't sound like her. But telling him where she was emotionally seemed more important than her pride. The kiss was a total surprise. Any modesty she may have had disappeared. Brooks had peeled back her shield and she felt like a flower waiting to blossom.

The tease needed to end. The sooner she got the information for the article the sooner she could move on to what could no longer be ignored, enjoying her time with Brooks.

She allowed him to direct her to their table, steering her by applying just enough pressure at the base of her spine. His light touch could have been stroking her inner thighs. The response from her body was the same. She struggled to breathe, without gasping.

Her mind floated several inches above her head. The purpose for the evening wasn't to get freaky with Brooks, but to write a story. But even with that thought pressed in her head she couldn't stop thinking about feeling his muscular body on top of hers.

Cat waved them over to the table.

"She looks like she should be at home packing her hospital bag," Geeta whispered over her shoulder to Brooks.

He held the chair until she was seated before sitting next to her.

"It's about time you guys got here," said Cat. "I thought you might have changed your mind."

"I was a little late picking Geeta up. I had some business I needed to finish." Brooks volunteered then dropped his arm over Geeta's chair. His fingers skimmed across her bare back.

"Ignore Cat. Since she's going to be a mom, she thinks everyone needs mothering," Geeta said.

"Very funny." Cat pushed away from the table and grabbed Jeremy's hand. "Come on, baby, dance with me."

"I was only kidding with her. Do you think she's mad?" Geeta asked Brooks.

"I don't think she's mad. Pregnant women can be a little sensitive."

She turned to Brooks. "Do you like kissing in public places?"

"I like kissing everywhere. Since you've been playing hard to get, it only amps up my need."

"I haven't been in the last few months. I've been trying to be a lot more discriminating. You can tell from my last boyfriend it was a quality I really needed to cultivate."

"But you don't have to use it on me. I'm pedigreed."

"What does that mean?" She wiggled closer to him, enjoying the playful teasing.

"It means I'm serious about you. Always have been." His hand drifted across her back, slow and meticulous, making frequent stops and applying gentle pressure.

"I see. And how can I tell the real thing from the fake?"

"You're going to have to trust me. If you live your life in a closet, look at all this good stuff you're going to miss."

The dimple in his chin taunted her urging her to place her index finger in the indentation. She wanted to take him at his word, but there was so much about him she still didn't know.

"Let's dance." He led her to the dance floor. "You're here to get a story. I need to make sure your experience is wonderful."

She wanted to assure him she was having a good time. Better than she could have imagined. When the band finished the song, they stayed on the parquet floor. Wrapped in Brooks' arms, the intoxicating scent of his cologne, the music, his gentle touch, all made the evening magical.

She placed her arms around his neck. The whiskers on his cheek had grown out enough to scratch her face. Instead of pulling away, she pressed closer. The rub felt good. What started out as an assignment was turning into a special evening.

When the event ended, the night wasn't over.

"Tonight you were supposed to ask me about the charity. I'd hate for you to leave and still have questions." Brooks eased the car out of the hotel lot and into traffic.

"How about we go back to my place, for coffee?" She detected lust in her voice, but hoped he didn't.

He rested his right hand on her thigh. "I was going to suggest the same thing."

Chapter Ten

The dialogue in her head was very different from the words in her heart. Geeta thought she wanted him because she was horny, but that wasn't true. She liked him. Maybe, more than liked him. She unlocked the door with Brooks standing behind her. On the quiet street she could almost hear every breath he took.

Was he as nervous as she was? Probably not. Brooks was capable of piling on the charm and she was knee deep in it tonight.

She stepped inside and turned on a lamp in the living room.

"Where's your roommate?" Brooks walked toward the kitchen with one hand in his pocket. On the way home he'd loosened his tie and now it hung around his neck.

"She went to Washington this weekend to visit her parents. Some political thing her father was throwing tonight." She dropped her clutch and wrap on the sofa before strolling into the kitchen. She flipped on the switch, flooding the area in bright fluorescent lighting.

Of all the men she'd invited over for coffee that she had no intention of perking, Brooks was the most handsome. One corner of his mouth lifted, the reassuring smile erased the apprehension locking her limbs.

"You know I'm not here tonight for coffee, right?" He sauntered towards her.

"And I hope you know I never planned to offer you any."

"Then we're on the same wave-length." His face hovered above hers for a moment as if he was taunting her with something delectable. The moment their lips connected, a surge washed over her doubt, carrying the questions away like the tide. The uncertainty about being good enough, or what might happen in the morning, or their compatibility were even less important as his tongue swirled around her mouth. Instead of thinking too much about what was about to

294

happen, she eased her body against his. The unexpected tenderness in his caress made the moment right. She didn't hold back, her instincts took over, guiding her hand up his chest.

Yesterday, the thought of holding onto Brooks for more than a few sexy moments never crossed her mind. But tonight when he showed up on her doorstep looking strikingly handsome, like the prince in a fairy tale, the thought wouldn't leave her alone.

She eased the silk bow tie from under his collar, and dropped it at his feet. Next she tackled the tiny white buttons on his shirt, liberating one at a time and punctuating each release with a peck on his lips. The playful game was both enticing and sensual. Her loins grew heavier with each kiss.

Amusement danced in his eyes. His shirt fell free only to reveal a sleeveless undershirt. She tugged the white cotton band from his pants to feel his warm, hard skin. The impressive size of his muscular chest was no surprise.

Everything about him was superb, even the way he possessed her tongue. Brooks might look low-key, but when it came to arousing her body, there was no question he knew how.

He looped his hand under the strap of her dress and pulled it down without liberating her tongue.

Instead of allowing him to control the moment, she pulled her tongue away, focusing attention on his belt. Once she maneuvered the complicated buckle, she unclasped his pants, and slid her hand inside.

"Do you know what you're doing, princess?" he whispered in her ear. "Don't unleash the monster unless you plan to tame him."

"That's exactly what I had in mind." She gripped his shaft, running her thumb over the tip.

He buried his head into the curve of her neck, licking her flesh. First his tongue was light, barely connecting with her skin, but as her moans grew deeper so did the pressure. She expected to hear a sizzle each time his cool tongue made contact with her. The gentle licking made it hard to concentrate on anything else. Maybe part of what she was feeling was pure desire. Six months on her self-imposed hiatus was a long time, but she knew it was more than that. She knew where her heart was going. She knew this time was different. Even if she wanted to say no to him tonight, to keep the pledge with Egypt, she couldn't.

He slipped the other strap off her shoulder, and wiggled the gown over her hips. After she stepped out of the dress, he leaned back. The admiring gleam in his eyes fixated on her breasts. He took his time with her body, cherishing it like he'd found the most exquisite piece of art and wanted to enjoy the unforgettable beauty.

His large hands cupped each breast, before he lowered his head and pulled a nipple into his mouth. The slow roll of his tongue over the hardened tip stirred every cell in her body. Tonight she intended for them to finish what they'd started on that warm spring night at the reception.

The palms of his hands braced her hips, but she couldn't hold still. She released his belt from the loops, and tugged at his pants.

"If I'm naked, you need to undress, too," she said.

"You're not quite naked yet." He reached for her thong, dragged it down her legs, and helped her out of the silky confines.

"Now it's your turn." She removed his cufflinks before helping him take off his shirt and t-shirt. "These have to go, too." She pointed at his pants.

He kicked off his shoes, shucked his pants and boxers at the same time. His heavy erection aimed at her as he trailed a finger down the center of her body. When he reached the gap between her legs he stroked her tender entrance. The back and forth motion synchronized with the sway of her hips.

Her back pressed into the wall, allowing him to ease down on his knees. His finger slipped inside of her moist folds. The sudden movement made her gulp to catch a breath. In less than twenty minutes, they'd stripped and she'd exposed more than just her body to him. He had seen her desire, too.

He parted her thighs, his tongue found her nub. The moment the two connected, her body ached for satisfaction. He continued to tease the hardened nugget, weakening her knees, until she almost fell onto him.

"Brooks…"His name was barely a whisper.

"Almost, baby," he promised but he didn't ease the pressure of his tongue. The taunting continued for what seemed like forever, before he pushed deeper into her. The motion was enough to rocket her into ecstasy.

Her arms and legs went limp, but Brooks held her up. From the pocket of his pants he produced a condom, and slipped it onto his erection. With the ease of curling a five-pound weight he lifted her onto the kitchen counter. The cold granite stung her butt, but the promise of having him was more important.

He pulled her forward, to the edge and inched inside of her warm cavity. Enjoying the pleasure. She pressed her mouth to his and clawed his back. She wrapped her legs around his back, driving him to buck against her like a wild stallion trying to break free.

Almost in unison he gripped her hips, pinned her in place. Her body exploded against his, shaking like a miniature earthquake.

Brooks collapsed on top of her, bending her flat against the hard surface. Her chest heaved up and down with each breath.

"I know this isn't comfortable for you," he said between gasps.

"I know, but I can't move," she responded.

"Let me carry you to a softer surface."

"Is that your way of saying you want to get in my bed?" She pushed up on her elbows. Moisture glistened between her breasts.

"Yes, that's exactly what I'm trying to say." He positioned his arms under her legs and helped her off the counter. She stretched out her back. He removed the used condom and disposed of it in the trash.

"Of course I'll let you in my bed." She led the way out of the kitchen.

Chapter Eleven

Brooks followed her up stairs. A perfectly round mole dotted her left butt cheek. He pressed his index finger against the flawless blemish.

"That tickles," she said over her shoulder before sprinting down the hall.

She jumped into the bed. Her brown skin against the white satin covering was beauty in contrast. For a moment he stood over the bed admiring her sleek body.

"How long are you going to stand there and stare at me?" She wiggled over and patted the empty space beside her.

He climbed in next to her, propping his body on one elbow. "Geeta, you know I'm serious about you, don't you? For me, this is more than a fling."

She wrapped her arms around his neck, pulling him down on top of her. "I thought we were being genuine at my sister's reception. But you disappeared. So what's different this time? Don't feel like you have to say that because we had sex."

He twisted a lock of her hair through his fingers. Was she upset with him? Staying away from her had been difficult, but a trip to Quantico and new cases had kept him occupied.

"Your sister told me to give you some space. She said you were going through a tough time. I didn't want to be the rebound guy."

"I should have known Cat had something to say." She collapsed on the pillow. "Has Cat given her okay this time?" she asked with sarcasm.

"From now on, you and I will make the decisions in our relationship." He nuzzled her neck. "Let's leave everyone else out."

"You've got yourself a deal." She squealed with delight and pulled him into an embrace.

299

She attacked his tongue with the same vigilance she'd used in the kitchen. Only this time he couldn't take his time or draw out the need. It was well past the time to confirm their status. He wanted to claim her in a way he'd never claimed a woman before. This wasn't just a date.

She flipped on top of him. With each kiss she planted on both sides of his neck, he had to concentrate to hold back his desire. Her tongue flitted across his feverish skin. With her body flat against his, she inched her way to down his chest, down his abdomen, until she took his member into her mouth.

He arched slightly, spreading his legs as she positioned herself between them. Each touch was like an awakening, bringing his senses to a higher level. Nothing in his memory prepared him for this moment. Her tongue traveled up his length leaving a trail of unbridled bliss.

She over-stimulated him. He willed his brain and heart to work together and enjoy the pleasure she provided, but the blood rushing to his loins ignored the warning. The gentle rake of her teeth pushed him to the edge of his tolerance.

His fingers tangled in her tresses. The tide caught up, washing over him with ecstasy that he couldn't restrain.

He splayed on the bed. Nothing on him could move. After several deep breaths his limps relaxed. With her head resting on his thigh, he heard her take a deep breath, like a big cat, satisfied with the hunt.

"Come here, Geeta." He tried to grab hold of her, but she pulled away.

"I'm not done yet." She sat up. Her breasts stood at attention, like perfect matching melons. "Can you get the condoms out of the nightstand drawer?" She pointed.

"Are you going to let me catch my breath for a moment?"

"From the looks of things, you don't need a breather." She trailed her finger along the length of his shaft.

"I thought you said you were celibate."

"I was until tonight, but that doesn't mean I didn't have hopes." She bounced on his thighs.

Brooks opened the drawer, and fished inside without looking. His hand landed on an odd object that he lifted out to examine.

"Do you want to talk about this, Geeta?" He waved the huge vibrator at her.

She clambered over his legs to snatch the weapon from him. "A girl has to take care of herself. And my finger wasn't good enough. Do you have any better suggestions?"

He glanced in the drawer and found the condom. "You've got me now, so you can get rid of that thing." He removed the vibrator from her hand and dropped it on the floor.

"Let's not get rid of my buddy yet. We'll keep it around in case you act up."

He placed his hand on top of hers as they rolled the condom into place over his throbbing shaft.

"If you let me, I believe I could spend the rest of my days here in your bedroom, pleasuring you." He gripped her hips, holding onto her so she couldn't escape. Ever.

"Is that a promise?" Her lips puckered.

She eased down on top of him. The slow, steady rotation of her hips would have made him promise her every cent in his bank account, his first-born and his soul. For once the odds seemed to be working in his favor. Patience had paid off.

When her muscles contracted around him like a vice, he couldn't help but reach for her. Pulling her mouth to his to take her tongue and her essence at the same time.

####

Geeta pretended to be asleep so he'd continue to kiss her neck. The caring way he held her in his arms was better than anything he could have said. Besides, she'd heard some pretty smooth lines from some of the best talkers in Philly. This was so much better.

"You'd better wake up if you plan to get to the community center to meet the kids. Don't you want to finish your story?" His lips were warm against her ear.

She turned over to face him. "Yes, but do I really have to move now?" She caressed his neck, loving the feel of him.

"As much as I want to—and I really do want to—I can't make love again this morning. I'm sore."

"Good, because I don't have any more condoms."

"But give me some time and a glass of orange juice and I'll be ready."

"I have a question to ask you and I want you to answer truthfully." She sat up in the bed.

"I wouldn't think of answering any other way."

"At Cat's house a while back, you made a comment about my attire. My tight jeans and my crotch gasping for air." She swallowed hard, forcing herself to continue. "Are you ashamed—"

He gathered her in his arms. "Oh no! I only said that because of the comment you made about my style of dress. I actually think everything about you is perfect."

He planted several kisses on her brow and eyes and neck and mouth. "You're perfect, Geeta. I mean that."

She nodded and punched the pillow. "I've got an idea. Let's dress. Go down to the center. Meet the boys and girls. Have dinner, afterwards. Come back here and pick up where we left off."

Chapter Twelve

Geeta clasped her hands in front of her, allowing Brooks to open the solid glass doors to the Steak House Restaurant. The wish granted by her fairy godmother had extended beyond the charity event, into a whole week. A week so perfect she'd floated through it while her stomach tried to keep up. They bounced between his place and her place, whichever granted the most privacy.

No matter how much she wanted to ignore the bloom of love for Brooks, it occupied every thought. As if they had gotten caught up in some big hurricane and landed in Oz, every available minute had been spent with Brooks.

After she took her seat, the waiter handed her the napkin and hurried off to another table.

"Did you get your article submitted on time?" Brooks reached for her hand across the table.

"Just barely. But the editor loved it. He said it was one of my best pieces."

"Do you want to thank me now or later?" he asked.

"I'll be thanking you tonight. The question is, will it be at your place or mine?"

"Well, your roommate is coming back today and since you've turned into a screamer I think we ought to spend the night at my place."

She swatted his hand, but couldn't help laughing. The freedom to be herself was so easy with Brooks. He never judged or tried to adjust her into something she didn't want to be. "Don't you think it's amazing that I only became a yeller when you came into my life? I've always been the meek, mild mannered one."

"I'm not complaining. I love my women with a little fire."

She leaned towards him without looking away. "Then you're going to love what I'm planning for us tonight." She licked her lips, hoping to entice him.

303

"You'd better be careful. If you keep that up we both will leave here hungry tonight and I'll take you in the backseat of my car."

"I love it when you talk dirty to me."

She glanced up to see the waiter standing at the table. After he took their orders his brisk departure made her giggle.

Geeta ran her hand over her face. "I can't believe I said something so naughty in front of a perfect stranger. I'm embarrassed."

"Don't be. I'm sure he's heard worse."

"This week has been perfect. Between spending time at your beach place, the superhero movie marathon you made me watch, and the time we've spent between the sheets, neither of us has gotten much work done."

The waiter returned with their drinks. After placing them on the table he left without making eye contact.

"I'm glad our schedules allowed us to hang out. But next week I've got to go away. Work."

"I've been meaning to ask you about that. What do you do for a living?"

He picked up his glass. After taking a sip he gathered her hands between his massive palms. "I've been putting off this conversation for some time. I don't like to talk about what I do, because people often get the wrong impression."

She pulled her hands away and fell back against the chair. Her heart picked up speed. Why did everyone have a secret? As much as she wanted to hear what he had to say, a small part of her didn't. For now, the status quo would have been fine.

"Whatever it is, just tell me." She tapped the table with her fist. "I asked you weeks ago if you were into something illegal. Why—"

"Hold on, Geeta. Don't let your imagination take you on a wild ride. I work for the Drug Enforcement Administration. DEA. I don't talk about my work because some of what I'm required to do is secretive."

Relief gathered in her shoulders like a flock of nest birds. She exhaled. "Whew. You had me worried. I can

304

handle that. At least you're on the right side of the law." She slipped her hands back into his. "Where are you going or is it a big secret?"

"I'm going to Quantico, Virginia. For some training, briefings. You know, work stuff. I'll only be gone five days."

"Sounds impressive and dangerous. So even though you dress like a royal conservative, you've got it going on." She gave him an admirable nod. Brooks had so many layers. Each one peeled away, revealing more about him to adore.

"Coming from you, I'm going to consider your comment a compliment. My job requires me to dress a certain way to fit in sometimes. Undercover. When I'm not working I dress the way I do to separate my two worlds. I need the transition."

She positioned her chin into her palm. "Tell me about your biggest case. Do you wear a gun? Have you ever shot anyone?"

"The last thing I want to do on this date is talk about work. I'm here with an amazing woman and tonight I plan to have enough of you to last me through a long, dry week."

"Just answer one question. "Do you carry a gun?" She wanted to compare him to Donny, but she wasn't sure how she wanted him to reply. The idea of Brooks carrying a gun wasn't as foreign as Donny having one shoved in his pants.

"I have a service weapon. I carry it most days and all the time when I'm working. But I'm always discreet."

In the span of a few months her life had changed. Men with guns.

"To us." She picked up her glass and tapped it to his. Being with Brook promised to be a helluva ride.

Chapter Thirteen

The drive from Quantico took longer than Brooks planned. Traffic on Interstate 95 North snarled outside of D.C. as usual. Under normal circumstances the delay wouldn't have bothered him, but he'd been counting the hours until he wrapped his arms around Geeta and tasted her. The things she promised to do to him kept his imagination in overdrive.

According to the reports, Donny hadn't approached her and there was talk of pulling the team off the surveillance. Maybe Donny had found someone else to sit in the courtroom and look like the doting girlfriend.

He pulled into the parking garage of his condo, turned off the car and climbed out. Before he closed the car door, a car pulled behind his, blocking his driveway. The blackened window hid the occupants, but he knew Donny's car. He'd seen it often enough in the last few weeks.

Donny stepped from behind the driver's side. "We got some unfinished business, man."

Brooks settled his hand on his holster. Donny's visit wasn't a surprise. He hadn't become a drug kingpin by being lazy. "No. I don't think we do."

"You've been following me. Checking up on me. At first I thought you just wanted my girl. But I had my boyz do a little investigating—"

"It looks like you've been doing a little tracking, too. You've got some nerve coming to my place." Brooks rearranged his jacket, giving better access to his gun.

"I do what I have to do."

The image of Donny as a two-bit punk dissolved. Somewhere in the last several months he'd picked up the hardened edges of a well-worn criminal. "Can we cut the crap? What the hell do you want, Donny?"

"It doesn't feel so good, having someone dogging you around, does it?" Donny eased around the car. His noted swagger had to be a show for the thugs inside.

Brooks widened his stance. "If you have something to say, then say it."

"Does Geeta know you're hanging around her to get to me? Does she know you're a cop?"

Donny crossed his arms as if waiting for Brooks to show surprise from the revelation.

Brooks took a step closer to Donny. Even with his oversized jacket, Donny's bulletproof vest was noticeable.

"Geeta knows everything she needs to know. And I'm not a cop." He poked his finger into Donny's chest. "Expecting trouble?"

"You'll never know. I'm being prepared like a good scout." He paused. "I figured out where I know you from now." He lifted his chin. "You helped bust me, that day. You were in the room."

"What do you want, Donny?" Brooks shifted his weight to his toes.

"I want my girl back. Geeta is special. I ain't gonna let some two-bit cop steal my woman. Besides, I can give her nice things."

Baited by the best, Brooks dismissed his declaration. "Not from prison, you can't."

"The only thing you can give her is heartache from wishing she'd dumped you. What can you buy her on a cop salary?"

"If we're done here, I've got real stuff to do. Don't you have some corner that needs your presence?"

"Like I said the last time I saw you, we ain't done, man." He backed away until he reached the driver's side of the car. Before getting inside he pointed his index finger at Brooks. He drove the car out of the garage as slow as he'd entered.

Donny was a two-bit thug. His threats were his power. He'd try to keep his nose clean until after his trial.

The concern was Geeta. It hadn't taken the whole week to realize she was more than a girlfriend. Brooks drew a deep breath, trying to erase the tension in his shoulders. All week his brain spun with ideas for a future with Geeta.

Something permanent. Until Donny was behind bars something would always be hanging between them.

####

The moment Geeta heard his keys in the door she loosened the knot on the silk robe. On her way to greet Brooks, she picked up the wine flutes. Before he could drop his bag she kissed him, transferring all her pent-up desire. He tasted like coffee and honey. She nearly spilled the drinks when he pulled her closer and tried to suck her tongue from her mouth.

After several moments his grip slackened enough to let her catch a breath.

"God, you feel good." He buried his head into the side of her neck.

"I really missed you, too. So I thought I'd surprise you." She handed him the glass. He drained a third of the wine in one gulp.

"What do you have in mind? Because a whole week without you was nearly unbearable. I might not let you leave my side for a month." He slipped his hand inside her robe. The way he caressed her breast, her whole body eased into his. She didn't know how much she missed him until his warm hand touched her skin. She placed her glass on the entry table and then took his glass, too.

"I want you to unbutton my shirt like you did the night of the ball." His voice was loaded with lust.

"You liked that, did you?" She planted her lips against and reached for his collar. "This is going to be fun."

She continued the routine until he was completely undressed. His moans stirred her desire.

"Follow me." She dropped her robe into the pile on top of his clothes. With his hand in hers, she led him into the bedroom. When he stopped at the foot of the bed she said, "Not yet. We're going into the bathroom."

"What do you have in mind?"

She pushed open the door, revealing the soaker tub, filled with soft fluffy bubbles.

"Girl, you really know how to spoil me. Are you getting in with me?"

She ran her hand over his chest. The hard planes of his body pulsed in her palm. How she missed this man. The only thing she wanted right now was to please him.

"You go ahead. I'll get our wine and be right back."

"Hurry up," he said. The bubbles parted as he dropped into the water.

His eyes were closed when she returned, but he heard the light slap of her feet on the tiled floor. Before breaking into his thoughts she studied his face. The soft music, wine, bubbles and, her naked body should have placed a serene look on his face, instead it was etched with tension. The urge to erase the lines buried in forehead overwhelmed her. Every night while he was away he'd talked to her until she was ready for bed. His soothing heavy voice was like a melody ushering sleep into her limbs.

"The week wasn't so good, huh?" she climbed in the tub, behind him. After wrapping her legs around his, she massaged his shoulders. Her small hands were hardly expert enough to release the knots at the base of his neck

"Oh, baby, that feels so good. You have miracle hands."

"You looked like you need to loosen up."

"I've got a lot on my mind." He slid lower, his shoulders disappearing under the bubbles.

"Want to share?"

"No. The only thing I want to do is enjoy my woman and this bath." His hands ran along her thighs then inched higher. The easy glide of his expert fingers started her core to warm. "How are things at the paper?"

"Like you said, let's not talk about work." She maneuvered her arms around his neck down to his chest. The silky hair on his lower stomach laid flat against his skin.

"You're talking my language. But I need you in front of me." He spun around facing her. With the same tenderness

309

Dating Just Got Serious

he used on her legs he held her breasts. Behind his eyes burned an intensity that wasn't there a week ago. They seemed to want to tell her something, and it better be something good. Something about the future and the two of them.

Chapter Fourteen

Brooks opened one eye.

Just one.

The room was gray, much like the murky sky visible through the crescent-shaped window in front of the bed. Geeta's body curved around him, her delicate arm draped over his waist.

He should have told her. At the wedding practice, at the rehearsal dinner, at one of Cat's many game parties, he should have told her the part he'd played in Donny's arrest. Maybe it wouldn't have mattered to her, but at least it wouldn't have become this phantom, lurking over his shoulder threatening to destroy their budding relationship.

Keeping secrets never worked in his favor. Hadn't he learned that before? The hard way. Secrets ended his relationship with his college sweetheart. The girl he thought he was going to marry. She'd objected to his decision to join the DEA, so he'd kept it from her until he received his first assignment. She refused to relocate to Seattle by throwing the diamond ring across the room and nicking his cheek. Packing his clothes and every-other-word mixed with *liar*, had gone on for eternity. The way she slammed the door on her way out let him know that trying to explain was useless.

Tonight. He'd tell Geeta tonight. She meant too much to him to lose. No matter what the circumstances, he'd find a way to let her know the two of them had nothing to do with her bum ex-boyfriend.

Geeta stretch her legs, her toes poking through the foot of the sheet. "Good morning, handsome."

"Hey, beautiful." Even this early she looked like a goddess. Her flawless skin reminded him of perfection, the kind that only existed in museums. Letting his college sweetheart storm out of his life had been upsetting until the rush of the first case filled the void. But with Geeta it would be different. Spying on a drug lords or breaking a big case couldn't erase the hole she'd leave in his life.

Geeta closed her eyes, pulling the sheet under her chin. He shook her gently. "Wake up. You wanted me to get you home early, remember. You said you had a piece to finish."

"Yeah, but I didn't know we were going to make love all night."

"Why not?" He kissed the soft flesh on her neck.

She giggled, but didn't stop his advance along her collarbone. "If I'm late with another article my editor will start to regret the promotion."

"Let's stay in bed today and play with each other. I need some more of you."

"Hmm, I'll come back, tonight. I'll bring take-out and a movie that I get to pick. After the movie we can pick up right here."

He hesitated to taunt her. As long as she was suggesting being with him he was happy. "Sounds perfect. But before you go can we just…one more time." He ran his tongue along her neck, his hands roamed across her flat belly. He could have been an octopus using everything he had on her.

"Okay, but promise you will let me get home before noon."

"Not only will I promise. I'll take you." His index finger slipped between her legs. She had her hook in him, but nothing ever felt so good.

By the time he pulled into her driveway, his limbs were sore, but having her holding onto him so tight satisfied another desire. The ones that had nothing to do with sex.

She pulled off the helmet, holding it by the chinstrap. "I don't believe you brought me home on the bike. You know I'm afraid of this thing."

"Then we need to ride it more, not less. I haven't taken it out all week. After a stay at Quantico I always cut loose by taking a ride. It's a stress reliever for me."

She placed her index finger under his chin, scratching the scruff growing there. "I thought I worked out all your kinks last night and this morning."

312

"Oh baby, you did." He planted a kiss on her finger. "But this is a habit now."

"Does that mean you're picking me up on it for dinner?"

"I'll get this out of my system this afternoon, and then pick you up in the car. Instead of having takeout food, I want to take you some place nice for dinner. We'll go to that Mexican restaurant you like on South Street."

She stepped closer, released his chinstrap and then pulled his helmet free. She braced his face between her palms. "Sometimes I wonder if you're too good to be true. You spoil me."

"Geeta." He paused. "You're very special to me. I think I'm falling for you." The words were like glue, sealing his mouth shut. He'd said too much.

"Yeah, sure you are." She gave him a tender kiss. "I've got work to do."

"What time should I come back to take you to dinner." Brooks asked without turning off the bike.

"Give me a few hours. I should be ready about seven."

He watched her unlock the door before pulling away.

Falling for her. What exactly did that mean? Did he want them to be exclusive? Was that the new jargon to make her okay with being his screwing buddy? What she wanted to hear was he loved her. She didn't want to be the only person in this relationship developing real feelings. The last time she did that, she was almost arrested.

She bit down on her tongue. No matter what, she wouldn't say she loved him until he said it first. He'd have to define what he meant by falling for her.

The interior of the house was dark. Geeta turned on the table lamp. Egypt sat on the living room sofa, a wad of used tissues piled beside her.

"What happened?" Geeta dropped her bag on the table near the door.

313

"He's married. He said I was fun, but he can't leave his wife and children. He has five kids. How does a man with that many children have time to hang out in a club, anyway?"

Geeta plopped down next to Egypt. She pushed Egypt's hair back, revealing her red-rimmed eyes. "You just met him, so you can't love him. Why are you so upset?"

"Why do I keep meeting jerks? Do I have a sign on my back that says 'kick me'?"

"All his money was in his mouth. What did he have a gold grill?" Geeta laughed.

"It's not funny. You can laugh because you've found someone special." Egypt shifted to face Geeta.

"Brooks is pretty special. I think I'm falling in love with him. But there's something between us, keeping us from really connecting. I can't put my finger on what it is."

"Geeta, don't scrutinize this relationship looking for reasons to pick it apart. I thought Brooks wasn't your type. But as we both know, I have no instincts. It's a good thing you didn't listen to me, huh?"

Geeta rubbed Egypt's shoulder. "You'll find the perfect person when the time is right." Geeta swallowed. She hadn't made it easier for Egypt by flaunting her relationship with Brooks. "I guess I ought to tell you I broke our pledge."

Egypt pushed Geeta's arm. "Ahh, I thought so. The last couple of weeks you stopped complaining and I think I even heard you humming to yourself a few times. I know I didn't hear the steady buzz of your friendly vibrator."

Geeta rolled her eyes. "Shut up. How about you? Are you still keeping the pledge?"

"Yes, I am. It's a good thing I didn't give in to Jay, the lying bastard." She wiped her nose with a used tissue. "I saw a palm reader today. She said the same thing."

Geeta drew back to stare at her friend. "A psychic? You saw a fortune–teller about your love life? Did she give you the winning lottery numbers, too?"

"I'm glad you think my situation is funny. But something she said resonated with me. She told me I needed to find fertile ground. So I'm moving to D.C. I think I need to get away. Out of Philly."

"You're going back to your parents?"

"Until I find my own place." She wiped her nose. "Will you be okay here by yourself?"

"I'll be fine. With my promotion I can afford the lease, now. Besides—"

The doorbell interrupted her. "One of the first things I'm going to do is change that annoying bell tone." She pushed off the sofa. "It's probably, Brooks, he must have forgotten to tell me something."

"Do you want me to give you and him some privacy?" Egypt stood.

"No, stay there. He won't be long. He's taking his bike for a long ride."

Egypt returned to the sofa, folding her legs under her and nodded.

Geeta opened the door. Donny leaned against the doorjamb with a toothpick between his teeth. She jerked her head back. Her tongue was thick, refusing to help her form the scream at the back of her throat. With both hands she rushed to close the door. He was faster, slipping his thick work boots into the opening and shoving his shoulder against the door.

What she ever saw in him escaped her now. The half ass smile he wore now only meant he was up to something. "Donny, what do you want?"

He thrust his face so close to hers she could smell his breath. "Is that any way to talk to someone bearing gifts?" He held a small box topped with a big red bow.

She ignored the present. "Donny, what do you want?" she repeated.

"Don't you want me to come in? I have something very interesting to tell you."

"Tell me from there." She nodded to the porch.

"Oh, baby, you're going to want to hear this. Inside." He tipped his chin toward the living room. "It's about your new boyfriend."

315

Chapter Fifteen

Geeta stood in the middle of the living room, her back stiff. The room felt cooler, charged with a new energy. Even before Donny, spoke the blood in her veins turned cold. His unfocused eyes spelled trouble.

"Whatever you have to say, Donny just say it and get-to-stepping." She wanted to sound tough but her legs were weak.

"Do you know your boyfriend is a cop?" he asked with a satisfied smirk.

Geeta released a shallow breath. "He's not a cop, he's a DEA agent. You didn't need to come way across town to share that bit of news." She reached for the doorknob.

Donny placed the box on the table, beside her purse. The smug expression was still on his face. He strolled around her as if he had the million-dollar prize she coveted.

"Did he tell you he was one of the cops who busted me? He helped break down the door. He was probably the one who escorted your naked ass to the closet to put on some clothes. So even though you think your new man is all about you, he's only getting close to you so he can get to me." His eyes narrowed like a snake about to strike.

Her stomach tightened in a hard knot. Her knees weakened, making it hard to maintain her balance. His declaration buzzed in her head like a fly against a window screen trying to get out. Donny would say anything to get what he wanted, but usually when he lied he turned his back to her, avoiding eye contact and lowering his voice. He spat out these words like poison. Even if everything wasn't true, there was some truth in what he said. She locked her knees to keep from being sucked into a drain.

"What have you told him about me?"

Donny grabbed her by the collar of her shirt, yanking her closer, whipping the gun from his waistband so fast she expected him to strike her with it.

Egypt jumped off the couch.

316

"You better sit your ass down, Egypt, before I knock you down. This is between me and Geeta." He tightened his grip with one hand and pointed the gun at Egypt's forehead. "Give me your cell phone," he yelled. In the quiet interior his voice sounded like danger.

"Why?" Egypt's voice was low.

"Because I said so. Now hand it here," he snapped.

Egypt reached for the phone. It slipped from her hand and clattered against the table. She picked it up again and extended her hand to him.

"Stupid. Put the phone on the floor and kick it over here."

Egypt eased back on the couch. She obeyed him. Her hands and shoulders shook. His warning must have left her mute.

He released Geeta long enough to shove the phone into his back pocket. Instead of fear she felt numb. If what Donny said was true then nothing mattered. Not him and not Brooks. They both had used her, pushing her around their game board like a useless pawn.

She tried to wrench away from Donny, but his grip was too strong. The sleeve of her shirt ripped as he snatched her closer.

"Let me go, Donny!"

"I told you, you belong to me. I even waited for you to come around. But you're acting like your empty-headed roommate. So now you don't have a choice. You're coming with me." His fingers dug through the thin cotton into her arm.

"I'm not going anywhere with you." She tried again to pull free.

He leaned closer, rubbing the barrel of the gun along her throat. His hot breath assaulted her ear. "Bitch, you'll go where I tell you to go." Squirming only made him tighten his hold.

"So while he's screwing your brains out, is he pumping you for information about me?"

317

His face pulled into an evil sneer that left her speechless.

With one hand, he shook her. The knot in her stomach went rigid with resolve. Any little-girl innocence remaining in her heart evaporated. Somewhere inside she'd find the toughness to take care of herself. No more depending on others to look out for her interests.

"You don't get it, do you? You're coming with me. You should have known better, Geeta." He bored down on her as if she were a naughty child who needed punishing.

"What are you doing, Donny?" she croaked.

Ignored her, he focused on Egypt.

"Don't even try to call anyone. The phone lines have been cut and if you step foot outside that door in the next hour, you'll regret it," he barked at Egypt, leveling the gun at the center of her chest this time.

Egypt curled her legs closer to her body, nearly disappearing into the cushion. Her brassy exterior disappeared. Geeta couldn't protect them both, Egypt had folded. Maybe Geeta would have done the same thing if anger wasn't pounding in her chest like warrior drums, making it hard to think.

He shoved her against the wall. "Open the door," he yelled.

Her shoulder blade throbbed from the sudden blow. He hoisted her around the waist, keeping her feet off the floor. She fought the fury brewing in her chest, trying to hold onto the pieces of Brooks she thought were true and good.

"Don't do this, Donny. Brooks and I don't talk about you," she yelled. "I don't know anything about your illegal activity so I have nothing to tell. If you're so tough and you want to know what he knows, ask him."

"Too late, honey."

Brooks turned onto her block. After scanning the street and not seeing the marked car, his grip on the steering wheel tensed. He'd hoped to talk with his superiors before they pulled the surveillance. If the government wouldn't protect her he'd hire someone else to do the job.

His right eye twitched when he pulled next to the dark sedan. He never ignored his senses. Without being able to see through the windows it was hard to know if anyone was inside or where Donny might be. Brooks kept his foot steady on the accelerator, until he reached the corner. After almost ten years of working law enforcement, no one he cared so much about had needed him to put his training to use. With no personal involvement he was able to manage his emotions through any situation. Tonight his breathing was fast and short.

After parking the car, he radioed for back-up. He pulled the hefty SIG from the holster and checked the magazine. Habit. Of course it was fully loaded.

With the gun positioned low at his side he doubled back between the townhouses, staying in the shadows. From the protection of the shrubs, he inched closer to her house. His breathing was the only sound in the stillness. Without slowing his approach he took a deep breath. He drew closer to the townhouse. The weight of the gun fortified his resolve.

The street remained quiet. Nothing had changed. He dropped lower, almost to his knees.

The muffled sound of an angry male voice hung on the still night air. Brooks secured the gun handle in the palm of his hand, his index finger on the trigger. His right eye continued to jump, sharpening his attention.

Waiting for back-up could be too long. If he'd been honest with Geeta, he could have prevented this episode. She needed to know how dangerous Donny was now. No longer a two-bit punk, hiding under beds. If he'd been honest he instead of lurking in the dark he could be warming her bed. If he'd been honest she'd know he loved her. The fine line between taking care of Geeta and his feelings for her blurred his ability to do the right thing.

The front door opened. Donny stepped through, his hand around Geeta's arm, his focus on the car. She flailed like a fish on the end of a line. Donny barely held on to her. Brooks tried to stay pressed against the house, unnoticed, but Geeta caught sight of him. She gasped.

"Shut the hell up, Geeta." Donny pulled her down the stairs without her feet touching the ground.

Before making his move Brooks followed Donny's gaze to see if someone was waiting for him in the car.

"Let me go, Donny. Let me go." The terror in Geeta's scream shook him to the core. Her voice echoed in the quiet.

With Donny distracted, Brooks stepped from the shadows, behind him with his pistol aimed at Donny's head.

"Let her go, Donny. Now!" Brooks yelled.

Donny swung around, locking eyes with him. "What you gonna do man? Try to save her?" he sneered.

Brooks didn't reply.

"I told you she's mine." He used Geeta as a shield.

"I don't belong to either one of you jackasses. Get the hell off me Donny." Geeta yanked on her arm, shrieking with each twist and turn. Her attempts to break free failed. Just when she seemed to run out of energy, her fisted hand connected with Donny's nose. The blow was so fast he looked startled, as if blinded by a camera flash. A thick stream of blood poured from one nostril.

Donny fumbled his gun. His grip on Geeta loosened enough for her to scramble away on her hands and knees. The cold, evil glare in Donny's eyes signified he was beyond reason. He tried to level his gun in shaking hands.

"Don't move, Donny. Don't do it man." Brooks cocked the trigger. Within seconds a squad car screeched to a halt from the left and another from the right. Donny spun around, facing a dozen officers with guns drawn.

"Drop it, or I'm going to drop you," Brooks commanded.

Donny lowered the gun, dangling it from his index finger. The officers approached him, kicking his feet apart until he fell to his knees. The incoherent babbling coming from him was the only sound filling the air.

Dating Just Got Serious

Once Donny was in the back of the squad car, Brooks went in search of Geeta.

Chapter Sixteen

Geeta sat in the middle of the queen-sized bed wrapped in the white down comforter. She couldn't stop shivering. She drew the wrap tighter, burying her chin into her chest. Trying to sort out what happened downstairs made her head throb.

A large hand had swatted at the sky, stopping time, stopping sound and stopping movement. She sat perfectly still, no more shaking. Instead, a hollowness ballooned in her like a mushroom cloud, tearing out all her dreams and replacing them with empty promises.

Brooks had seemed so sincere. If he wanted information, then of course he'd be charming. It was hard to determine which hurt more, his betrayal or having it all exposed by Donny. She wanted a big blackboard eraser to obliterate the last year of her life.

She dropped her chin. How could she have been so wrong? Was it all make-believe? How much of what Donny said was true? He wasn't above telling a lie if there was a benefit for him.

She reached for the blanket at the foot of the bed and draped it over her legs. Moving to turn up the heat seemed insurmountable. Doing anything worthwhile required more strength than she had. She rocked back and forth. The motion brought her comfort.

A soft knock at the door stopped her motion for a moment. "Go away, Egypt. I want to be alone," she croaked.

"Brooks is downstairs. I told him you didn't want to see him but he won't leave." Her voice was barely a whisper.

Several seconds ticked by. Uncertainty gripped her the same way Donny had earlier. Another lie might slice her in two. Maybe she should send him away, but she wanted to know for sure. She wanted to hear him say the words. She wanted to know if his betrayal was as thorough as Donny claimed. She couldn't move forward without knowing.

"Did you tell him what Donny said, Egypt?"

"I did. I hope you aren't mad at me, but I thought...I—"

"Don't worry about it. It doesn't matter. Tell him to come up," Geeta said.

In an instant Brooks was in her bedroom. She turned her head to him. His suit and tie reminded her they were supposed to go to dinner. She'd planned to ask him about their relationship, but now she had the answers. Never had he directly asked her a question about Donny, but had she volunteered information without knowing? She clutched her stomach, trying to rule the pain.

"Is it true, Brooks? You busted Donny? You were in the apartment that day?" There was no emotion in her voice, there was nothing left. Asking the question drained the little strength she had left.

"Yes, Geeta, but let me explain."

She shook her head. "No, Brooks. There's nothing you can say." She turned her back to him. "Good-bye."

He rushed beside her, the bed sagging under his weight. He placed his hand on her arm. Every time he touched her, her body reacted. Welcoming the feel. But she pulled away, feeling betrayed by him and her common sense.

"Geeta, I don't know what Donny told you, but what we have...what we're building has nothing to do with him or his case. It never has."

Her eyes stung, but she refused to cry. The little innocent girl couldn't afford to fall for his smooth talking good looks or charm.

"Then why didn't you tell me from the beginning? What was the need to keep the secret? You must have thought it was pretty funny seeing me standing in the middle of all your DEA buddies, butt naked and babbling like a baby."

"I'm sorry if I've hurt you, but it was never like that." He locked eyes with her.

She wanted to believe him. Life would have been so simple if she could erase Donny's words. But crawling back into the safety of her cocoon held an even better advantage.

She drew in a deep breath and squared her shoulders. "Brooks, I've heard so many apologies in the last few years. The one thing they have in common was none of them changed the past or erased the pain. I want you to go now. Now." Her voice was steady, filled with the determination she needed to move on.

Chapter Seventeen

Geeta pushed the vase to the other end of the table with all the other roses Brooks sent every day. White ones, pink ones, red ones. Even the dead ones from two weeks ago still sat at the end of the table, their heads drooped over like they were in mourning.

At ten every morning the florist arrived with another bunch. If only the disappointments in life could be wiped away with the sweet smell of roses.

She checked the caller ID before answering the ringing phone. A new habit since Brooks continued to call.

"Cat, what's up?" she said to her sister.

"Do I have to waddle over there to see you or are you coming to my get-together tomorrow?"

"Stop being so dramatic. I saw you two days ago."

"I miss you. Watching the games isn't the same without you here. Brooks promised not to show up. He doesn't want to come between us. So I don't understand why you keep refusing." Cat was due any day. The closer she came to being a mother the needier she became.

"Cat, you're wasting your breath and time. I'd rather not take a chance of running into him. Not yet, anyway. I'll come see you day after tomorrow. I promise."

Cat huffed. "Is he still sending flowers?"

"Yes. And he calls. He was in my driveway when I came back from a meeting last week." Geeta rested her elbow on the table.

"What did you do? Did you talk to him?"

"No, I kept driving, right by the house."

"Could you be wrong about him? I don't think he would use you."

"I guess we'll never know the answer to that question, will we?"

Cat sighed heavy enough to make her point over the phone.

Living her life to please others was something she used to do. Cat would come around, one day.

"I've got to go, Cat. This article won't write itself. I'll come by day after tomorrow. Hide some chicken wings in the fridge for me." Geeta ended the call.

She stared at the computer for several minutes without touching the keys. Donny's information must have clobbered her muse. She hadn't written anything decent since that night. If she didn't hand in a dazzling article in by the end of the week her editor would probably put her back on in-house sales.

Happiness was an abstract concept. The last time she was really happy was at her sister's wedding when she thought she'd met the perfect man. Brooks had poured more attention on her in one night than a whole host of boyfriends had in five years. To expend that much time and energy to win a case seemed like overkill.

The doorbell chimed, breaking her fixation on the keyboard. The florist was right on time.

She opened the door and held out her hand for the flowers.

"Good morning, Geeta." Brooks' hands were clasped in front of him. His eyes were sharp, clear, beautiful. She missed him, but her common sense overruled her desire.

Without giving him a moment to start talking, she snapped her wrist to swing the door closed.

Brooks shook his head. That's exactly the reception he expected. But one closed door wouldn't be enough to keep him away.

"I'm staying out here until you open the door, Geeta. Sooner or later the two of us will sit down and talk. You're going to hear my side, if it's the last thing I do." He waited.

Thirty minutes later he was still on the outside. "You can't avoid me forever and you can't stay in the house forever. So you're going to have to come up with a better plan to avoid me," he yelled at the door.

The heat under his collar traveled down his spine. The cotton shirt stuck to his back. He pulled his cellphone from the breast pocket of his jacket and watched the minutes tick off.

"I'll be back tomorrow, Geeta. And the day after that. And the day after that." He headed to the car. Sitting surveillance provided stamina for all kinds of incidents, including this one.

He backed out of the driveway. This time he wanted to fight for her. He'd let his college girlfriend slip away without fighting for her. But not this time. Not Geeta.

Chapter Eighteen

The editor of E-News motioned for her to sit in his office before exiting to refill his coffee cup. Geeta repositioned her butt in the chair facing his desk. Waiting was a strategy for Hal. The anticipation was supposed to break her down for whatever piece of information he wanted to impart.

Geeta closed her eyes. If Hal had any idea what had happened to her in the past two weeks he would have adopted another tactic. She wasn't the weak girl he hired a few years ago. If she could stand up to Donny and ignore the urge to answer when Brooks called four or five times a day then she could take a stiff talk from Hal.

"Geeta, I'm glad you found time in your busy schedule to come in today." Hal took his chair. With the little stirrer clamped between his lips, he set the coffee cup on the desk.

"Hal, I know you wanted to see me last week, but I've been really busy covering the bridge scandal in Jersey. This story is not one of those fluffy pieces like the charity events for the basketball team. What happened over there could end someone's career." She leaned closer, banging her index finger on the desk to make her point.

"You still need to make the staff meetings. Also, if you don't get the article to me on time, I'm going to start giving the prime assignments to someone more reliable." Hal stuck the chewed up stirrer in his full coffee cup.

Geeta popped up out of the chair. "You can count on me. I went through a pretty bad break-up, but I'm over it now."

He held up his hand to stop her. "Yeah, aren't we all? Get the assignment to me by the end of the week then, take some time off."

"I don't need any time off. I've got this, Hal. Don't you like the stuff I've written so far?" Her scalp tingled. Was he getting ready to fire her?

"Don't worry, Geeta. You're one of my best. I want you to recharge your batteries. If your life has taken a wrong turn maybe you need to step back for a moment. Look at it from a different environment. Take a few days, enjoy Christmas with your family, then come back in here, ready to write and ready to turn them in when I say so." He picked up his cup. "Now go."

She gave him an appreciative nod. "You know you're like my dad away-from-home."

"Yeah, yeah." He waved her away, but not before she saw his seldom-revealed dimple.

Geeta said good-bye to the staffers. At least she had all the data she needed for the article. The problem was keeping focused long enough to get the information on paper.

Every few minutes Brooks popped in her head. The way he used to hold her breasts like he was weighing them in his palms, or how he touched her, the smell of his skin when he snuggled behind her in bed. In the short time they'd spent together he'd become embedded in the fibers of her life. But they couldn't have a relationship without trust. Even if his feelings for her changed over time, he'd started out in the wrong place.

She pushed away the image of Brooks. Soon he'd be a distant memory. She hoped.

####

Brooks shut off the car engine and climbed out. He spotted her car as soon as he pulled into the open-air lot. Sooner or later she'd have to come out of the building.

He leaned against the driver's side door, folded his arms over his chest. With nowhere to go, he could wait. And wait. Cat said her sister could be stubborn, but he hadn't pictured her being unforgiving. The cold, narrow stare she gave him before closing the door without giving him an opportunity to say anything was like a spear in his gut.

Geeta bounced around the corner. With her focus on the ground she didn't see him until she neared the driver's side of the car. She stopped short. Her hand went to her chest.

"Brooks, you scared the shit out of me. Why are you here? Why won't you just let this go?"

He took a step toward her. "Because I want us to talk. I want to explain everything to you."

She held up her hand. "Stop. I've heard so many explanations in my lifetime, how about I pull one out of my handbag and read it to you? So how easy was it for you to trick me? That must have given you something to laugh about, huh?" Her voice took on a cruel timbre.

He stretched his hand toward her. "Geeta, what we shared never had anything to do with Donny's case. The only thing I can credit Donny with is leading me to the special woman you are. I couldn't control the circumstances of how we met, but from the moment we did, everything I said and did was genuine. If you could stop being angry long enough you'd realize I'm telling the truth." His voice didn't waver.

Brooks' career was based on being able to read people, to know what they were saying with their bodies and not their words. And he was good at it. Geeta's words were sharp, but her eyes were speaking a different language. She wanted to believe in the miracle that could happen between them. He only needed to give her time to turn off her force field.

"Are you going to let me get in my car?" she asked without looking at him.

"You believe me, don't you?" He touched the sleeve of her coat.

She produced the keys from her purse. "I used to believe in Santa Claus, too."

Chapter Nineteen

Geeta popped the cork on the bottle of champagne. Bubbles ran over the top and down her fingers. She licked each one.

The table had been cleared of all the dead flowers.

"Come on, Egypt. Dinner is ready. Let's get this celebration started," she yelled from the kitchen.

Egypt came into the room carrying a big gift-wrapped box and with a big grin spread across her face.

"What you got there?" Geeta asked.

"I can't leave here without giving you something. You let me move in here with you and you've been a godsend for me. I know I have some work to do but, I'm a whole lot better thanks to you." Tears appeared in her eyes. "Maybe it's a good thing, me moving to D.C. Two sad sacks in one house would be too pitiful."

Geeta pretended to think about Egypt's comment for a moment. "Yeah, I guess you're right. Now hand me my present." She ripped the paper, lifted the lid off the huge box. She pushed aside the tissue paper. "Egypt, you bought me a Louie. It's gorgeous. I love it." She gushed.

"Sure. Every girl needs a Louis Vuitton bag. It's just a small token." Egypt flopped onto the chair. "Now tell me what smells so good. Did you cook my favorite meal?"

"Of course, crab cakes, twice baked potatoes and asparagus. " Geeta dished the food. "Guess who I saw today?"

"Mmm, I hope it wasn't Donny."

"Donny won't be seeing anyone for a long time, unless it's from behind glass. Brooks. He was outside my office after my meeting with Hal." She took the seat in front of Egypt at the table.

"That's awesome. Did you guys make up?"

Geeta put her fork down to contemplate her response. The night he admitted the truth, she made a decision. No matter how much her stomach fought the choice, she

331

wouldn't change her mind. No. We won't be getting back together."

Egypt chewed a mouthful of food, sipped from her glass, and maintained a neutral expression. "He likes you, so who cares how the two of you got together? I'd take a man if the stork dropped him on my doorstep. You and your sister are extremely picky. It must be nice to have men lining up for you to choose from."

Geeta's heart sped up. "We are not picky. We're discriminating. And how do I know Brooks wants me for me, or if he wants me to get some info on his big drug case? What happens after the trial? How do I know this isn't something he does to get what he wants?"

Egypt lifted her fork to her mouth. "Fine. Examine everything with one hundred questions. That will keep you busy when you're all alone." She shoved a forkful of potato in her mouth.

"I can't be like you, Egypt. You accept behavior I would never tolerate, the gold teeth, being stood up, forgotten birthdays. I don't want another boyfriend, I want someone to take me serious." Geeta pushed her plate away.

"You have to start somewhere. That's all I'm saying."

The phone rang. At least she didn't have to respond to her roommate. The two of them were good roommates, but their take on life was very different.

"Yes, Cat," she said into the receiver.

"The babies are coming. I'm on my way to the hospital," Cat said between breaths.

"Okay. I'll leave the house now and meet you there." Geeta dropped the phone and turned to Egypt. "Cat's in labor. I've got to go."

"Okay. Get out of here."

"I'm sorry about missing your special dinner." She kissed Egypt's cheek before dashing out the door.

####

Dating Just Got Serious

Geeta stood at the large window overlooking the hospital parking lot. The agitation in her stomach slowed a little, but until Jeremy told her Cat and the babies were fine, the feeling wouldn't go away. Between the waiting, Egypt's cutting comments and running into Brooks, the day spilled over with excitement.

Cat always found something wrong with every guy she brought home. Cat's instincts on Donny were spot on, but she was too close to Brooks to see his faults. Cat thought he was the golden boy.

One day she'd forgive herself for being so gullible, falling for his charm. But she'd walked into the relationship with her heart open. Too bad he hadn't.

"Geeta, there you are." Jeremy picked her up and swung her round.

"Tell me! Tell me!" She giggled with delight along with him. "What did she have?"

"The most beautiful girls in the whole world. They are absolutely perfect." He settled her back on the floor. The joy and happiness dancing in his eyes made her grin. He grabbed her hand and pulled her toward the maternity ward.

"How is Cat?"

"Your sister is amazing," he said over his shoulder, with his broad smile still in place. "She was nothing like the women on television. No screaming and cussing. She kept telling me how much she loved me. Every time I think I love that woman, I realize I love her even more. Does that make sense?"

Jeremy talked so fast understanding him was difficult. Geeta nodded. How could she disagree with him on anything? He walked on a cloud ten feet off the ground built for just him and Cat.

Jeremy pushed open the door to the private room. The large bed was positioned in the middle of the space with a small bassinet on each side. Pink and blue teddy bear wallpaper adorned the wall. But the way Cat beamed, was the only thing Geeta could focus on. She held a baby in each arm and made it look easy.

Geeta dropped Jeremy's hand to slip the white gown over her clothes and sanitized her hands before approaching the bed. She always imagined she'd rushed to her sister's side the day she gave birth. Instead she inched toward the bed. The whole scene seemed surreal, like walking on a high wire. She brushed a kiss on Cat's forehead. Being a mom elevated Cat, putting her in a sacred category, somehow. Finding love, getting married and having a family gave her life the perfect stamp.

"Which names did you guys decide on?"

Cat looked over at Jeremy, before answering. The weight of the emotion exchanged in their glance was like watching a summer flower bloom for the first time.

"We're going with Simone and Sami. After Grandma, and Jeremy's grandmother," Cat responded with her gaze locked on Jeremy.

Jeremy positioned his body half on the bed and half off. He eased one of the tiny bundles from Cat's arm like an expert. He stuck his pinkie finger into the baby's palm and her tiny little fingers curled around his.

"Can I hold her?" Geeta whispered.

"Of course you can, Godmother."

Geeta eased into the chair near the bed with the baby cradled in her bent arm. The uneasiness from earlier faded enough for her to focus on her niece's tiny features. Until the moment Cat passed the child to her, she'd never thought of wanting children or wanting to be a mother. The growing urge took root and as her niece fisted her tiny hand, the feeling came over her like someone had draped her in wanting.

"Why are you crying?" Cat leaned in her direction. Her voice held a new tenderness that must have come with motherhood.

"I'm so happy for you two. It's like you are all grown up." Geeta settled back into the big leather chair. "You're a mom, Cat of two beautiful daughters. I'm speechless."

"I know, right? It's so amazing. I don't think I've ever been happier."

"Hey, wait a minute," Jeremy protested.

"You know what I mean." Cat stroked his hand.

Geeta looked down at her sleeping niece. The pint-sized cutie was too small to determine which parent she favored. Both girls had their father's straight nose. Jeremy was right; they were perfect. Everything about the tableau in front of her was beyond anything she'd ever seen or felt.

The gaping holes in her life seemed magnified with emptiness. The meaningless dates, the sitting in bars only stalled her from getting to the life she wanted. She tightened her hold on the baby, coveting the sweetness and innocence. Wishing couldn't bring this kind of joy. Settling wouldn't bring this kind of happiness. This kind of joy was carried on wings of love, the one emotion that seemed to be allergic to her.

Chapter Twenty

The last encounter with Brooks had been successful. No more flowers, no more calls, no more unannounced visits. If only that had meant no more tears then life would be improving, too.

Geeta caught the escalator up to the train platform. The icy finger of winter had already touched Philadelphia. Outside, the gray overcast sky promised snow later. Leaving town for a few days was harder than she'd imagined when she made the plans. Sitting around Cat and Jeremy, sponging off their happiness needed to come to an end. Neither of them would dare tell her to give them some space, time alone with their new babies, but she knew. The way they gazed at her when she rocked one of the twins to sleep or the fake smiles they wore when she walked into the room.

Egypt had tried to cheer her up before she left for Washington a week ago. When her efforts failed, her parting gift was a blind date with a guy she claimed was fabulous. The only question was if he was so great why didn't Egypt snag him? Why couldn't she find someone in Philly for Geeta? What good would Mr. Right be if he lived in New York?

Geeta unfolded the piece of paper that Egypt had given her. Printed in Egypt's careful script was his name – Rowan. They were supposed to meet at a small restaurant in SoHo for an early dinner. According to Egypt, he was the perfect guy for her. Geeta scratched her nose. Maybe Egypt was right because picking the right guy proved to be a skill Geeta couldn't master.

Lies had changed the direction of her life. One moment she was frolicking around, enjoying a relationship with a man she loved and the next an undercurrent pulled her out to sea. Even the small townhouse seemed different, like it had multiplied in size, giving her plenty of room to ramble around in her loneliness. Brooks must have finally gotten the message. She hadn't heard from him or seen him in five days. She missed his persistence. Even though she kept ignoring him, a part of her wanted him to keep trying, to fight for them. His disappearance hadn't been a total surprise, it was only a matter of time before he picked up the scent of another woman or work pulled him away again.

She flipped her wrist to peer at her watch. She had exactly three minutes to board the train to New York. She couldn't look away from the couple kissing good-bye on the opposite platform. They could have been shooting a love scene for the latest romantic comedy.

Geeta shook her head and stepped into the train car. She took the nearest window seat, happy not to be able to see the love scene anymore. After checking to make sure her phone was on vibrate just in case Cat called, she closed her eyes. This trip was about relaxing, changing her perspective, finding a new starting point.

Dodging Brooks for a full month was like working two jobs. The man was like a ninja showing up at her house, at the office for her weekly meetings and calling every few hours. The last few days he'd gone mute. Nothing. She should have been happier. After telling him to leave her alone so many times, he'd finally decided to follow her instructions. It's what she'd been asking him to do, so she should have been prepared for the desolation. Instead of breaking through the barrier she'd constructed, he walked away.

The welcome vibration as the train chugged away from the station lightened the agitation simmering in her gut. With her tongue pressed against the roof of her mouth, she sighed. The luxury room, the massage and the shopping spree waiting for her in Manhattan might help put her in a better frame of mind. After a few days away she would take a fresh look at her future.

The seat next to her sank from the weight of a passenger settling into the cushion. Without opening her eyes she hoped it wasn't someone who wanted to chat on the phone or engage in conversation. For once she wanted to be selfish, do only the things that made her feel good, and talking right now wasn't one of them.

She turned to face the window before opening her eyes. The landscape flashed by in the normal fall hues of brown and almost browns. Dull, uninspired scenery, much like her spirit.

"Hello, since this seat isn't taken, I hope you don't mind me sitting here?"

She jumped. That voice, she knew it like she knew her father's voice. The baritone quality was both beautiful and dangerous. The acceleration of her heartbeat went from ten to one hundred in seconds.

"Brooks…what…how…why on earth are you here?" She knew the answers, but his presence left her without the ability to ask sensible questions. She wanted to hug him for his persistence but didn't dare move.

He stuck out his hand. "I'm Brooks DiNardo. You must be Geeta Preston. Since we took a wrong turn before, let's start over again."

She ignored his outstretched hand, but he seemed unperturbed by the slight. He rubbed his strong, square chin. "The first time I saw you, you were butt naked in the middle of an apartment of a drug dealer we were looking for. Even when I tried I could not erase the image of your gorgeous body. I couldn't get you out of my mind. I'm glad we have this opportunity to meet on much better circumstances."

For several moments she said nothing. Instead she stared into his beautiful eyes, wanting to believe everything he said. Hoping their relationship had begun as simple as he made it sound. The anger in the pit of her stomach fizzled.

"You expect me to believe that's what happened?"

"I expect you to know. I'm telling you the truth. I omitted some information, before. I'll never do that again." His voice was matter-of-fact, but he leaned close enough to kiss her.

She needed to say something, see something other than his lips, tempting her closer. "I'm going to New York."

"I figured that much. The train is heading in that direction." He pulled her hand into his and folded his fingers around hers. The liberated woman in her wanted to pull away, but being claimed stirred her cautious heart. Trapped between him and the window of the moving train, there was no escape.

"Okay, so you know where I'm going. But where are you heading there?"

"I'm doing whatever I have to do, to win you back. We hit a bump and instead of fighting for us, you sprinted."

"Is that what you think happened?"

"I want us to have the kind of relationship you fight for. There is always going to be something standing in our way, but if you turn and run every time then we'll never know how good we can be together." He rolled his thumb over her knuckles but he didn't take his eyes off her. The message in his gaze found its way to her heart.

"You really saw me naked during the bust?"

"As naked as the day you were born, but baby, you filled out in all the right places."

The only smile she could muster was a weak one. Some details of that day were very vivid, others she wanted to forget. If they managed to crawl through this challenge and stay together for ten years, she'd probe him for other images he might remember.

"So what's the plan? For us?" Geeta asked.

"You're going to forgive me for not telling you everything. Then you're going to let me tear down the wall surrounding your heart. Then you're going to let me love you like no one else can."

####

Brooks couldn't suppress the smile tugging at his lips when Geeta slipped her hand into his as they exited Penn Station. The only sign of hesitancy left was her tongue pushed against the inside of her cheek, like a snail crawling under a blanket.

"Have dinner with me tonight," he asked. "After all, we've said we were going to give it a shot, right?"

"I'm supposed to meet someone for dinner. I have no way of letting him know if I change my plans. It's a blind date Egypt set up." She shrugged her shoulders. "I'm going to be here for two nights. We can have dinner tomorrow."

They moved to the end of the line of people waiting for taxis. Brooks ran his hand along his chin. "You're meeting someone named Rowan, right?"

She dropped his hand to stare at him. Her eyes full of questions searched his face. "How did you know? Egypt told you?"

"I'm your blind date. Brooks Rowan DiNardo. Egypt set up this rendezvous before she left."

They inched to the front of the cab line. She turned to face him with a look of surprise. A stiff wind whipped her hair across her face.

"So even though I thought you'd given up, you hadn't?"

"No. I never had any intention of giving up. I'm not a quitter. There is so much about me you still don't know."

"I've got an idea. Let's take it one date at a time until I know everything." She pressed up on her toes, placed her arms around his neck, and slipped her tongue into his mouth.

Epilogue – One Year Later

Brooks brought the motorcycle to a stop. Balancing the machine between his legs, he dropped the stand. In the last year so much had transpired, but never could he have imagined all of this.

He turned off the bike and removed his helmet. After unsnapping her strap he helped her remove her helmet. He pushed a lock of hair behind her ear, before planting a kiss on her cheek. No matter how long they'd been together he'd never get enough of touching her.

"Are you nervous?" He held her face between his palms.

"I'm not. But no matter how old I get, I think Cat will always see me as the little sister. When I tell her we're married she's going to go ballistic."

"With two toddlers, I think she'll be happy she didn't have to help plan a big affair."

"Yeah, but I think it's the rest of our news that going to make her head explode. Her get-togethers have become legendary. I can't imagine spending Sunday any other way. "

Brooks climbed off the bike and helped her down. "She's going to be just fine. We'll start our own memories. Let's do this." He grabbed her hand and led her into the building. She continued to fidget on the ride in the elevator. He hoped she'd never lose the wide-eyed innocence she displayed at that moment.

Before he knocked on the door, Cat snatched it open. "I'm so glad you're here. I need help with the dip and the girls won't sit still for longer than a few moments."

Jeremy appeared at the entry, a child in each arm. "It's about time you guys got here. Cat has been checking the door every two minutes." He shifted the girls to Cat and grabbed Geeta in a bear hug.

"How's my favorite sister-in-law?" he joked.

Geeta swatted his arm before embracing him. "Jeremy, I'm not going to let you pull my chain today. I want to see my nieces."

Both Jeremy and Cat greeted him. The affection between this close-knit family tugged at his heart. All he wanted for him and Geeta was the kind of happiness filling the condo. Geeta had opened her heart, and let him back in. The blissfulness surrounding them exceeded his imagination.

The girls wiggled their way out of Geeta's arms, each staggering off a different direction like drunken sailors.

"You two are beaming." Cat wrung her hands. "What's up?"

Geeta looked at Brooks before facing her sister. She expelled a deep breath. "Okay, I'm just going to say it." She glanced at Brooks again.

He placed a hand on her knee for reassurance.

"Brooks and I got married last week."

Cat's mouth dropped open, but for once alarm didn't blaze in her eyes.

"Congratulations, man," Jeremy said.

"I knew something was up with you two. I couldn't reach either of you when I called. Where did you get married? City Hall?" Cat demanded.

"We didn't want the big fancy wedding, and all the hoopla. It's just not me. We spent the week in Saint Thomas. Just me and Brooks a minister, and one witness on the beach, with the sun setting behind us. It couldn't have been more perfect."

Together they'd practiced this speech. The most difficult part of the conversation was his. "There's more." He cleared his throat. "I just received a new assignment. We're moving to Texas...Houston in a few months."

Cat sucked in a quick gasp, drawing the air from the room. A silence fell over them. Even the toddlers seemed to stop their constant jabbering. For several quiet seconds nobody said a word, but gazes transferred from one person to the next. His heart beat slowed, waiting for Cat and Jeremy to give their blessing. What they thought meant a lot to Geeta, and he wanted her content, joyful about the next step in their marriage.

"Cat, did you hear Brooks?" Geeta asked.

Cat placed her hand at her throat. "I did, but I—I..."

"It's a promotion," Brooks inserted.

"Of course I'm happy for you two. It's just a lot to take in at once." Cat stood and embraced them both. Tears appeared in her eyes.

"Don't start crying Cat. It's just a temporary assignment. We'll see each other as often as we can. Brooks and I plan to start our family real soon, so I'll need lots of sisterly advice."

Geeta's comment must have provided the okay for Cat to give into her tears. Cat pointed her index finger at Brooks. "You take good care of my little sister."

"That's exactly what I plan to do."

Except from Speed Date

Egypt Carrington's heart beat a zillion times faster as they neared the nightclub. The thumping sound of the live music the thickening crowd and the date waiting on the inside were like a magnet pulling her forward. She glanced over her shoulder at her slow moving girlfriend. "Renee hurry up or he'll be gone before I get to the door."

"Have you ever tried to walk fast in stilettoes?" Renee's voice was tight, as if the effort to keep up required her full concentration.

"I'm wearing this tight mini skirt, and my heels are higher than yours."

"You've got legs like an Amazon, so that doesn't count."

"I'm finally going to meet him." Egypt slowed her pace enough to allow her friend to catch up. "He's perfect in every way. Tall, with dark hair, employed. He likes to travel, he has a condo facing the Potomac and he wants to settle down." Egypt talked louder, over the pounding music echoing across the block. Now wasn't the time to tell Renee what else he had.

"You have never met this man. You only know what he told you on a few phone calls and the speed dating website. Don't put him in the perfect category until you've met him face to face. People lie on those dating sites."

"I haven't been intimate with anyone since I left Philadelphia." Egypt lowered her voice. "When I made that pact with Geeta I had no idea it would be so long. I'm wound up so tight I'm about to burst. I have a special feeling about him. We've been in communication for three months. If he wasn't really interested I'd know." Egypt forced her voice to sound normal. "From his pictures his good looking with soft brown eyes. He's got a David Beckman quality about him, including the scruff on his chin.

Renee shrugged one shoulder. "You're just horny. It happens to the best of us. Just because your psychic said you'd find true love doesn't mean Slade is the one. Nobody takes real relationship advice from a woman with a scrunchie, a gauze skirt and a full beard."

"Stop making fun of my lady. It's not a full beard." Egypt grabbed her friend's hand to pull her the remaining few feet to the entrance. The darkened double glass door made it impossible to see inside. Egypt took a deep breath. The first time Slade saw her in person she needed to look like she had her life together.

Renee nudged her arm and angled her head at the handsome hunk heading toward them. He looked tall enough to be Slade but instead of jet-black hair, his was the color of sand.

"Do you think that's him?" Renee whispered.

"I wish." Egypt willed her mind to find something familiar in the figure coming her way. "Slade said he'd be wearing a black button-down shirt and black slacks." She hesitated long enough to give the man another look, more thorough this time. Slade was good looking, but compared to the perfect specimen coming toward her, he was a runner-up.

"Good evening ladies, let me get the door." He jerked the heavy handle with little effort.

"Would you happen to be Slade?" The grin on Renee's face was as bright as the all-night gas station on the interstate.

"Slade? No, I'm Declan. Declan McKinney," he said to Renee, but looked at Egypt. His pretty rows of teeth were encased in a smile that could melt leather. "And you are?"

"Egypt Carrington. Please ignore my friend. She hasn't had a drink and she was hoping you were someone else."

"That's delightful. Why don't I buy you both a drink?" His eyes were glued to Egypt's breasts pushing at her strapless bustier.

"Thanks, but we're meeting someone." Egypt wanted to ignore Declan, but it wasn't easy. She adjusted her top just in case the girls were spilling out. "Maybe another time." She eased past him, gently brushing her shoulder against his chest.

"Sure thing." Declan allowed them to enter the club ahead of him. Then he crossed the club, weaving between elbows. His blond curls touched the collar of his shirt.

They inched through the crowd trying to get move close enough to the bar rail to get the bartenders attention.

"I don't see him." Egypt stood on her toes to see over the crowd. Arriving a little late was supposed to be the right strategy. She wanted to walk up to him, let him glimpse her curves and shapely legs as she approached. Everyone always said they were her best features.

The plan had failed.

Nobody in the club even came close to looking like Slade.

"That man keeps looking at you." Renee used her head to indicate the cluster of small tables across the room.

"What man?"

"The one who held the door for us. I think he likes you."

"Focus, Renee. I'm here to meet Slade. You know, my dream man."

"Forget that. Declan is a hunk." Renee rubbed her hands together she must have been anticipating a miracle. "Maybe he's a prince."

A quick glance over her shoulder confirmed Renee was right. Declan was precisely the type of man she'd normally go for, but this time she was determined to follow the advice of her psychic. Her own counsel never seemed to give the results she wanted. Her own counsel had left her heartbroken and almost in bed with a married man. Her own counsel was the reason she was back in Washington D.C, still single and horny as hell.

****

Declan McKinney positioned his chair to give him the perfect view of Egypt. She was as exotic as her name. Too bad she was taken. From the curves on her body and the thick curls framing her heart-shaped face she could have easily become his next distraction.

"If you stare any harder your eyeballs might stick to her ass."

"Am I being obtuse?" Declan turned to face his cousin across the table.

"You're being a McKinney." Richard sipped his drink. "Nothing is ever off limits to us." Richard's voice held the familiar tone of a man happy with his position in life.

"I want to have fun. She looks like she could provide it in several different ways."

"You're hoping to razz the family. She's tall, attractive, and has that African princess thing going on. You like trouble and she looks willing to bring it. Didn't you say she was meeting someone?"

"I don't like being told who's right for me." Declan glanced at his watch. "Besides, she's been waiting an hour. Maybe it's not working out."

"And you find that even more interesting. Don't you? It's like she just upped the ante. You'll start pacing in about five minutes." Richard narrowed his eyes. "What happened to Bernadette? Last month you fancied her."

"She was the typical debutante. I was a check on her scorecard." He held up his hand and spread his fingers. "Meet successful man. Check. Date successful man. Check. Marry successful man and have two babies-preferably twins—while maintaining her figure and her status at the Country Club. I wasn't going to check that box." Declan shifted his attention back to Egypt. Her tight skirt rode up, exposing her slender sleek thighs.

"And you think this one will be different?" Richard asked. "Can you imagine your family's response if you bring that one home to London for the family Christmas party? Your father's heart will collapse for sure, but not before disinheriting you and leaving the company to his delinquent brothers. My father would be first in line."

Without diverting his gaze, Declan said, "Who said anything about taking her home to meet my parents? I'm not opposed to a vigorous romp between the sheets. Make that two or three if she's as lusty as I imagine."

ABOUT THE AUTHOR

Jacki Kelly has written dozens of short stories and several books. She lives in the North East with her husband and one loveable dog. She loves hearing from her readers so please contact her.

Connect with her online:

http://www.jackikelly.com
http://twitter.com/Jackikellybooks
http://facebook.com/jackikelly-Author

If you enjoyed reading Blind Date, please tell everyone you know. Please post a review for other readers on Goodreads or other forums.

JOIN THE JACKI KELLY NEWSLETTER!
So you can stay tuned to new releases, appearance and events and prizes.

DATING JUST GOT SERIOUS!

Read the series

Blind Date
A Single Date
Date Me
One Date At A Time
Speed Date

www.ingramcontent.com/pod-product-compliance
Lightning Source LLC
Chambersburg PA
CBHW020825180626
46814CB00001B/108